Carnival in Brooklyn is where it's at.

The Labor Day Murderer danced

on Eastern Parkway, Brooklyn.

Even in the last chapter

I was still guessing,

"Who's the murderer—

Which woman?"

Printed in USA

Lloyd Hollis Crooks

GRENADA GHOST

Romance...Suspense...Murder...

Lyle Gordon begged for his meals in his native Trinidad and Tobago, but dreamed of being ringside to watch John Wayne and Cochise battle for turf. In his odyssey, Lyle enjoyed the virtues of beautiful women, and slept on the bunk bed of Rikers Island prisons. A humane story...A Must Read!

Wayne Brathwaite Publishing

A Novel By Lloyd Hollis Crooks

Wayne Brathwaite Publishing

Post Office Box 1617
Bowling Green Station
New York, N.Y. 10274-1617
E-mail: Enid@worldnet.att.net
Tel: 1-718-693-0769; 1-718-361-3536

Library of Congress Catalog Card No. 98-93701

ISBN 0-9666296-0-4

Printed in the United States of America

Book Cover Art: Reba Ashton-Crawford

Book Typesetting & Design:
Carlos & Portia Thompson
Tel: 1-718-859-5093
E-mail: Jtsvcs@aol.com
Address: 1294 Fulton Street—#227
Brooklyn, New York 11216

A blend of intrigue and culture mix...British humor...This is more than a novel of simply telling connected stories, but also an anthropological/sociological odyssey of Lyle Gordon's life...colorful and interesting.

—Professor Clinton Crawford,
City University of New York
Author: *Recasting Ancient Egypt in the African Context*

From behind Norway maples with their bright green foliage wives got a glimpse of their husbands' mistresses...That is an ingredient in West Indian Carnival.

Dr. Obasegun Awolabi
Medgar Evers College, CUNY

This is a work of fiction. The events and characters portrayed are figments of the author's imagination. Their resemblance, if any, to real-life counterparts is entirely coincidental. Names of real places are intended to give the author's work a sense of reality and meaning.

"Caribbean Daylight"

Mr. Rohit Kanhai

Success is you. One love.

10/30/99

Dedicated to my brother Paul who scratched beneath the smooth veneer, Mr. Cheeseman who gave me my First Primer, and to the Butlerites of Fyzabad who blocked the Red House gates in Port-of-Spain, Trinidad and Tobago, and though beaten and bloodied by Massa's emissaries, demanded "Justice!" from the colonial powers.

ACKNOWLEDGEMENTS

My sincere thanks to all of my professors at Medgar Evers College of the City University of New York. You made learning a joy, and your encouragement gave me wings. Also, thank you, Ms. Bernadette Bibby-Smith, for deciphering my hieroglyphics, and my sincere thanks to all the Computer Technicians in Room 2014 at Medgar Evers. You answered my every call.

Obrigado, President and Mrs. Joaquim Chissano, for graciously welcoming me into your country, for allowing me in my research to witness firsthand the beauty and culture of Mozambique, and especially for letting me know why the familial birds dance and sing, "*Xiku tsigua! Xiku tsigua!*"

To those who prefer to remian unnamed, you have my sincerest commendation.

Finally, it must be noted that *Grenada Ghost* could not have been completed without the help of my entire family. To them, I owe my heartfelt gratitude for allowing me the space and time that I needed to pen my thoughts.

"She was a mother without knowing it, and a wife, without letting her husband know it, except by her kind indulgence to him." Inscription on a tombstone in Plymouth, Tobago, West Indies.

—Unknown

"The Alzheimer's disease is even more baffling than the Plymouth tombstone, and I pray God that there'll soon be a cure for this brain crippling disease."

—Lloyd Hollis Crooks

"A Detective's Paradise"

—Hear Our Voices Magazine

Chapter One
Fyzabad

Forty flaming flamingoes fluttered from the mangrove, flew skyward, and alphabetized themselves as they winged their way at sundown towards their swampy habitat. The game birds had returned from fishing for frogs. Lyle Gordon took a cursory look at the birds' flight for they signalled the close of day for Grandpa and many laboring field hands. Lyle also knew the birds' course, and he kept running—running in their direction as a bearer of good news. He ran under pumping jacks and derricks; he whisked by sunburned oilfield workers on their way home from work; he ran abreast fast pedalling cyclists who felt the raindrops; and he flew past steam rollers that levelled the axed timber on the macadamized roads. Unbelievably, Lyle ignored his friends who pitched marbles with their dusty knees and knuckles, and only made a hand sign to his brother Paul who danced his kite in the breezy sky and eluded his foes in kite-fighting battles.

In a jiffy, Lyle was off the main road. Barefooted, he raced through the shortcut. He trampled up the mud tracks, cut through rice lagoons, sloshed into snail infested ravines, and toppled basket traps that were set for crayfish. Lyle balanced his body on narrow logs over the swollen river, and parried stray dogs and grazing bulls, but he never stopped running. His patchy shirttail flapped endlessly as the songs of early owls and toads echoed through the woods. Lyle's last hurdle, the feared stinging nettles, were brushed through like a grasshopper.

Finally, he reached his destination. He saw his grandfather packing the food carrier and hiding his hoe in a banana patch. From the sugar cane embankment Lyle shouted hysterically to his grandfather as if in hot

1

pursuit by the Devil from hell. "Grappa! Grappa! Aunt Lily come...She come from America...She really come...True! True!" He panted, tripped, and fell. Fate loves children. Lyle wasn't hurt. His dog Flossy licked him. Grandpa picked him up, and quickly packed the reaped produce on the donkey cart.

Aunt Lily had at long last come to take Lyle out of Fyzabad. He had to share the news.

Fyzabad was the only place Lyle knew. It was a saucer-shaped village lodged south of the Godino River in the Republic of Trinidad and Tobago (Trinbago). Trinbago was also known as Pitch Lake Country to the Southern patois mouths. Fyzabad had history, and it exported oil and comedy. In Fyzabad, sabotaged oil wells periodically blazed; every citizen was nicknamed; and babies christened in the white churches' fonts were named after colonial governors, biblical heroes, or after Tubal Uriah "Buzz" Butler, a.k.a. the Chief Servant. The Chief Servant was Fyzabad's god, Fyzabad's mouthpiece, and, unequivocally, the 1940's one-man trade union whose word was the gospel.

It was picturesque to watch the peasantry houses of red tapia mud, sticks, and thatched leaves meander up the red hills of Fyzabad. In those comely abodes, neighbor John's personal life was better known by neighbor "Grapevine" Rosa. Trade unionism got instant recognition from the oil magnates when Charlie King, the feisty lawman sent by the colonial governor to quell the oilfield riots of Fyzabad, was set on fire and burned like dry chips. The Chief Servant negotiated on behalf of the underpaid oilfield workers. He asked the oil companies for one penny on every barrel of oil. The oil companies refused to pay that penny. Instead, the beefy-oilrich barons shipped Fyzabad's oil wealth to England to feed the King and Queen, and the barons used their English influence to have the Chief Servant imprisoned for his ceaseless agitation on behalf of Fyzabadians.

Incidentally, Grandpa was mulling over Fyzabad's history when he rushed to the embankment, picked up Lyle, and stretched Lyle's back. "Happiness kills m'boy," Grandpa said. "America have no use for boys with broken bones. Sickness come in aeroplane and leave on jackass cart." He massaged Lyle's body thoroughly with his muddy fingers, and Flossy, the dog, looked on. "How you got here so fast, Lyle boy?"

"I flew with the wind, Grappa."

"I can see that."

"Is my bone broken, Grappa?"

"Boy, if you continue running, it surely will." Grandpa lifted his grandson and put him on the donkey cart. Grandpa had known all along that Aunt Lily was expected, but he was too sad to broach the subject before. "You's leaving us, boy, before you know our history? If the people in America ask you about us, you don't even know what to say to them, Lyle boy."

"I know a lot about Fyzabad, Grappa. I know about the Chief Servant, the greatest man in this country...I know about those Chinese people, especially Chinee Chin who gives thirteen ounces to the pound, and whenever I go into Chinee Chin's shop, he chases me out, and he tells me, '*No hap, hackwai*' in a disgusting way. I know that *hackwai* means black boy, and he never has whatever I ask for...I know about sickly Portuguese Alves who says, 'Bad pay kills trust.' I hope Portuguese Alves dies soon because Grandma says no matter how much money she pays Portuguese Alves, her account never goes down; and that is the reason why Grandma can't buy a new pair of gym boots for me to wear to Sunday school.

"Grappa, I even know about Mr. Sabga who sold Grandma 'bargain-bargain,' that cheap cloth he carries around on his back. Grappa, you remember when Mr. Sabga came to pick up his money for that bargain-bargain that he sold to Grandma?"

"Sure!"

"You remember that Grandma called me and told me in my ear to tell Mr. Sabga that she was not at home, and Mr. Sabga said to me, 'Little fella, tell your Grandma when she leaves the house she must carry her two feet too?'"

Grandpa laughed heartily. "Yes, that was my fault. I should've build the folding blind much longer so that whenever Grandma hide behind the folding blind her two feet wouldn't show. Your Grandma Leoni was right to hide from Mr. Sabga...Them Syrians sell their cheap cloth too damn dear...Bargain-bargain me foot!" Grandpa sucked his teeth, tugged at an overgrown shrub, and wiped his sweaty face with a clump of sweet bush. "What else you'll tell them people in America about us, boy?"

Lyle began to reply in textbook English, but resorted to a mixture of English and home patois. "Grappa, for sure, I'll tell the people in America about them high-color people in Apex Oilfields who think they are better than we...And I'll tell the people in America about them bigshot high-brown people who robbed Uncle Dodo of his cocoa estate because Uncle Dodo couldn't read and write...And I'll tell the people in America about you...You're a nice Grappa...And about Grandma...About Aunt Gina...And about Mr. Tellymack, my headmaster.

"Grappa, I hate Mr. Tellymack. He beats us...All Mr. Tellymack teaches us little children are how to speak correctly, and about a stupid poem called *Abou Ben Adhem*. He, Mr. Tellymack, wants us to recite that stupid poem just like him...'Boys and girls, diction, diction, please!'" Lyle mimicked his headmaster. He and Flossy jumped on and off the cart. "Boys and girls, diction, diction, please!" He mocked Mr. Tellymack repeatedly; and Flossy barked repeatedly.

Grandpa bridled the donkey, and Lyle and Flossy jumped on the donkey cart. Grandpa was in his glee, and he continued to test Lyle's knowledge of Fyzabad. "Boy, so you's not going to tell the people in America about the great Tintin?"

"Like what, Grappa?"

The cite-me-and-relate-me archives had their griot records. Tintin was a legend. She was a proxy of the Chief Servant and was aware of all of the Chief Servant's trade union activities. Tintin was just fatter than bones and had never slept on her bed. Her wooden bed, decorated with a cornstraw mattress, a lily-white embroidered sheet, and four pillows as hard as Goodyear tires, was a showpiece. Tintin plastered a no-trespassing sign on the dirt wall next to the bed.

During the Fyzabad disturbance, the anti-riot squad raided Tintin's shack in search of the Chief Servant. The government wanted the Chief Servant dead or alive and had a posse of 2,000 English soldiers in search of him. A police sergeant in full battle dress pulled Tintin's door, and the marline twine which secured her door popped in the sergeant's hand. Tintin, cuddled on the floor, shouted, "Where you going, Mister Corkhat Sergeant? You better don't go near me bed!"

"I don't want your bed, Tintin," the vigilant sergeant said. "I want that strike instigator...that self-styled Chief Servant...that illiterate son of a bitch. Tintin, where's your hipshorted man?"

"The Chief Servant don't live here...and the Chief Servant ain't no *illterate* because he know when hungry belly is groaning for food; and even if he *illterate*, he's our Chief Servant."

"What you said, Tintin?"

"I said the Chief Servant is fighting for all we poor people in this country. He is the only man with the courage to face up to England and to those prejudiced French creole who think they is white. The Chief

Servant, Papa Butler, is a godsend!"

The newly-promoted sergeant touched Tintin with his cold bayonet, and she shivered on the floor. "You talk what you don't know, Tintin," the sergeant said angrily. "Your Chief Servant is *not* my godsend. For that matter, let me see if he's below you." He pushed Tintin with his polished boots.

Tintin rolled over. The space she reluctantly vacated would have fitted only a cricket bat. "Mister Shinebutton Police," Tintin addressed the sergeant, "you ain't see the Chief Servant ain't here in me house."

"Shut up!" the sergeant replied. "Do you want me to carry you down to the cell and lock you up for disturbing an officer in the performance of his duties? Say one more word!" The sergeant ransacked Tintin's one-room shack. He ripped down a portrait of the Chief Servant that was nailed to the dirt wall, and he checked for clues that would have led him to the Chief Servant's hiding place. The sergeant became irate. "I'm giving you one more chance, Tintin," he said, "to tell me where your nigger man is...that troublemaker...that no good son of a bitch who wants to change this country and run out all the white people...Don't you know that the white people did so many good things for Trinidad and Tobago? Where do you think the dress you are wearing came from?" He looked at her. "Tell me, Tintin, otherwise..." The sergeant shifted his gaze to Tintin's perfectly neat bed. A copper penny would have rebounded off of the treated flour bag sheet.

Tintin's voice pitched. "I ain't know where the Chief Servant is...Don't touch me bed nuh! Ah warning you, Mr. Shinebutton Police."

The lawman took no heed of Tintin's warning. He bayoneted her mattress, the bed sheet, the pillows, and the cedar bed frame. Each got a single incision. He looked at Tintin on the floor. She was crouched in a prayerful pose, but her hands were stretched below her bed. The sergeant marched up and down Tintin's cozy room. His boots shook the windows and doors, and loose cow-dung plaster fell from the dirt walls. He scoffed at Tintin as he dusted his tunic uniform.

His next mission was to wreak havoc to Tintin's bed. The dutiful sergeant did not know that the Chief Servant's scouts—some were lawmen who hated the white administration—had spread the news of the impending police invasion. Tintin, a confidante of the Chief Servant, she, more than anyone else, expected the anti-riot squad would search her house. Every Fyzabadian had a weapon lying in wait for the unfriendly incursion of Her Majesty's brutal policemen.

Tintin's weapon was unique. As the sergeant trampled her floor, her hands found her weapon. It was her nightpot. She uncapped it, and the instant smell of fermenting feces and urine combined pierced the sergeant's nostrils. The smell was pungent. The smell was rank. The smell was disgusting. It was ineffable—words couldn't describe that smell. But, indeed, the smell that came from Tintin's nightpot rocked the sergeant's head backwards; and he immediately forgot that he was on Her Majesty's mission. The decorated sergeant retreated. He held up his gun in a safe stance, and the attached bayonet shone from a glimmer of sunlight that permeated Tintin's thatched roof. The sergeant backpedalled and pirouetted in one movement towards Tintin's front door. He jumped off her top platform step that connected five broken steps, and he fell on the muddy ground. He stuck his bayonet into the ground, pressed his hands on the base of the gun, and raised himself off the mud. He scampered into a waiting police van, and commanded the uniformed chauffeur: "Touch the accelerator, private! Get off the fucking brakes! Speed! There is poison gas in Tintin's house."

Tintin came outside and pranced in the water-soaked yard with a heroine's smile. Her uncovered nightpot was in her hand. She waived it to the speeding police van and hailed, "Take that! You son of a bitch! You damn red-nigger-horn child playing you's a white man, and you don't even know who your father is." Her words echoed off the roofs of the zinc tenement in the valley below. Half an hour later, Tintin's bed was again a showpiece for the villagers to admire. That night, too, Tintin slept on the dirt floor on a crocus bag.

Grandpa ended his discussion of the escapades of Tintin when he met the spring. "Woh, donkey!" he said. The donkey stopped. He jumped off the cart with his empty food carrier. He cleared the moss in the spring and dipped water. "Drink, Lyle boy, for that nasty fall." Lyle gulped from the carrier and gave the rest of the water to Flossy. Grandpa got on the cart. "Hi, donkey!" he said, and the donkey moved off willingly. "You want to hear more of Fyzabad to tell the people in America, boy?"

"Tell me more, Grappa."

"I'll only tell you more, boy, if you'll behave yourself in America, and you'll tell the people in America about us."

"Yes, Grappa."

Grandpa was game. "Lyle boy, we have plenty of history in this little oilfield. I can belch you history for days without stopping. Before you was born, worthless Craig used to live in the back of me and Grandma. Craig said he fought in the 1914 war, and people say Craig is still shell-shocked, but I ain't believe any of that story. I know personally that whenever lazy Craig wanted a plate of free food, he used to lie down on the hot pitch and pretended that he was shooting Mussolini with his bony fingers. Your Grandma Leoni used to feed Craig, but left to me alone, Craig would've died from hunger."

"Who else, Grappa?"

"Then we had Hot Ones. Hot Ones was not so

famous, but if you go by Hot Ones, even at midnight, you could get a hot piece of bread, and he didn't have no oven."

"Well, how come Hot Ones always had hot bread, Grappa?"

"God in heaven knows...I don't have to tell you about Grenadian Pearly and Shango Elaine. Them two people have been cussing before you was born about who is the real owner of that sour piece of land they's living on. Once Mr. Kelly, the big oilfield driller, did get lost when he was passing through the shortcut. He asked a little boy just like you to show him his way. You know what the little boy told Mr. Kelly: 'Mister, just keep on walking until you meet two people cussing, and the oilwell that you's looking for is just opposite them two women...And, Mr. Kelly, if you's looking for that oilwell in the dark night, don't bother because them two people does keep their windows open to cuss in their sleep.' You know the little boy was right. When you come back from America to look for us, if Pearly and Elaine isn't dead, they'll still be cussing for that sour piece of alligator land."

"Who again, Grappa? Give me more history. Flossy wants to hear, too." Flossy barked. Lyle put the dog in his lap, and listened to his Grappa.

"You won't be around to see God-Send-Rain kneeling in the savannah and praying to God to send rain. God-Send-Rain always prays to God to send rain whenever he bet all of his wife's rent money on Shell Football Team only to see Shell is losing badly. He knows if it rains the referee will postpone the match, and he'll get back all of his wife's money that he done bet."

"That makes sense, Grappa."

"Boy, I's damn sure Bag-o-Sugar would be dead when you come back from America to see us. She'd be dead because of the amount of dew that does fall down on her head at nights. Every night she does go out the road and stand by the market in that same twalala dress for the oilfield workers to provoke her for her to get the opportunity to cuss them, and to boast that she have family in high places. She does boast and say that she have a cousin—I's sure he is a fifth cousin—who is a magistrate in the City of Port of Spain. Bag-o-Sugar likes to boast and say that her magistrate cousin does wear white Arrow shirts, and not blue dock and khaki like them oilfield workers. I don't know why Fyzabad people does trouble Bag-o-Sugar to hear the same thing over and over again."

"Grappa, I troubled Bag-o-Sugar many times, and she did not tell me that same old thing."

"What she told you, boy?"

"She told me that you and Grandma used to bathe in Gower's well naked, and you..."

Grandpa changed the topic immediately and moved on to another famous citizen of Fyzabad. "Lyle boy, you must definitely tell the people in America about Eveready Jools who does balance a tray of hops bread on his head while riding his bicycle down that skiddy Delhi Road hill. Eveready Jools have a good balancing head, but that man don't ever believe in God."

"I know! I know, Grappa. I heard Eveready Jools say that the Virgin Mary gave Joseph a horn child. What is a horn child, Grappa?"

"A horn child is like neighbor Harry's son. Neighbor Harry is black black like a tar baby, and his wife Miss Florry is blacker than a pot; yet their son Jimmy is yellow like a Chinese! Little Jimmy have nothing from Harry's nature."

"I heard Jimmy is Chinee Chin's child, Grappa. Neighbor Florry went and begged Chinee Chin for a piece of sol fish and cornmeal, and that is when she got the baby Jimmy."

"*Mamayo*! When you heard that, boy?"

"Grappa, I heard that since I was little. One night Grandma thought I was sleeping, and I heard her whispering that to Aunt Gina...Jesus is really a horn child, Grappa?"

"Eveready Jools say that, probably he know. But you, boy, don't you ever believe anything that that godless man say! And don't let any woman in America give you a horn child when you be a big man!"

"No, Grappa! And you know what else I heard Eveready Jools say?"

Grandpa was scared to inquire of Jools. He was afraid that atheist Eveready Jools, his schoolmate, might have leaked some of his, Grandpa's, unpleasant past. Effortlessly, he said, "What that godless man said, boy?"

"Eveready Jools said he ain't believe that bible talk about faith can move mountains because Apex Oilfields only used tractors and bulldozers whenever they wanted to cut down a mountain or clear a location to put up derricks to drill for oil."

"Boy, how come you know so much about that godless man? You does go by his place to thief his mangoes?"

"No, Grappa. You forget Eveready Jools doesn't put water in his mouth to talk. He's plain talking just like you, and I like Eveready's interpretation of the bible."

Grandpa sulked. "*Carrajo!*"

"What's wrong, Grappa?"

"Coming to think of it, I's really glad you's leaving from near that godless man, and from near them ugly Sullymans, too. Soon your nature will grow, and it will put you into lots of trouble with Madame Sullyman. I may have to even kill Madame Sullyman."

"But why, Grappa?"

"Because Madame Sullyman have a voodoo chair...She does practice obeah. As ugly as Madame Sullyman's girl children is, whichever boy who got hard nature sit on that chair and sex any of her daughters, that boy got to marry Madame Sullyman's daughter overnight. I could never forget that Miss Buelah used to boast and say that her boy-cock-son Rothan could tread any of Madame Sullyman's daughters and nothing would happen to Rothan. Your Grandma wanted to keep Rothan away from trouble. She did pick fresh limes from behind the house and did give Rothan to suck. Those limes was to cool down the heat in Rothan's nature, because Grandma saw that Rothan was always eyeing those ugly Sullyman gals...Rothan was so rude and mannish; he didn't suck the limes. You know what happened, boy?"

"What happened to Rothan, Grappa?" Flossy barked as if he, too, wanted to know.

"Rothan did go in Madame Sullyman's house and did sit down on that voodoo chair even before he tread any of them gals. Nobody, not even his mother Miss Buelah, did know when Rothan got married to Jean Sullyman, the one with the long mouth and long teeth. Little boys, especially when their natures start to grow and get hard and spring water, must listen to old people. When little boys have hard natures, they must definitely listen to old people to prevent their damnation."

"When would my nature get hard and spring water, Grappa?"

"Whenever that be, let Aunt Lily know so that she'll give you some limes to suck."

Lyle pondered for ten seconds, then he blurted: "Grappa, what you say about little boys' damnation is true, but big people like Miss Buelah must not brag and boast that they can outsmart voodoo or obeah, because only goodluck can beat obeah especially when your boy child nature is hard like a rock."

"Sure's right, son...Let's go and look for Freddy since we's passing so close to his house. Poor Freddy, he lost his job for cussing his boss. I always told Freddy when he's cussing a white man he must cuss him like a

Bajan."

"What do you mean by cuss like a Bajan? Is a Bajan a person from Barbados, the land of the flying fish?"

"Yes...And to cuss like a Bajan means to cuss a person very soft, or to cuss him in your mind so that only you can hear. Freddy was right to cuss his boss Mr. Mowll because Mr. Mowll short pay him, but Freddy was not smart to cuss Mr. Mowll very loud because Mr. Mowll, that dog!, heard him and fired him. Mr. Mowll even blackballed Freddy. Freddy should've done like me. I cussed Mr. Mowll many times, but each time I cussed him like a Bajan. I cussed him soft, soft. I's sure them white people in America is different; and they's fair people. You won't have to cuss them white people in America at all because they's different from them white English people in the oilfields."

"How you know? You went to America before, Grappa?"

"No...But I know so. And I know everything in America is big, so big. You'll see big, big houses touching the stars. I don't have to tell you, because soon you'll see for yourself. *Mamayo*!" Grandpa exclaimed in Trinbago patois. "Warm silver snow does fall down in big chunks in America! You don't have to go to Miss Beran theater here no more to see screen stars. In America you'll be right there to see real screen stars...right on the spot to see John Wayne shooting down them Indians...And, boy, so I'll be boasting about you when I imagine you up there sleeping under that silver snow...But you know I could never be ever prouder than when you climbed up that greasypole and got to be the champion on that greasy Monday, Mister Adult Nigger."

* * * * *

Lyle and his grandfather Braffit Gordon, seated on the donkey cart, daydreamed of that greasy Monday when Lyle was given the nickname Mister Adult Nigger.

It was an Easter Monday in festive Fyzabad. The remains of Judas's Good Friday effigy were still kicked about by toyless children when the greasypole flag was hoisted. The well dressed boys wore gym boots which had been whitened for several days in advance. Their pants, styled with gun-mouth bottoms, made of English tweed, were in vogue; and round neck polo shirts, with made-in-Hong Kong labels, sucked the perspiration from their athletic bodies. On the boys' waists were leather belts with glittering, metal buckles. Those buckles of various designs, which were turned out by apprentices on the oilfield lathes, shone as brightly as the coconut oil on their shin bones.

On that gracious Easter Monday the girls wore brightly-colored bodices and flair skirts which barely touched their knees. Their socks were immaculately white and matched their spotless Bata shoes. The rich and the sophisticated were dressed in clothes bought from Montano Stores in San Fernando, the industrial capital of Trinidad and Tobago. Every attire was indeed a showpiece.

In Fyzabad, climbing to the top of the greasypole was always the premier event. The greasypole was a 40-foot pole pasted with tallow. It was firmly planted into the red earth. Mr. Mondesir, the organizer of the sports meet, had begged and got three prizes. The prizes were nailed and tied with wire on the top of the greasypole. Shopkeeper Chinee Chin gave a bottle of 100 percent proof rum; shopkeeper Portuguese Alves gave two florins; and the journeymen Syrians and Lebanese pooled their resources and donated a 5-pound picnic ham encased in tar paper. The picnic ham was the most coveted prize.

Lyle had competed in every track and field event and lost; but he was determined to be a winner that day. The last sports event was the climbing of the greasypole, and top honors for achieving such feat were shared by "Nigger Champ" Spree and "Coolie Champ" Chatoor. On that Easter Monday about which Lyle, his Grandpa, and even Flossy daydreamed, Chatoor, a meek Indian boy, had declined from the climbing competition. He was in mourning because his uncle had recently died.

Mr. Mondesir traversed the savannah and shouted on that memorable Easter Monday for competitors, but only Spree answered the call. Mr. Mondesir again shouted to the top of his lungs, and he waited on competitors. Lyle disappeared from the crowd, and then reappeared with greasypole paraphernalia.

Spree was about to give a solo exhibition when Lyle came forward with two pieces of rope. The milling crowd was shocked. A spectator passed his hat; Mr. Mondesir dropped two numbers in the hat's sweaty belly; and Spree pulled to climb first. Spree smiled and looked up at the prizes donated by Fyzabad's generous businessmen. The prizes hung temptingly from the greasypole; and they swayed in the slight breeze that blew.

Cocky! Spree licked his lips. He had foreseen a victory climb which would have given him an opportunity to taste ham for the first time in his life before Christmas morning. The rum was earmarked for his stepfather who had handpicked special friends for the tasting party; and the money was for his mother, Miss Mary. She had already budgeted five cents for Spree to go to the movies and sit in balcony with the oilfield middle class. The rest of the money was to shop in style at Chinee Chin, and to pay Portuguese Alves a deposit on their lifetime debt.

Spree's focus was on the gifts of the prosperous merchants. He donned his gear, filled his pockets with sand, and placed a jackknife in his mouth a *le* Tarzan. With his handrope and footrope in place, he began his climb. Spree was half way up the greasypole when he slipped down. "Breda" Paul (Lyle's brother), "Starboy" Shenko, Zack, Irwin, "Joiner" Jan, and "Godino" Kenwyen—they called themselves "the Boys of Fyzabad"—burst into senseless laughter. Kenwyen, his mouth as wide as the river, screamed as though he sat on a twirling feather which fitted—you know where. The Boys' collective laughter echoed.

The itinerant climber pretended that his stumble was prearranged. As Spree wormed up the greasypole in his second attempt, his footrope fell, and he lost grip. He slid down, and brought down an avalanche of tallow grease with him. Spree didn't panic for he trusted his ability, and each climber had three chances. "The coolie champ would've never slid down. Coolie is always better than nigger," a spectator, engulfed by his kith and kin, heckled Spree. Spree paid no heed to his detractor because the "Coolie Champ" Chatoor was in mourning, and Lyle, the competition, was unheard of.

Confident Spree blew a kiss to the game crowd, and resumed his ascent as a greasypole great. Spree really looked great. He powdered the pole with sand, and climbed up, and up. The sight of his ascent was unbearable to the Boys. The Boys wanted to see Lyle, Spree's junior, get his chance. Like politicians, the Boys thought up a trick when Spree was an arm's length away from the wind-swayed Syrian-Lebanese donation which drooped on the greasypole.

Unrehearsed, Zack squeaked. His squeaks falset-toed. Breda laughed at Zack's squeaks; Irwin laughed at Breda's; Shenko joined in; Jan laughed at Shenko's; and it seemed as if the Godino River had broken the sluice gate and the torrential waters had come down when Kenwyen opened his mouth. "Spree," Kenwyen shout-ed, "you just like a Grenada Mongoose. You only know how to suck eggs. Your sore foot mother, Miss Mary, the *soucouyant*-vampire, taught you how to suck people too? Wha' you doin' up there, vampire boy? That cooked ham ain't have blood." The Boys laughed louder and louder, and their laughter became contagious. The raucous cacophony of the thousands of laughing voices could have muffled the exhaust siren of the Apex Oilfield power plant; even King Kong, with both feet planted in the ground, would have lost concentration, and so did the mortal, Spree. He, too, laughed to hide his hurt. He completely lost all his concentration. He slid down the pole faster than olympian Sonja Henie on ice skates, and was disqualified.

Fyzabadians worshipped heroes. Immediately Spree fell from grace. The hurt to Spree and his family was disastrous. The crowd no longer cheered Spree; they jeered him and chased him around. Spree's supporters were few, but they took faith in the fact that Fyzabadians are like elephants: if it takes a million years they will repay in kind, or worst; but, for sure, the aggrieved or his offspring will "get even." "*Payback*," as it was called, was a tit-for-tat phenomenon of Fyzabad.

Lyle could not believe Spree's plight. At that moment he was bothered most by the fact that he had learned from his spiritual baptist Leader Gerrol that retribution means: "Souls reap on earth what they sow on earth." Now he was sure that one day one of the Boys, or all the Boys—he included—would reap the fate of Spree. Nonetheless, he quickly buried the thought that burdened him. He summed up his courage and looked at the huge savannah. The savannah was filled with the Who is Who in Fyzabad. The grandstand housed dignitaries. Fyzabad's two-tiered middle class, who lived in different sized and colored bungalows owned by the Apex Oilfields Company, was in attendance. Their sobriquets, "Playing White" and "Acting White," were whispered by those who thought they were "Really White." The three shades of skin color, who, except for today, would have ostracized themselves from Alex Haley's roots, flanked Colonel Hicklong, the Englishman of German blood, the *kopf von den kopfen* (the boss of bosses) of the oilfields. The Colonel, forever diplomatic, in his reserved seat under the arch of the grandstand, resembled a stick of white chalk glued to a blackboard. Mr. Tellymack, the headmaster, wore his new suspenders that held up his size forty pants. He was ushered in by Miss Tookin, nicknamed Young-and-Old. (Young-and-Old won her nickname because the shy, young men of Fyzabad lost their virginity on her bed.) Chinee Chin didn't need an usher. With a flow of fractured English, Fyzabad patois, and philosophy, he smiled his way to his reserved seat next to sickly Portuguese Alves. Portuguese Alves coughed, spat in the hot sand, and he covered his dusty saliva with the tip of his sandals.

The only donors who missed the sports meet were the Syrians and Lebanese. That day, too, they pedalled their "bargain-bargain" deep in the Cocoa, the backwoods of Fyzabad. To the Syrians and Lebanese, making money to send back to their homeland was more important than the Fyzabad social event. Conversely, Fyzabad negroes viewed that Easter Monday was going to be proof of a victory climb by Spree, and further proof of their superiority over the East Indians. The negroes rhymed calypsoes and sang, "Chatoor is in hiding./We sure his uncle isn't dead or dying./" The East Indians retorted, "Nigger is a nation,/Full of perspiration./They lazy like hell,/And they live in the police station./"

From sunrise the people of African descent beat spoons on bottles, drank liquor, and boasted of their superiority over all the other races. The negroes referred to themselves as proud Africans. The proud Africans called Chinee Chin a thief; the prouder Africans scorned sickly Portuguese Alves and called him consumptive; and the oilfields' middle class got the spleen that came from all the Africans' tongues. The onlookers who voiced that Chatoor, the "Coolie Champ," was better than Spree, the "Nigger Champ," were soiled with tallow grease thrown by the brazen Africans. The African people of Fyzabad reminded the East Indians that they (the East Indians) came indentured from India, and toted their (the Africans') bundles on their heads.

God-Send-Rain, Paymaster, and Mr. Songbird, the noblest of African gamblers, showed their disdain for the East Indians. Those noble African gamblers shouted to the East Indians, "All you came from Calcutta, and now you uppity coolies get so fresh...Get out of town when Spree come down...." The African gamblers pooled their money and jewelry and placed heavy bets with Dadoo Maharaj, the Hindu pundit and pawnshop owner. The "cock-sure" African gamblers gave Dadoo Maharaj lofty odds, and took Spree to win. The Africans acted; they danced; and they put on impromptu plays. Hamlet? Could be! "We're going to bust your business, Dadoo, and run you fresh coolies out of town," the African gambler-playwrights said repeatedly. That was the way the first act of the Africans' script should have ended. Nay! There was a blind curve in the road. The antagonists won. The African protagonists ran Spree out of town the moment he slid down the greasypole.

There was commotion galore!

The commotions in the crowded savannah unnerved Lyle. The straw pole had made no prior mention of a little boy named Lyle Gordon. He was invisible except to the hand-to-mouth people who nurtured him. On that unforgettable Easter Monday, Lyle walked to the greasypole with Grandpa's hog rope which he dare not lose. The Boys milled around him with doses of courage and faith. The Boys were like that mother who shielded her baby from a lion with her hairpin as her weapon. The Boys' hopeful, Lyle

Gordon, his weapons were bits of rope, sawdust, and a dull hacksaw blade. Lyle tied his footrope and handrope in a grip Uncle Lookup, the scoutmaster, had taught him. He put the hacksaw blade below his cloth belt, and he tied a pouch of sawdust around his neck. Barebacked and barefooted, Lyle Gordon began his ascent on his greasy Mt. Everest without a Sherpa Tensing.

He was half way up the pole. The Uncle Lookup knot slipped continuously, but he held on to the same spot on the greasypole until he was tired. He became frustrated and was about to slide down. The Boys sensed his troubles. They hollered with urgency, "Lyle, Lyle, Mr. Immanuel is coming up behind you!" (Lyle had once stolen Mr. Immanuel's mangoes, and Mr. Immanuel had gone up the tree like a tiger behind him.) The Boys' reminder of Mr. Immanuel gave Lyle new wind, and the name Immanuel also did the trick. From then on, the unknown greasypole climber went upward and picnic-hamward with few slips, and he profited from Spree's clearing of a great deal of the tallow grease.

Lyle touched the three prizes. In doing so, he abided by the Mondesir Law of Greasypole Possession; *i.e.*, a contestant must touch all the prizes to claim ownership. He heard the spontaneous ovation below, but his Grandpa's voice echoed: "Lyle boy, you's doin' good, but don't leave me hog rope of there nuh." Lyle sawed the ham from the pole with his hacksaw blade. Breda caught the ham, smelled it, and made sure that it was really an edible product. Ham in Easter? Breda thought. A ham in Easter was the equivalent to the "Missing Ball," the country's biggest sweepstake worth Three Hundred Dollars. With the thought of a ham in his hand, Breda grinned from ear to ear. The wind swayed the pole, but Lyle maintained his concentration. He ripped the pouch with the money and pocketed it. Only the bottle of rum gave him a little problem, but he eventually freed the rum from the wire with his teeth. Alas! the task was over; and Lyle slid down the greasypole to the thunderous applause. A proud greasypole great was he!

"Likkle Lyle...Lyle! Lyle!...That's ah we boy...That's our boy...The new nigger champ!...That little black boy who was up there on that greasypole is neighbor Braffit's grandson...The adult nigger...." Words of praise came from the tree tops, hanging branches, from the galleries that overlook the savannah, from the covered and open bleachers, from the grandstand, from the East Indians, from the expatriates, from the hated Apex bungalow people, from Chinee Chin, Portguese Alves...But the loudest holler came from Grandpa himself.

Lyle received the coveted Mondesir gold belt, the highest sports medal in Fyzabad. The belt was presented to him by Tubal Uriah "Buzz" Butler, the Chief Servant himself, who, earlier that day, was released from the Royal Jail after serving time for disobeying his ban from trade union activities. "What shall we call this little fella almost as great as me?" the Chief Servant shouted to the crowd as he lifted Lyle like burnt offering high in the air. "Mister Adult Nigger! Mister Adult Nigger!" Grandpa's voice echoed above all the mixed voices in the foot-beaten savannah.

* * * * *

Lyle and Grandpa's daydream of that Easter Monday ended when Flossy barked. Flossy smelled cooked bones, and Grandma's voice was heard in her kitchen. "Lily, they're back from the field. I am sure Lyle went to burst the news to Braff."

In the plum-laden yard Breda heaped the dry leaves with a coconut frond. "Breda, who won the kite battle?" Lyle asked as he steered the donkey into the yard. "Me," Breda replied. A sudden thought hit Grandpa as a pile of leaves blew on him. "Mister Adult Nigger, get off the animal. I want to ask you something."

"What, Grappa?"

"What's Spree's real name?"

"I don't know, Grappa. Everybody called him Spree before he and his family were chased out of town. I'm glad because I was afraid of him. He called me Smelly because I smelled things before I ate them, and many times he picked me for a fight."

"You didn't make him fall down the greasypole and lose his title so don't be afraid of nothing." Grandpa injected another odd question. "Boy, do you know who was eating my cashew nuts in those sealed tins?"

"Rats, Grappa!" Lyle avoided that question. "Let me tell you about Spree, Grappa. He is a good stick fighter. Even if you have a long piece of iron, and he has a small stick of chalk, he can hit you ten times, and you can't hit Spree once. Spree's father is a stick fighting champ, and he taught Spree how to stick fight and how to butt with his head. Spree butted a boy one day, and red blood came from that boy's head!"

"That is past tense, boy...Tell me, who was that brown-skin gal with a big bow of ribbons in her hair? She had on a red dress on the day that you climbed the greasypole." Grandpa pretended he did not know the girl about whom he inquired. "That little gal who shouted your name, 'Lyle! Lyle! don't slip down...' Who was she?"

"Grandpa, you can't remember her? She's Miss Brownie's daughter, Elizabeth. We are in Mr. Tellymack's class. You can't remember when I put a small mirror on the floor to spy under her dress, and she caught me? You remember after Mr. Tellymack beat me real good, Grandma wanted to murder me again just for that little prank. You remember

Grandma told me that the proper way for any man to get to see under any woman is to approach her from on top, and the way to do it is..."

Grandpa cut him short. "That's Grandma Leoni all right." Grandpa changed the subject again. "Lyle boy, anyway, you don't have to bother about Spree again because you's going to America...Boy, this coming Christmas am going to miss you to help me varnish those chairs."

"Grappa, varnish early this year because last year you varnished late Christmas eve and the chair stuck on Mr. Wilson's bottom on Christmas morning."

"I was sure glad that did happen to that no-good Wilson serge pants. He is a man who's always coming in my house to look for my wife when he know I ain't home...Woh! Woh, donkey! Woh!" Grandpa pulled the ass to a complete halt. Lyle and Flossy jumped off the cart and darted to the house. "Lyle boy, don't go and tell Grandma what I just said nuh!" Grandpa shouted aloud as he unloaded the produce from the cart. Breda, with a big grin, with his broom in hand, raced after the wind-blown leaves. He, too, was always tickled by his Grandpa's frank talk.

Slowly, Lyle raised the backroom window with a short bamboo rod. He poked his head outside and whispered, "No, Grappa. I, too, know Leoni all right...I won't tell her what you said about neighbor Wilson." Lyle's voice became a mere whisper, and he made a sign to his grandfather to come closer. "Grappa," he said, "how come you didn't tell Flossy and me about Cousin Edderleen?"

"*Mamayo*! Boy, you know that 'tory too?"

"Grappa, don't trust me. I know every story."

"Boy, don't tell people in America about that 'tory nuh!"

"Why, Grappa?"

"Because that is fambaly business."

"I never knew that Cousin Edderleen was our

real family."

"Cousin Edderleen is my fambaly, and she's your Grandma fambaly. So you see how close she's to all of us. Don't tell America that 'tory 'tall, 'tall! Let fambaly business remain in the fambaly only."

"Okay, Grappa. I won't tell people in America our family story." Lyle raised his voice to a normal pitch. "Grappa, am going to pack my Mondesir gold belt in my gripcase." He rushed through the house and kissed Aunt Lily. "Go and wash up, boy, before I give you dinner," Grandma Leoni said. He ignored his Grandma and rushed to find his gold belt. It was the first time that Lyle had seen a tiny engraved *M* on the back of the gold-plated buckle.

It was an enterprising day, and after dinner Lyle packed more of his keepsakes in his gripcase. He finally went to bed and dreamed of America.

The next day Lyle awoke with a new zeal. He had to say "Goodbye and thank you" to the village, or, at least, to all the old people, especially those who were kind to him when his parents died. He had to find those kind people in whatever mud tracks they lived. He had to visit them and tell them, "Thank you, neighbor Rosa; Thank you, neighbor Meena; Thank you, Mr. Cheeseman..." The "Thank-yous" were enormous. Whether Mr. Cheeseman had bad dogs or broken bottles hidden in the grass that would cut Lyle's tender feet, Lyle had to find him and tell him goodbye. Not to tell the villagers goodbye was tantamount to bad breeding, and the villagers, in turn, would have called Lyle "ungrateful" even in their prayers when they asked God for forgiveness for their sins.

His first stop was at the Fyzabad Anglican School. He knocked on his headmaster's door. "Come in," Mr. Tellymack answered. Mr. Tellymack was not only the village school master, but the Buge, the poet, the preacher, the notary public, the counselor. To be precise, Mr. Tellymack was Fyzabad's yardstick. In

greatness, Mr. Tellymack was second only to the Chief
Servant. Many years ago Miss Saysay had dreamt that
whenever the day had come for Mr. Tellymack to die
he would get two burials. Yet with all of Mr.
Tellymack's fame, Lyle hated him, and he often cursed
Mr. Tellymack like a Bajan. Lyle cursed Mr. Tellymack
in his thoughts; he cursed Mr. Tellymack in his sleep;
but he never cursed Mr. Tellymack aloud for even the
woodpecker which hammered the immortelle tree by
his peep window to hear.

"Sir, I've come to say goodbye," Lyle, barely four
feet, said; and he looked up.

Mr. Tellymack was six-foot-eight. He was a natural
heavyweight. He was ebony all over, even in the palms
of his hands. The days Mr. Tellymack wore white buffs
of Clark leather his eyes were expressionless. On those
days every disobedient boy wished he were good; every
absent-minded girl wished she had worn coarse
bloomers; and the boy who played hooky from school
knew that he had to wear twin and padded khaki
pants. The Buge never spared the rod. There was no
Board of Education psychologist to handpick the
dyslexic, the late starters, or the undernourished. The
Buge was the doctor, and his medicine for learning was
his soaked leather strap.

Lyle, seated before Mr. Tellymack, instantly
remembered the day he hadn't learned the proper
diction for *Abou Ben Adhem*. In a flash, he again saw
the vision of Mr. Tellymack who had gripped him,
pulled the seat of his trousers to dead center, and
leathered his buttocks. That was the first time Lyle had
tasted his headmaster's soaked leather which the class
called "black power," and eversince Lyle had tried to
steal black power, though unsuccessfully.

"So you're going away next week," Mr. Tellymack
said to regain Lyle's attention.

"Yes, sir. I've come to say goodbye in advance."
He paid attention to his grammar. He dare not speak

Fyzabad patois or the pidgin English he employed to daily provoke Chinee Chin.

"I heard the news yesterday." News in Fyzabad got around in a minute, with or without the hand-pedalled telephones that were only in the white people's bungalows. Mr. Tellymack smiled incitingly and hoped his pupil Lyle would initiate conversation. Lyle did not.

The schoolmaster opened his drawer. "Here's your second testimonial for winning the recitation contest, young man. Your diction was just as I taught you and all my present and past pupils. Never forget *Abou Ben Adhem*. Never forget what that poem stands for. Apply it in your teaching, your preaching, whatever. I give all of my present and past students that advice."

"Yes, sir...Excuse me, sir. Sir, Grandma sent me in the shop to buy an ounce of butter to put in the bake. I have it in my pocket, and it's melting, sir."

Mr. Tellymack shook Lyle's hand and spoke at the same time. "Be a good boy, Loile, and remember that big world of America runs on toime...You've been late to my class, and that was to your detriment. Toime built America, Loile." His handshake twisted Lyle's brass ring, and his Barbadian accent grated Lyle's ear. "You'll remember what I told you, Loile?"

"Yes, sir," Lyle answered softly and politely, and he quickly walked away. He did not look back for he feared that looking back would have been a temptation for his headmaster to make him recite *Abou Ben Adhem* one more time. That time of the day was pal's time, not the school principal's time, and Lyle wanted to have no more dealings with "Black Power" Tellymack for the rest of his life. He cursed his headmaster one more time, but like a Bajan.

When Lyle reached "Joiner" Jan, his favorite pal among the Boys of Fyzabad, he was exhausted from the many hours of visiting teachers, friends, neighbors, and relatives. "Joiner" Jan and his mother, Miss

Delcina, anxiously awaited his arrival. He was on time to hear Miss Delcina leave her instructions. "Jan," she said, "watch the bake for me...Am just running to the shop to buy a piece of sol fish."

"Yes, Ma," Jan said. "Where are you going to buy the salt fish?" Jan had his reason for asking that pertinent question.

"Am not going by Chinee Chin to get cause to curse his Chinese creole children. Just because they have a little high color they talk down to the customers. For that matter, Chinee Chin's goods are too damn dear...Seems as if Chin wants us to help him buy back China. Am going by Portuguese Alves to buy the sol fish, the good kind of bacalao, to let Lyle taste my hand for the last time."

"Okay, Ma." Jan watched his mother until she was out of sight.

Delcina left a round, cornmeal-flour bake roasting on the baking iron. The bake was the full circumference of the baking iron. "Joiner" Jan cut out the middle of the hot bake and put it aside on the kitchen counter. He stuck the two crescent-shaped ends of the bake together. The heat of the baking iron and Jan's joining skills glued the bake perfectly. Jan rested the bake back on the baking iron to finish roast. The bake was round again, but it was much smaller in size.

"Joiner" Jan cut the extracted portion into two pieces, and used his both hands as a scale. "Take the bigger piece, Lyle. This is my gift to you."

The bigger piece of the stolen bake that Lyle chose was an atom bigger than Joiner Jan's. "Thank you, Joiner, for letting me choose first, but you should have let me cut the bake." They laughed at each other, and both pals ate the bake hurriedly with brown sugar.

Delcina returned from the shop. She was a red woman. Shocked by the dwindled size of the bake, she got redder. "How this bake shrink so!" she shouted.

"Ma," Jan said calmly, "it could be one of two things."

"What!" Delcina's curiosity peaked.

"It's either that sickly Portuguese Alves' yeast that you put in the flour is no good, or what Mr. Tellymack taught us in school about science is true."

"What Mr. Tellymack taught all you about making bake, boy?"

"Cold does contract things, and heat does expand things, Ma." Jan worked his mind and looked at Lyle for his blessed assurance. Lyle, with a blank face, worked his tongue; and he used his tongue to clean his teeth and the roof of his mouth. With the help of his saliva, Lyle swallowed the uncooked flour in slow motion.

Delcina challenged her son's logic. "Jan, well, how come the hot bake didn't swell and get bigger according to Mr. Tellymack's teaching?"

"Ma, because sickly Portuguese Alves' yeast is no good…Good yeast makes flour yield and rise." Jan moved his hands upward like a maestro with a baton conducting his orchestra in the last movement of *The Missing Flour*.

Delcina shook her head in total approval. She was so pleased with her son's I.Q. "God must bless that man Mr. Tellymack for the amount of knowledge that he is putting in all you brains," she said. "But that ofay, sickly, thieving, black-market Portuguese Alves, he must die with his eyes wide open for robbing we poor people in Fyzabad. No wonder why the people of Sangre Grande raised their red flag, ran him out of town, and nearly killed him!" Delcina went earnestly to her cooking. She sang, *God that Made Us Earth and Heaven*, and fried her salt fish in sweet oil and onions. She served Lyle first. She handed him an enamel plate with the salt fish wedged between the bake, and Jan poured his best friend a giant cup of lime squash. Delcina surveyed her guest while he ate. "Lyle boy, you know you already start to look just like a Harlem darkie."

"True, Miss Delcina?"

"So help me God, boy!"

Lyle belched suddenly. "Sorry, Miss Delcina, for my bad manners...And thank you again, Miss Delcina, for the nice bake and sol fish." He got off the table and put his utensils in the kitchen sink.

Miss Delcina kissed him. She looked softly into his eyes and said, "Behave yourself, and write us as soon as you get up in America...Lyle boy, I have some sol fish remaining in the pot, but if the flour did yield I would've surely given you a piece of bake and sol fish to carry to school to eat tomorrow during recess time."

"Miss Delcina, I stopped going to school because Grandma has to measure me to make new clothes to wear up to America...And Grandpa said that I have to go in the market and help him sell his produce to get money to help Aunt Lily pay for my plane ticket...And, believe me, Miss Delcina, the way my belly is full today, I would not need anything to eat until next month."

"Lyle, you know you're a joker just like your grandfather Braff."

"Everybody tells me that, Miss Delcina." Lyle told Miss Delcina goodbye. He made the victory sign to "Joiner" Jan, the bake bandit, and walked away with a hidden smile.

Lyle's last week in Fyzabad had come. It brought a minor miracle. "Bad Pay" Evena had come to settle a 20-year debt that she owed Grandma. That debt had come about in a strange way. Evena had obliged Grandma Leoni to deliver her dollar and *whe-whe* (illegal lottery numbers) to the *whe-whe* banker. On the way to the banker, Evena was stopped by an undercover policeman. Aware of the stiff penalty for transporting *whe-whe* numbers, Evena swallowed Leoni's numbers that were written on coarse brown paper. She also swallowed Leoni's dollar bill that was wrapped in the coarse paper.

Evena returned to the yard of eager ponters and told her story as if she were the biblical whale that swallowed Jonah. Everyone was convinced. Not Leoni! Worse still, one of the *whe-whe* numbers that Leoni had betted on that day had won. Twenty years had passed when Leoni had said, "Evena, you's a bad pay...You swallow me dollar like Mandrake so you have to shit it out like Mandrake...." The other words that came out of "Cussbird" Leoni's mouth were too offensive for even the carrion birds to alight on.

Lyle couldn't believe that he was seeing "Bad Pay" Evena at Grandma's door. He was almost eight years old and had heard about the Evena-Grandma episode ever since he was two. It was the first time that he had seen Grandma and Evena speak; and that, to him, was a miracle. "Bad Pay" Evena hailed, "Leoni! Leoni!" Leoni rushed out of her house. Evena paid her 20-year debt. She paid her debt without interest, and apologized to Grandma. Grandma kissed the blue dollar note, gave Bad Pay a bearhug, and invited her to join the table for dinner.

Everyone at the dinner table was happy to see the two *whe-whe* ponters together as dear friends again. Aunt Gina, pudgy and excitable, ignored Grandpa's presence and seated herself at the head of the table. She quickly said the grace before meal, served herself only, and ate everything that wasn't nailed down.

"Mammie Leoni," Gina said, after her first course, "I hope you didn't cook with plenty salt or grease because Dr. Littlepage stopped me from eating those calories."

Grandma was shocked. She was so shocked that her spoon fell from her dribbling mouth. Grandma knew only a few people like the expatriates and the oilfield middle class could have afforded a visit to Dr. Littlepage; and Gina certainly wasn't in that category.

Grandma knew that Gina got her medicine from the health clinic in bottles labelled, "Shake Well Before Using." Gina drank Fyzabad's *Shake Well* for all her complaints. She drank *Shake Well* for even her suspected cancer.

"What did you just tell me, Gina?" Grandma asked to test her perfect hearing.

Gina added, and repeated more of her don'ts. "Mammie Leoni, I hope you didn't put curry in this pot...I don't eat salty or greasy food...I don't ever eat much seasoning. I have a paper from Dr. Littlepage telling me what I should eat."

"Gina, I didn't want to say it, but you's the most liardest of all my three children. Since you join that Shouter Baptist religion, you's lying even more. My dear child, when you bring that paper from Dr. Littlepage, and let me read it with my own two eyes, I'd tell you what I put in the food that you done eat."

The diners roared with laughter.

"Well!" Gina said. She heaped her plate again and said, "I go have to take a very strong dose of epsom salt to wash out the pot salt and grease from me stomach."

Lyle grinned and choked. He couldn't help himself from remembering the day that he had worked for his Aunt Gina and was rewarded. He recalled that on that day after his loving Aunt had shared an ounce of peanuts among her nine children and him, and she still had peanuts left, she called him. With her cherubic face, Aunt Gina began her usual sad song before she rewarded him: "God is good...Likkle Lyle, you knows Godfather (Godfather was her husband) is dead, and I alone have to mind these children. But you cleaned up the back yard that these pickaninnies dirty up so good, that I must pay you today. Take this, boy, and don't open your hand till you reach home!" Her command was obeyed. Gina opened Lyle's right hand, put something in it, and then locked his fingers. When Lyle got home and opened his locked fingers, he found a farthing which smelled of garlic. He knew that he needed three more farthings to make a penny; and he also knew, being told by his Aunt Gina, that money mixed with garlic stays longer to spend.

Gina looked at Lyle. She sensed what was going through her nephew's racing mind. "Likkle Lyle, what you's thinkin' about?"

"America, Aunt Gina."

"You better had." Gina left the dinner table, and the diners laughed to their hearts' content.

Lyle's happiest day came when the Gordon family and few close friends fitted themselves in Mr. Wheeler's lorry bound for the airport. They reached their destination. Aunt Lily checked in her luggage at the British West Indian Airways counter. The first announcement for passengers travelling to the United States of America to board the plane almost stopped Lyle's heart. Aunt Lily smacked friends and relatives on their cheeks and tried not to smudge her lipstick. Lyle kissed Grandma and Grandpa, and tears trickled from their eyes. He hugged his brother Paul for a long minute. "Goodbye, Breda," he said.

"Did you pack your gold belt?" Breda asked.

Lyle fought the tears, but couldn't answer. He pointed to his gripcase, and shook his head affirmatively.

Spiritual Baptist Leader Gerrol purposely brought humor to the sad group. "Shepherd Lyle," he said, "you better leave before the tears from Baytee's people drown you."

Lyle glanced at Baytee. (It was the custom in Fyzabad to call any unmarried East Indian girl "Baytee," especially when you didn't know her name. The boy was called "Baytah.") He smiled at the attention that Baytee got. Baytee's relatives and friends who had come to see her off to America were almost two hundred in number. Some took pictures with Baytee, but the majority of Baytee's family and wellwishers were shedding tears because Baytee was going away to America to live.

"Brains!" Leader Gerrol said, and he pointed to his fat belly. "Tell them in America about me, Shepherd Lyle." Lyle knew the story about Leader Gerrol's "belly is not his brains," according to how it was interpreted, but he ignored Leader Gerrol's hint totally. What would happen if he lost the plane was Lyle's mindset!

Aunt Gina lunged forward. She meant to outshine the spiritual leader. Gina was both a shouting Spiritual Baptist and a Roman Catholic, a bit of chemistry unknown to the Vatican in those days. It was Ash Wednesday. Father Hennessy had earlier in the day blessed Gina's throat, and his imprint of ash on her forehead was as bold as the Imprimatur. Gina, unadulterated from the chemistry of two faiths, touched the talisman in her bosom, pushed spiritual Leader Gerrol aside, and sermonized in creole, in *deep* creole.

"Likkle Lyle," Gina began, "you knows you's stubborn, but you must always walk with God because you won't be likkle for too long again. Never burn your bridges...Always do as these Indians down here...These Indians down here in Fyzabad don't even know India 'cause they born right down here in Fyzabad, but you'll always hear them boasting 'bout India and praying to God to live long enough to go back one day to see India.

"Likkle Lyle, you must do just like them East Indians and boast about us negroes in Fyzabad when you go to 'merica. If you get fed up with the place, tell Aunt Lily to post you back down to me in a big box. Lily is my sister, and you's my horn; and a goat horn is never too much for a goat to carry." Gina turned to her sister Lily and addressed her. "When our brother died, you went to 'merica since you was a likkle girl, and I never heard from you. You's one who believe that my sense is nonsense. I've been carrying likkle Lyle for a long time, so if you get fed up with him, all you have to do is to post him back down in a big box to me."

Lily kept her peace. She remembered that she and Gina, as children, had fought bigger wars for less than what Gina had just said. Gina paused, and she looked at Spiritual Baptist Leader Gerrol. He was mum. He didn't wish to be the recipient of Gina's rebuke. Gina again addressed Lyle directly. "Likkle Lyle, you must remember the great peoples of Fyzabad like the Chief Servant..." She stopped abruptly.

Lyle knew his aunt so well that he knew why she stopped and cringed on the words "Chief Servant." The Chief Servant, the great trade union leader who fought for the working man's cause, especially those of the oilfield workers, was not a native Trinbagonian. Worse still, he migrated from the spice island of Grenada, and Gina hated Grenadians with a passion. She called Grenadians "Small Island Sufferers" when she was in their company; she called Grenadians "Outbocas" when she was alone; and when Gina was really pissed with Grenadians, she called them in one breath "Windjammer-mongoose-who-came-to-take-away-our-jobs-go-back-home!" Had J.O. Cuttridge, the Trinidad and Tobago expatriate Director of Education, heard Gina's emphasis on the "M" in the word "mongoose," he would have changed the word-rhyme method of education taught to his crown colony subjects for the look-and-say technique. Gina never stopped talking about her two bad experiences with immigrants from Grenada: One took her job for less pay with more work; and the other stopped lending her money because she never paid her debts.

Lyle looked at a plane in the sky and wondered if it would come back in time for him.

"Look at me, boy," Gina commanded him. "Not because you's goin' to 'merica I can't box you in your mout'...Now, I's talkin' to you one mo' time, and listen to what I's sayin'. You see our neighbor Baytah, that nice Indian boy, did take a plane and went away to study for doctor. Baytah passed all his exams overseas, and he

came back home doctorin' medicine. Baytah did not
change when he came back from Inglan; he behaved just
as usual and helped his mother, neighbor Meena, bake
roti when he came back from Inglan. When Baytah
came back from Inglan, he didn't behave like them
stoopit black people who ate out all the crabs from the
mangrove before they left to go away...Them black
people, when they came back to Fyzabad from Inglan,
they talked a lot of highfalutin Latin—*kaylatibus
kaypratibus...*"

Lyle had played ignorant of the knowledge of a
guarded family secret. He felt if he revealed that secret,
Aunt Gina would end her lecture and he wouldn't miss
the next plane. "Aunt Gina," he said, "how come you
talking Latin, and I heard you can't read or write? And
that is why you have to work like a tattoo and tote dirt
on your head for three cents an hour."

Gina didn't skip a beat. With one action, her left
index finger and thumb clamped Lyle's upper and
lower lips like a dress hooked on a clothes line with a
clothes pin. She continued with her advice as if her
nephew had never interrupted her. "When you go
away, boy, if all you do's just to write a likkle story
'bout us, we go be proud of you." She paused; she let
go his lips; then looked at him sternly. "...But you
must come back and behave just like Baytah..."

Again, with the pure innocence of a child, Lyle
interrupted his aunt. "I heard you told Grandma that
Baytah brought back a white-lady wife from England
to lighten his darkness, and Baytah broke the promise
to marry dark-skin Baytee under bamboo in their
religious Hindu rites."

"Gawddammit! What happen to you today, likkle
Lyle? Seems like you ate the parrot behin'!" All the
airline clerks raised their heads in unison and looked at
Lyle and his Aunt Gina. "Didn't I tell you never repeat
what big people say inside their houses, likkle Lyle?"
She led him away from the crowd.

"Yes, Aunty."

"Didn't I tell you never bad mout' big people in public, and never investigate big people?"

"Yes, Aunty."

"What did I tell you does happen to likkle boys with too much lip?"

"They does get it cut off, Aunty."

"Well, tell me beg pardon, boy!"

"Beg pardon, Aunty. I will never, never, do it again."

"Not even in 'merica! You hear me?"

"Yes...Not even in America, Aunty."

"I knows more than you. I's livin' in this worl' longer than you...Ah sayin' it one mo' time: Never forget us in Fyzabad, especially neighbor Meena, Baytee's mother, because you know why?"

Lyle remembered a true story about Baytee's mother and about her roti. He dare not repeat that story, but whenever he mulled that story in his mind he had mixed feelings. In a split-second, the story crossed his mind. The story was: Aunt Gina had sent him early one morning to beg neighbor Meena for roti. Neighbor Meena lived just one hibiscus fence away. She was a very charitable East Indian woman. Lyle met neighbor Meena kneading the roti flour in her urinal basin. He rushed back home, told his aunt what he had seen, and waited on her reply. "That is nottun," Aunt Gina said, "because Baytee's mother already told me that she does wash that basin with plenty of water, and she does scrub it with plenty of ashes...And didn't I tell you that big people don't lie! Go back right now and wait for neighbor Meena's hot roti if you knows what's really good for your likkle stomach!" Lyle immediately brought his thoughts back to the airport.

Planes were landing and departing, and he was worried. He knew that in Fyzabad when a passenger missed the last bus to San Fernando, that passenger had to wait until the next day. Lyle wanted his last day in Fyzabad to be today, but his Aunt Gina was his hurdle between today and tomorrow. He felt Aunt Gina's hand on his shoulder when she said, "You listenin' to me, boy, or you there thinkin' of something else?"

"Am listening to you, Aunt Gina."

"We may be likkle straws down here in Fyzabad but plenty likkle straws make baskets of hay. Even when you get married talk about us...Don't forget to walk backwards up the plane steps to prevent evil spirits from followin' you to 'merica...And don't forget to say your secret Baptist password when your foot touch the col' groun' in 'merica...And hold on to your religion. When you gets in trouble you must pray to God, and teach your children to pray to God when they gets into trouble, too. Prayer's the key. You's listenin' to me, boy?"

"Yes, Aunty."

"And don't grow up to be a numbskull!"

"No, Aunty."

Aunt Lily stepped forward to end the dialogue when she heard the final announcement for delayed passengers. Lyle was grateful for Aunt Lily's intervention.

"Take this, likkle Lyle," Gina said. Her body trembled as if touched by an outside force. "Ah sensing trouble in 'merica, likkle Lyle, but you was born with a caul over your face, and when people's born with a veil over their faces no trouble can stick on them." She held Lyle's little body, wheeled it around three times, then said, "Nothing bad and evil can follow you to 'merica now." She said it as a pre-tested guaranty. Gina held her loving nephew's hand firmly. She opened his fingers and said, "God is good...You knows Godfather is dead..."

Lyle knew what followed, or, at least, he thought he knew what would have followed. Disgusted, he hummed his favorite Baptist hymn.

"You knows I don't like to hear that hymn because

it does remind me of Godfather, and when they put him down in the grave."

"Yes, Aunty."

"And if you knows that, then why is you humming it?"

"Me mout' slip."

"Don't let your mout' slip again, boy." She pulled Lyle closer to her and applied the usual open-and-shut-sesame movements of his fingers. All Lyle's life Gina opened only one hand while he voluntarily closed his eyes. This time she opened both hands. With his eyes closed, she squeezed an unfamiliar object into his right palm, but he knew that it was money. In his left hand she placed a prickly object. He was curious but he dare not open his eyes. Finally, she locked his fingers in both hands. "Don't open your hands until you reach high up in the blue sky, likkle Lyle." She hugged Lyle tightly and cradled his little greased head between her lofty breasts. She kissed him, and kissed him. When Aunt Lily finally separated them, Gina cried her heart out. She was too spent to even look to see if Aunt Lily had walked Lyle backwards to the plane.

On the top of the ramp Lyle waived endlessly to the people of Fyzabad. A beautifully uniformed BWIA hostess curtailed him. The air hostess smiled, and closed the aircraft's door as the last two passengers stepped in. The BWIA plane taxied on the Piarco runway, and thousands of people waived at the silver beauty as it lifted to the sky.

Thirty five thousand feet above ground, airborne Lyle eased the slender fingers of his right hand, and he saw a dollar bill. "Plenty money!" He smiled with glee. He showed the dollar bill to Aunt Lily, but he didn't allow her to touch it. In his joy, he forgot to open his other hand, but as he rested his head on his left hand to sleep in his favorite fetal posture, he felt a sharp prick. He quickly opened his hand. He stared at the small, black, sharp, steel object. It was the hook from

Aunt Gina's rat trap. Lyle knew the significance of the rat hook, and he pondered on the past.

He focused his eyes on the peaceful clouds outside his window. The blue and white clouds looked original, and imaginary figures floated through the clouds. He looked at the rat hook again. The hook vividly reminded him when his parents died and Aunt Gina took him in. He remembered when, one quiet morning, Aunt Gina flew the cheese-baited rat trap that was hidden below her boxwood table. The trap made a loud noise in the still of that morning. Automatically Lyle's eyes went back to the billowing clouds outside his window and his head shook as if the noise of the rat trap were heard in his ear again.

He wanted to admire the serene clouds but the magnet of his thoughts forced him to look at the steel hook in his hand. He looked at the hook and was forced to remember a painful morning in his life when he had agonized by the fireside in neighbor Meena's kitchen. Of all the mornings that he had gone to beg neighbor Meena for her roti, that rainy morning he was ashamed of his condition. On that painful and unforgettable morning, all he first had for breakfast before going to neighbor Meena's kitchen were the cheese bait that the rats rejected and a cup of rain water. Suddenly, his full thoughts occupied his bitter-sweet past. He was entranced. He relived a fact: that if neighbor Meena had denied him her roti, the cheese bait left by the rats and the cup of rain water would have been his only meal for that day. That period in Fyzabad's history that Lyle survived was a season of dearth, and of ration, in a productive oilfield town where only the French creole and the expatriates from England had plenty. Native Fyzabadians had less than the crumbs.

With tears in Lyle's eyes, and like a child who had gone through Gethsemane, from his window, his eyes searched for God in the moving clouds. He gave thanks and prayed. "Dear God, bless neighbor Meena for all those days that she gave me free roti when I was hungry...And, God, forgive me for calling neighbor Meena that bad word—a coolie—even when I was in her kitchen and waited on her hot roti. Miss Meena, you are not a coolie...You are a kind lady, a nice lady, a good lady, and Aunt Gina called you a godsend. If Aunt Gina knew I called you a coolie, even though I said it in my mind, Aunt Gina would call me an ungrateful child. I'm not ungrateful, neighbor Meena. I like you very much, Miss Meena...And God will bless you and make you sell plenty of roti by the market...And, Miss Meena, when you get plenty of money don't forget to build a new board house; and you'll break down that old, dirt house with the fireside outside in the rain." He paused. "...And, Miss Meena, when God gives you plenty of money you'll buy a new basin from Chinee Chin—not from sickly Portuguese Alves—and you'll use that new basin only to knead your roti flour, not to pee-pee in."

Lyle again paused, like a preacher, contemplative. He became somber in his prayer. "Dear God, please bless my Aunt Gina and prevent her from not telling the truth...Use your power, dear God, and cure Aunt Gina's cancer with the health office *Shake-Well* medicine...Aunt Gina, I thank you for everything. You really knew the things that were best for me—me, this stubborn, likkle Lyle. Aunt Gina, you didn't tell me but I knew when you went to work in the white lady's bungalow that the white lady offered you milk to drink but you spat it out even though you like milk. You spat out the milk from your mouth when you remembered that you left me home without anything to eat. Me, this stubborn, likkle Lyle, will never forget you, Aunt Gina; and I promise you that I will remember all the people in Fyzabad who fed me when I was hungry, and those who showed me the way when I was lost at the crossroads."

He took an intense look at the rat hook, then he

put it in his hip pocket. He crouched his little frame on the inclined plane seat, and went fast asleep. His cathartic prayer raised goosebumps throughout Aunt Lily's body. She tugged her neck scarf and wiped her tears. The woman passenger who sat beside her hid her moist eyes with the palms of both hands. Aunt Lily took a blanket from the locker above, covered her nephew gently, and she, too, went fast asleep in the fuselage of the BWIA jet.

A voice awoke them. It was the captain's. "Ladies and gentlemen, you are now descending to Idlewild Airport."

At the International Arrivals Building a little girl broke the crowded line. "Lyle, Lyle," she said excitedly.

"Elizabeth, Liz...What are you doing here?" Lyle replied. "Where are you going?"

"My uncle is taking me to Brooklyn."

"I'm going to America," Lyle boasted.

"You're in America, Lyle!" She rushed over to her uncle. "Uncle Harry! Uncle Harry! You see that boy over there...He's my schoolmate...My friend Lyle...He and I went to Mr. Tellymack school...He's the boy I told you about who put the mirror...Never mind! He's the boy who climbed the greasypole and won the Mondesir gold belt...He recited *Aboud Ben Adhem* and won the two recitation prizes...He's a Spiritual Baptist in Leader Gerrol's church, and when he shouts and catches the power, he becomes a warrior in the spirit...Can he come and visit us, Uncle Harry?"

Uncle Harry measured and re-measured Lyle from his head to his brown Bata boots to fit in Elizabeth's total descriptions. He finally answered, "Sure...sure...sure...su...." His last word was a whispered dimuendo.

Elizabeth ran across to Lyle. "You heard what Uncle Harry said? Would you come and look for me?"

"If Brooklyn is near America!"

"Brooklyn is in America!" she emphasized. She was

proud about the fact that she had given a fellow immigrant his first lesson in American geography.

Lyle sought counsel from his aunt. "Is Brooklyn in America for true, Aunt Lily?"

Aunt Lily nodded.

"You see I ain't lie. You promise to come and look for me, Lyle, and to be my best friend?"

"Yes, I promise." He picked up his gripcase, looked back at Elizabeth, and followed on Aunt Lily's shoe heels.

Chapter Two

The Promise

Lyle was finally convinced that he was in America, and Brooklyn was part of America. On his first day of school, a warm day in September, he looked in the sky for snow, and hoped snow would fall in warm chunks as his knowledgeable Grandpa had assured him. He was more disappointed when he did not see the mighty John Wayne and the Indian, Cochise, battle for turf on ethnic Brooklyn's streets. What Lyle did witness, and firsthand, was his plight as a new immigrant in Miss Thebaud's class. He was snubbed, teased, jeered, and his heavy Trinbago accent was mimicked even by kids who first learned English in leaking boats on their way to America to gain their freedom from dictators. Nonetheless, Miss Thebaud, his grade 3 teacher, a patient woman, liked him; and she molded his confidence. Miss Thebaud programmed Lyle's energy, and made him read aloud every day in front of the class. Lyle hated the ordeal, and he hated her more, but when he realized that Miss Thebaud was interested in his welfare, he nipped wayside flowers and shrubbery, and sneaked them onto her desk to show his gratitude. Lyle thought he had concealed his identity, but each day when Miss Thebaud arranged her bouquet into her resurrected vase, she looked at him and smiled.

It was Alan's turn to flex his muscle. Alan wanted to test the mettle of the new boy in the class. Alan, the nine-year old bully, took extra liberties. He told his friends what he'd do to "that skinny kid." As the class scampered out of the room, Alan addressed Lyle. "You, skinny!" He thumped Lyle. That day Alan met his Waterloo.

Every morning after Lyle said his prayers Aunt Lily gave him a pep talk. That morning before he left for school, she told him, "Boy, in America, people test your strength, and if you are weak they'll beat you every day of your life." It was as if the day had come for Lyle to defend himself from the every-day-of-his-life beating when he jumped Alan from behind, knocked him to the ground, and scratched him the way his dog Flossy scratched the dry earth in search of a brazen mongoose burrowed in the ground near Grandpa's hens' house. Alan, wiser than his age, knew the American motto: If you can't beat 'em join 'em. Alan became Lyle's friend, and he looked for fights on the basis of Lyle's strength. Lyle ran from Alan's fights because he remembered the sternest of Aunt Lily's warnings: "Boy, if a giant hits you, I expect you to hit that giant back; but if you pick up your friends' fire rage and get suspended from school for fighting for them, you would be mailed back to Fyzabad in that big box in the corner." The conspicuous box in the corner had a roll of sticky tape, and it was brightly labelled in bold letters: TO AUNT GINA, IN CARE OF THE CHIEF SERVANT, FYZABAD, TRINIDAD & TOBAGO, WEST INDIES. Lyle dreaded to walk near that box for fear that the box might have a flying trap. He had had enough of all that was Aunt Gina's and opted to stay away from trouble in order that he would remain in his new home, Brooklyn, U.S.A.

Sending Lyle back to Fyzabad never crossed Aunt Lily's mind. Truthfully, Aunt Lily cloaked her real fears. For that matter, Lyle had outgrown that cardboard box. Her main reason for ensuring Lyle's sterling behavior was that she had overheard at her domestic day job what her boss said on the phone. Her boss said to the caller that, "It's a burning shame that there's a multitude of two more new negras in the same class with Katherine." Aunt Lily knew that Lyle was one of those referred-to "negras;" but uppermost in Aunt Lily's mind was the fact that her boss had clout, and her boss' words had political weight. She was concerned that if Lyle were deemed "unruly" by an impatient teacher, or if he had a "dispute" with Katherine, such misdemeanors of his would be enough reason for the School Board to show its muscle, and put Lyle in the Special Ed Program. Aunt Lily knew firsthand the pitfalls of Special Education because she was in the program. Lily, then a new immigrant, was classified as a slow and backward child, and her classification was based on the spasmodic findings of the experts—the school psychologist, *et al*.: "As a student, Lily Gordon never owned a library card, and she never cooperated with her peers in the playground." Aunt Lily remembered verbatim the psychologist's subjective findings as she remembered the provocation of her classmates who caused her to react vulgarly. Hence, she dreaded the thought that Lyle could suffer her fate, too. As the sole guardian, she became vigilant in her effort to safeguard Lyle from the dangers of school politics; and she used all her smarts to keep her fidgety nephew in check so that he would not be mistakenly stigmatized.

Time moved on. Lyle showed progress in his school work and behavior. He was named "Student of the Month" on many occasions. He was proud of his acquired American accent, but at times he relapsed into his heavy Trinbago twang, and talked two hundred patois words a minute to elude uninvited listeners to his conversations. Elizabeth Brownie was also a student in Miss Thebaud's class, but Lyle favored his new friends. He reneged on the promise that he had made to Elizabeth at the Airport, that he'd be her best friend.

In junior high school, however, Lyle renewed his interest in Elizabeth. Elizabeth's chest began to show growth; she was pretty; and her neatly pressed uniform curved on her teenage body. He waited for her at the busstop, at the assembly line, and brought Aunt Lily's sugarcakes for her to supplement the cafeteria's Gilbert-and-Sullivan lunches.

Elizabeth became popular in her class, and her teachers gave her monitors' duties. It was her chance to ignore Lyle and flirt with Jimmy, the rich kid, whose gifts were never generic. Jimmy offered Elizabeth an assortment of chocolates bought from The Milky Godiva. Jimmy was kind, and all his classmates wanted to be his friend. Elizabeth liked Jimmy but her heart belonged to Lyle. Lyle, however, liked all the girls in his class. Once he promised Elizabeth Aunt Lily's home-made cupcakes, but he gave them to Jennifer. His glib to Elizabeth was, "Jennifer looked hungry, and I felt sorry for her." He did not know that Jennifer had already told Elizabeth that he had used the cupcakes to introduce himself. Jennifer also admitted to Elizabeth that the cupcakes were delicious, and that she told Lyle where to meet her whenever he had more cupcakes. Regardless of Lyle's indiscretions, Elizabeth forgave him.

Lyle was fourteen years old when Aunt Lily moved to an apartment on Tilden Avenue opposite Holy Cross Cemetery. Aunt Lily continued to advise him every morning. The only place in the United States she knew was Brooklyn, but Aunt Lily always started her words of advice to Lyle with, "In America." As Lyle rushed out of their apartment with the hope of meeting Elizabeth at the busstop, and to prove to rich Jimmy who is who in Elizabeth's life, Aunt Lily called him back inside to counsel him one more time. He was furious.

"Boy, in America," Aunt Lily began her discourse, "you can play and have fun, but I don't want you to be gullible and quick to give information as you gave to all your partisans in Fyzabad: the warrant man, the wayside bankers, the cockfighters, everybody...In this country you see but you still don't see! I don't want you to put all your trust in black people, white people, brown people, the well-dressed, or the undressed..." She looked at him. Lyle immediately eclipsed his frown. All he thought of at that time was that Jimmy's probably bribing Elizabeth with brand name goodies that he'd never be able to afford with his meager pocket change. With a sudden change of the subject matter, Aunt Lily said, "Do you like white girls, boy?" She caught him off guard, but answered for him. "That's all right, boy, once the love is mutual. God made all of us. We are all equal—the air you breathe out, they breathe in, and vice versa."

Aunt Lily stepped closer to the big cardboard box in the living room. It was the very box once earmarked to mail Lyle back to Fyzabad. The box eventually became a clothes storage box. Lily edged herself so close to the box and the wall that Lyle thought she was putting on a Lucille Ball's act. It was no act. Aunt Lily was sincere about what she was about to say and do. Dear Aunt Lily was about to lay down some serious house rules. Swiftly she pointed her fingers in an uncanny manner. Lyle, from past experience, thought that she was showing him a newly dug grave in Holy Cross Cemetery from which the junkies took the dead man's wreaths and recycled the flowers. Observant Lyle also thought Aunt Lily's next procedure was that she would bite her fingers, as it was a superstitious custom for Fyzabadians to bite their fingers when they pointed at a grave. Fyzabadians did that to prevent the dead from visiting them in their sleep. This time Lyle's assumption of Aunt Lily's motive was dead wrong.

She had pointed in that fashion because she trusted no one who lived on that block—not even if he were Sir Winston Churchill outside her window with his advice to the Allied Powers. Lily had pointed in that obscure fashion because she did not want anyone who looked into her house to see in what direction she pointed. She raised her voice and demanded Lyle's attention. "You see those people in that corner house over there," her hand trembled from fear as she had pointed, "when you're playing on the street and your ball goes over their fence forget it! Don't go for it! Don't ask for it, and don't be fresh about it! For that matter, those people down there have a fair skin daughter who goes to Catholic school, don't even look in her direction when you see her on the street! If anyone asks you anything about those people by that corner house, don't open your mouth...Make sure you shake your head from left to right so that if any informer is looking at you, he'd see that you didn't divulge any information. You listening to me, boy?"

"But why?" Lyle inquired, and he added, "Aunty, when you'd stop calling me 'boy?'"

Aunt Lily was firm. "Because I say so, boy! I am old enough to know whether your little seeds in your pants are ready to be cooked." She spoke with such rapidity that Lyle wished he could have recorded her words in shorthand. She related him rumored stories about the occupants of the corner house; and he, too, eventually gained his own tattle-tale experience about them.

The people who lived in that big corner house were nine in number. No one on the block knew their family name, and the postman never made deliveries to the occupants of the corner house. Their visitors came by cars, and a remote-controlled door gave the visitors admittance into the garages of that corner house. The Tilden Street Block Watchers' underground census accounted that there were a mother, a father, four sons, a daughter, and two elderly women who lived in that corner house. Ever so often a male member would be chauffeured out of the enclosed premises in a huge black car with dark tinted windows. The car sped in the direction of the Belt Highway. Immediately thereafter, all the blinds were drawn, and all the women in that private building were heard as they wailed in grief. Their matriarchal instincts told them that male child who departed in the black car would never return.

Two days before that nameless family moved from that corner spot, the only male member seen was a gaunt-looking, old man. His wife, too, had gone through a metamorphosis. She had become fat and gray, so different from when Lyle first knew her. In the past when Lyle disobeyed Aunt Lily and had peeped through that nameless family's forbidden fence, he had seen the old man's wife as a manicured specimen. She was fashionable then, with bouffant hairstyles, heavy makeup, high heels, and flowing gowns. She was a moving billboard. In those days, Lyle was in awe of her looks. He had, only once, made the mistake and said, "Aunt Lily, when I become as rich as a city bus conductor, I would buy you a dress like the one that pretty lady at the corner house wears." That day Aunt Lily went ballistic. She screamed at him and said, "Son of a bitch, not that dress for me!" She threw the frying pan at him, and the pan left its mark on him and on the partition. Lyle immediately realized that he shouldn't have known what that lady in the corner house wore that day, or, for that matter, any day of her life.

The curious block watchers speculated constantly about that private family's lifestyle, but even long after that unknown family left the neighborhood, the Tilden Street Block Watchers, dressed in auxiliary police uniforms, with batons, whistles, and flashlights, were still afraid to walk near that vacated corner house which was partly hidden with overgrown rose bush.

Fittingly Aunt Lily taught her teenage nephew the ways and rumors of the street. He quickly learned why the Oath of Omerta was important, and why the words "Never again!" were significant. But Lyle knew, without coaching, when the meaning of the salutation, "Black Brother," was swilled down like cheap wine, when it became as insincere as Madonna's hair rinse, or when that salutation "Black Brother" was as solid as a rock. Lyle was raised by a single black woman; and his insights into the American psyche taught him that sons raised by single women must sharpen their perception and learn quickly because they are the sit-ins for their absentee fathers. Sons become men by evolution: first, by mimicking; then, by looking at their shadows; and, finally, by masking their fears. It was evident to Lyle that manhood became endemic with the onus of responsibility thrust upon sons who became surrogates for their missing fathers.

Lyle masked his own fears but his barometer was always on success. Grandpa had told him he'd be successful in America, and Aunt Gina had told him that no evil could follow him. He believed them. As a naturalized American, he had new ideals. He no longer felt comfortable with the nickname "Mister Adult Nigger" given him by his Grandpa after he had won the greasypole prize, but he couldn't wipe that nickname from the tongues of Aunt Lily and Elizabeth.

He had witnessed fisticuffs for the utterance of the word "nigger." He never understood why it was wrong when white Jimmy said the "N" word under his collar, but it was okay when black Tom, with a gleeful handshake, hollered, "Nigger!" to his black mate. Nevertheless, all those images and anomalies shaped Lyle's adolescence. He chose what he liked, rejected what was offensive, and when he was unsure he sought the advice of his Aunt Lily. Lily was unequivocal when she told Lyle that he wasn't always wrong, and that others hadn't the right to be always right. Aunt Lily sometimes reversed her advice to suit the circumstance.

There was another redletter day. Lyle and Elizabeth graduated from Tilden High. There were no limousines to drive them to the prom as both families barely eked out their existence. On graduation day, Lyle and Elizabeth did not introduce their parents. For that matter, they hardly spoke to each other. They drifted off in different directions at the end of the graduation exercises, but made plans to meet at their rendezvous.

It was Lyle's eighteenth birthday. Elizabeth was to meet him at their rendezvous at three in the afternoon at Brighton Beach. Suddenly, she got a brainstorm: She showed up at Lyle's door at two o'clock instead. She was dressed in a white cotton blouse fitted into a multicolored wraparound skirt. Her strap shoes had low heels. Her toenails, painted in bronze, protruded comfortably through the thin straps. Her coarse hair was oiled, tightly brushed into one plait, and a gold brooch held the plait close to her perfumed neck. She strolled to Lyle's house, and the sun turned her color to dark olive. Her shoulder bag matched her complexion.

This was enterprising Elizabeth's first visit. Her visit was unannounced; she was uninvited; and she wondered what would be the outcome of her intrusion. She quickly dismissed her negative thoughts; and, with a deep breath, she mumbled a four-second help-me-oh-Lord prayer and pressed the Gordon's buzzer. A split-second delay would have changed her mind.

"Lyle, I hear the bell. Do you expect anyone?" Aunt Lily said.

"No," Lyle replied.

Aunt Lily went to the door and opened it. "Hi," she said to Elizabeth.

"Good afternoon." Elizabeth paused. "You, you won't re-remember me." Her words bucked. She anticipated Lyle would have come to the door.

"No. I don't remember you. Are you one of those vulgar girls who live next door?" Aunt Lily spoke as a warden who was ready to discipline the prisoner.

"Yes, no, not far away." Stage fright engulfed Elizabeth. Her answer was contrary.

Aunt Lily studied her a bit. "Well...what is it, Miss?"

"You last saw me when I was eight."

"Where?"

"When Lyle asked for your permission to visit me." She shifted her shoulder bag to gain momentum.

"I'm lost." Aunt Lily engaged a slight smile that had no semblance of a welcome.

Elizabeth groped for words. Why am I here, God...Help me, dear Lord, she thought.

Lyle helped her. He shouted from inside. "Who is it, Aunt Lily?"

"A young lady." Aunt Lily knew he'd come without delay. She knew a new girl on the block always perked his interest. The girl's race, color, or creed did not matter to him. Lily knew her adolescent nephew was the opposite-gender man.

Lyle rushed to the door. A beach towel covered his showered body. His eyes met Elizabeth's. "Oh no! Let her in, Aunt Lily." He rushed back inside, and he nervously dressed himself in his favorite summer outfit.

Aunt Lily apologized to Elizabeth. "Am sorry for letting you stand outside in the hot weather, Miss."

"It's all right," Elizabeth said. "You can't be too careful, you know." She stretched her hand, and Aunt Lily shook it politely. "My name is Elizabeth Brownie. I'm eighteen now; but ten years ago we travelled on the same plane. We had embarked at the Piarco Airport in Trinidad, West Indies." Elizabeth gave a quick resume of herself.

They were in the living room. Aunt Lily looked at Elizabeth. "Wait...Wait...Wait a minute!" Aunt Lily shook her head, then blurted, "Are you the little girl from Pitch Lake Country who was so expressive?...That little girl with all those variegated ribbons in your hair?...That little girl who excitedly gave Lyle's biography as quickly and as crisply to your uncle at Idlewild Airport?...What's his name again?"

"Uncle Harry." Elizabeth blushed.

"Can't believe it! Can't believe my eyes! How old are you now?" Aunt Lily went into her mix of patois and American English. "Gyul, girl, turn 'round leh me see you good to make sure dat is really you...Girl, gyul, you look so nice. *Mamayo*! You have grown so lovely...Where have you been? What are you doing now." Aunt Lily's behavior was synonymous with Elizabeth's behavior and excitement when Elizabeth, unexpectedly, had seen Lyle at the Airport ten years ago. This time Elizabeth was the one in awe of Aunt Lily's excitement. Aunt Lily became repetitious. "Girl, gyul, Lizzy, leh me pinch you. You are beautiful, Elizabeth...You are adorable...You're...." Lily hugged Elizabeth like if Elizabeth were her lost lovechild that she found on the Oprah Winfrey Show.

Lyle came into the living room and interrupted the two women. "Aunt Lily, meet my friend Elizabeth Brownie," he said, and sat on his favorite chair. He called it, "My cool chair." It was the chair with the least plastic covering. Aunt Lily hadn't sufficient money to cover that chair completely to preserve its durability.

"We have already met, Lyle boy," Aunt Lily said. "Isn't Elizabeth gorgeous?"

He nodded.

"May I get you something, Elizabeth dear." Aunt Lily showed polish in her courteous remark.

"A soda would be fine. Thank you." Elizabeth's smile was infectious.

Aunt Lily rushed off to the kitchen. She mumbled, "Can't believe it! She's so lovely. I can see inward spiritual grace in Elizabeth's good breeding." The first time Lily heard of "inward spiritual grace in good breeding" was when she first came to Brooklyn in the thirties. Mrs. O'Donnell, Lily's aunt's employer, said those words to describe little Lily when Lily sat quietly in the servants' room.

Elizabeth said, "Lyle, I hope you don't mind what I did." She did not wait for his answer. "This is for your birthday, honey."

Lyle was still shocked. He took the gift, and dropped it behind the half-covered plastic chair.

"Open it," Elizabeth said.

Lyle obliged. "A T-shirt?" He tried to end the conversation before Aunt Lily returned.

"Turn it over, please, and read what is written on it, Lyle."

"I Missed You." Lyle read the words softly. He heard Aunt Lily's footstep. He folded the T-shirt and invented a blank look for his face.

"Here's your soda, Elizabeth dear," Aunt Lily said. "Yours is in the can, Lyle." She resumed her position next to Elizabeth, looked at Lyle, and smiled.

"In the can for me, I see," Lyle said. He interpreted Aunt Lily's coyish smile. He knew her eyes could glimpse a needle in a haystack at dusk, and he was sure his aunt read the words on his T-shirt.

The trio recreated their ten-year old meeting which first began at Idlewild Airport and chatted freely about life at present in New York City.

"Excuse me, folks," Aunt Lily said. She read their thoughts. "It's time to see *I Love Lucy*."

"Quite." Elizabeth answered and stood. She waited until Lily left. "Do you like my gift, Lyle?" She raised her back from the warm plastic couch.

"Very much. I thank you for the gift."

"You're welcome."

It was mid-August. The vine maples with toothed lobes turned orange and red. Some in symmetrical rows still had patches of green leaves, but the orange and red leaves interspersed between wove a pretty pattern. Among the mixed hues, chameleons, camouflaged, crawled on the branches. The sky was pale blue, and foamy white clouds anchored on the blue as if they rested there for a short respite. The sun was not seen, but its rays were felt. The fire hydrant operators sprayed passersby. The passersby did not complain for their bodies needed to be cooled, and their cars needed to be washed.

Lyle, and Elizabeth, too, preferred to have their bodies cooled outdoors. Their minds were on their rendezvous.

"When last have you screamed your lungs out on the roller coaster in Coney Island, Liz?" Lyle asked.

"Since you stood me up, Lyle. To be exact, it was the week before graduation...The last week of high school when you sent me a note, wrote part of it in shorthand, and you knew fully well that I couldn't read shorthand."

"Not that again! I told you why I couldn't make it, Liz."

"I heard otherwise, Lyle."

"What you heard?" Lyle asked softly. He never trusted Aunt Lily's make-shift walls.

"That you dragged out Billie's tonsils after her graduation," Elizabeth said even softer. "You couldn't wait around after our graduation to be introduced to my parents, Mister Adult Nigger; but I heard where and how you partied at the private graduation. Would you care to divulge the full name of your escort who graduated from Midwood?...Forget her name...I'll settle for just the block in which she lives." Elizabeth smiled, and she sipped her ginger ale as if it were a nectar. She took a piece of sweetbread from Lyle's hand and ate it. Playfully, she said, "My eyes are closed, Lyle. Take a piece of ice, honey, and write on the ice your other woman's street address, not her name."

"Get off of it! Let's hit the boardwalk, and I'll tell you something that I told no one before."

"Sounds interesting, but not before I say goodbye to Aunt Lily."

"I'll get her in a minute," he assured her. "I'm pumping iron now. How do I look, Liz? I weigh a solid one fifty."

"With your round, dimpled, black face, you shouldn't carry such a bushy, black head. Why not dye your hair red like the English beatniks?"

He smiled. "How do you like my goaty, gyul?"

"Goaty now? You're forcing grass to grow on bottle, boy. How tall are you?"

"Five nine. Haven't you anything nice to say about my new look?"

"I want to be outdoors when I talk about your Flatbush look...You know, something: Somehow, I was scared to come, but I like Aunt Lily very much. How old is she?"

Lyle went into a general discussion. He spoke of his aunt, and his relationship with her for the past ten years.

Aunt Lily was sixty five years old, full of vigor, of medium height, with a full nose, and deep nostrils. She was a hard worker. She received no Social Security benefits because although she contributed towards the Social Security Fund through payroll deductions, her many domestic employers did not apply her deductions nor their own contributions on her behalf to the Social Security Fund. Some days Aunt Lily cooked in the dark when she expected the Florida-based landlord at her door. Lyle knew her plight, and showed his gratitude. He asked Aunt Lily for nothing, and secured a job as a packer at Bohack Supermarket. Aunt and nephew loved each other. They appreciated each other's company. Lily blessed the day that she brought Lyle to America, and she knew that she needed her nephew as much as he needed her. She cooked the dinners Lyle liked, and was thrilled when he gained weight.

There were times when she and Lyle fought: when his school grades dropped, when he came home very late without a suitable excuse, when he did not want to attend the Methodist Church, and when his friends' perspiration and football shoes stained her plastic cushions. Worst still, Aunt Lily and Lyle fought when Lyle's countless girl friends did not meet her approval. He once showed his disdain for the way she treated his girl friends, and she retorted in distinct patois: "Boy, not because you's pissin' on the wall, and it is frothin', you think you is a man. In my house you is no man! I is the man, and I is the 'oman...You is the chil'. Jus' keep that in your pipe an' smoke it." Aunt Lily took a breather to calm her asthmatic flare. "Boy, of late, it seems as if them young girls thief you brain." She censured him in patios, and added some of the blue vernacular, the Trinidad and Tobago flavor. When Aunt Lily resorted to that diction, Lyle knew that was no time for him to be feisty or bombastic. Worst still, that was not the time to remind her that he, the grown-up Lyle, was not a 'boy.'

Elizabeth giggled softly throughout Lyle's tales of his Aunt Lily. "So that's your history with Aunt Lily for the past ten years?" Elizabeth commented. "Very interesting."

"Liz, I hope I didn't over report, because Grappa did tell me that ah mus' not talk about we *fambaly* 'tall, 'tall."

Elizabeth amusingly said, "Me grandmudder did tell me when mout' open 'tory does jump out; so me must keep me mout' closed to protect me *fambaly* business."

They laughed about the way they imitated their grandparents in the vernacular.

"Liz, had I known you about two minutes longer, I would've told you about me Cousin Edderleen." They laughed..."But everything I told you so far is the gospel...Just by the way Aunt Lily catered to you, I know she likes you. Tonight I'm sure to hear that you have 'good breeding.' I hate that colonial word. The way Aunt Lily likes you, am sure she'll give you communion without confession."

"I have nothing to confess about, Lyle?"

"Are you sure?"

"More sure than you, lover boy?"

"Me is a lover?"

"Let's not go into that...Why do you say Aunt Lily likes me?"

"My Aunt Lily can make me out of mud; and I can make her out of cardboard. Somehow, though, I think Aunt Lily is over touched with insularity. She hates my American friends. She feels a West Indian man should marry a West Indian woman."

"It could be preference rather than prejudice?"

"Ha, ha! You're good at semantics, gyul."

"Boy, this gyul is prejudiced against only one American woman."

"Is it because that woman is American-born, or is it because of your stupid jealousy?"

"Make your pick." Elizabeth stood up, and she looked at the children who sprayed each other with water guns filled from the spouting fire hydrants.

Aunt Lily walked in. "So you two are about to go gallivanting?"

Elizabeth answered. "Lyle and I have decided to hit the pitch to celebrate his birthday."

"You're no longer in Fyzabad," Lyle chimed in. "The boardwalk has no asphalt."

"Thanks for the correction, Mister Adult Nigger."

"You're welcome, Miss Black Caribbean America." Lyle finally felt relaxed with his aunt in their midst. "Keep talking to Aunt Lily while I hunt for my wallet, Liz."

"Shakespeare's? 'Who steals my purse steals trash?'"

"Nah! Leigh Hunt's, espousing about angels writing in a book of gold."

"You still remember that *Abou Ben Adhem* poem?'"

"Sure! How could we forget with the amount of blows we got from Mr. Tellymack for that poem. Remember the Buge said that poem could be our salvation, our sermon, and we even acted out the significance of that poem. As small as we were, the Buge stuffed our heads with Shakespeare, Chaucer, Longfellow, Gray, Hunt, name it...The Buge felt only education chalked up success."

"I remember. Fyzabadians should erect a monument for Mr. Tellymack." She turned to Aunt Lily. "Aunt Lily, does Lyle still boast about that greasypole stuff?"

Aunt Lily quickly answered. "Liz gyul, are you talking about Grandpa's Mister Adult Nigger?...Are you talking about the champ who won that Mondesir gold belt?" She danced on her arthritic legs.

Lyle chuckled, but Aunt Lily and Elizabeth kept a straight face. It was comic opera on Aunt Lily's plastic chairs.

Elizabeth continued to address her audience. "Grappa's Mister Adult Nigger won the greasypole prize unfairly, Aunt Lily. I was there, and I screamed my lungs out for him to win, but I knew he won unfairly. His brother and his friends teased Spree until Spree lost concentration and slid down the greasypole. Lyle's friends vulgarly shouted to Spree and told Spree that his mother, Miss Mary, was a *soucouyant*, a vampire— whatever they called the poor lady on that Easter Monday. The negro gamblers lost their money on Spree, and those sour losers chased Spree and his family out of Fyzabad. Fyzabad is a strange place, Aunt Lily. Aunt Lily, do you know that after that day the nickname Vampire stuck on neighbor Mary. People really believed that neighbor Mary sucked them at nights. Even black black Nellie Jools on whose body you could not see white paint in daylight, she, too, got up one morning and said, 'Ah sure this blue-black mark on me belly is from Vampire Mary's mout'.'"

Aunt Lily laughed and laughed. She could have died from her fits of laughter. She held on to her heavy chairs for vertical support.

Elizabeth went on, and reported more of Fyzabad's happenings of the past. She clowned as she performed, going in and out of the Trinbago patois. "Did Lyle tell you that he used to steal his Grappa's raw cashew nuts to bribe the bad boys in the district to protect him from Spree's wrath? Did Lyle tell you that when his Grappa went for the cashew nuts to sell them in the market, his Grappa found just a handful of nuts in the sealed tins. His loving grandson—I beg your pardon—I meant the Mister Adult Nigger told his Grappa that the greedy rats opened the sealed tins with their sharp teeth and ate all the cashew nuts."

This time Aunt Lily had the full support of her large and unrepairable couch. Her laughter turned into an almost endless cough. Lyle shook his head endlessly. He had never seen his aunt in such a happy mood. Aunt

Lily eventually recovered from her hysterics of laughter. She spoke in dead earnest as if she had a premonition: "What is joke for children is death to crapaud...Boy, all I know is that I'm a born Fyzabadian, and I still believe in *Payback*."

Lyle knew the import of Aunt Lily's statement, but since Aunt Lily was no Aunt Gina, the oracle, he ignored Aunt Lily's remarks about *Payback*.

The chitchat increased. More ginger ales and home-made sweetbread were consumed. "How's your Uncle Harry?" Aunt Lily asked. Lily wanted to learn more of Elizabeth's background so she used her roundabout approach. The old folks in Fyzabad were adept about finding out about their spouses' families. A background search was a must; and Fyzabadians found out each other's past by gleaning information from every Tom, Dick, Harry, and his parrot cockatoo. That was the villagers' 1930's internet; and it worked. "How's your Uncle Harry?" Aunt Lily repeated the question.

"Not as robust," Elizabeth replied. "Uncle Harry is depressed most of the time, and he's under heavy medication because..." She cut her sentence.

"What's his problem? What's wrong with Uncle Harry?" Aunt Lily insisted.

Reluctantly, Elizabeth said, "I can't be too sure...But after Uncle Harry came back from his vacation when he brought me up from the islands, he lost his job at Mr. Goldberg's bakery. I think Uncle Harry took it on. He had worked at that bakery for over thirty years. Mr. Goldberg told Uncle Harry, 'I own the bakery, and I can't go on a vacation, but you can go down to the islands and have a good time...You don't need this job, Harry. You have money to frolic with those buxom sweathogs down there.' Mr. Goldberg fired Uncle Harry in a-snow-ball-in-hell minute. I heard Uncle Harry, on bended knees, begged back for his job, but to no avail. Other than that, Uncle Harry is fine. He now looks forward for his social security check on the third of every month, and spends it on his grandchildren. The good thing is: My uncle, once an atheist, has accepted the Lord. He goes to church twice on Sunday now, and he prays to God before he eats his meal."

Aunt Lily wished she hadn't inquired of Uncle Harry. Uncle Harry's plight re-confirmed what she had told Lyle the very first day that he had worked as a wrapper at Bohack Supermarket: "Boy," she had told him, "never talk success stories in front of the white man, especially if he is your boss."

Lyle was glad when Elizabeth and Aunt Lily's conversations ended.

Elizabeth, with poise, stood erectly and stretched her hand to say goodbye. Aunt Lily held Elizabeth's hands and used them to embrace her body. She embraced Elizabeth affectionately, kissed Elizabeth, and said, "Liz gyul, don't let it be ten years next time. You are family now. You are so different from those young girls who stand in front of the building with their dirty mouths. I can see you're from good breeding."

Elizabeth's visits became common place. Lyle reciprocated Elizabeth's visits; and both families became telephone pals. Elizabeth remained faithful, and kept all of her spare time for Lyle. On the contrary, Lyle shared his time. He exploded when Elizabeth told him of rumors about him and Billie Zellars. "You don't know Billie, so you shouldn't listen to dogs who bring bones," Lyle often said. Nonetheless, Lyle dated Billie up to the day she left for France to study political science. On that very day Lyle shared his time with Billie and Elizabeth; and his separate arguments with both women were stormy, and stormier.

At dinner time Lyle sought his aunt's advice. Lily questioned him instead. "Boy, whom do you prefer— the American woman or the Caribbean woman? I don't have to tell you who's my choice." Aunt Lily, in a B flat pitch, sang, *Praise Him in the Morning, Praise*

Him in the Evening.... She ended the hymn in the middle of the verse, and said, "Whom do you love? I don't want to hear that Cyrano de Bergerac shit that you 'fall in love desperately and each time the effect is the same.' Black folks have melanin, boy." Lily's nostrils quivered when she spoke.

"I'm not going to say that Cyrano shit today, but about those two spicy ladies, one jars, and one soothes. Both effects suit me just fine...and," Lyle paused, "neither woman knows the other."

Lily's swift reply followed. "Nothing hides forever. Take my word, boy!"

The day Lyle proposed to Elizabeth, localized showers fell in sections of Coney Island. Sea Gate was wet; and the boardwalk was bone dry. Elizabeth, dizzy, got off the roller coaster, and was unsure of her bearing. She found Lyle among the Puerto Rican drummers and female salsa dancers. "Would you marry me, Elizabeth?" he said without warning or drama.

Elizabeth choked on her saliva, and gasped for breath.

"The dizzy ride or my proposal caused that, honey?" he asked.

She did not answer. The drummers drummed louder. She embraced him, and moved him away from the beautiful Hispanic woman who rolled her midsection like Coney Island waves. Hand-in-hand, Lyle and Elizabeth uttered not a word as they strolled on the boardwalk from West 28 to Brighton Beach. They looked at the ocean. The big boats on the Atlantic headed for the Bay. The amateur fishermen threw their lines from the jetty, and a little sea plane flew above the boardwalk and dragged behind it an advertisement of an emboldened coca cola sign. The life guards left their high chairs on the beach; but bathers, sun worshippers, the anorectic with implants, and lovers with beautiful bodies in bikinis refused to go home. Lyle and Elizabeth walked on the beach and touched the cold water with their toes. The tide ebbed, and the moon in its second phase followed them to their rendezvous.

The base of a weeping willow tree was their rendezvous. The willow's densely-leafy canopy allowed little light to penetrate it, but there was enough light for Lyle and Elizabeth to admire each other's body. The hanging branches were the curtains to their earthen bedroom, and that night the bugs and mosquitoes stayed away. Other lovers who often shared the willow tree were absent that late evening. Lyle and Elizabeth kicked off their shoes, hustled off the bulk of their clothes, and embraced lovingly. They had never before enjoyed so immensely the luxury of this hanging willow. Both knew the weeping willow beautified Brooklyn's Little Odessa, kept nests for squirrels and robbins, and lost its verdure in the late fall. But that evening, that tree that grew in Brooklyn gave them comfort. Lyle and Elizabeth were uninhibited. They talked; they giggled like kids in Miss Thebaud's class; and they were like Adam and Eve in the garden, but they didn't hide their sins from God. The lovebirds heeded the call of their desire. Energized, a rivulet of perspiration bathed their bodies and mixed their scents on that blissful night.

Neither Elizabeth nor Lyle wanted the night to end. They dressed and went again on the boardwalk. Elizabeth stood still, and Lyle admired her under the pole lights infested with sandflies. He spoke with his eyes and saturated her beauty, but never said a word. She understood his taciturn behavior in those times because she knew that he savored his energy for their physical interaction. Lyle embraced Elizabeth, and she rested her head on his shoulder. He stroked her hair and broke his silence. "I love you, Liz," he said. "Love has no meaning without you, Elizabeth. Whatever you think, whatever you feel, whatever you are told, you are who I want today, tomorrow, and forever. Believe me, honey, whatever I do, wherever I go, in my pain, in my joy, you'll be at the fore of my memory. I'll never let you down." Lyle raised her head off his shoulder and looked into her beautiful eyes. "I want you to know Elizabeth Brownie that you are the future Mrs. Lyle Gordon." He slipped a ring on her finger. The ring fitted as perfectly as Cinderella's glass slipper.

Amazed, Elizabeth looked at the tiny diamond. "From Woolworth's?"

"No. From Bohack's." They laughed.

"Let's walk," she said softly, and she looked at the dim diamond.

He put his hand on her shoulder, looked around, and saw no one nearby. He slid his fingers into the space between her netted brassiere. She looked at him. "Look at the ring, gyul," he said. They giggled. Lyle's hand felt the thumping of Elizabeth's firm breasts. They stood in the middle of the boardwalk and kissed tenderly, then cravingly. They kissed till their palates ached.

Elizabeth spoke. "Would you always want me like this?"

"Always," Lyle assured her.

"Are you ready for my reply, honey?" Elizabeth said. She leaned on the cracked rail, unmindful of its strength, and gazed at the Atlantic. Speed boats bumped on the water. Police launches cruised along. In the distance, for the first time, a lone row boat was seen; its single inhabitant, enroute to the Bay, sculled in a slight breeze, and the moonlight showed the boatman his way. Lights flickered from the Verrazano Narrows Bridge; the expanse of its unsupported structure seemed longer than that recorded in the archives. The waters on the Atlantic rippled in peace. Lovers oblivious of their surroundings curled in the sand below the dank and dark boardwalk. Two elderly couples, the men wore yarmelkes, the women wore long dresses, walked by in single file, and spoke softly in Yiddish. A man yelled for joy from the concessionaire game booth. The man, in his sixteenth attempt, at last won a prize. Joy welled Elizabeth's heart for she was truly in love, and Lyle was her prize.

Elizabeth also knew her competition, Billie Zellars, had left for France. She looked into Lyle's welcoming eyes; her loving gaze lingered; and she lengthened her trademarked smile. Her smile was slow, sweet, and warm as that summery day. She spoke in a whisper, as softly as a pompom: "I'll love you forever, Lyle honey. That's my promise."

"That's my promise, too, Liz. You're my only love."

They kissed. Their kiss was as long as the tail of the comet that pitched over the Atlantic Ocean. They finally went home.

America, once Lyle's distant daydream, had become a reality. Grandpa was right: Everything's big, so big in America. The expanse of the American landscape, the loftiness of its skyscrapers, and the engineering feats all around, kept Lyle in awe. The abundance of the American crops was phenomenal in his eyesight; and although Lyle had setbacks and saw injustice in its many forms, he was enamored by the kindness and concern of the American people. Lyle knew that he lived in the greatest country in the world, and his greatest proof of that belief was that he caressed the American largesse, not in troy weight or currency, but in dreams richer than his deceased Grandpa would have imagined. It was only the decibel of Brooklyn's bells left to be heard.

Lyle was twenty three years old when the Methodist Church bells rang for him and Elizabeth. Aunt Lily proudly hooked her handsome nephew and escorted him up the aisle. Uncle Harry, with his flashy cane, followed proudly with his gorgeous niece, the bride, at his side. Uncle Harry gave the bride to the happy bridegroom, and Reverend Beresford Moore performed the wedding ceremony.

Mr. Lyle Allister Gordon took Miss Elizabeth Cynthia Brownie's hand in marriage. He unveiled his bride; and he kissed her deeply. They became man and wife.

Nine months to date, Elizabeth gave birth to their son. He was named Nigel Atiba.

Chapter Three

The Appointments

It was a steamy Friday morning in August when the cuckoo clock alarmed in the Gordons' Vanderveer apartment which was lodged between Nostrand Park and Ralph Laundromat in East Flatbush. The alarm was not needed, for from the Vanderveer complex the boom boxes of calypso, soul, and reggae music rocked the graffiti walls. Lyle snored in bed near his peep window. In dire need for that apartment with a panoramic bedroom view of four bustling avenues— Foster, Nostrand, Newkirk and New York—Lyle bribed Sammy, the superintendent of the complex, and Sammy gave him the apartment when the white tenant vacated it. Noises came persistently from Vanderveer men and women who originated from south of the Dixie, the Caribbean, and Central America. They argued as they washed their clothes in the giant machines. Their loud arguments were not about management's reduced maintenance services since they became the majority of the tenants after most of the whites had moved out, but about who, among them, spoke black English right. From the park, the sounds of raucous voices came through Lyle's cracked window. The voices that morning were those of bearded ball players, some on permanent holiday. These masculine bodies exuded their favorite curse words, "Blood clat," and exited through a man-size hole in the link wire after their game of basketball sociology, often interrupted by grass-smoke communion. Lyle was used to the early milieu of the Vanderveer chatterboxes. The ball players' chatter did not disturb his sleep. In fact, not even the heat generated from his damp blanket disturbed his sleep for he was exceedingly tired from consecutive nights of moonlighting in his gypsy cab "Leaky."

Elizabeth woke. She lit her candle, knelt, and prayed. She prayed to the Lord for guidance. The day had come for her appointment; Lyle's, too. She touched Lyle gently. "Honey, it's time to get up else you'll be late for your job interview. You need that job if we are to buy a house this year. You know where we came from nearly everyone owns his or her own house, even if that house is made up of two sticks propping an umbrella."

"Eh heh!" Lyle grunted, and balled himself under the perspiration-drenched blanket.

"Wake up, honey," Elizabeth said softly. "I want you to drop Hettie and me to Mount Signal Spiritual Baptist Church before you go for your interview. We are going to meet Leader Dollon there." Elizabeth shook Lyle harder.

Between a dying sleep and a long yawn, Lyle answered. "Who?"

"Leader Dollon."

"Who he that? How did you meet him?"

"Through my new friend Hettie...She, too, is from Pitch Lake Country, our sweet Trinidad and Tobago. We're both going to join Leader Dollon's congregation." Elizabeth was excited. "At last, we've found our kind of Spiritual Baptist Church. Now Brooklyn can truly be known as the Borough of Churches."

"Eh heh...Goodluck," Lyle said.

"Lyle, your interview is eleven o'clock so you have sufficient time to drop us with Leaky before you go on your interview."

"What time is it now, Liz gyul?"

"Almost eight...Lyle boy, I prayed to the Lord this morning, and I told Him that if I take fellowship at Leader Dollon's church my contribution will be flowers. I'll provide all the flowers for the church. That will be my responsibility, nobody else's."

"Liz, when last have you contributed anything towards Leaky? Leaky works on gas. I can't even afford to pay her insurance, and I may end up in jail if Leaky knocks down a pedestrian."

"What if I fill Leaky's tank with super?"

"Am still not taking you. I have an appointment with a bread-and-butter job this morning. You have to watch before you pray, so my job interview comes first."

"Says who?"

"Me. That was my Grappa's motto: Watch before you pray. Grappa was as smart as King Solomon."

"Because your Grappa cussed like a Bajan, that made him as wise as King Solomon in the bible?"

"Because he was practical. Grappa knew his priorities. He knew he had to feed his donkey if he wanted his donkey to work."

"Please, please, Lyle darling, take Hettie and me to the church. It is just on Nostrand Avenue. You'll be blessed, Lyle."

"I ain't going. Over thirty years I haven't gone into a Spiritual Baptist camp. Why now?"

"It isn't an illegal church camp like Leader Gerrol's where you and Aunt Gina had to hide from the police in Fyzabad. It is a registered church with a big sign for the world to see. Are you taking us?" She pulled off his blanket, and he pulled it back on him.

"Not even if my Leader Gerrol were there in Mount Signal, and he was sharing bogus food stamps under the altar." Lyle raised the blanket slightly over his head. "For Christ's sake, let me sleep, 'oman!"

"No! It's time to get up. When you lived in Fyzabad, the sun never rose on you; you had to get up before the cock crowed to go and beg neighbor Meena for a piece of lighted charcoal to light Aunt Gina's fireside. That was the only way that you would have had a fire burning to make your bush tea. The traffic noise is New York's cock, and it crowed all night on Nostrand Avenue...Get up, boy, and light my fire!" Elizabeth dug her finger into his side.

"Go away, 'oman, and light your own fire. You just

disturbed a nice wet dream that I was having."

"If it were the woman who calls my house and leaves parables for messages whenever I pick up the phone, you would have got up, lit her fire, and then use Leaky to drop her to Timbucktu."

"No such woman exists."

"Liar! What she has that I don't?"

"You tell me, sweet leg."

Elizabeth softened her tone. "Honey, you know I love you only. I swear. Can you?"

"I told Reverend Beresford Moore when he married us 'I do,' but I didn't sign a fidelity clause with him on your behalf." Lyle stretched below the blanket and waited on Elizabeth's retort. He knew his wife, and he also knew she would not take what he just said as mere words. He was always the recipient of Elizabeth's acid tongue, but he, too, pulled low punches.

The cuckoo clock continued with its croaky sound. It was a very old clock, and the alarm was faulty, but Lyle refused to part with the clock. It was a gift he received from Aunt Lily before her death. From beneath the blanket, Lyle peeked at the disturbing clock, which any antique dealer would have bought for his tricky trade. He pushed his hand through a hole in the blanket and pulled Elizabeth's leg.

"Why is it that every morning you want me to stop that dumb clock. Why don't you stop it sometimes." Elizabeth got up, turned the clock upside down, and the cuckoo's croaks ceased. She yawned, and spoke at the same time. "Why did Uncle Harry bring me to this cold country?"

"You always blame your deceased Uncle Harry whenever winter is approaching. Why don't you go back to dead Fyzabad?"

The Fyzabad remark riled Elizabeth. "I'm waiting on you to take me back to our birth place. It seems as if you've burned your bridges unknown to Aunt Gina. You Caribbean Americans are more American than the Red Man. What's the big deal here? You've to drive a fifth-hand, leaking car without insurance to earn money...You were laid off from your last job the week before you would have been vested...In another job it was all right when your boss saw you reading Superman, but he fired you when he saw you reading Shakespeare. The statue with the lamp is for all shipwrecked...probably not for you, Grappa's Mister Adult Nigger!"

"I'm doing fine, Sister Elizabeth. Amen. Sister Elizabeth, you really need some of the Spiritual Baptist gospeling to put you straight. It's really time to meet and greet your new Leader Dollon, so you all can sing, clap, jump, dance, and scream when you're in the spirit."

"Hear who's talking! Don't you hear the other people when they rejoice in their churches, mosques, and synagogues?"

"Those rejoicing adherents don't scream as if God is deaf. You Trinbago Baptists could really make an earthquake with your stamping and shouting."

Elizabeth shook her head. She had pity for Lyle and the way he reasoned. "Look what this country has done to you—set you apart from your religion. You should have remained in Fyzabad and be that God-fearing shepherd boy."

"Liz, I'm sorry if I blasphemed in any way."

Elizabeth changed her approach to get his favor. "Honey, I have a little money put away. I'll buy Leaky's gas in order that you can take us to church."

"I know you have plenty money hidden away... probably your dead Uncle Harry is the benefactor of couple of your bank books. The majority of all you Caribbean women have at least two secret bank accounts unknown to your husbands; those bank books are always in somebody else's name. How many bank books do you have, Ms. Smarty?"

Elizabeth did not contest Lyle's statement. "Please, please," she said, "drop Hettie and me at Mt. Signal."

She applied her coquetry. She always won with it. She kissed Lyle through a hole in the blanket, and he opened his half-shut eyes wide. He threw off the blanket, ran his fingers through her hair, and he kissed Elizabeth down to her romp. She liked what Lyle did to her body. She pulled Lyle closer to her; and she felt his body contortions. Elizabeth was now certain that Lyle was like a dog in heat, and she could bargain with her body. "Honey, are you taking us to the church?" she asked softly, and the breath from her nostril tantalized his midsection. She sat on Lyle's chest, and he felt the velvet part of her body.

"Now? In this state, honey?"

"Yes, now. You know what Fyzabad riddle comes to mind right now—can you guess which riddle?"

"No."

"Lyle, if you guess which Fyzabad riddle is on my mind, you can have all of me."

"Liz, the riddle is: What's the price of Mr. Lett's house?"

"Dummy! Mr. Lett used to put up his house for sale every year, and whenever people came to buy his house, Mr. Lett chased those interested buyers away, and said: 'All you Fyzabad people are so unreasonable. Where all you long-eyed people want me to go and live? In the sky?' Honey, I'm not like neighbor Lett; I'm not an unreasonable person; I don't want you to live in the sky; I'm selling my merchandise; I want you to live on earth near me; and I really want you to buy my merchandise, honey. I'll give you another clue, Lyle." Elizabeth rubbed her body on him. "How do you feel, honey?"

"Good, honey...Good." Lyle wriggled the lower part of his body.

"Now, tell me, my loving husband, what Fyzabad riddle we can apply at this minute?" She took his fingers, passed them gently over her breasts, and down to her belly button. "What's the answer, honey?"

"Addoknow."

"You mean you really don't know that riddle, Lyle. Think, dummy, think." She relaxed her thighs. "It's all yours the way you like it...not too dry, not too wet...Yummy." She slackened her cotton robe and flashed the meaty merchandise.

Lyle still couldn't unravel Elizabeth's riddle. "Give me another clue, my cruel Sphinx," Lyle said, "because I really want to enter Thebes."

"This is not that silly Greek mythology, boy. This is for real...This is Fyzabad's homegrown massala." Elizabeth eased slightly off of Lyle's hairy chest. She took his fingers, and put them between her legs. "Don't you like the feel of the massala, honey?"

"Yes. It's warm and nice, gyul."

"Now, boy, this is your last chance. Let's suppose we were in the tall grass below Immanuel's mango tree in Fyzabad and a mango fell...You got the mango, and I wanted it. How could I have gotten that mango from you—and you know you'd kill for a mango? How could I have gotten that mango from you without a fist fight? Every gal who has a hairy bank knows how to get deposits made at the expense of the customer without getting into fist fights...Be it bedtime, or any time."

Lyle smiled and showed his white molars; they were still spotless from the soap vine he once used as a Fyzabad boy to scrub them. "Honey, my lovely Grecian Sphinx, if I unravel your riddle would I be able to make a deposit in the hairy bank this sticky morning?"

"Sure, my handsome prince. I cross my heart." Elizabeth crossed her chest with both hands, opened her legs wider, and brought them closer to his chin. "Answer my riddle, and you can enter into the depth of Thebes, honey boy."

Lyle whistled two lines of calypsonian Lord Kitchener's *My Pussin'*. Then he shouted: "The answer to the Sphinx's riddle is when dicky's hard, heart's soft; when dicky's soft, heart's hard. In Webster's English that means when we're not blinded by sex we see correctly; but when we are blinded by our sex drive we go for the shadow and not the substance."

"Smart boy...You are smarter than your Grappa and King Solomon put together," Elizabeth said. She quickly jumped off his chest, and she crossed her legs as tight as the entwined bamboo roots in the rain forest.

"Can I make my deposit in the Sphinx Bank now, honey?"

"Eh, eh."

Lyle used his right hand as a craftsman's chisel to pry open Elizabeth's legs, but her legs were padlocked. Samson, with his uncut hair, in possession of all of his strength, could not pry open her soldered legs. "That ain't fair, 'oman," Lyle protested. "I answered the riddle, so I should be paid."

"'All's fair in love and war.' Answer one more question, honey, and you'll be paid. Is your dicky hard or soft?"

"Can't you feel the pummelling?"

"Sure! Are you going to drop us to meet Leader Dollon on this hot and sticky morning?"

"After I make my deposit into the hairy bank."

"No way! Because after you get my honey, and your dicky gets soft, you'll change your mind; and you'll not drop us at the church. I know of you Fyzabad men. No matter how long you remain in America, you all never divorce your sneaky Fyzabad habits. Fyzabad oilfield men, Joiner Jan included, are the pits. Thank God Joiner Jan didn't come to America to make you worse than you already are."

"I can assure you, my dear, that I was only bluffing. I didn't really want anything from your kind of unfriendly bank."

"Not the way your Mr. Dicky felt. Be reasonable, Lyle. You know I have no more birth control pills or condoms; and you also know fully well the doctors' fees and the monstrous hospital bills that we paid when I was pregnant. That money could have bought a house. Right now you don't even have a job with insurance benefits. How do you expect me to take a chance without protection. Didn't you just advise that we should watch before we pray?"

"Honey, I'm going to charm that interviewer today, and the Gordons will have insurance benefits before the day is over. We'll buy Pastalaqua's house that's up for sale. I'm so happy that another Italian is leaving for exurbia to admire glacial trees in winter and to get the National Guard to shovel his snow. Good for him! Better for us! Pastalaqua's price is good! Honey, I heard Pastalaqua will take as little as one hundred dollars as downpayment on his three-family brick house. The brothers mugged racist Pastalaqua last week. If the brothers mug him again this week, just for my sake, he'll probably drop his downpayment to fifty dollars." Lyle looked at Elizabeth with a sad face and said, "Don't mug me as the brothers mugged Pastalaqua. Can I have a taste of your honey, please, please...just a little taste for goodluck at my interview today?" Lyle displayed the hump in his boxershorts.

"Lyle, can't you wait till tonight? I'll buy a pack of condoms on my way back from my appointment with Leader Dollon. Would you take us to church? Please, please, honey, please."

"You didn't keep your promise, 'oman, when I answered the riddle. That reminds me that the Chief Servant, my Fyzabad hero, once said, 'If I spell K-N-O-W for N-O, I still mean N-O, even if addoknow how to spell it.' Get my drift, honey chil'? The answer is N-O, once; N-O, twice; sold to the highest bidder—N-O!"

"Business man Lyle, is your lousy heart hard, or soft?"
"Stone hard!"

"What a convenient heart." Elizabeth touched his penis. "I see Mr. Dicky's now as soft as the Pillsbury doughboy. Honey, you know when Mr. Dicky wants, and Mr. Dicky doesn't get what he wants, you always get pains in your..." Unexpectedly she pulled Lyle's scrotum; he winced; and Elizabeth continued with her clinic "...and they become swollen. You have a slight pain now, but the plague upon thee is next."

"That's all right with me, dreadful Sphinx. Zeus will punish you."

"Leader Dollon believes in the God of Israel, and he'll come to my rescue."

"Leader Dollon or the God of Israel would rescue you?"

"Whomever...So we're even now: No ride for me, and no hairy bank deposit for you...Let's all travel by the subway together. Be early for your appointment for once."

"Who says I was ever late for a job or an appointment. Aunt Lily gave me that cuckoo for punctuality because at my first job, as a grocery packer, I was always on time."

"You were on time for that packing job because if you were not there on time, the other eager-boys-in-waiting would have got the job. And oh how you needed that job to get candy change to bribe me away from Jimmy, the Robert Taylor of Miss Thebaud's class!" Elizabeth long wanted the opportunity to throw that remark at Lyle. She felt satisfied whenever she reminded him of the hard times in his life. "Go get dressed, Lyle, and travel with Hettie and me on the subway. We'll get off at the Church Avenue stop, and you'll continue to Wall Street. Hettie is one building away, and I can call her on the phone."

"C'mon, now! You know I hate Hettie, that no good Trinbagonian woman...that troublemaker...that imbiber. For that matter, the IRT conductor on the Big Underground 4 may get a heart attack if he didn't see me running to catch his train."

"Seeing you running to catch his train, or seeing you with a new escort—me, the unknown?"

Lyle stuck his head below the balled-up blanket,

and he left his body exposed like the ostrich's. Elizabeth pinched his hairy leg. "Who told you of my regular escort?" he mumbled.

"Look me in the eye, Lyle. You know I'm psychic."

"I've heard you say so, Liz. Your boss at Chase knows that, too? That is why he gave you the day off to go and buy flowers for your new spiritual leader— Leader Dollon?"

"Forget about that now. Someone told me that you travel with the same woman whenever you take the train. Remember what you have to buy is what I have to sell."

"What's your price—a ride in Leaky?"

"Cut the crap out! Who's the woman you travel with every morning?"

"I'm sure Hettie Campbell, after she took her fifth brandy, told you. Hettie always tells you what she doesn't know. She just got to know you, and already she'll jump in fire for you. She'd even—I better not say it. What you did to her? You spat in Hettie's mouth, and that is why she's so loyal like Lassie to you?"

"Women bond differently from men. We know a good thing. That's all it is."

"That is why I'm not taking you to meet your new spiritual Leader. You'll put him against me, too."

"Don't stray from the subject, Lyle. I want to know about that bitch who escorts you to the train every morning! Hettie told me not one goddamn thing about her! Don't try to talk yourself out of it. I'm losing my patience. What's that bitch name?"

"Ms. Breeze."

"From where? Is she your high school sweetheart, the one who went away to France?"

"Remember you wanted to know on what block she lived? She lives on this block."

"And I don't know that bitch! I'm going to join the block association tonight."

"Aren't you the nice, holy lady who's going to see Father this morning to get spiritual guidance?"

"You know fully well that in our Baptist faith we don't call anybody 'Father.' The spiritual title is 'Leader.' Why am I telling you this. You were a screaming shepherd in the Baptist faith...a hungry-Baptist-shouter boy who grew up eating left-over church food and Miss Meena's roti. If it were not for their meals you wouldn't have had the strength to climb that greasypole...Ungrateful son of a bitch!...You tell your son everything about your past, except that of your hungry days when you were as skinny as Ghandi."

"I'm so proud of my wife, Lady Elizabeth. Lady Elizabeth grew up with maidservants, and she got her ovaltine in bed. Lady, you just gave me a brain storm, sweetheart." Lyle jumped off the bed, and went and nailed Aunt Gina's rat hook over the front door. Elizabeth followed him. Lyle spoke to himself as he stood on the chair. "Don't nail the rat hook this way, likkle Lyle; this way is better, likkle Lyle...Ouch! Liz, see how you make the hammer pound my rude finger." Lyle showed Elizabeth his index finger, and he manoeuvered his index finger as if it were a piston going in and out of an engine block.

"If God were like man He would have pounded your useless balls, too, for lying so early in the morning."

"Those are not holy words, Liz gyul. You have to wash your mouth before you go for spiritual guidance this morning...How do you like the way I hung Aunt Gina's rat hook, Liz?" She ignored him. "Liz honey, all the rat hook needs now is a piece of rancid cheese, or sol fish, the good kind of bacalao. Don't you agree, rich girl?" Lyle got off the chair, and he pulled Elizabeth on the bed.

"I'm not amused, jigger-foot boy. I still want to know who's Ms. Breeze?" She was mad with anger. She faced him.

"Her?" Lyle grinned.

"Yes, her! Where did you meet her—that fucking bitch?"

"Through serendipity?"

"Who the hell is she?"

"Fate."

"Stop the bullshitting. If you know for how many years I wanted to put my hands on that bitch. I hope Ms. Breeze has long hair so that I can pull out the roots. If she wears earrings that would be even nicer. I would rip them out of the lobes."

"That's heartless! I thought you once said that you'd never fight any broad for any guy, even if he's as handsome as I." Lyle passed his hands gently over his bristled chin.

"Shit! You call yourself handsome?"

"Ms. Breeze does. She blows in my ear."

"Next it will be in your crotch."

"Won't that be nice, holy girl." Lyle touched his groins. "Oh, they are swollen from non-use...Omm." He feigned as if he were in deep pain; then he burst into laughter.

"So you, Mister Niggerman, you refuse to tell me that bitch name?"

"If you had attended the last block meeting you would have heard her name."

"I wasn't there, so you tell me."

"Foster A. Breeze is her name."

"That's a man's name! Are you into sexual variety? Is that something you learned in your jazz haunts."

"Don't be a chauvinist pig."

"Where did you meet the other pig—Mister, Miss, Mrs. or Ms. Foster A. Breeze—whatever that he, she, or it is?"

"On Foster Avenue. Every morning Ms. Foster escorts me to the subway to catch the BU4, and she's so nippy. Yesterday she was in front of me, and I lost the nine-fifteen train...And that's why I have to go back for the second part of the interview today. If that law firm's second interviewer likes me, she'll hire me. I always prefer a white woman than a white man to interview me. White women are softer on black men. White women don't use their office as their men folks and snipe a black man in his face."

"Is Ms. Breeze white?"

"Wouldn't you want to interview me if I were a prospective employee in your employ? I'm sure Ms. Foster A. Breeze would."

Elizabeth unwound. She was no longer taut. "Wait a minute!" She spoke to herself. "We live on Foster Avenue...the breeze on Foster is always very strong...so Lyle married Foster Avenue and the Breeze and came up with the name Ms. Foster A. Breeze." She looked at Lyle; and she burst into laughter. She jumped on Lyle's back, and hit him playfully.

"Police! Police! Help! Help! This no-good Brooklyn broad is abusing me." Lyle rolled all over the bed and enjoyed his mock persecution.

"I'll never abuse you, honey...I'm sorry, honey, for being such a fool." Elizabeth kissed Lyle, and kissed Lyle. "Oh, my nice husband...There's none other like you."

"It isn't I who named hurricanes after broads. Don't tell the women libbers Betty Friedan, Gloria Steinem, and others that I called women broads."

"So what! I call all men stinking dogs. Anyhow, let Ms. Breeze be my only competition. What about that old flame who left for France? Is she back?" Elizabeth did not wait for Lyle's answer. "Lyle, I thought you said you are now an early bird, and you no longer run for the BU's? I've seen a man drop dead running for the big underground 4. He still did not get on that subway car. Poor soul, he just made himself early for the next world. Lyle, your heart will give up if you continue to run. You'd die, and you wouldn't be able to search for my many bank books to put them in your name." She smiled. God sees sin in those kinds of smile.

Lyle expected that bank-book rebound, for he knew his wife never left a stone unturned. It was his option to 'Let sleeping dogs lie.' He said, "Liz, when I die, or if I'm in jail, only so I'll stop running for the BU's to take me to Manhattan. Faithful Leaky is a one-borough car."

Elizabeth got off his back. "Die, yes; but jail, no," she said. "Mister Adult Nigger will never go to jail to let Grappa turn in his grave."

"You may never know, Liz."

"Not you, Lyle. You love your freedom much too much. In jail, you'll miss your gallivanting Saturdays that turn into Sundays in Jacki's jazz class."

"So you don't believe that I hustle in Leaky at nights to get our downpayment money for Pastalaqua's house? Do I have to get a bill of rights from you?"

"You know you wouldn't be AWOLed from jail, except you break the bars with your white teeth?"

"Do I need your approval to listen to jazz, 'oman?"

"No, sir." Elizabeth was contrite. "Would you let me explain, kind sir?" She paused. "You have been trying to write a hit song since you were courting me at Uncle Harry's, and the money from that imaginary song was to pay for a trip for us to go back home on a grand holiday in Fyzabad. Mister Adult Nigger, a/k/a Lyle Gordon, the budding songwriter, leaves every Saturday morning to buy manuscript paper to jot down what is in his blank, musical mind...And up to this day, Lyle, the man who follows his dreams, has not bought a scrap of any kind of paper."

"How do you know? You searched my toolbox again?"

"Your toolbox has nothing that is important. May I continue, Mr. Music?" She applied a prayerful stance. "Dear Lord, would a bird-free man like the Mister Adult Nigger go to jail? Mr. Music, if the good Lord calls with the answer, please call me. I'm nearby." Elizabeth stepped out of her slackened cotton robe, and she walked naked to the bathroom.

"I'll choose a life sentence in Rikers Island instead of six feet below the col' groun'." Lyle spoke without conviction, and when he said the words "col' groun'," Aunt Gina crossed his mind.

Elizabeth shouted from the bathroom, "By the way, lover boy, what sex is Jacki? That he, she, or it, is hard to figure out on the phone...I guess Jacki X doesn't even have a fingerprint."

"You should know; you're the psychic one, Baptist girl."

Elizabeth came out of the bathtub. She stood dishabille before the life-size mirror in the bedroom and creamed her chocolate body with a perfumed ointment. She cuffed her breasts and caressed them from the base to the tip of the nipples. Her breasts, like Sunkist oranges ripened in the California sun, the teats swarthier than the pulps, were pointed temptingly to Lyle. Elizabeth, painstakingly, ransacked her clothes closets in search of the "right" dress for the occasion. After her appointment, she intended to visit an old friend.

"May I choose the dress for today?" Lyle said.

Elizabeth answered Lyle with teasing body movements. "Is this how the P.R. chick did it on the boardwalk in Coney Island?" Lyle smiled, and Elizabeth put on her garments in an odd manner. Only her stockings, high heels, and an undersize panty which revealed pubic hairs were on her streamlined body. She picked up her pocketbook and placed a neatly wrapped gift into it. "What about this dress, Lyle?" He smiled his approval. In a pretty red dress that rested just above her knees, she finalized her makeup with care. "Honey," Elizabeth said, "stop staring at me as if we are below the willow tree in Brighton Beach." She looked into the mirror as she spoke.

"Liz, I owe my manhood to that weeping willow. That's how a man in love looks at his woman, honey. Right now I have all my sap for thee. Each day I love thee more." Lyle drew his chair to the back of her, and he passed his hand gently down her sheer stockings.

Elizabeth put down her makeup, looked at her

craving husband, and then at her candle. She was aroused by Lyle's loving words. For months, he hadn't spoken tender words of love. At bedtime, he made signals. He usually waived to her after he climbed on and off her body as if his movements were by rote. Most nights Lyle's love signals were as confusing as the traffic light at the intersection of Foster and Nostrand Avenues. At that intersection pedestrians were knocked down regularly because the traffic light's mechanism was not right. "Are you all right, Lyle?" Elizabeth evinced a silly smile, and Lyle treated her question as a pun.

"I'm more right than Nostrand's traffic light," he said.

"Who else gets your love, Lyle?"

"No one else, honey."

"Not even Ms. Breeze?"

"Not even Ms. Breeze."

"Were you ever jealous of me?"

"Nah."

"Not even when I flirted with Jimmy in Miss Thebaud's class and in Mr. Phillips' homeroom?"

"That freckled-face white boy? Never! I was jealous that I hadn't his kind of goodies to bribe you."

"Howdoah look?" Elizabeth asked, and waited to get Lyle's "as-usual" compliments. She also expected his total absorption in Howard Cosell's sports commentary which came static-filled from their ancient, one-band radio.

Lyle shocked Elizabeth again. He turned off the radio without a moment's hesitation. He looked into his wife's eyes, and he answered his wife like a man who, for the first time, felt the intensity and the magic of a woman's love. He said, musically, "You couldn't have looked lovelier, Mrs. Gordon."

Elizabeth was dumbfounded. "Me? Mrs. Gordon." Elizabeth questioned her own identity. Lyle, her husband for over ten years, hadn't said such soothing words to her in ages. At bedtime, they often applied the

Venn diagram. He slept in his favorite fetal position, clockwise, on one side of the bed, and she slept in an arched posture, counterclockwise, on the other end of the queen size bed. Their only commonality was the blanket that warmed their bodies. Now Lyle's words were music in Elizabeth's ear, and she had to reciprocate in kind. She had to answer her mate's love signals. In her age of reason, she was "bugging out." Elizabeth picked up the phone to cancel her appointment with Leader Dollon. On impulse, she put down the phone. Heck it, she thought: It was better to remain at home with her husband; it was easier to call his interviewer and report that her husband is seriously ill; because, after all, if her husband got the job on Wall Street, he was just going to be a black stenographer who would be employed as a showpiece in a white law firm to satisfy the Equal Employment Opportunity's quota. Lyle's romantic words danced frivolously in her brain, and her brain rocked her entire body out of keel. She had zero resistance against her own will power, and was ready for their physical interaction. In the mood for sex, she began to strip as a street urchin. She always fantasied being her husband's mistress, shipwrecked on a barren island. She cherished that thought because her trusted friend Hettie Campbell had told her what a mistress does in bed and what she receives in return from her suitor. Immediately Elizabeth imagined being that mistress; she felt like "wines on the lees," aged, cured, refined, down to the dregs; her liquid would be drunk by her man, and he would be satisfied; forever satisfied, after he moved from her lid to her crease, and applied the tantric techniques of delaying his climax for her sake. Her fantasy was nigh, albeit not on a barren island, but in a barren room, bereft of furniture, but with a soiled carpet that would cushion the motions of their sticky bodies. They would shipwreck their bodies on the floor, and she would feel Lyle's liquid heat in her canals, regardless of her devotion to logic and birth control. Elizabeth, the protem mistress, held her man and caressed him. Her foreplay was truly masterful with her moist fingers and talented palms. She touched her man's already-risen organ, and said in Fyzabad lingo, "Nice, hard nature, boy?"

"Yes, gyul. I know from under-the-weeping-willow-tree days that's the way you like it, hard, hard. Now, I truly believe that only luck can beat voodoo and obeah, because I never thought I would have got an opportunity to make a deposit into your money box this morning." Lyle dropped his brief in one action. "Yes, Grappa," he became nostalgic, "it's hard nature. Grappa, I'm gonna sit on Madame Sullyman's chair just like Rothan without drinking my lime juice."

"Honey, I thought I was beautiful. Am I as ugly as Madame Sullyman's gyul children?"

"Sweetheart, you are more beautiful than all the gods on land, in the sea, or in Hades."

Elizabeth kicked off her shoes. She went to her man, and he took off her brief panty and combed her pubic hairs with his breath. The romance thermometer rose as she lifted her dress half way over her head when a knock was unbelieveably heard on their bedroom door. Her jaws drooped, and her saliva parched. "Damn!" Elizabeth said. She dropped her dress down as if it were on an antique clothes rack, and slipped on her shoes in a hurry.

"Who's it?" Lyle inquired.

"Me, dad. You always want to inspect me before I leave for school."

"Sure, son. Wait a minute, daddy's little boy. Come in." Lyle said the three short sentences in one breath. He snatched his striped robe from the dirty clothes bin and put it on backwards. He kicked his boxershorts and Elizabeth's skimpish panty below the bed with one sweep of his toes. Finally, Lyle exhaled the remaining air in his lungs and sat down on the edge of the bed.

Elizabeth couldn't speak. She struggled to regain

composure, and fiddled with her makeup.

Nigel walked in. "Daddy, why don't you drop mommy and Miss Hettie to the church?"

"Another day, son. I have an appointment this morning. I'm going to get a new job today to have money to buy a house just like the Sullivan's; and, beside, I'd promised to tell you the rest of those Fyzabad stories...Remember? Let your mommy run off, and I'll see if I can squeeze a short story before you leave for school."

"Daddy, I like the story about Leader Gerrol who pointed to his stomach and called it his brains. I promise to tell Lord Meath that thriller."

"Who's Lord Meath?"

"My friend Tommy Sullivan. That's my new name for him."

"Why did you change Tommy's name?"

"Because Billy called Tommy a shanty Irish, and Tommy told Billy that he, Tommy, has rich cousins in Ireland in County Meath, and some of his cousins are lords...So after Tommy's quarrel with Billy, I changed Tommy's name to Lord Meath."

"But why?"

"Because Tommy likes that name, and when I call him Lord Meath he does my math homework."

"Can't you do math, daddy's little boy? Your mother is good in math. Why don't you let her help you, son?"

"I prefer Lord Meath to help me. I always go by his big house, and his mother likes me. She's a lawyer. She has a piano. She's teaching me chords, and how to play *Chopstick*. Lord Meath's mother, Miss Kate, said I'm a fast learner."

"Suppose Lord Meath isn't around, who'd do your math?"

"He'll be around. He's going to be a detective. He can really fight good. Lord Meath did Billy like this...and then a karate...and then a punch. Lord

Meath and I are going to be detectives." Nigel acted out the fight scene.

"Your pal Lord Meath probably wants to be a detective because his father told him a police story."

"Eh, eh. His father ain't told him no police story."

"How do you know?"

"I never see no father since I'm going in that house, but I know everything his mother told him."

"His father could be away on business."

"Lord Meath would've told me that, too, because I told him everything about our family. I told him about you...about mommy...about Fyzabad...about how your Aunt Gina couldn't read nor write. I told him about how your Aunt Gina was called a *tattoo* because she toted dirt on her head, and she was paid three cents an hour. I told him that your Aunt Gina was a hard worker and the fastest *tattoo*, and she moved more dirt than the tractors. Lord Meath did not believe that your Aunt Gina moved more dirt than a tractor. He told me that I was fibbing. We had a big fight, and I beat him up for not believing what I told him."

"That's no good, son. Even though you disagree with a person, there's no reason to fight. Tomorrow I want you to apologize to Lord Meath."

"Why?"

"Because you beat him up."

"You know how many times he beat me up, and his mother never told him to apologize to me."

"What else you told Lord Meath about us?"

"I told him because of the amount of trays of dirt Aunt Gina moved on her head, Fyzabad oilfield got better roads...Then he asked me a dumb question."

"What was that dumb question?"

"He asked me what was the weight of each tray of dirt that Aunt Gina carried on her head?"

"What did you tell him?"

"I gave him a dumb answer, of course."

"Like what?"

"I can only say it in Bajan."

"All right. I got the picture, son. What else you told Lord Meath about the Gordons?"

"I told him about how you and mommy are sure to fight whenever you all speak that dirty Fyzabad patois instead of English."

"My god! You really told Lord Meath everything."

"Even about your toolbox, I told him. Everything! Lord Meath's mother told him what to tell Billy about Billy's mother. Billy always bothers Lord Meath in school whenever Nancy is flirting with Lord Meath."

"What's flirting?"

"Like flying around like a blind bat."

"I see...Did Miss Kate, Lord Meath's mother, say something nice about Billy's mother?"

"Promise you'll not tell Billy's mother when you meet her in Parent-Teacher's meeting?"

"I'll promise, if it is not about a murder."

"It's about the police, but it is no murder."

"Then, what is it, detective?"

"Miss Kate told Lord Meath that when Billy's mother goes out at nights to clubs she always dresses up."

"Isn't that normal? Isn't your mother dressed up today? Doesn't your mother look pretty?"

"Mommy looks as usual."

Elizabeth looked at Lyle. The "as-usual" compliment rang a bell. "Then why isn't it normal when Billy's mother dresses up, son?" Lyle asked.

"Because Billy's mother always comes back very late at nights, drunk, staggering, and when the police comes up to Billy's mother, she tells the police, 'Look at my fine clothes, officer, you can see I ain't no bum.'"

"That's a joke, Nigel. I heard that joke before. Lord Meath's mother, if she didn't invent that joke, heard that joke, too; and she recycled that joke in her house. Your wise Lord Meath gave you that joke as a fact."

"That's no joke. That's a fact!"

"Then what is Billy's mother's name?"

"Miss Bound-to-Drunk."

"I mean her real Christian name?"

"Addoknowdatfact." Nigel sounded like Lyle, especially when Lyle spoke pidgin English fused with Fyzabad patois and the Brooklyn lingo.

"I told you that I want you to be a surgeon." Lyle studied his son as he advised him of his future vocation. "I want you to work in Kings County Hospital to help sick people."

"I don't want to be a surgeon because when you come home late from jazz lessons somebody says," Nigel looked away from his mother, "that she wished I were already a surgeon to cut off daddy's...you know what?" Nigel picked up his book bag, threw it on his shoulder, but he did not move.

Lyle looked at Elizabeth. She bit her smile. Lyle controlled his laughter with the aid of a recitation. He immediately recited *Aboud Ben Adhem*. Elizabeth echoed him, but she stopped at the beginning of the last verse. Lyle preached the last verse in the vernacular. Elizabeth and Lyle's diction and mannerisms were identical. "That's Tellymack for you in part one," Lyle said. "And that's a Trinbago Spiritual Baptist preacher emphasizing the long vowels in part two," Elizabeth said. They applauded each other.

"Who is Mr. Tellymack?" Nigel asked wryly.

"Our headmaster in Fyzabad." Lyle and Elizabeth answered in unison.

"He made everybody recite that poem the same way?"

"If you passed through Mr. Tellymack's class, you better...Otherwise!" Lyle and Elizabeth answered again in one voice.

"That's dumb!" Nigel said.

Lyle zipped the side pocket in Nigel's book bag, and Nigel settled the bag on his shoulders. "Son, nothing is dumb," Lyle said. "Believe me. Even a clock, stuck on yesterday's time, works. Why? Because that time on that stopped clock would be correct twice when tomorrow comes. So think! before you say anything is dumb. A dumb action today could be a fact tomorrow."

Nigel nodded half-heartedly, and he walked out of the room without kissing his parents. He, too, had an appointment, and he was running late for it on that humid August morning.

Elizabeth said, "Lyle, I'm saying chow before the devil creeps under my dress again." She gathered her things and retrieved her panty from below the bed. She also made sure the gift was in her handbag.

"Liz, I really wish the dear devil creeps there more often. Don't forget Nigel needs a sister to play with."

"Get it from Jacki."

"Not with this doughboy."

"Bye, Lyle." She kissed him. "Wait till later, doughboy." She touched Lyle's flaccid penis.

"What is the gift that are you taking in that little box, Liz?"

"If you take Hettie and me to church you'll find out."

"Enjoy your appointment, dear. Tell Leader Dollon that I said howdy, and tell him I'll buy the vase to put your flowers." Elizabeth was about to say something, but Lyle cut her short. He whispered his true feeling in Bajan: "Me! buy a vase. You wish! God will have to send down Jesus to get me back in a Spiritual Baptist church, especially in Brooklyn, New York."

"Lyle, be on time for your interview. Take a clean shave. Don't go looking like Barabas. Remember Pastalaqua's house is our goal. Take a real bath...not a *Starboy Shenko*, that dry-cloth wash...Remember what white people say about us when we aren't around. Also, don't use that loud perfume that the brother sold you on Fulton Street; it smells like rum vomit."

The front door was suddenly pushed open. Nigel rushed inside, and he kissed his parents.

"We knew you'd come back for your allowance," Lyle said. "Here's a dollar for two days, young man.

Why do you always leave Lord Meath downstairs? Isn't our house good enough for that little lord?"

"Miss Hettie is the only person that I see who comes into this house."

"That's the reason why you never invited Lord Meath inside our house?"

"Eh heh...You invite him."

"Is Lord Meath downstairs?"

"Yes."

"Your mother and I want to be introduced to him."

"Well, hurry. We have an appointment with Eggie and Bob to price some boxes before we go to school. Lord Meath said that we'll move those boxes this afternoon if the price is right. Eggie and Bob own the new candy store on Nostrand Avenue. They're foreigners. We laugh at their accent."

"What!" Lyle hit the roof. "You laugh at people! I can't believe I'm hearing that from the son of an immigrant, and he's living under my roof. *Carrajo*! Grappa always said, 'What ain't meet you ain't pass you.' Imagine my son is laughing at people's accents! I can't believe it! *Mamayo*!" Lyle put his hand on his head in the same way his Grappa did. "*Mamayo*! *Mamayo*!"

"Those foreigners really talk funny, dad. Lord Meath can imitate Eggie and Bob very good...We'll wait just five minutes for you downstairs." Nigel looked at his wrist watch, and ran downstairs. He did not wait for the elevator. He knew that it may never come; but he was sure if the Vanderveer elevator did come, its smell of urine would stifle him.

Elizabeth reached downstairs before Lyle. She introduced herself. "Nice to meet you, Lord Meath." Elizabeth smiled graciously. She held Lord Meath's perfectly clean right hand longer than usual. She looked at Lord Meath's left hand to see if it were just as clean.

"Nice meeting you, Mrs. Gordon." Lord Meath exhibited his chummy smile and looked at Nigel, who was the diplomat observer with a poker face.

Lyle came crashing like the waves. He barely spent three minutes to wash his hands and find appropriate clothes. "Where is..." He forgot Tommy's nickname.

Elizabeth stepped forward and said, "Lord Meath, this is my husband, Nigel's father."

"Nice to meet you, Mr. Gordon." Lord Meath stretched his hand. His proud stature was that of a statesman.

"Nice to meet you, Lord Meath," Lyle said. "I hear you'll be working with the foreigners in my neighborhood this afternoon."

"That's after we do our homework." Tommy's manner was businesslike, but his voice was sincere. "I'm contracted with Eggie and Bob's, but the workload is too much for me now."

"That Eggie and Bob, the foreigners, are they fair people?"

"We've had our disagreements."

"Like what?"

"I'd rather not tell a third party." Lord Meath's eyes, blue as Sinatra's, didn't blink. He spoke with them.

"Am sorry, Lord Meath, for my indiscretion."

"Sometimes we do make mistakes...Can Nigel work with me as an equal partner?"

"Sure! Sure! Why don't you do your homework at my house sometimes."

"Give me a chance to think about it. Goodbye, Mr. and Mrs. Gordon."

All the parties went their separate ways.

Lyle ran upstairs. He intended to take a quick nap, but he fell asleep on the dishevelled bed. At the tenth hour the phone rang. He snatched the phone and said, "Who you want? Heysoo? No livin' hay. Me no habla Spanglish." He hung up the phone and said, "*Gracias*, Heysoo, but next time let your Mira Mira call you ten minutes earlier." Lyle was running late for his interview. He rushed to the bathroom with a *Starboy Shenko* in mind. The *Starboy Shenko* was a quick bath named after

Shenko, the burliest of the Boys of Fyzabad. Shenko, asthmatic, often went to the Oropouche River with the intention of going in the water to bathe, but, instead, Shenko sat on the river bank and drycleaned himself with his red-flannel underwear. The day that Shenko went into the water, he took a bath in less time than the starboy Frank Sinatra would have taken to tie his trademark Sinatra knot.

Lyle chortled when he turned on the shower. Though he lacked the *Shenko* touch, he had Jesse Owen's speed in dressing. Lyle darted out of the shower and pulled the towel quickly over his body. He unlocked his toolbox and got his socks and shoelaces; that was his safest hiding place from Nigel on gym Friday, and from Elizabeth who searched for women's clues. He was dressed in an instant. He looked in the mirror and said, "This is a real nice tie that you brought back from France for me, Billie...I hope Wall Street likes my Sinatra knot...Am sure Liz knows that you're back from France, Billie, but Liz is playing it cool. My sweet Elizabeth is playing dead to catch you alive." He smirked at the thought.

Lyle hid his toolbox, and broke his fast when he nibbled a piece of cheddar cheese and gulped from the juice bottle. He blew out the candle. "Liz, I know you want the candle to be kept burning to brighten your day, but the Mayor got rid of Ladder 19. The Mayor said the city has no money." He locked the door in two positions, jumped three treadles of the step, and his Tom McCan brogues pounded the pavement. Foster Avenue breeze was behind him in its intensity, and it pushed him to the subway. The sound of the No. 4 train was heard. It tunneled underground, and halted at the Newkirk Avenue stop. He rushed down the stairs. He dropped his token into the turnstile, wheeled the turnstile with his hip, leaped into the car, and the train conductor smiled when he closed the sliding doors on Lyle's heels. Winded, Lyle touched his lusterless

Mondesir gold belt as if the belt gave him assurance. He slumped on the cold seat, and was subwayed to the Wall Street firm of South Opnorth, Pickdom & Cotton to fill his appointment.

Lyle got the job. Miss Gennoyer walked him to the elevator, and he shook her hand with a firm grip. He controlled his emotions throughout the forty nine flights down. In the Chase Manhattan Bank concourse, he shouted, "Hallelujah!" and raised his hand in the air. He raced through the beautifully variegated concrete flooring of Chase Plaza adorned by a Japanese wishing-pool and headed down Nassau Street. He ran to the nearest public phone banks on Wall Street to call Elizabeth. All the phones were visited by afternoon lovers. Lyle waited on a vacant phone and in the meantime recited, "Mrs. Elizabeth Gordon, on Monday I'll be a Wall Street stenographer...with insurance...with overtime...with free meals...with taxi service...the works...Pastalaqua, here I come with my downpayment for your house...Time to move to Long Island, Pastalaqua! Oh, there's a vacant phone."

An office clerk darted out of the Stock Exchange, and he grabbed the vacant phone. He hugged the phone for thirty minutes, and fed it with quarters, dimes, and nickels until there was no more loose change in his pockets. The chatty clerk dug into every crevice in his pants, shirt pockets, and uniform jacket. He finally found a dollar in his breast pocket. "Change a buck for me, boy." He addressed Lyle as if Lyle were his obliging neighbor's cat.

Lyle always hated cats, and he chased them away with mighty rocks, even Miss Meena's cat suffered at his hand; but Lyle always loved dumb insolence as a personal weapon, and he applied dumb insolence with greater force than the force he used to throw rocks at cats. In Wall Street, for sure, Lyle knew he could not throw rocks at the feisty Stock Exchange clerk even though the clerk looked like a cat in business attire.

Thus, he opted that Friday, to him a Friday as sacred as Good Friday, to combat the Stock Exchange clerk's insult with a dose of *Shake-Well*-Lyle-Gordon's-dumb insolence. Not even did he say, "Get thee hence, Satan," his favorite scripture quote. His chart and compass were, "If speech is silver, silence is gold."

"What are you doing down here, boy?" Lyle's antagonist again stressed the word "Boy." He dropped the phone, and it dangled by the cord. He signaled the middle-finger curse to Lyle as he walked into the Exchange entrance on Broad Street.

Lyle cleaned the phone painstakingly with his tie for his antagonist to see, and he said softly, "Seems this French tie gives me goodluck, but I always get in an argument whenever I wear it...Now," he paused, "I shall tell my loving wife that I'm bringing home the condoms, and she should buy the wine." In spite of the slight tiff, he was exceedingly happy to be among the participants who bustled in three-piece suits and sunk into grottos that lead them to the Wall Street subway.

He phoned Elizabeth.

"Hello. This is the Gordons' residence. May I help you."

The voice that answered was a strange voice, but Lyle recognized that voice nonetheless. In fact, Lyle recognized the voice immediately. He hung up the street phone gently without saying a word and whispered to himself, "What a classy kid, that Lord Meath...Seems as if the two detectives are already at work. I wonder who'd be the third party in their detective story." He looked at the clock on the eves of the black walls of Trinity Church that bound Wall Street on the west. The clock read 5:00 p.m.

That eventful Friday began Lyle's business life in the silk stocking district. He was now part of a new culture—the culture that was Wall Street's. On Monday, Lyle Allister Gordon would roam the rich canyons on the southern tip of Manhattan Island.

Chapter Four

The Passing Years

The Gordons kept their appointments: Nigel with his friend Lord Meath; Elizabeth with her church and bosom friend Hettie; and Lyle with Leaky and alias Jackiass. In Lyle's parenting hours he told Nigel many Fyzabad stories; and he also made it incumbent on Nigel to express himself freely. "Nigel," Lyle often said, "my Aunt Gina was great—may God bless her in the grave—but I was too afraid of her. Many times I hid my true feelings from Aunt Gina, sometimes to my detriment, son."

"Thanks, dad," Nigel said. "I'll always talk my mind like my great Grappa."

"Your great Grappa said, 'Plain talk is not bad manners.'"

"Lord Meath speaks his mind to me, and I speak my mind to him...nothing but plain talk."

* * * * * *

Elizabeth and Nigel returned from church, and Nigel said, "Mommy, why dad doesn't ever come with us on Sundays?"

"Because your father goes gypsy cabbing in Leaky."

"You really believe he goes moonlighting on Sundays?"

"Yes. Don't you?"

"If you say so...Why was everybody dancing in church, mommy?"

"That wasn't dancing. They had the power. The Divine Spirit was manifesting in them."

"What is the power?"

"When the spirit comes in us, and we shake and call the Savior in strange tongues."

"Where does the spirit come from?"

"No one knows. The spirit is like the wind."

"When the spirit was in Miss Hettie, what language was she speaking, mommy?"

Lyle walked in and overheard the conversation. "Why all these questions, Nigel?"

"I'm practicing to be a detective. And why don't you come to church on Sundays?"

"I have to drive Leaky to get extra money to pay for our new house. You saw how Pastalaqua damaged the walls and the commodes before he left for Long Island. We got the Pastalaqua House for sure, but with a lot of deliberate destruction. God is good, son..."

"I hope so."

"I know so, son. Don't you like your new room with your own television? How would I get money to pay your way through college, and then through detective school, if I don't moonlight in Leaky? Lord Meath's mother is a lawyer. Do you know what she charges her clients? I know what Wall Street charges their clients per hour. Only the rich can be Wall Street's clients." Lyle took out his day's earnings as a gypsy cabdriver, and he placed it on the table.

Nigel looked at his father and at the money on the table. "That's all the money you made, dad?...Mommy," Nigel said to his mother who absorbed the father-and-son conversation, "what did Leader Dollon preach about tonight?"

"People who are too busy to find time for God...money grabbers...whoremongers..." Elizabeth walked to the bedroom and ended her sentence. "And liars!"

"Dad," Nigel said, as he pulled off Lyle's boots, "I hope I didn't get you in trouble?"

"Not at all, son. Plain talk is not bad manners." They laughed, father and son, and slapped their palms.

"Dad, today I was playing in Sunday school. I hid behind a door, and I disappeared. Sheila couldn't find me because that door led me upstairs right into Leader

Dollon's robing room."

"Shame on you, Nigel," Elizabeth shouted. She came out of the bedroom. "I sent you to Sunday school to learn of Jesus, not to play..." She paused, looked Lyle in the eye, and ended her rebuke, "...jazz in Jackiass' bank...It's time for bed, son...Tomorrow I don't want you to go with Lord Meath at Eggie and Bob's unless you can write me a letter stating all the things that a carpenter puts in his toolbox. A good detective can imagine what's in any toolbox without even knowing about the journeyman's trade."

"That's a great assignment, mommie."

"Then do it!"

* * * * * *

The years quickly rolled by. Nigel did all of Elizabeth's assignments, and he ingested Lyle's Fyzabad stories.

Nigel Atiba Gordon and Tommy "Lord Meath" Sullivan worked towards their goal; and they achieved their dreams. Their friendship grew during their school years, but one incident cemented their brotherly love more than any other.

It was the norm every afternoon when Marine Park Junior High School was over that the black kids, moreso the boys, scampered from school. The black boys hid from the white bullies, and they took the long route through the park to get the crosstown Avenue U bus on the other side of south Brooklyn. On Avenue U the black children transferred to another bus, and then finally to the B44 bus that took them home. Most of the black boys got home late and bloodied. Lord Meath brought Nigel's crosstown ordeal to an end.

The bell rang; and Lord Meath rushed upstairs to see his math teacher. "Nigel," he said, "wait for me. I'll be back in a minute." As Tommy spoke, Nigel concealed a stone in a brown paper bag. That stone was his hidden weapon to ward off his white assailants.

"Got to go before Ricco and Pollie find me, Lord Meath."

"What do you mean by that, Nigel?"

Nigel did not answer.

"Nigel, how come you are always late for work at Eggie and Bob's. Eggie said that two boys want our job. I am always there on time, but I alone can't do everything. It is just a hop and a jump to the busstop. I wait at the busstop for us to travel together, but you never show up. Where do you go, Nigel?"

"For the B3."

"The B3! That's a crosstown bus to Kings Plaza. Your bus is the downtown B44, and it is right there on Nostrand and Avenue S. Why am I telling you this...You know that."

"I don't want my face to be bashed in by Ricco and Pollie. They told fat Harry that he's too black for Marine Park, and he should stick with the jungle bunnies in Bed Stuy. Did you see Fat's face this morning?"

"Fats told me that he rode into a post. His bike had no brakes."

"He didn't tell me that."

"Ricco and Pollie did that to Fats?"

"Who else?"

"You're travelling with me today. I'll handle them."

"How?"

"You'll see."

"You have a switchblade, Lord Meath? Pollie and Ricco aren't afraid of you."

"Neither am I afraid of them. My mother represented them in court more than once. She told me what they did was not right, and they could have been sent to jail."

"What Ricco and Pollie did?"

"My mother did not tell me. She said that was lawyer-client privilege. The law dealt with them in a special way."

"Would the law be around to see when Ricco and

Pollie hurt me, Lord Meath?"

"Trust me, Nigel, Ricco and Pollie won't harm you after today."

Nigel waited for Lord Meath in the school yard, but debated with himself: "I better leave now through the park." He lifted his bag and was about to leave when Lord Meath appeared.

"Let's go, Nigel."

Nigel turned toward Marine Park, an extremely large playground, which bounded his junior high school on the east.

"We are not going for the B3. We are going to Nostrand Avenue for the B44. Eggie and Bob expect us early today," Lord Meath said.

"Okay, if you say so." Nigel was hesitant. Fear of the unexpected made his book bag heavier than it was.

At the intersection of Avenue S and Nostrand Avenue, Ricco entertained his friends with smut jokes. Pollie was on another mission that day. Lord Meath touched Ricco. He actually accosted Ricco. "Ricco, you're a chump," Lord Meath said aloud.

Ricco stood still. He was shocked. He flexed the cobra tattooed on his needle-pricked arm. In front of Ricco stood Lord Meath, a wonderfully handsome kid with a clean cut and clean hands; he was a little thirteen year-old David before Goliath. Lord Meath's weapons were his eyes. They were blue, but fierce. Ricco passed his palm on his slick hair.

"Paco," Ricco said to his thug friend, "hear this before I smack this fresh kid escorting his jungle bunny." He addressed Lord Meath. "Yo! What you say? Yo!"

"If yo didn't hear, then yo not only a dump chump, but a deaf chump, too, Ricco." Lord Meath stressed every syllable. "I know yo. My mother wrote an affidavit for yo and Pollie. Yo listening, yo! What did both of yo sign when my mother notarized the affidavit, yo?"

"Yo! Yo! That lady lawyer is yo mother?"

"Yes, yo! And yo surely won't want me to say more for my jungle bunny and Paco to hear what letter of the alphabet yo and Pollie used for yo signatures."

Ricco looked at Nigel sheepishly, then he addressed Lord Meath. "Yo! That's cool, man. Yo mother is a genius lawyer, man. Everything is cool, yo."

"Everything is cool, yo. Tell Pollie and yo hate gang that, too, yo! Yo listening to me, yo."

"Yo, that's cool, man."

"That's cool, Ricco."

Ricco hustled Paco away and said, "Paco, let's go play pool man. Paco, I owe yo a beer for that pool game last night. Let's have it, man." Ricco hushed his voice and said, "That blue-eyed kid is crazy, man."

Tommy, that blue-eyed kid, was crazy for the preservation of his friend's rights. Nigel was never again late for his assignment with Eggie and Bob. After school, he took the shortest route home, and hugged his pal on the way to the B44 bus.

Fate and serendipity are neighbors with different goals, and neighbors with different goals sometimes meet. When Nigel met Ricco again, they were both men. Nigel was the schooled detective. Ricco was the civic-minded juror whose decisive vote in a criminal case decided the ill-fate of an innocent man.

Chapter Five

South Opnorth,
Pickdom & Cotton ("S.O.")

Gertrude Gennoyer, the stenopool supervisor, was the warden in pants suit, with a gait like a penguin. She was a woman of high morals and exceedingly fair in her official dealings. She was transferred from S.O.'s office in Silly Pond Road, South Carolina. Her code name was GG, and she was slow to understand risque literature as the GG snail train was fast to come up the track on subzero evenings. The office celebrated Lyle's fifty-third birthday, and Jodi Dapray bought him a birthday card. The card read:

A birthday toast to a music man!
If your private organ droops in a duet,
Use your strongest finger.

Jodi deliberately rested the birthday card on the floor to draw GG's attention. It did. GG picked up the card, read it, and with a smile of approval said, "Lyle, isn't that nice. My nephew Carl got a similar card on his birthday, and since then he has been practicing his arpeggio." GG handed Lyle the card and left the room. The stenopool was grateful that she quickly left the room. Lyle's hernia pained from his controlled laughter. Jodi had bloodshot eyes, and the stenopool was in hysterics. It was Lyle's twenty-first year with the law firm, and he was convinced that he kept his job, not on account of the company's policy which was unwritten as the British Constitution, but because he loved to be a part of all that was GG's.

The morning dragged on. Jodi, the queen of mischief, was also the office housewife. She sat down to lunch before the official lunch time. She was a wizened woman, almost bloodless, but she was a health food freak. Before her were four bags; each contained seeds, greens, oils, and the ageless, brown bag had her entree. Jodi appetized on cottage cheese, shredded carrots, mixed greens, raw okras, garlic, raw nuts, and brown water. She opened the bag with her main menu, and she went after her lunch with avarice. Instantly, members of the stenopool gasped and rushed for the closest windows. They needed fresh air to ward off the smell of Jodi's entree. Her entree was not only rank, but it stunk.

"What's that?" Phillo Liman asked.

"*Poisson frais*," Jodi answered with a stuffed mouth.

"More like poison, Jodi." Lyle corked his nostrils with both thumbs.

"It smells like stinkin' sol fish!" Daniel Cake said. Daniel Cake was a stenographer of few words. He shied away from Lyle, and Lyle didn't care for him either.

"How did you call Jodi's food, Daniel?" Lyle asked.

"Stinkin' sol fish!"

"Where are you from?"

"Is that your business, Lyle?"

"Not really, Daniel."

"Am an American."

"Naturalized?"

"Are you S.O's census man?" He looked at Lyle's waist over and over.

Lyle felt stupid. He moved from the window, and pulled up his Mondesir gold belt. "Sorry," Lyle said and whispered to himself, "Only a Fyzabadian pronounces salt fish as *sol fish*."

GG walked in. "What's going on? This is an airconditioned office! Why are these windows opened? Close them! There is work to be done. Daniel, see Mr. Dempsey...Phillo, take off the belt from the dictaphone...Miriam, make these corrections for Miss Bellamy...Jodi, here's the Lysol spray...Linda Joans, where's your timesheet? Why are you always late with it, Linda? Don't you know that we have to bill the clients, and your charge is equally important as the lawyers'. This is the last time I'm going to tell you this, Linda Joans...Lyle, Mr. Pinwick needs steno. He's in a rush...Remember that he's a Harvard scholar, and Harvard gave America five Presidents so far."

"So what!" Lyle said beneath his breath. He knew S.O. hadn't a union, and Hazel Parris was fired for being sassy when told of another lawyer's background. Lyle particularly remembered that it was Friday, the last day of the working week, and the Labor Day weekend followed. He collected a stenopad from the supplies locker and rushed off to Mr. Pinwick.

"Lyle," GG said aloud as he returned to his desk, "you had two callers. One sounded like your wife; one wasn't. This is office hours."

He didn't thank GG. Instead, he looked at her two innocent pools of blue eyes, bounded by mascara. Miriam, the new employee, sneezed. No one said, Bless you. Miriam said it for herself. She backspaced on her typewriter until GG went into her office and closed her door. "Lyle," Miriam whispered, "that frustrated woman's telephonic relays are always like that?" Lyle shook his head, and concentrated on the marked-up prospectus and the shorthand notes before him. "Thank you, Lord," Miriam said, and made the sign of the cross. She made the sign of the cross again, and said, "Thank you, dear Lord Jesus, that that old hen who sits on her eggs on Fridays did not pick up any of my calls today." Jimmy, Mario, and Caesar had called her in GG's absence. Jimmy and Mario were Miriam's ex-husbands with whom she battled on the phone for child support; and Caesar was her disco partner who was always in need of a weekend loan.

It was 4:30 p.m., and GG was frustrated as there was no work for her to distribute to the stenopool. She looked at the transcription banks located on the wall and wished for their green lights to appear. The green lights indicated that the lawyers were dictating work on their IBM transcription sets for the stenopool. It was the habit among lawyers to buzz three times on those sets when they had a rush job; nonetheless, GG treated every job with urgency. She loved to hear the "beep-beep-beep" shortly before the end of the working day. That beep-beep-beep sound gave her power: power to keep her typists and stenographers in to work late, and also to show management that her stenopool on the forty ninth floor was more productive than the other two stenopools. There was petty rivalry among the three stenopool supervisors. Phillo, S.O.'s alias Rona Barrett, the Gossip Columnist, rumored that GG's first taste of power was as a Sunday school teacher, and that she treated the stenopool as an extension of her Sunday school.

Alias Rona Barrett proved his point again. At five minutes before five the buzzes were heard, and GG's countenance brightened. She smiled, and her smile broadened. Higgory Zumzum, Esq., a lawyer with nocturnal habits, gave four long buzzes that echoed through the stenopool. The pool people looked at the clock on the wall and sheepishly looked at their synchronized wrist watches. Yes, it was true. Those buzzes echoed five minutes before the witching hour—the time for them to leave for home to enjoy the long weekend.

Everyone became pretentiously occupied. Lyle put in a blank sheet of paper and typed ASDFLKJ a dozen times. Linda pressed her hand on her chest, located her ulcer, swallowed two giant-sized capsules without water, and recited the Twenythird Psalm. Madeleine stared at the buzzer vent. She was a partner's secretary who was demoted to a pool stenographer because she refused, on instruction, to tell clients that her boss was out of town when, in fact, he sat in his office and skulked. The buzzer met her telling Phillo, "Jehovah's Witnesses cannot lie," and Phillo replied, "You mean cannot lie down straight?" Their dialogue ceased. Phillo chalked up two firsts: He left their argument hanging like a fox tail, and he cleaned the ball of his typewriter for the first time in five years. Daniel made a sick face. Yet he looked stronger than Popeye the Sailorman, who just consumed two bowls of spinach. Miriam packed, and unpacked, her stationery in her drawer. Those in the johns flushed, waited on the tanks to refill, and flushed again. The toilet chains clanked, and clanked.

The stenopool knew that four buzzes meant a Zumzum's super rush. They hated his rush and him equally. Higgory Zumzum had a penchant for longwindedness. He wrote a memo to say that he expected a memo, and wrote a follow-up memo to say that he received the expected memo. His legal advice were Canterbury Stories. He dictated his advice in the passive voice, re-dictated it in the active voice, changed adverbs to preposition, and gave instructions on the dictated belt to refer to what he said in a previously dictated belt. With the ear plugs that often burned their ears, even the new stenographers eventually learned the Zumzum ropes: The new stenographers kept a carbon copy of Zumzum's first draft, because they were sure that his tenth and final draft would be almost verbatim to his first dictated letter.

All GG's pool people trembled in their boots as the echo of the prolonged buzzes tickled their ears. No one dare cover his or her typewriter or dictaphone at that hour, a sure crisis hour for GG. Jodi knew the rules, but she covered her typewriter and locked her dictaphone.

On that Friday, Gertrude "GG" Gennoyer meant to close the week's curtains with a bang. She cleaned her brass nameplate; angled it on her desk to face the employees; and raised from her swivel chair as a lady in a Southern pantomime. She stood in the middle of the room, and knew that her presence was not an encore. GG studied her audience. Jodi, aware of GG's antics, delved into her bag of nostrums, and nibbled the remains of her *poisson frais*. Every stenographer needed air to ward off the horrible smell that came from Jodi's corner, but no one opened a single window for fear of drawing GG's attention. Jodi did the unobvious: She opened the windows as if the day had just begun, and said, "Isn't the air refreshing?" No one answered; no one wanted to be conspicuous, especially Lyle Gordon whose mind was on the coming Labor Day festivities in Brooklyn when people from the blue waters of the Caribbean dance on Eastern Parkway (the Parkway). "Carnival Monday," he called it.

The Zumzum buzzes actually met Lyle striking off Elizabeth's name from his weekend itinerary and replacing it with Billie Zellars'. Lyle continued arduously with his mock typing, and he banged out ASDFLKJ like an automaton. Jodi even refused to pretend that she was occupied with any of the lawyers' private typing of their wives' Christmas club shopping lists. (Such typing work was labeled as "Office Charge, No Billing," and GG had no control over the lawyers' indiscretions.) Phillo whispered to Jodi, "Do as if you are typing Mr. Mordecai's girlfriend's research papers. GG has a crush on Mordecai." Phillo's words fell on stony soil. Jodi opened her drawer, took out a discolored jar, and dipped first the larger of her thumbs into a creamy substance. She spread the substance on her right elbow, and she massaged from her elbow up to the tips of her fingers. She alternated the process just as slowly.

"What's that...slight smell...Jodi?" GG paused twice. The first time that she paused, her mouth was more appropriately shaped to say 'stink smell.'

With the utterance of clinical authority, Jodi answered her supervisor. "It's cottage cheese. I'm taking out the toxins from my bones. May I," she stared her supervisor, "Miss Gennoyer?"

"Sure! Sure!" The stenopool supervisor, the proper

and petite Southern lady, had the last word but not the last bit of strategy to combat Jodi Dapray, a native New Yorker. With her sweet-and-instant smile GG said, "Jodi, you have to work late tonight. I must remind you that Mr. Higgory Zumzum graduated summa cum laude...Transcribe his belt so that it will make sense as if it came from him." GG stepped away as if she were on a dais and was followed by flood lights.

Jodi frowned outwardly but laughed inwardly like Braer Fox who pleaded not to be thrown into the briar patch. She had over budgeted on her next paycheck, and she desperately needed overtime to buy an earth shoe.

"Goodnight. Enjoy the Labor Day weekend," GG said.

"Goodnight. Same to you, Miss Gennoyer." The pool people replied with instant reciprocity. They had hidden smiles for they knew the Confederate had lost another indoor battle to the Yankee.

With fits and starts, Jodi put on her earphone, slipped Mr. Zumzum's dictated belt into her dictaphone, rolled in a sheet of letterhead paper into her typewriter, waived to her peers, and said, "Here beginneth thy overtime on the Zumzum chronicles. See ya on Tuesday, guys!" Her fingers touched the keys and, she, singly, disturbed the peace with her efficient typing on overtime hours.

"T.G.I.F. (Thank God It's Friday). Mr. Diarrhea of the Mouth had us quaking in our boots again." Phillo clowned. He recited, in part, the beleaguered wordings in one of Mr. Zumzum's dictaphone belts that he had transcribed: "Take this letter. Dear Sir...I mean, Dear Sirs...Make it, Gentlemen...Erase that...Dear Sir or Madam, Enclosed please find...Erase that. Herewith are...Jodi, have you met the *de facto-de jure* clause as yet?" The stenopool went wild with laughter. They were more than familiar with Higgory Zumzum's *de facto-de jure* expression which eventually turned into the DFDJ Fan Club.

Phillo rushed to the elevator, trailed by his cohorts, and each stenographer recited tidbits of his or her favorite passage of dictation that over the years came from the Zumzum's buzzes. The work week ended, and stampeding feet blocked the already packed elevator. The grimness of Friday faces was gone.

"We've got a so-called native on board with a Squaw Valley accent." Lyle spoke from his squeezed position in the back of the elevator.

"Living in New York? They're devils. My second husband is from there," Miriam shouted.

"Why didn't Mr. Squawky take a bus to Hollywood. Who the hell is he?" Phillo asked.

"A someone who referred to Jodi's *poisson frais* as sol fish!" Lyle stuttered, deliberately, and spoke in a heavy Trinbago accent.

There was a disorder of laughter. The elevator shimmied down and hit the street floor. It could have been a disaster but South Opnorth, Pickdom & Cotton's people didn't care. It was a Fulton Street fish market gathering. Only one person was mum.

Daniel Cake bored his way out first. Lyle Gordon trailed Daniel's footsteps, and shouted, "Sol fish Cakey! You's a fresh water Yankee."

Daniel looked around. He again looked at Lyle's waist. He said not a word, but his eyes revealed vengeance.

All were bound for home. All had plans for the Labor Day weekend.

Chapter Six

Billie Zellars

Billie Zellars, a graduate of La Sorbonne, was a political consultant to a black underground movement which sought to rid America of its bias policies. Billie was other things, too. She was a part-time model, an agitator, and she was Lyle's woman. She hated the color gray or any axiomatic conclusion which was derived from or based its premise on conjecture. "It's either black or white...Oh how I hate the open-ended stuff," she'd say. She was attractive, of medium height, brown eyes, bleached hair, light complexion, and her graciousness was overpowered by her uneven temper which she struggled to keep in control.

She and Lyle were driven back to Building 122, her Bedford Stuyvesant brownstone. Her apartment was spacious and inviting, but her north wall was a riddle. That wall was adorned with silhouetted profiles of twelve black men and a woman; and those profiled people were the architects of her growing underground movement. She called them Generals-for-the-Cause or the GC's. Three of her poster generals were dead; and those living, she felt, would make life uneasy for the powers that be, because they would fight for the rights of the black people of America. Billie's argument was, if the black people of America were not free, other black people of the world would never be free. "America is the rhythmic Mecca of the swarthy skins" was her one-liner. Her professor, a Dr. Awolabi of Medgar Evers College on secondment at La Sorbonne, instilled in her that "in the world of politics there are no permanent friends or permanent enemies, but there's only permanent interest." Billie liked her professor's philosophy, and she fed it to her underground group who meshed that philosophy with their own. The underground group devoured Dr. Awolabi's philosophy; and they used it as their springboard to leap into their every position— political or nonpolitical—to achieve their sometimes questionable goals.

As Billie walked into her foyer she echoed what Dr. Awolabi in a puckish moment would have thought of the white cabby who chauffeured them from Manhattan and chatted endlessly about his black girl friend. Lyle tipped him handsomely because he was the only white cabby who did not ignore their outstretched hands and signals when they waited for transport on Seventh Avenue.

"Lyle, after all these years, ever so often Dr. Awolabi crosses my mind for the things he'd ad lib. He's so quick on the draw. Whatta professor!"

"Let's not talk of him today."

"I promise. Did I tell you thanks, honey, for getting me out of the house and treating me to a Broadway matinee? Neil Simon's play was interesting, but I would have preferred to see Amiri Baraka's *Dutchman* instead, and get away from any kind of political fodder today."

"Are you serious? We saw *Dutchman* before, and it is filled to the hilt with social politics. I hate *Dutchman* because of Clay. He is just as stupid a black man as most of your GC's. Clay unmasked himself in that play, and that's why the white woman Lula made a fool of him. That is still a weakness today among black men. They get comfortable with white women, strangers or not. That general," Lyle pointed to Billie's wall, "I know him personally. He will drop his guard, unmask himself, and forget his sacred assignment as soon as he sees the bulge of a white woman's nipples in a silk top. That's why am always fascinated by Frederick Douglass' journey. Douglass knew when not to take off his mask. Your generals," he looked up, "addoknow about most of them!"

"All these men have shown their mettle." She counted them silently as she bobbed her head.

"By the way, Billie," he unbuttoned his shirt halfway, looked at her wall, and admired her body, "what made you so sure that none of your GC's is 'running with the hare and chasing with the hound'? Is it because you are their mulatto leader?" He knew his tease would set her on instant fire.

Billie surprised him. She did not blurt her reply. Without smudging her hair and makeup, she undressed slowly out of a fine-tailored, navy-blue outfit. She slipped into a transparent negligee and smiled her way to the fridge. She took a cold coke and drank it slowly. "Oh how I needed this a long time ago to cool my anxiety...Honey," she addressed Lyle, "I want you to write this in red ink and hide it in your toolbox in a spot where your wife, Queen Elizabeth, could find it." She spoke calmly, her diction perfected. "Let the QE and others know that I'm a black American woman. I'm not like you island people who boast of your brown skin and soft hair to benefit from your friendly societies."

"What's new, girl?"

"Of late, every weekend you get on my back. What's your problem?" Her voice pitched.

"I'm getting off your back right now. My favorite jazz pianist, Errol Garner, is on." He turned up the volume on the radio in the study and sat on the loveseat.

Billie switched off the radio and sat next to him. "For the rest of the evening you've got to listen to my kind of jazz till night falls."

"This Sunday? I prefer to work Leaky and make money."

"You'll work Leaky after you listen to my kind of jazz this evening."

"I know your kind of jazz, and it's worse since you returned from France. Seems you've adopted France's anti-foreigners ways. You give me the inclination that your soul bruvvers (brothers) are only those born here in America. To you, West Indians are not bruvvers; they're foreigners—wetbacks."

"Don't put words in my mouth." She got up. "This is Marcus Garvey. Where's he from? Jamaica!" She pointed at a dark profile on her wall. "You should be carrying the banner of what he stood for instead of debating my skin color." She sat down.

"I'm from Pitch Lake Country—sweet Trinidad and Tobago."

"There you go again isolating yourself as that short-sighted politician, Admiral Burnham, of Guyana. He is always boasting that he's not a West Indian, but a South American. He refused to join the West Indian Federation to make it strong; but he found that it was more expedient to make his jungle accessible to Jim Jones and his cult."

"If you know your geography, you'll know that Guyana is hooked to South America."

"Big deal! What does that brother gain with all that vast amount of unproductive lands. Venezuela is fighting to own Burnham's jungle. Coming from Pitch Lake Country I don't expect you to have much sense. You migrated from that port where the unsceptered, political King Bill said, 'One from ten leaves nothing.' Your Aunt Gina was one of his jesters who cheered his 'rithmetic. What a ploy King Bill had to break up the West Indian Federation because Count Manley from the land of wood and water first pulled out of that budding Federation of ten islands. Had that West Indian Federation been given a chance to germinate, today it would have been a financial broker for the black Caribbean and even for the black Americans. Such an accomplishment in post-Rule Britannia times would have been in our history books but those two major Caribbean *jefe civil*—King Bill and Count Manley— aborted the birth of a Caribbean federation. They favored their only love child named 'My Own Sovereignty.' King Bill and Count Manley, two scholars, who shot so many arrows and poison darts at colonialism were too power drunk to recognize that they could better handle the global issues as a bloc. Probably, who knows, Bill and the Count were subconsciously still in awe of the days when they stood in the broiling sun with savoring smiles and waived their miniature Union Jacks and sang *Rule Britannia, Britannia Rule the Waves* on King George V's birthday. Don't you think that might have been a probable reason why they aborted the Caribbean Federation, because, as you know, they hated Britain's policies towards its colonies? Don't you agree with me, black man?"

"Don't use me as your sounding board, brown-skin gal. I'm an American." He ribbed her.

"Naturalized. Remember?"

"I remember now. What else is news on Radio Bed Stuy?" He went for a beer. "Hold your reply until I return. Need a beer, too? I forget you don't like beer because it looks like your brother Ruff's piss...I'm back. What's the latest on Radio Bedford Stuyvesant?" He touched her with the cold bottle.

"My generals' resolve. Don't forget that my generals—the elder statesmen—did the ground work for people like you who tote briefcases with homemade sandwiches on Wall Street."

He laughed at her humor. "I thank them most kindly; and I do appreciate your reminding me of my portfolio." He went closer to her north wall and scrutinized the caricatured people on it. "Only these two and probably this one would have risked their safety to speak for a black cause. The others are hot air blown into a coalpot in the Sahara. Talk, talk, talk, and more talk. According to Grappa, they're *kakarats*; they're full of shit."

"All you really know is how to prevent Leaky from leaking and to criticize my effort and my heroes' noble intentions."

"Them?" He pointed to the wall. "Most are akin to

the bruvvers on the Lexington express who watch a black grandma straphang in front of them, but offer their seats to the blonde exurbanite who did not ask them for their seats, and did not thank them either. Your generals talk black Brooklyn, but act German *Long Giland* as the ultra new immigrants once called Long Island."

"Not my generals! Not those proud men who fought and are still fighting the cause. Your kind of bourgeoisie down in the Caribbean, no doubt!"

"Your kind! The homemade grits, well done. They moved out to exurbia and have to call their Brooklyn bruvvers to keep their company on the phone...so I'll expect them to swap their seats for friendship, Pinky."

"Do not call me Pinky. I saw that movie. I did not disown my roots, and there's no imitation in my life."

"Sorry, dear. May I ask a question? That brother's picture that you ripped off the wall last week, the brother whom the movement no longer trusted, why did you distance yourself from him?"

"Too much corporate blackness. He talks communist but his pocket is capitalist."

"Who among us isn't? You couldn't be serious giving me that as a reason for getting rid of a general? To me, he was practical. His ideas sounded fresh and better than those also-ran fossils you venerate." Lyle pointed to Billie's decorated wall. "That one uses his church for bazaars; that one equivocates on matters of blacks' concern; I heard that one cheats on his wife, and he refused to let his illegitimate children know where he lives. You want me to continue? Anyone who lacks basic family values would compromise political values; so your kitchen cabinet of generals is already compromised. Tell them when you meet next Thursday what I said. I don't care if they bomb my house! There are only few of them I'll trust with my interest."

"What's that story about first taking out the mote in your own eyes...or was it about a gnat...or was it about people in glass houses...or was it about 'He who is without sin cast the first stone'? You want me to continue? Pot's telling kettle that kettle's bottom is black."

"If you're referring to me, I'm not in the running to be a general to speak to and for the black people of America. Why don't you read a good book and let me listen to my jazz station."

"Read about your favorite Eurocentric history?"

"You have European blood, so that's cool."

"I'm African."

"'The Africans of Africa consider you as the daughter of a slave.' You never heard that before?" Mockingly, Lyle looked at his black hand. "You, African? Not like me." Lyle again pointed to her wall. "You read of him, the brother with the mustache, and the headlines that he's making in the newspapers these days?"

"Yes, I read about the movements of Mr. About-Face-of-Unsoul Ice—that prodigal son who returned. He abandoned the struggle. Traitor! The nerve of him telling Jesse Jackson who remained in the struggle to go back into the woodshed for another season." She ripped his portrait down and shredded it.

"I recognize that general even though he is penciled in abstract art. Getting rid of him, too? That leaves you with eleven darkened faces. Seems as if this is the purging month. Before the 1984 Democratic Convention is over your wall may be empty at the rate that you are going." Billie kept shredding the portrait. "How much more can you shred that general's portrait? Wasn't he a fighter in the sixties?"

"He's no longer for the cause...He's now a businessman flowing downstream with the other opportunists."

"What he's into now?"

"I heard he was designing sexy pants to show his crotch. That venture probably failed, so he's seeking attention by attacking bruvver Jesse Jackson."

"You mean the bruvver you shredded to bits should agree with everything another bruvver says."

"You don't know what's going on in America, man, otherwise you'd never ask such dumb questions. In this country, when you learn the rule, whitey changes the rule. What did you really learn since you left your Aunt Gina?"

"I learned from Aunt Lily who came to America before you were born that once you don't interfere with America's heroes—their John Waynes, their Billy Grahams, their Jesse Jameses and their pocketbooks—you're safe." Lyle looked at Billie. She was still shredding a past general into atoms. "Billie, it seems that that bruvver changed because he went to other climes and moved away from the familiar brick and mortar and from people like you."

She went for another coke. She returned and fixed her eyes on him.

"Let me finish, Billie, before you give me those vengeful eyes. That Mr. Unsoul Ice brother whose portrait you crushed with a vengeance, don't you think that that bruvver, having gone away and compared the good and evil of other systems with America's, don't you think that overseas exposure gave him an opportunity to rethink about his brashness? Some of us think in school, and some of us think when we try to swim upstream and fail. When do you think? Is it when you are moonlighting?" He took cognizance of the look on her face and changed the conversation. "By the way, I saw an old film of you on the Paris runway. I loved your catwalk and the way you made money to earn an education. I, too, wanted to be a model. You are really beautiful. The brothers who come for political advice, are you sure they aren't hitting on my woman?"

"I'd be glad if they did." She looked for a jealous reaction from Lyle but he had none. "I left Fanon's *The Wretched of the Earth* on the table. Did you read it and prove my point?"

"Why should I? Fanon is not a brother. He's a foreign black. Remember your definition of a bruvver. Honey, I wanted to obey you, so I only read about American bruvvers?"

"Lord Lyle, I knew where Franz Fanon's from. But didn't he advocate violence for what was needed? Didn't he tell the Third World not to create institutions which drew their inspiration from the white man?"

"You just spoiled a good jazz tune. You only read the first chapter of Fanon's, or you purposely left out the bridge. Do like James Brown, sister: Take it to the bridge, and you'll realize that wartime tactics cannot be used now."

"Hold it!" Billie shouted. "Who told you that the war was ever stopped on blacks. It is just that we don't cry as others, and we don't have the means to make motion pictures for others to continually remember the plight of sixty million of our foreparents through the Middle Passage. Blacks also don't have the means to show the plight of our people who suffered from physical slavery, and that of mental slavery as exhibited by your ignorance; and your ignorance mounts and rises every second like the national debt does." She sipped her coke as a party girl.

Lyle retorted swiftly. "Who's preventing the black millionaires from making movies about our plight? Take, for instance, the black millionaire who came on public TV and said that he cocked over two thousand women. A dollar from each cockee could have started a means fund. What a jackass of a cock man!"

"It takes thick tolerance to discuss with people like you who are immunized witnesses to the truth. Dr. Awolabi's intimated..."

"Leave that innocent doctor out of this! You and your generals are forever using his work of scholarship as chopped logic. Where I came from permanent interest is..."

Billie screamed. "Stop right there! Don't say another word! You are not referring to that Pitch Lake Kingdom, I hope, where everyone is afraid to tell King Bill, the Treasurer Extraordinaire of the Public Funds, that he's naked? Let me tell you what I researched about your homeland. You want me to dramatize the carnivalistic see-saw down there in that oil/banana Republic?" She put down her coke. She cleared a table that was laden with curios and stood on it. "Lyle, should I wear a mask or unmask myself like Clay of Baraka's *Dutchman*?"

"You are already acting so why ask for my approval. Do as you please. Use your Katharine Hepburn's voice to complete the show."

"Ladies and gentlemen, Act One." Her voice was Ms. Hepburn's. "My clothes are transparent and you can see through me, so if my nose grows like Pinocchio's throw powder on me. Should I sing the national anthem of Pitch Lake Country, Sir Lyle? I know the words but I forget the tune. Would you help me?"

"No!"

"Well, ladies and gentlemen, I shall start without further ado. In Pitch Lake Country, learned ladies and gentlemen, also known as the Republic of Trinidad and Tobago, on any given Sunday, the King sitting in his Whitehall, in a good mood, will knight an old buddy and call him Sir CLR because his old buddy is cultural, learned, and responsible. Think of the acronym CLR, ladies and gentlemen. But, on Monday, when the King wakes up with milk in his bloodshot eyes, the King will find it expedient to unknight Sir CLR and put CLR under house arrest to be alone with the crickets. Why, ladies and gentlemen? Because, the King, being an obeyer of all of his dreams, will interpret his dream about Sir CLR to mean that Sir CLR now has a neo-Colonial slant and that makes Sir CLR conniving, lecherous and riotous. CLR's testosterone level reveals, me thinks, ladies and gentlemen, that he has enough balls to rob King Bill of his kingdom.

"Ladies and gentlemen, if I sometimes speak in the first person, it is because of my burst of passion." Billie telegraphed a cunning smile to Lyle as if she really were Katharine Hepburn and he were Spencer Tracey. She jumped on and off the coffee table and assumed several identities. Her last concocted identity was that of a Trinbagonian who faked his graduation from Eton. "But, ladies and gentlemen, the process doesn't end there." She poured herself a glass of wine. "Ah, this tastes better than the import I got from the Palace." She smelled the wine like a connoisseur. "What was I talking about, Sir Lyle?"

"You were indeed talking about King Bill, the Treasurer Extraordinaire of the Public Funds of Pitch Lake Country, who sat in his Whitehall Kingdom and devoured the mud fish cascadura."

"Ah yes! That King. There are others in the blue waters, ladies and gentlemen, but for now let's concentrate at this moment on King Bill, a short man, a little deaf, with ideas bigger than his size. Those ideas he cultivated on English soil, at Eton and at Oxford. Let's go in order as the British have taught us. We have finished, ladies and gentlemen, the patterns of the King's dream on Sunday and Monday. Lest I forget to intimate you, ladies of gentlemen, King Bill also taught in the United States at Howard university. Let's go on to Tuesday.

"On Tuesday morning, because of a nightmare, King Bill would command his full court of jesters to sign in advance an agreement to accept punishment should they appear ungrateful in his Wednesday night's dream. Are you following me, Sir Lyle?"

"Sure! Suppose King Bill really has another nightmare?"

"*Auto da fè!*" Billie dramatized voicelessly in pain. She slashed her hands across her throat, fell, and fluttered like a choked fowl in an Orisha Shango feast. She became as silent as soaked silk until she heard Lyle's voice.

"Self-execution? C'mon. You should be re-writing Shakespeare's tragedies."

"Am I going too fast for one of the King's overseas jesters who vote by proxy?"

"Bullshit! Where's the TV guide? It's time to listen to a more sane discussion on ABC."

"Don't you like my short wave news, or do you prefer to listen to the edited version of the Chicago Black Muslim Minister's speech on Channel 7? Probably tonight the Liberals may hound Jesse Jackson to cut that Muslim minister loose."

"That is not unlikely. Liberals or not, they would expect Jesse to cut ties with a man who said, in reference to the Jews, 'Hitler was wickedly great.' Don't you think they should?"

"The Black Minister was provoked into saying that!"

"Generals should show their mettle when they're provoked by their detractors."

"Who's your Rabbi, Aaron Lyle?"

"Moses, Miss Hepburn."

"What do you expect from a black Republican who writes shorthand for a living on Wall Street and bootlicks to get overtime to buy a house?"

"Then my deceased Grappa was a Republican, too. He told me since I was in knee pants that it was better to cry than to speak with a loose tongue when provoked because only the excesses of your speech would be remembered."

"So you, too, wanted the Minister to cringe and cry! Never! I'm tired of the constant calumny heaped upon that Chicago Black Muslim Minister. I'll bet my last dime that you cannot repeat the full text of what that Black Muslim said. You are no different from the white media and black copycats who take a person's speech out of context."

"I can't repeat his full text, but any figure of speech using Hitler as a metaphor for justice was in bad taste. That Black Muslim Minister who condemned slavery so vociferously should know that other people have feelings, too. The Jews have already said, 'Never again!' for Adolph Hitler and the atrocities that were heaped upon them, and I know the Jews will never forgive that Black Muslim Minister. Mark my word."

"There you go again playing God. How large a mote do you have to build around the Black Minister, Aaron?"

"Miss Hepburn, you are a La Sorbonne scholar, not a numbskull like likkle Lyle. Please be informed that I held the Black Minister's ship rudder until he threw down the Hitler anchor. Miss Hepburn, please be silent about the Minister's loose tongue, and Aaron will treat your silence as a *mea culpa* on the Black Minister's behalf. Your minister's talk power is destructive to his flock."

"What's wrong with you? Sure you're not a kitchen slave? You are one of those niggers who don't want to rock the boat, so don't you say one fucking word about that Black Minister. Continue to smoothe feathers, but smoothing feathers will never make you a man. With all the headaches that you and Elizabeth have, ABC will never give you a headache commercial. I know you like golf, but you'll never be given a club to play at the Masters. Not even George F. Grant, the black brother who invented the golf tee, was invited there. I'll also bet my life that in your Wall Street firm there's not one black receptionist, and if there's one, she's placed on the floor that only welcomes messengers. Lyle, it's time to unload your Aunt Gina's baggage and start probing the higher-ups. If you disagreed with what the Black Minister said, I invite you to come to our meeting and get it off your chest. What you are doing is 'throwing out the baby with the bath water.' When you stop holding his rudder, you weaken your base; and that is what the uppity blacks don't know, but they find out sooner or later when the fall comes. 'Pride comes before the fall' is my advice to you. That's the difference with you, others like you, and the Black Minister. Our underground movement needs talk power to fuse the spark, and big talkers for the cause is a must, black man." Irate, Billie looked at her wall of generals. One general in particular looked down at her.

"Big talkers who talk in a hurry may talk you up a gum tree, and the cost to take you off that gum tree may be mortifying. The bat used his wings to communicate; and the bat flapped himself up a gum tree. That wise, nocturnal mammal, to ease himself, turned upside down, and shit in his own face."

"Consider yourself in the Witness Protection Program!"

"Is that your threat or theirs?"

"I'm tired of your fucking Aunt Gina creole stories. When did you tell me you learned those stories? I remember when. It was when you and Aunt Gina picked small pebbles out of raw rice before your frugal midnight meal. Imagine, after all these years, you're still living by Aunt Gina's rules. You refuse to investigate people in high offices. You no longer walk on Massa's spit because you can afford shoes in white America, but it was better when you did, because you now play every day, knowingly, in Massa's saliva. Why, Lyle? Why?"

"Because people should be loyal to the broader culture."

"What culture? Milt Coleman's. Milt Coleman is not under the bed with his *Washington Post's* notepad ready to report on you as he did on Minister Jesse Jackson; so you have nothing to be afraid of. Why are you stuck only in the gratitude mode, Lyle?"

"And why all this politics, Billie? I might not have objected to your choice of generals had you included Dr. Martin Luther King, Jr. up there among your heroes. Your favorite heroes are those burn-brother-burn bruvvers and those who quarterback after the burning."

"Peaceful Martin died from a peaceful bullet because his strategy was that of a simpleton who turned the other cheek in a dog-eat-dog world. Those brothers'," she paused, "approach will be...Let me not reveal their plan to Mr. Johnny-come-lately. He may go tell it to two people—the marish and the parish."

"Sure, I'll tell the marish and the parish of you and your generals' chopped logic and save them from a bloodbath." Lyle looked at the eleven questionable profiles on Billie's wall and shook his head in wonder. "Billie," he said, "if your personal philosophy is the gun, you'll be out gunned by the majority's bullets. Seems as if your underground generals love creating Harlems and South Bronxs, slums and sores, that will keep their hate campaign going until the Repatriation Bill is passed in Congress."

She did not answer him. Instead, she spoke to the woman's portrait on the wall. "Should I throw another pearl?"

"This swine won't stand in your way, girl."

Billie further addressed the walled woman. "Only a fool thinks that the victim is guilty of the crime. Certain foreign people," she looked at the woman's portrait and then at Lyle, "should stop their daydream. The Red Man is still living on the reservation without basic amenities, and this Afro Saxon thinks our salvation will come around the bargaining table. The Afro Saxon knows the answers so well." She again addressed the woman's portrait. "You, scarred and tarheeled, picked the cotton, but the cotton buoyed others, but you. You knew, without knowing how to read, that New York, way up north, is just as South of the Dixie, way down south. How they say it again in patois? Massa bull massa cow—one and the same—homozygous. I guess Pollyanna," the corneas of her eyes searched Lyle, "will learn the hard way one day. He'll get up and wonder why he's in handcuffs."

"Billie, the way you talk it seems that I'll never learn enough about this country. I should go back home!"

"Get off that vehicle, Lyle! You're letting down your buckets here, so talk about here. Get out and fight the system's bogus and racist policies. Don't only think of making money and buying real estate. The powers that be say people live below the Brooklyn Bridge and eat in soup kitchens by choice. Forget Pitch Lake Country, your Trinidad and Tobago, and talk about America, the land of plenty. You live here!"

"Your American countrymen spermed all over Pitch Lake Country when America had a naval base there to protect America's interest; and while the Americans were raping and procreating over there in PLC, they were also boasting about their 'My America' on foreign soil. At that time your American countrymen were using the country of my birth as a seaport to watch their enemies."

Billie laughed as a victorious war general, then used her pet Latin quotation. "*Quis custodiet ipsos custodes?*"

"You're asking me who'd guard the guards? Don't you know that the nation of Pitch Lake Country is still administering penicillin to get rid of your countrymen's biological culture? Thanks to your American soldiers!"

"Thanks to your political King Bill, the deceased Prime Minister."

"King Bill got rid of the Yankees."

"A big sham! Your King Bill, political doctor, patient, and medicine—a perfect trinity! The foremost of research scholars that the world had known! It was he who again invited back the Americans, after he chased them away, for a tax-tree holiday with pioneer status. King Bill's rationale in bold legislative jargon was, 'INCENTIVE FOR INVESTMENT.'"

"What a forgiving King."

"What a dumb businessman! He scrapped a viable railway; twelve years later he put eight miles of asphalt on

the said railway track, and renamed it an 'Expressway.'"
Billie laughed mockingly for a few minutes. "And, what's
funnier, is the fact that the Expressway runs alongside an
already existing road, and both routes end in a car park
without parking meters...Ladies and gentlemen, I thank
you for lending me an ear and for allowing me to recite
the unsung bio of King Bill who lost his day job with the
Yankee Government. When the Yankees needed King
Bill no more, it was then King Bill chose to be a servant-
politico of Pitch Lake Country, to his benefit, I assure
you. Then it became the season of sour grapes for our
dear departed King Bill. May you rest in peace, Billy Boy,
and may your headstone read: KING BILL, PLC's
ROBIN HOOD." Billie bowed gracefully.

Lyle applauded. "My poor King. Ms. Zellars
flavored your life with bias. It's a pity that such a great
man died."

"Surely not as a pauper, the Little-Doctor-Know-
It-All. In my research on your vindictive king, I read
where he said when he was in his glory, 'Had your
Chief Servant (Tubal Uriah Buzz Butler) died ten
years before his death, Butler would have died a hero.'
King Bill's quote of the Chief Servant could be
applied to himself. It all goes to show that the future
belongs to the Man in the big kingdom upstairs only."

"Ms. Zellars, I don't care what you say about that
Pitch Lake King, but his people rallied behind him for
over thirty years because he was very good to all his
subjects. For sure, I can foresee that one day couple of
your Presidents will burst their crypts and come forth
and prostitute the Lincoln bedroom for greenbacks to
pay the Devil in hell."

"In one breath you're an American; but as soon as I
attack the King of the country of your birth you
become riled, and forget that you took the oath of
allegiance to this country. Did your psychic wife tell
you that a few of my deceased Presidents would burst
their tombs, come forth like Lazarus, and privatize the

Lincoln bedroom in a joint business venture?"

"Ask her."

"Are you taking her to the Labor Day parade tomorrow, Lyle?" She unbuttoned the last hook on Lyle's shirt and played with the gray hairs on his chest.

"No."

"Are you taking anyone else to the parade?"

"What a dumb question."

"Let's drink to that, honey." She filled both glasses. "No more politics. It's a long time you haven't brought me up to date on Nigel and Lord Meath."

"They're private detectives."

"When?"

"Sometime now."

"You...You, son of a gun; you kept that from me. Why? I always thought you told me everything. Why you hid that?"

"I didn't think it was important. Right now they're working for the Nicholby Private Investigating Agency, and soon they'll be on their own."

"You better hide your toolbox before they break into it."

"They're not the type."

"Is Queen Elizabeth as inquisitive as I, still beautiful as Mrs. Burton, or does she prejudge the opponent like Elizabeth in *Pride and Prejudice?*" She patted Lyle's matted Afro and smirked. "Eh, eh! Don't force an answer, my dear. I know you never talk about the women you love. You're a man with confidence in the women you love."

"And you're a woman I love regardless of your foibles."

"A woman, or *the* woman?" She stressed "the."

He didn't answer. He opted to return to the politics of New York City and her politics of poverty. "Honey, you know I'm beginning to see some of your points." He looked at her and smiled. "I have an easy question for you."

"Shoot, honey."

"Suppose I'm attacked by people who hate your heroes, your generals, all your GC's for whatever reason?...You know sometimes people get hurt because of the company they keep. Let me beat about the bush a little. We are now in 1984."

"I know that, Lyle."

"You remember about five years ago a Puerto Rican boy was killed about two blocks away from Building 122 by a policeman. I never told you what I witnessed as a carry-over of that incident."

"Today I'm getting to realize that you hid a lot of things from me. Anyhow, go-ahead, Lyle-in-the-confession box."

"Honey, I knew what your reaction would have been then, but I'm going to say it now. Well, when I was going home ten days after that young Puerto Rican boy got killed...when I reached the corner of Gates and Nostrand Avenues, it could have been after eight in the evening on August 27, 1979." Lyle took out his address book and checked that date and other information that he had noted. "Police car number 1785 stopped, and two white policemen came out...You see how disjointed I am in relating this incident...I don't even like to talk about this...There was this young white man who led the blacks and Puerto Ricans in a protest march against the policeman, who it was alleged, killed the Puerto Rican kid. I really don't like to relate this incident because it brings tears to my eyes." Lyle stopped, and debated to himself whether he should relate this incident to Billie.

"Don't get me interested and now cut me off. Go on, Lyle."

"As the protest march by the blacks and Puerto Ricans led by this young white man ended at the corner of Gates and Nostrand Avenues, the people who lived in the neighborhood scattered and went their separate ways. The young white guy who headed the blacks and Puerto Rican march waited on transportation to take him home. The burlier of the two policemen, a hulk of a man, came out of police car number 1785—I guess they followed the march to control traffic. That hulk of a policeman took out his baton and beat that young white man without mercy. Every time that white policeman hit that white guy who headed the black parade, the policeman mumbled something...."

"Lyle, I can tell you what that pig told his victim: 'Is you a nigger lover, boy? Well, take this night stick and learn from these blows that you don't belong here with them niggers, white boy.' That is just what that spineless, racist amoeba said in his crucifixion of another white man whom he thought broke his crease, as they say in that British sport called cricket."

"That savage cop hit his prey with his night stick. That savage cop whupped his prey, and whupped him with all his force, until his prey fell speechless. The other savage cop looked on at the live theater on the streets in black Bedford Stuyvesant where his brutish pal performed. Both criminals drove off in police car number 1785 with satisfied smiles on their faces. The black people who milled around, picked up that beaten white hero, and put him in a car. I don't know whether his black friends took him to the hospital or to the morgue.

"For many nights I couldn't sleep, for I saw the hands of that huge monster divining punishment to a human being who did nothing but exercise his constitutional rights. I developed a strong hatred for white policemen; but, with time, I realized that those two evil policemen did not represent all the men in blue in the New York constabulary...I started off by saying suppose...I can't really remember what was my original thought."

"Lyle, you began this sad story by saying suppose you were attacked by the forces who hate my heroes, whether it was those two dirty cops in blue, whomever; and if I were around, and unarmed, what would I do. I know for sure that if you thought that white good Samaritan was beaten mercilessly by a white cop, just imagine what would have happened to black like you. Then and now, I'd protect you and face the consequences." Without giving a hint, Billie put her left hand below her pillow, and she pulled out a revolver. She placed the barrel on Lyle's forehead and pulled the trigger twice. She moved the gun from his forehead, pushed her hand into the pillowcase, and retrieved two bullets. She loaded the two bullets into the chambers of the gun. Effortless she said, "The third chamber is loaded. Isn't the answer easy? See, I'm a good girl scout. I'm always prepared. Always at your service, sir."

Lyle lost his speech and his blood.

"Go-ahead and talk. You are alive, honey. Tell me about that police brutality stuff which, I am one hundred percent sure, you did not report to the Commission on Police Brutality or to any Ombudsman...Like other West Indians, 'you come to drink the milk, not to count the cattle.' That's what my generals are against. Injustice! Whether it is from black or white. My generals don't hate Jews; they only hate those who justify injustice whether it came from Hitler or Idi Amin. We as gentiles don't hate an Italian because that Italian discovered America, if he did; but we'd hate him if, having discovered America, he brutalized the natives of America who didn't *need* anyone to discover them. We don't hate Paul because he isn't Peter, but we'd hate Paul if, because of him, Peter has to pay for Paul's deeds." She poured three drops of wine on the floor. "These drops are for the spirits of our ancestors. Do you go to Coney Island to pay tribute to the Ancestors of the Middle Passage? I go every year to the ceremony on West 16 Street and the Boardwalk. You should follow me and the GC's and go there and think. When do you think, black man? Go there and look at the Atlantic Ocean, the biggest grave yard of Africans." She did not wait on an answer. She saluted the silhouetted images on her wall. "They are for that cause. Go-ahead and talk, bruvver. Give me an explanation for why you watched a brutal act and behaved as the good Christians who were noncommittal when Hitler burned the Jews in ovens." She waited patiently on his reply.

The heat from the incandescence of the mantles in Billie's beautiful apartment brought blood into Lyle's face. He tried to make sense in his bewildered state, and he unconvincingly tried to show that he was not perturbed by her gun play. Yet his professed macho did not match his voice, for he sounded as if he had lain in bed with Rip Van Winkle. He eventually shook off that feeling and spoke. "No, No...I didn't report the incident, and I regretted it; but whe-when," he stuttered, "you and they," he pointed to her north wall, "seize power from whomever, what would the movement do?"

"Pledge allegiance to us, and you'll know. You see the kind of people who come here for consultation on Thursdays—blacks, whites, yellow, people of the rainbow, all kinds. You see their determination. You are privy to that. They are men of substance, not of straw."

"You, they, and your Generals-for-the-Cause walk on water, but only when the dam is burst?"

"Yeah! It takes a Lyle Allister Gordon, the collar-and-tie boy in Wall Street to make such an analogy. What's your real hobby horse?" Billie's light skin became red. She moved away, threw her wine glass in the sink, and crouched on her bed. Above her was a woman's portrait. The eyes of that portrait looked down on her.

Lyle followed her to the bedroom. "What's yours for black bruvvers mugging black bruvvers? Oh yes, I remember: It's only a century since slavery was abolished and, like the cooling earth's crust, your black bruvvers are still shifting and fitting themselves on the earth's shrinking interior. Did I quote you correctly?"

"Ask columnist Jack Anderson. He may tell you that if they shift, we'll shift. Your case is sad. As great as Paul Robeson was there's hardly a footage of film of him in the Library of Congress at this time. Or if it's there, there's no real effort to find it. Think of how the powers that be prevented Robeson from making a living to feed himself and his family."

"What's the relevance?"

"Did you know that Robeson ate the bread that the Devil kneaded because he went to Russia. Today everybody in Congress wants to go to Russia to greet the enemies who live in that 'Evil Empire'; and today they are praised for doing thus. Blacks always had foresight, man. That's the relevance, Lyle. I guess the next thing you'll tell me is that if the Indians had invested the twenty four dollars they got for Manhattan Island, they would have been able to buy Richmond today with the interest from that twenty four dollars. Your Aunt Gina must have fed you with too much rat food."

"Dearest friend, was that last nail to my coffin necessary? That's what happens when we tell our friends our past; they throw it back in our faces."

"I'm sorry, honey" Billie said. "I'm truly sorry. Would you take me off that gum tree? Please, I beg you, honey."

Lyle shook his neck. He crawled up the bed, lay his head on a pillow, and looked up at the portrait that looked down on them. "Who's that lonely lady with such chiseled features?" He showed concern in his expression.

"I prayed for the day when you'd ask me that question. After all these years, alas. She was my mother—half Indian, half white. My father was black. Both my parents died fighting for the cause of justice in divided America. While I was in France my father informed me of everything that he agitated against in this country. You may not believe this, but regardless of who is or was the architect, affirmative action was always at the fore of my father's memory."

Lyle's forehead gathered lines. He leered at the portrait of the elderly woman on the wall. He, too, had aged since their dialogue. He was confused, but he spoke. "Billie," he was apologetic, "tell your Generals-for-the-Cause that this Pitch Lake emigrant, this American immigrant citizen, this Pollyanna, this Johnny-come-lately, this Afro-Saxon says that he may not like everything they stand for or their method of approach to their objectives, but also tell your GC's that he understands their hurt.

"Tell your GC's that I'd lived in a black country that was once ruled by white expatriates. In that country, at the age of six, I had to run from my church because the white expatriates in power sent their black policemen to raid our black Baptist church at midnight. We worshipped at nights because we had to hide to serve our God. The white man was allowed to practice his religion day and night but we, the black spiritualists, were not allowed that privilege. Our religion was outlawed. It was banned! The white man's religions were legal. The white man's Tridentine Mass, with the priest's back turned to the congregation as he recited the Hail Marys, was of God. The white Protestants' liturgies were of God. All the Spiritual Baptists' prayers and prayer houses, to the white man, were of the Devil. Just imagine the white man said that our prayers which beamed in us and which came from the great spirits of the Upper Volta were illegal! Tell your generals that my Aunt Gina and I hid in slimy gutters with worms when our church, deep in the forest, was raided. Still my Aunt Gina and I obeyed the powers of the spirits of our foreparents—those in the motherland, and those who travelled for 300 years on European ships and are entombed in crates in the bowels of the Atlantic Ocean. We refused not to obey those spirits because the white law said so. Aunt Gina and I purposely disobeyed the law of the land and went to Leader Gerrol's Baptist Church which evoked those spirits.

"The white man came to America and sought religious freedom, and after he got wings he came to the country of my birth and denied me my religious freedom. The white man's scale of religious freedom was always tied to a surprise package. It took just one brave Baptist spiritualist to challenge that archaic law, and today black spiritualists throughout the Caribbean can worship as they please. I hope one day I could say that it took just one of your good generals to do the needful and the thoughtful.

"Billie, tell your few good generals that if they want to succeed they should follow the resolve of the Jews who vowed, 'Never again!' and meant 'Never again!' If your generals adopt any other policy, they'd be just spinning their tops in mud. I know your general's hurt. I know what it is to mash Massa's spit, and to be judged not only by Massa, but also by Massa's orphans. I know what it is to be laughed at, and to be put at the back of the class because of my black skin. I know what it is to be told, 'You're nobody.' I know what it is to be denied, and to be hungry.

"I know what it is to watch the American soldiers pleasure with the flesh of my family in exchange for a 'mess of pottage.' I know how your generals feel. Believe me. I don't only moonlight in Leaky; I also moonlight with the living literature of life. I've been there, sister. Believe me, I know. My concern is not your diligent commitment; it's your cabal compromise, sister."

Billie applauded Lyle's speech. She refilled their wine glasses, danced to the *Electric Slide*, and stopped. "Brother Lyle, whatta speech! I'm truly impressed, but I don't believe your sudden awakening. Do me a favor: Save your breath for the Labor Day carnival tomorrow, and your empathy for the soft-back snails that cross the busy freeway at noontime."

"Believe me, I mean it, Billie."

"I know a guy with your kind of empathy and belief, Lyle Gordon. Tomorrow I'm going to introduce you to that dude who graduated from Harvard, but I'll purposely make the mistake and say, 'Lyle, meet a friend of mine who graduated first class from Howard University.' You'll see my friend Jack's hurt because I say he graduated from a premier black university instead of from Harvard's. Jack hurts just the way you hurt, Lyle."

"Is his picture on your wall, or did you rip him off as you did Mr. Unsoul Ice?"

"When we meet on the Parkway tomorrow you can ask him."

"What costume you'd be wearing, Billie?"

"Let me surprise you, honey."

"Just don't be naked, girl."

"I'd love to, knowing that island boys love to play skittles, their favorite hide and seek, but hate to get caught. Of all the men I've known..."

"Including your French encounters of course?"

"Including my French encounters of course, island men are the biggest playboys and the worst hypocrites."

"What's the recipe for me, this hypocrite, not to be caught?"

"Call all your women Honey, Lyle, so if you happen to call me Honey in your sleep, Queen Elizabeth will think you are referring to her. By the way, does the QE know about me?"

"I'm sure Elizabeth does."

"Via your toolbox?"

"Our triangle is since high school. The QE may be dormant, but I assure you that she ain't dumb."

"How does Elizabeth refer to me?"

"You really want to know, Billie?"

"Sure!"

"Before she says her prayers, she calls you by the Muslim name, Jacki X; and after she says her prayers when she's really psychic..."

"Don't say it. Let me guess. She calls me by the other variable, Jacki Y."

"A variable all right, but it is: 'Jackiass, that he, she, or it, without a fingerprint.'"

Their laughter echoed throughout the brownstone, and for the first time they hugged in the early evening.

"Dear woman of this unfriendly society," Lyle addressed her, "for all that armchair politics today, am gonna perform so good on this workbench," he patted the bed decorated with cotton sheets and fluffy pillows, "in just a few minutes that you'll scream the two vowels that made soul bruvver James Brown rich, rich."

"And I'll behave like Fyzabad's girls and say, 'No, no, no,' even when the gristle is in the hole and they're moving suggestively to the gristle. If your Grappa had lived in America he would have been jailed so many times for thinking that Grandma's 'no' meant 'yes' when he tripped her on the muddy banks of Gower's well."

Lyle rolled off the bed crackling with laughter. "Go tell that on Johnny Carson's."

"And I'll tell Johnny Carson that you heard that at nights when Grandma and Grappa thought you were asleep." She kept as serious a face as a wooden judge. "Lyle, I guess you'll ask me who told me that Calypsonian Sparrow from Pitch Lake Country made money from two words, too. Remember he sang the ditty *Jean and Dinah* to get recognition from his peers...There's something that bugs me about Pitch Lake Country, your sweet Trinidad and Tobago, with its calypso mentality."

"What?" He put his nostrils in her armpits. "Oh, this aphrodisiac is heavenly."

"Stop it, and give me the answer to what bugs me."

"What? You tell me."

"Lyle, even though the black bruvvers invented the steel piano, the black bruvvers of Trinidad and Tobago didn't get recognition until the white brothers and their mulatto friends like me—ha! ha!—learned the art of beating pan. Only then the black bruvvers were invited into the uppities' backyards and to Government House to beat pan."

He moved his nostril from her armpit and looked at her. "Who told you that? Professor Awolabi? I got the feeling that you were teacher's pet."

"Since you don't want to answer my question, I hope this name calling isn't a ploy to whip up a new argument and give yourself a reason to jump into Leaky and go and hustle passengers. Many times you left me at the mercy of my candle. Elizabeth's candle is religious; mine's sexual."

"I ever did that—left you horny and ran?"

"So many times you jumped in that gypsy cab and left me with my imagination."

"Naughty girl. That was my way of hitting back when I found that you spent too much time with your underground generals and their homework."

"You just said black men talk too much, so why don't you stop talking and do what every hot blooded American—black, white, or the naturalized—does?" She rubbed her warm body on him.

"I'm Afro-Saxon. Remember?"

"For now, you can apply the drums and the sax. I don't care how you mix them. Just mix them erotically."

"What if I apply the drums from Africa, the banana from the Caribbean, the little Saxon nuts, and the sweet promiscuous pea from Louisiana for *lagniappe*?"

"What's *lagniappe*?"

"You didn't research that? Think of *lagniappe* as a baker's dozen, an extra pea would be thrown in."

"That sounds good, sugar pup. Throw everything in."

Billie came off the bed, and Lyle tugged her back on it. Her negligee that drooped on one spaghetti string, dropped. She, like an over-wound doll which burst its spring, glanced at Thoreau's *Walden*, the only hardcover on her library shelf. She ended her talk of "fateful lives" and proved her feminine mastery on top of her cotton sheets. "I love you with all my heart, bruvver," she whispered in Lyle's ear. "I'm confident one day you'll join the cause and be a trusted general." She gasped in sweet pain.

He flushed her body to his, and dried his tongue on her perfumed ear. She spoke again, but it was impossible to understand her gibberish until she said, like the king of soul, Mr. James Brown, but in a sweeter octave, "Oo! Ah!"

"I do love the sound of your long vowels, honey," Lyle said. "Queen Elizabeth's is just as long and just as sweet sounding." He released himself from her grip, and looked at a portrait overhead. "Hope it's all right with you, Mama."

Billie looked at that portrait and grinned, and they rested quietly for several minutes. "Since you like my performance so much and you made me perform in front of Mama," Billie said, "am making a last ditch effort to get you to join our multiracial movement. Listen to what I'm about to say, and don't interrupt me, Lyle. You know our secret code: That we can answer a question without speaking. I'll touch that certain part of your body, and you'll answer with your eyes. If you look to the left, the answer is no; and if you look to the right, the answer is yes." She touched that secret part of his body, and he looked neither to the left nor to the right. She was neither angry nor surprised at Lyle's indecision.

Their evening of theater, politics, and romance ended.

"It's time to change into my Leaky garb and hustle young riders in search of basement parties this Labor Day weekend. Don't move, Billie. Let me collect my clothes and fly from your jazz room."

"I'll get your clothes for you, honey."

"You never let me go into your closets. What are you hiding?"

"Nothing. It's the duty of the host to fetch your clothes...Here's your Leaky clothes. It's a nice disguise for a man who just laid a woman."

He smiled with his teeth. "Where's my belt?"

She looked around. "Sorry. It fell." She bent for it; she paused; then said, "Oh, I'm cramped. Pick it up for me, honey."

He did. "As ordinary as this buckle looks, Billie, it's gold or gold plated, you know. Touch it."

"No."

He kissed her gently and buckled his waist.

"See you at our rendezvous on the Parkway tomorrow, Lyle."

"Sure will, beautiful." He ran down the balustraded steps of her parlor floor and went into the warm air outside. He looked at Leaky parked below a giant weeping willow and smiled at what was in his thoughts. Leaky had only one oil-drop stain on the concrete below her. "Let's go, Leaky girl. Sorry you didn't know Grappa's donkey. You two are more faithful than most human beings I've known."

Lyle was out of the Bedford Stuyvesant neighborhood. He was delayed in Crown Heights as a crowd of Orthodox Jews marched on Eastern Parkway, west of Kingston Avenue, and held banners which read, MOSHIACH IS COMING. "I hope the cops come and clear this traffic," he mumbled.

Eventually, he reached Flatbush. In Flatbush, as he turned on Nostrand Avenue and headed south, a sudden thought weighed him down. It was the thought of the clicks from Billie's pistol on his brain. Instantly his mind went haywire. He talked to himself: "Was that what they called Russian roulette? Was that gun really loaded, or was Billie bullshitting me? What kind of woman would play with a man's life then fuck him! That's not the way to convince me...All this confusion politics—lining up Hitler on the same side with his victims...Booth strapping the facts... Blaming everybody for our sins, except ourselves...Europe underdeveloped Africa...The Pope gave Africa to the Portuguese and his other friends...The white man caused all the famine in Africa...They brought us here as slaves...All these textbook lectures from her and her generals...I've been hearing those lectures since I got off the plane with my greased feet in cheap Bata shoes and my processed twalala shirt stuck in my off-the-nail knee pants.

"How come my knowledgeable Grandma who interpreted dreams for the neighbors didn't know all these things about Africa?...Was she that ignorant? Grandma cursed Bad Pay Evena and called her a fuckin' African. She cursed Mr. Jools and called him a no-god Zulu. She cursed Miss Loo and called her a bow-foot Pygmy. When I was a boy the words African, Zulu, and Pygmy were blue words in Grandma's mouth. What would Grandma do today had she lived to hear that the words 'black and beautiful' go hand in hand. Grandma, I'm telling you that the world has changed. Are you hearing me, Grandma? Black and beautiful are now related, Grandma."

Lyle drove, and his thoughts shifted to his long deceased Grandma and to the genealogy of the black man. As he approached the intersection of Nostrand and Snyder Avenues, a motorist broke the red light. Lyle pulled away and avoided a fatal accident. Without missing a beat, he shouted blue words like his Grandma would have. "You fuckin' African-Zulu-Pygmy bitch! You colorblind or you can't see!" His emphasis on each word was Grandma-perfect. Ten seconds later a broad smile sweetened his face. "My god!" he said. "Grandma, that's your ghost who just talked for me and prevented me from being the author of myself...I don't ever say such things, Grandma." He changed the pattern of his smile and spoke again. "Africa, oh Africa, the shape of your continent is a question mark. That's why we are all guessing. Someday there would be correct answers. Billie, who knows, your kitchen cabinet of generals may provide those answers for Africa. You always say, Billie, 'When it comes to Africa and Africans, water runs, but blood clots.' You may be right. What the hell does numbskull likkle Lyle know! I'm already brain damaged by Grandma's literature, Grappa's genes, Aunt Gina's do-as-I-say doctrines, and my artificial intelligence."

Dozens of costumed passengers on their way to pre-Labor Day parties flagged Leaky but Lyle did not see them. He drove Leaky aimlessly, turned off Nostrand Avenue, and found himself back on Nostrand Avenue again. His past suddenly came before him, and he tried to strain the bitter from the sweet of his boyhood days. His eyes burned, became misty, and two strings of tears rolled from them.

In his rearview mirror he barely saw the bold church sign behind him. He braked suddenly, reversed, read, and re-read the sign. He immediately felt guilty about his lifestyle. He attempted to drive off, but his legs cramped. He could not drive past the church. Elizabeth was inside that church with that bold sign. It was the church that gave her spiritual guidance and helped to mould his son Nigel into manhood. Lyle, at that moment, knew that he, too, needed spiritual guidance.

"Leader Gerrol," he whispered as he clutched the steering wheel, his eyes still moist, "I wish you, too, had come to America. You were once my North Star. I need help, Leader Gerrol. Should I accede to Billie's request? If I join Billie's generals, would I broaden their horizon or cloud mine?" As he spoke, his body shivered, and he said, "Lord, only prayers could stop this shiver...It's time for my kind of Baptist religion."

He parked, switched off Leaky, and thought of the past, the present, and tomorrow, as he walked towards the church.

Chapter Seven

The Church

MT. SIGNAL SPIRITUAL BAPTIST CHURCH, ELIAS S. DOLLON, LEADER, was the bold sign in front of the brick edifice on Nostrand Avenue. Lyle sluggishly walked towards the church door. He was conscious of his casual attire. A little abashed, with a portable tape recorder tucked below his arm, he looked at his damp shirt and taxiing shoes. He opened the door noiselessly, stood in the middle of the aisle as a lost sheep, and he gazed at the worshippers dressed in different colors which, to the knowledgeable, revealed degrees in spiritual heights and depths in the Spiritual Baptist faith. As a backslider, Lyle was unsure of his heights or depths, but he instantly remembered that in Fyzabad when he was under the tutelage of his spiritual Leader Gerrol, he was a shepherd in the faith, and that he had worn white clothes to church. He stopped thinking of the past when the rejoicing congregation gripped his attention. The congregation, like a response meter, sang, clapped and stamped; they accented the strong beat and evinced a rhythmic pattern as they swayed. There was no seen metronome, but there was precision in the adherents' movements. Lyle moved from where he stood and was about to take a seat near the church's decorated centerpole which, to spiritual Baptists, signified the universe and the godhead. The sudden and spontaneous manifestations of the worshipping congregants and the handbell ringing had a decibel count intolerable to Lyle's ears for he had grown unaccustomed. He was confused and stood on the said spot.

Leader Dollon, with his eyes closed, stood erect at his unevenly built altar and talked in strange tongues. Hettie Campbell rushed Leader Dollon a glass of water; petals of a white rose floated in the crystal glass, and Leader Dollon sipped and swallowed, water and petals.

His second taste from the crystal quenched his carnal thirst, and he opened his eyes. There was joy in Leader Dollon's visage. He tipped over the pulpit and beckoned to Lyle, the stranger, to draw closer. Lyle obeyed the Leader and moved to the front pew among the spiritual hierarchy. Elizabeth raised from her knees after a session of prayers for strayed souls and was shocked to see her husband in their midst. "Thank you, Lord, for showing my husband the way!" Elizabeth said. She said it three times; the congregation shouted "Hallelujah!" and showed their appreciation for the visitor's presence. Elizabeth triumphantly raised the hymn *Precious Lord*. The full church, with members regaled in their colors, burst forth in loud mixed voices, and Lyle's tenor voice blended beautifully.

The offertory was next on the program.

"Amen...Amen...Hallelujah! Welcome to that new soul," Leader Dollon said, and began his sermon.

Lyle became nervous because he knew he was that "new soul" whom Leader Dollon welcomed. He thought the sermon would address his adulterous life because he remembered that when he lived in Fyzabad, Spiritual Baptist leaders with clairvoyant eyes singled out members in the congregation and preached on them. He resigned himself to his fate. He depressed the record buttons on his portable cassette; he closed his eyes; and he hoped that Leader Dollon would preach on anything but about him.

"Dearly beloved in the faith," Leader Dollon began, "I address you in the name of Jesus Christ...Visiting shepherd, mothers, pointers, provers, stargazers, believers, and members of the body of Christ, a blessed good evening."

"A blessed good evening to you, too, Leader Dollon," the congregants replied.

Leader Dollon continued. "We are all spiritual and born of the womb of the water. How nice it is for us to dwell together in unity...How nice it is for us to rend our hearts and not our garments."

"Amen," Lyle said.

"Let the church say Amen," Leader Dollon said.

"Amen," the congregation said.

Leader Dollon continued. "The wonderful foundation lesson is taken from the First Chapter of Ezekiel which tells us of the visions of God. It also tells us what is the spirit and why we catch power. Comrades! many times we sit in our corners and tell ourselves that we are spiritual, but how many of us are really walking the spiritual road. We call ourselves Spiritual Baptists and yet we don't even know what the spirit is. Behold! Ezekiel tells us about us. And, according to the First Chapter, Ezekiel tells us that at one time he was at the River of Chebar where he saw visions: a wheel into a wheel into a wheel; and there was a living creature that bore four faces. A real mystery!"

Lyle was puzzled by the text, but members of Mount Signal were not. They softly hummed a hymn as background music.

"...On one side of that creature, believers, was the face of a man; on another side, an ox; on the third side, an eagle; and on the fourth side, the face of a lion." Leader Dollon shook fiercely. "Sons and daughters of Mt. Signal, do many of you really understand what the First Chapter of Ezekiel is telling us? Even well-grounded spiritualists doubt themselves when the Divine Spirit manifests in them—in common parlance, when the power goes in them and shakes them until they shout and talk in unknown tongues. Many of us experienced these feelings and do not know that the Divine Spirit is operating...."

Lyle looked at his watch and his tape recorder. The time was l0:00 p.m.; and the mini cassette was recording the sermon from Mt. Signal Spiritual Baptist Church on Nostrand Avenue.

"...Have you checked, children of Christ, how many faces were there on that creature or how many wings were there among the four living creatures? According to my understanding...." He paused.

"Couldn't be...Couldn't be...A carbon copy," Lyle mumbled to himself.

"...I repeat, according to my understanding," Leader Dollon pointed to the congregants, "the creature had sixteen faces and sixteen wings because four times four make?"

"Sixteen," a prover shouted. He pumped his body, and then he let his Leader continue.

"Amen, brother...Each living creature had two pairs of wings, and they never turned wherever they went; they went straightforward. The same time that they were going east, they were going west; the same time that they were going north, they were going south. A real mystery, comrades! Why? Because the spirit of the living creature was in the wheel so wherever the wheel led them they went; they had to follow the spirit.

"You must obey the spirit. Many of us do not want to be identified with Spiritual Baptists because of new-found earthly joys. Such joys often stifle the power and kill the spirit...Many of us refuse to wash in the chilly waves to be reborn...Many of us would hold on to worldly gifts, but sons and daughters of Christ when you go your separate ways don't forget to read Ezekiel. Read your bible and check the gospel, and it is only so that you'll know that I was not reading from a cookbook.

"If our interpretation is the same, and in this faith it must, because in this faith we must be evenly yoked...."

There was a sudden clacked sound. Lyle's cassette ended its recording. Nonetheless, he listened attentively to the sermon to the end. Lyle did not understand the sermon, but his scrutiny of Leader Dollon's antics, mannerisms, the way the Leader juggled words, and his application to some key phrases gave Lyle an uncanny feeling.

The Gordons drove home. So overjoyed was Elizabeth to see her husband in church that she said nothing about his overnight jazz sessions. "Lyle," she said beaming, "why did you run out? Leader Dollon always inquired about my husband, and there you were. Just as I was about to introduce you to him and to the other members, you pulled off your belt and hustled out of the church as if you were going to fight. You always use your belt as a buffer. You use it to blush also. You looked as a nervous person. How many functions that make-believe gold belt has?"

"Liz, coming to think of it, I really don't know; and I wasn't aware that I'd taken off my Modesir belt and ran out of the church as a nervous man."

"You ran out of the church as if you and Leaky saw a passenger across the street waiting on a car to go to the airport." They laughed. "Tell me, Lyle, why did you run out of the church?"

"I wasn't dressed in my spiritual garb, and I felt odd."

"Rend your heart, Lyle...Regardless of your attire, Leader Dollon and the other members would have been glad to be introduced to you. I always talk about you and Nigel. Most of the members remember Nigel, but only Hettie knows you. Hettie told me..."

"Eh, eh! I don't want to hear what Hettie told you."

"Leader Dollon always wanted to meet you."

"If Leader Dollon so wanted to know me why didn't you invite him home?"

"You are never at home. Remember?"

"Liz, how does Mt. Signal survive on the small offerings that you Caribbean people give? Rev. Ike will never preach to you all."

"Because Rev. Ike likes to see big bills only in the collection plate. That's not what the church is all about...For the twenty four hours that I'd not seen you, and I knew that my faithful husband was on the road hustling, I'd expect to hear that a fifty-dollar bill at least was put in the collection plate. I'll ask the treasurer if there was one."

"Liz, I can assure you that I gave much more than the two brethren who sat on my left and on my right. One gave a shiny quarter; and the other brethren who was filled with the holy ghost power and who, am sure, has two apartment buildings in Flatbush, gave a crisp dollar. What did you give, Liz?"

"I gave the flowers. I always supply the flowers regardless of the occasion and the cost of the flowers. Not one cent from the collection plate do I take to help me buy flowers, and you saw how many vases were there. I've been doing that for years. What else do you have to criticize, Mr Backslider?"

"Mt. Signal has a crooked altar."

"What else, mister critic? I know you are good at criticizing, if nothing else."

"Nothing else."

"How do you like the Leader?"

"Mr. Muscle? He was fluent. Sometimes his accent changed from Caribbean to American, vice versa. My Leader Gerrol hadn't his style and diction, but whenever my Leader Gerrol opened his mouth, I used to feel the spirit making waves in me...Strange...Strange, if Leader

Dollon had ever lived in our hometown Fyzabad I'd say that I'd seen a carbon copy of..."

"Don't say another word! Stop it!"

"Liz, why won't you allow me to finish what I was about to say?"

"I don't want to hear whatever you have to say. You always hallucinate when you come from your haunts and joints...no doubt, a whorehouse you call jazz. If the spirit didn't manifest in you as it did in me tonight, it was because your body was unclean from whence you came...probably from Jacki's hairy bank. Goodnight!"

"Goodnight, honey. Don't cook for me tomorrow. I'm eating out." Lyle went into the bathroom.

Elizabeth shouted from the bedroom. "We shall both be eating out. We'll be evenly yoked on the Parkway tomorrow."

He didn't answer. She turned off the lights, and in the darkness Lyle thought of a way of eluding Elizabeth tomorrow.

Suddenly the lights were turned on. "Lyle," Elizabeth shouted, "why did you smell the water in the lota before you drank it?"

"Liz, we'll talk about that tomorrow. Goodnight."

"Okay...Tomorrow." Elizabeth pulled the sheet over her head and mumbled, "Even Leader Dollon noticed him."

Chapter Eight

Carnival in Brooklyn

"This Labor Day's weather is fine. The sun appeared earlier than usual as if it promised the revellers on the Parkway that it would be there for them," the WLIB announcer said. "Just stand on the Parkway between Utica Avenue and Grand Army Plaza and you'll probably see all the Caribbean-Americans and their roots squeezed into the corridor of Crown Heights. I call today bacchanal Monday, so I'll kick off my show with my favorite calypso." The WLIB disk jockey spliced onto his turntable the Mighty Sparrow's *Sol Fish* and raised the volume.

Lyle was up early and was dressed in his one-piece khaki jumper with a bold sign labeled on it. He tuned into every news station to verify the weather, and he had breakfast, befitting of President Ronald Reagan's after his military victory over the spice island of Grenada. Nonetheless, Lyle's mind was on two women; mainly, how he'd get rid of his wife Elizabeth for that day without getting a blessing from her acrid tongue. Billie was waiting for him at their Parkway rendezvous, and Elizabeth was locked in her bedroom where she put on the final touches to her makeup and costume.

A brainstorm hit Lyle as he munched his toast. He muttered, "This is it! We'll never be evenly yoked today, Elizabeth honey." He swallowed two gulps of his coffee. "Aaah," he said, and threw the rest of his toast in the garbage bin. He moved quietly from the table and went through the back gate to make sure that he wouldn't run into his son Nigel who was expected for breakfast that morning.

Half an hour later Elizabeth opened her bedroom door and hummed Lord Kitchener's calypso *Flagwoman*. "Honey," she said, as she danced towards the kitchen table with a miniature Trinidad and Tobago flag in one hand and an American flag in the other, "how do you like my costume? Honey, I have a surprise for you, and I'll present it to you on the Parkway." Lyle was not at the table. "Where are you, honey? We'll be with others on the Parkway today. Guess who?" She danced towards the bathroom, waived her little flags, and twirled them like if she were the famous flagwoman that led the oldtimers' carnival band in Trinidad and Tobago. "Lyle, Lyle, did you see the placard that I made to display on the Parkway today? I cannot find it. Where are you?" She went to the spareroom and searched. "I must have left it in the church closet or in the taxi. Did I bring it home, Lyle? Did you hide my placard? Stop hiding, and don't be a child." Elizabeth searched in vain for Lyle. She was furious. She was enraged—so enraged, that her brown face became as red as the dirt of Malehice, Mozambique. She spoke to herself. "So that's it! Lover boy, you don't want to be evenly yoked with me on the Parkway. You already made plans with that sinking whore, Jackiass." The air from the whisper of Elizabeth's voice was only felt and heard by her bottom lip.

Lyle had already reached the Parkway dressed in his one-piece costume. He gazed at everything and at everyone. The brownstones structured with marble, elaborately carved stone ornaments and high ceilings for the first time got his attention. The brownstones' row formation reminded him of the workers' barracks in Fyzabad oilfields in the forties. On rooftops were ebony children who counted the bands seen in the distance. Lyle waived to them. In a storefront was a green grocer who had just raised from the floor. His body was turned towards Mecca and passages from the Koran came from the green grocer's mouth. He ended his prayers, and yelled in Arabic to members of his family to get busy and serve the wave of customers who poured into his store.

Across the street, Beverly, a Jamaican woman, shouted to her friend Hilda. "Me soon come, 'ilda."

Hilda replied, "Beverly, me leaving me yard now. Me 'ear the steelband beating." Hilda and Beverly raised their voices above the pan storm of high tenors, first tenors, double tenors, double seconds, triple seconds, double guitars, cellos, six-pans, tenor bases, nine-bases, and twelve-bases skillfully played by boys and girls as young as seven years old and adults as old as Methuselah.

"Hurry fas', man. I want to get a place near the Labor Day judges," a man said, and grabbed his food basket and folding chair.

"Am is," his South Carolinian woman replied.

Lyle was thrown into the festive mood from the spicy street conversations. He jovially said to himself, "Me soon come, Billie honey. Don't lose your patience because am is only two blocks away." He felt rejuvenated as he walked against the flow of carnival traffic, and he obeyed the spontaneous directives of dancing traffic policemen. A woman masquerader, separated from her band, burdened under the weight of her wire and feather headpiece and the opposing wind, shouted to an admiring ABC News cameraman. "My name is Vera. Make sure you take me picture good. You like me mas', Mr. Photo-takeouter? I got a dream from God to play this mas' this year." Lyle turned; and he looked at Vera. He was one hundred percent sure masquerader Vera was a "Trini," a native of Trinidad and Tobago, as he was. He recoiled at Vera's dreamy remark, but then he reasoned that Trinis say the darnest things, in jest, or otherwise! In true West Indian carnival spirit, Lyle shouted, "Vera gyul, give ABC News plenty bullshit talk because ABC does report anything on black people and call it prime time news! Give it to them, Trini! Vera gyul, before you leave don't forget to tell ABC that you already got a dream from Noah, and Noah told you what mas' to play on the Parkway next year...Put ice in their ice!"

In true carnival spirit, Lyle chipped off to the music

and ambled on the sidewalk.

The sidewalk was transformed into the world's largest mardi gras market. Everything potable and edible carried a black flavor. Bodegas carried deep and hot aluminum pans filled with tacos, black beans, fried pork, yellow rice and white rice. Southern entrees were pushed on wheels. The savory aroma of Jamaican curry goat dishes clashed with the scents from Guyanese pepperpots. "Nostrand" Sylvia stood before her giant-size pelau pot, seasoned it, and watched it consommé. "Sugar Finger" Gloria heated baskets of roti on a baking iron beneath a make-shift shed of tarpaulin. "Pantry" Clive added hot and sweet peppers to his pots of callalloo, tested his ground provisions with a fork to make sure that they were cooked, and tasted a piece of roast beef that was hung from long steel skewers. "Tobago" Eurice chopped cucumbers and spiked her pig souse; Granny Eulah warmed her coconut bakes and blood pudding in an iron pot, and her daughter Sheila added nutmeg and flavored her home-made hot chocolate. "Ah! Ah! Ah smelling Mother Enid's pot," a reveller said to his mate. "It's time to drink some soup, gyul." Mother Enid's cowheel soup, left to simmer, was inhaled by Crown Heights' kosher people who would have exchanged Jacob's coat for Mother Enid's cowheel recipe.

Countless vendors, except Tony, were cooking, selling, and dancing on the Parkway. Tony, his accent as thick as his pizza sauce, left his cart unattended. Under Tony's umbrella was *un chiodo curvo* (a bent nail) brought from Italy for goodluck, but Tony ignored his goodluck charm and went to Papa Son's jinx-removing booth in search of black chutzpa. In the adjoining booth Madame Pierre hailed in creole, "*Gaddè! Gaddè!* Good griot, rice and banana." Her call was heeded. The peasant-looking Haitians bought griot and cooked green bananas; the exiled bourgeoisie ordered mixed rice which they ate last (to show their upper breeding and table manners), and Madame Pierre crowned their plates with griot and Uncle Ben's. She reminded the exiles that she should not be forgotten for her good deeds on the Parkway when they returned to Haiti and overthrew the Dictator.

Yes! The day that Lyle Gordon had eagerly awaited had come. It was the day of Caribbean connections, the biggest Woodstock/USA. It was the only day in the year that the Parkway became a treasure trove for Caribbeanites. In its east-west corridor, a not-seen friend for over fifty years could be run into. On this corridor, Caribbeanites who were written off as MIA's were found. Here deadbeat dads took the risk to come and parade knowing fully well that the warrant man may be lurking under a mask, and they could be apprehended; but still the deadbeats risked dancing on the Parkway. The Parkway, that three-plus-mile stretch of asphalt, sheltered by silver maples, London planes, pine oaks, black oaks, red oaks and elm trees, became the world's largest theater. The elm trees spiralled breeze down their branches to the gyrating and competing dancers: heavy-set mothers tried to outdo their slim daughters with their belly movements. From behind Norway maples with their bright green foliage wives got a glimpse of their husbands' mistresses. There were drums, drums everywhere; and pretty gals were dressed in guitar strings which hid their broad tops, and two-ply napkins covered their broader bottoms. The women's attire perked the men's male sap.

Lyle paused for a minute and joined the resident tourists from Long Island, New York, who, every Labor Day come off the Expressway and sightsee on the Parkway. Jostling for space with the resident tourists, in awe, Lyle marvelled at the footworks of the *Garifuna* people. The *Garifunas*, descendants of the Caribs of St. Vincent, West Indies, danced the Chumba, Wanaraguwa, Punta, Hugu-Hugu, Paranda, and Sambi. "All you could dance, Ilayulei gyul," Lyle shouted to his friend, the lead dancer of the *Garifunas*.

"Am sorry I can't stick around because am on my way to meet my honey."

He was one block away from Billie when, strangely, he remembered the gun Billie put to his head last night. With that thought he became furious and fearful of her. He reasoned to himself: "Last night Billie put a gun to my head, and today I'm going to meet her for her to put the bullets in my brain. Lyle, Aunt Gina would say that it's all right to be drunk, but it's not all right to be that stupid." With that thought, Lyle turned around immediately. He walked in the opposite direction and a woman caught his eyes. Lyle scoped the woman. She was an attractive white woman who had already developed a pre-midday Parkway tan. She held a camera in one hand; a handbag was strapped to her blouse; and her pegged pants barely rested on her Italian-leather pomps. The white woman's golden hair, wet braided, was carefully cornrowed. She looked like a child in a woman's body; her freckles on the swell of both cheeks and below both eyes could be mistaken for carnival confetti; and her eyes searched for information in the bacchanal crowd. Instantly, Lyle remembered Trinidad and Tobago carnival, the great leveller, had worked magic for his Grandpa, and now he wished that Labor Day carnival on the Brooklyn Parkway would work magic for him, too. With his thoughts racing he came abreast of the woman that he surveyed, and he approached her. "Hi, Bo," Lyle said with his captivating smile, "how's the space, Mama?"

"Me? What space?" she inquired.

"Yes, you, with those braids."

The woman smiled. She checked the wording on Lyle's costume before she spoke. "Bo Derek cannot travel without John, Mr. Adult Nigger. Didn't you read that in the *Inquirer*?"

"I didn't. My name's in the *Inquirer*, too, madam."

"It's written on your costume," the woman said.

"Oh, I forgot." He looked at his khaki costume.

"Are you subbing for comedian Richard Pryor?"

The woman's eyes roved down to Lyle's torso.

"Maybe. And are you subbing for my sister?" His eyes took in her beauty.

"I don't get it! Why your sister?"

"As a child my sister always unbraided her cornrows to look grown among her peers at school, but on her way back home my sister braided her hair back in cornrows so that she would not receive Grandma's paddle. Are you on your way to or from school?"

"I'll only answer if you'll tell me how I would have looked in front of your Grandma."

"Grandma is dead—God bless her soul—but she'd surely come to life to see the plantation children—I mean the owners'—in cornrows."

"Are you racial or funny?"

"I'm neither. I'm just, in a roundabout way, trying to tell you that your cornrows are beautifully done."

"Thank you, but flattery doesn't pay. That's all you wanted to tell me?"

"I can add that the Parkway is a big school where you'll observe a lot of Caribbean customs and costumes. You'll even hear some revellers from the Caribbean say, 'Drinking rum is our culture,' but don't take them seriously; take me." He smiled. "My name is Lyle Gordon. Call me Lyle."

"You disappointed me, Lyle. I really wanted to call you Mr. Adult Nigger." She smiled. "Constance Wagner. Call me Connie."

"I like your sense of humor, Connie. Are you on your way to meet your husband?"

"I was socially married, happily divorced, and now widowed."

"A three-in-one combination meaning?"

"I'm alone."

"Me too!"

"Don't you belong to a band of more adult nigg..." Connie reshaped her mouth and brought out the sound "niggroes." She was about to reconstruct the complete sentence.

"You don't have to. Anything goes on carnival day." Lyle assured her that there's no slip of the tongue on carnival day.

Connie smiled. "Thanks for saving me."

"You are welcome."

"Why that name on your costume, Lyle?"

"To remember my Grandpa and the good times we had. Why not jump up in true Caribbean fashion with me?" He looked at Connie and telegraphed his special smile—a smile as if they were already confirmed pals.

"Is it safe? I don't even know you."

"C'mon, Connie. You couldn't be safer. I've brought no one; I'm meeting no one; and I expect no one."

"Then what are you doing here?"

"I should ask you that question! You don't look salsa to me, Connie."

"I can dance salsa."

"You dance salsa like this?" Lyle whistled and tiptoed to the tune of the *Blue Danube Waltz*.

"The Adult Negroes would be waltzing today?"

"Who are those negroes?" They laughed.

Connie replied. "I'm a reporter for the *Daily Remedy*, and I guess my boss chose me to cover this Labor Day beat. To think of it, I'll need help to interpret the concise imagery of the West Indian tongue."

"Here's your hired hand, ma'am."

"At minimum wages?" They laughed. "Let's turn back and walk this way," Connie said.

Lyle thought of Billie, and he hesitated.

"My hired hand is afraid of something?"

"Of course not. I just felt a gravel in my shoes." He slipped off his shoes and shook them.

"Lyle, I didn't see or hear any gravel."

"Connie, it's not a matter of hearing or seeing, it's a matter of feeling...Let's go, ma'am." He whispered in Bajan, "She's smart like Grandma."

The U.S. Army Steel Orchestra came along with

pannists who read the music score *I Love America*. Orchestrating behind them were countless steelbands and brass bands. Some were resident bands; others came from the archipelago which stretches from the Bahamas in the north to Trinidad and Tobago, the birth place of the steelband, in the south. Panamanians of Central America and Guyanese of South America were also proud to be a part of that archipelago of carnival revellers. The countless bands played Lord Kitchener's *Flagwoman* and the Mighty Sparrow's *Sol Fish* as theme songs. Lyle and Connie were sandwiched between pans and people. Some revellers' perspiration, high as aeroplanes, was relished, as that, too, was part of the carnival thing; other revelers, their perfumed bodies, drenched with sweat, gave off an amourizing odor that aroused their partners' sex glands; and their aroused partners, oblivious of their surroundings, deep kissed and fondled their lovers' flesh. The extra sweet-smelling masqueraders indeed brought a balance to the Parkway's air.

Lyle and Connie intermingled among the disguised masqueraders, the summer soldiers in camouflage khaki, the ganjaceros who drank booze from soda bottles, the genuflects of the Caribbean, the natives, the lawabiders, the offenders, the ex-offenders, the good, the bad, the ugly, and the priestly. The Parkway was a sea of imposters of American Indians, robbers, minstrels, sailors, men of space, fantasy, and clowns. One clown achieved the impossible: He bore more medals than the deposed Jean-Bedel Bokassa of the Central African Republic.

The Caribbean spirit was livened with dancing on the streets, and personal digs, known as *pickongs*, were thrown as friends greeted each other. Lyle and Connie became comfortable with each other and began to tease each other with *pickongs*. "Whitey," Lyle called Connie. "Blackboy," she called him. They were true participants. Whitey and Blackboy fueled their stomachs with roti and root beer. "Is that white meat yours to eat like the Frenchman, bruvver," a reveller asked Lyle. "No, brother," Lyle replied, but bore a suggestive smile as he chipped to the sweet music. More than a million shoe soles moved in unison toward the judges' platform located to the north of the Brooklyn Museum. Judging the best band or best costume was indeed a difficult task.

Music galore! The pingpong soloists played the high notes on their steel pans; the artistes on the second pans strummed off the beat; the bassmen played on the beat; the revellers danced to calypso music on the first and third beats, and to reggae music on the second and fourth beats. Drums sent out telepathic messages, and women held on to their men. Lyle held Connie protectively. He was in his glee and had no thoughts of Elizabeth or Billie. He took his belt off his waist and hooked it around Connie's waist.

"Isn't it lovely," she said. "Where did you get it, Lyle?"

"Consider yourself a champ now, Connie. I'll tell you more about it later. I know that you're ready to interview the revellers to get info to pad your by-lines for the hot press tomorrow."

She laughed. "I'll do just that." Connie interviewed the Caribbean revellers and onlookers. Some Caribbeanites told her that they hunted the fertility of the American crop as America hunted theirs; some boasted of their chief ministers, prime ministers, and presidents who were the juggernauts of their countries' independence and release from the metropolitan pawnbrokers; but there were those masqueraders who felt that the Caribbean Ayatollahs took the whip from their colonial masters and cracked it louder. Whatever the masqueraders' views, their Caricom feet danced, and their alcohol intake, if exchanged for water, could have washed Flatbush Avenue clean of its dirt.

The hovering clouds tricked the revellers as it tricked the weathermen. Rain came. Then the sun followed. The pannists changed keys as the weather changed moods. The pannists revved their pingpong sticks and touched thirty-secondth notes with speed and grace. The foot traffic was heavy and the bands swelled into the side streets. Noise and music were synonymous.

A reveller yelled excitedly, "O god Ezla gyul, that's you!"

"Yes, Shellyann girl, that's me. Long time nuh see."

"I's so damn tired. Let's take a quick rest by Fyzabad Corner, dig the scene, and mind people's business," Shellyann said.

Fyzabad Corner, earmarked by a giant-sized yellow banner, at the intersection of Rogers Avenue and the Parkway, was an oasis. Just being in the vicinity of Fyzabad Corner was like being inside a mailbox for you were sure to collect news and be in a position to relive nostalgia. The popular custodian of that famous Corner, Newsworthy Henry, once plied his tailoring trade in Butler's Fyzabad, and Fyzabadians from all walks of life dropped in and danced under Henry's mildew tarpaulin. Fyzabadians touched Henry, squeezed him, slapped him, hugged him, kissed him, and replenished their booze buckets and food carriers in Henry's stall. Henry's old girlfriend, now an English professional mourner, in good humor, remarked, "Oh god Henry! you still have that big mutton?" Henry laughed like a fisherman with a big evening catch and replied in his squeaky 55- year old voice. "Seems as though you missed having the big mutton, Dora. Come and squeeze it, gyul." Dora looked at the bulge beneath Henry's apron and smiled.

What the serenading Fyzabadians needed most, and got from Fyzabad Corner, were the latest unrecorded global news and tidbits from Newsworthy's file. The multitude of serenaders left, but started gossips that Newsworthy Henry embellished, embroidered, and fanned for the rest of Labor Day.

Ezla and Shellyann shouted, "Mutton man!" Henry waived to them from his stall, and shouted equally loud,

"Bad tongue women!" The two women embraced each other, kicked off their soft shoes, and sat on a concrete slab that the city workers left akimbo on the service road. Connie and Lyle took a cue and rested, too. Connie and Lyle sat on a smooth root stump and faced Ezla and Shellyann. Connie took out her small tape recorder from her bag, concealed it with her purse, put it on record, and eavesdropped on Ezla and Shellyann.

"Girl, what's happening?" Ezla asked.

"Gyul, you really want to know what's happnin? Am here catching me ass in New York," Shellyann replied.

"How long are you living up here?"

"Five years, and am trying to get me citizenship."

"Me ain't want citizenship; me ain't want fellowship; all I want is a big ship to ship all me things back home to Trinidad and Tobago...And when are you going back home, girl?"

"Gyul, I don't know. And you?"

"Next week all this time am down under the tropical sun."

"Why so quick?"

"Me stay up here! I don't like nothing up here. I don't understand the wrong-sided laws...the politics...the free for all...Thieves broke open my apartment four times; they stuck me up twice and took my money. Thank God they didn't rape me! Me stay up here! I already bought ten jumbo barrels to ship my belongings down home. Girl, I ain't staying one day longer in this rat race. I rather go home and *lime* (hang out) below a breadfruit tree than to stay here."

"Gyul, I wish I could've talked like you, but I have so many irons in the fire."

"Fuck them irons! Irons or no irons, am running from here pronto. I ain't even paying my credit cards. If Mr. MasterCard and Mr. Visa want their money, they could send a warrant man down home to me in Trinidad and Tobago to my unknown address."

"By the way, you know who I ran into just now, gyul?"

"Whom?"

"Lord Chilly. You know he have a child with Sarah?"

"He has a child with big mouth Sarah! That man has about forty illegitimate children. I don't see what a woman sees on that man. That man is as tight as a frog's behind. He doesn't give woman money. And furthermore, he can't move his waist in bed! He ain't have a good face; and he ain't have grace."

"Ezla gyul, how you know that? You was with Lord Chilly too?" Ezla didn't answer, and Shellyann changed the subject. "Ezla gyul, I want you to take down home a ham for me mother. I hear a ham cost so much money down home."

"The ham down home must cost money! Girl, what do you expect when those young people down home smoking all the grass that the hogs should get to eat."

"Ezla gyul, you know I never thought of that."

"Girl, commonsense should've told you that. And to make it worse, the stupid Indian Opposition Party in Parliament is blaming the government for those weed smokers in Trinidad and Tobago. The day that that coolie Opposition Party holds the rein of government, we niggers will have to go back to Africa. You mark my word! This black government is the best government we ever had. This present People's National Movement government is patterned on King Bill's policies. God, please bless King Bill in his grave." Ezla looked up in the sky. "King Bill is dead, but he brought Trinidad and Tobago from scratch to something. I always remember when King Bill fought the American Government to get back our land. Could you imagine that England had given America our land in Chaguaramas to be used as a military base during the war without consulting us? Could you imagine that America gave England an old battleship just good to hatch eggs as a collateral for our land at Chaguaramas?"

"White man to white man, they don't care how they trade away our lands. The same thing they did with Africa. King Bill fixed America's wagon good and took back our land before he died! But what was worse was when the Americans used to fly their flag on their embassy, and they didn't fly our flag as a mark of respect. King Bill compelled the Americans to fly our Trinbago flag. 'That was blatant disrespect by the Americans' King Bill told us in the Peoples' University of Woodford Square. King Bill was really the best man who ruled Pitch Lake Country. Ezla gyul, King Bill had so much brain. I never see a small man with so much brain in his head. He made we black people feel proud of ourselves. Them Chinese! them Portuguese! them Syrians! and especially them French Creole! who used to walk all over black people, hated King Bill's guts. Why? Because King Bill let them know that 'Massa Day Done.' That is why I believe King Bill one hundred percent when he said in the Peoples' University that 'the white man did not abolish slavery because he felt sorry for his slaves...It was because it became too expensive for the slave owners to feed and maintain his slaves.'"

Out of the blue, Shellyann said, "And gyul, did I tell you the calamity about me breda?"

"Your brother! Girl, what happened to him?"

"You know me stupid breda left his good wife for a Yankee 'oman...And the thing what does hurt me is to see that Yankee 'oman huntin' me breda down all about. Me breda can't even breed."

Connie touched Lyle with her toes and tried to imitate Shellyann's twang. "Ah hope yo could breathe...Who's huntin' yo down—yo wife or yo Yankee 'oman?"

Lyle didn't answer, but he sheepishly looked into the crowd for Elizabeth and Billie. He got rid of his thoughts when a masquerader dressed like Big Bird of *Sesame Street* fame displayed her headpiece.

"Ezla gyul," Shellyann said excitedly, "you see that 'oman showing off her headpiece...That is the 'oman I was telling you about. That is the 'oman who was coming out of the motel with her sweet man, and when she saw her husband going into that same motel with his sweet 'oman, she scrambled her husband and said in the Queen's English, 'I knew I would have caught you here today, Harry.' And you know that her *cunumunu* (foolish) husband didn't even ask his wife what was she doing with a man in the motel."

"Girl, when those asshole West Indian men are in love that is how they behave. Am looking for an asshole man, too, and believe me whenever I get one not even you can take him away from me."

Connie looked at them and couldn't stifle her laughter any longer.

Shellyann read Connie's eyes and lips and said, "Ezla gyul, that whitey's taking all the words out of our mout'. I's sure as daylight that black man with her have a good job, and he's making lots of money…Gyul, when them black men have some kind of pedigree, they does always run and pick up a white 'oman and forget their own kind. I have a nephew who does say that he go marry a high brown 'oman or a white 'oman to lighten his darkness, but I done tell me nephew that I may settle for a high-brown gal, but don't bring any white 'oman by me for dinner. I already let my nephew know in plain Inglish that I ain't cooking for no whitey after I get my green card from Uncle Sam. That cheap white bitch in Jersey who does only cook kosher franks and have me working cabaret hours would be the last white 'oman I'd be working for after I get my immigration papers from Twenty Six Federal Plaza. Mark me word!" Shellyann's diction spoke for her sincerity and integrity.

Connie lost control of her laughter. She threw herself on Lyle for support. She was red; and he, pretentiously, in broad daylight, looked for stars near the sun; but he still couldn't detain his laughter any longer.

"Mout' open 'tory jump out," Ezla said.

"Let's us move from here, gyul," Shellyann insisted,

"because it looks as if we have an audience. Gyul, leh we move from these two nosy people who's looking at us. Let us go and look for the *Grenada Ghosts*. I have a friend who's playing in that band. That band is bad! They's up to date in their politics, and they always have a debate on which calypsonian's tune should be used for the road march."

"But Shelly girl, don't forget that debate always ends up in a fist fight every Labor Day parade."

Connie whispered in Lyle's ear. "What's the road march?"

Lyle whispered back to her. "That's the theme song. That's the most popular tune; and that tune will be the tune that the *Grenada Ghosts'* musicians will play for their masqueraders to dance on the streets."

Shellyann touched Ezla and spoke loudly. "Gyul, you see that nigger dog is whispering to that white fowl about us." Unrehearsed, Shellyann and Ezla got up, kissed the palms of their hands and rubbed their pouted derrieres for Connie and Lyle to see. The two best friends then chipped off to the strains of Sparrow's *Sol Fish* played by Despers USA Steel Orchestra.

Connie stopped her recorder, and she looked to see where Ezla and her pal headed. She pulled Lyle off his derriere and said, "Lyle, let's find the Ghosts."

"Is it the band of Ghosts or those two women who suit your fancy?"

"Both would make good bedfellows for my news report on Labor Day Carnival in Brooklyn. Let's find the Ghosts, Lyle." Connie and Lyle eventually found the talked-about band after they bored their way through the hectic crowd.

The *Grenada Ghosts*, a masquerade of race, was a band with approximately two hundred revellers. They assembled on the surface road at the intersection of the Parkway and Franklin Avenue. The participants were robed completely in gowns, not even their fingers were seen. Halloween and African masks covered the ghosts' entire heads. Only their eyes were seen. Each ghost held a placard on a short pole, and Connie and Lyle read their placards aloud. The placards told in soundbites what each masquerader thought of America's invasion of Grenada. There was also a placard about a turmoil on the African Continent, and it was written in Portuguese.

DID PRESIDENT REAGAN BOMB GRENADA BECAUSE GRENADA TALKED TO CUBA, OR BECAUSE BLACK CHILDREN MUST BE SEEN BUT NOT HEARD? BECAUSE THAT'S AN EASY QUESTION, DON'T ANSWER IT.

SHAME! SHAME! AMERICA IS CALLING THE BOMBING OF GRENADA A MILITARY VICTORY, YET YOU CAN'T EVEN SEE GRENADA ON A WORLD MAP.

7000 AMERICAN SOLDIERS INVADED GRENADA; 8790 GOT MEDALS FOR THEIR GOOD DEEDS. THAT'S REAGAN'S KIND OF NEW MATH!

RONNIE, YOU WENT TO GRENADA AFTER THE RUSSIANS SHOT DOWN FLIGHT 007. YOU DID NOT HIT BACK THE RUSSIANS. I SEE YOU ENJOY BEATING THE WEAK.

CUBA INVADED GRENADA WITH DOCTORS, NURSES, AND ENGINEERS.

MY MOTHER LIVES IN GRENADA AND SHE JUST SENT ME A LETTER TO SAY THAT THE PEOPLE PREFER THE AMERICANS MORE THAN THE CUBANS EVEN THOUGH THE AMERICAN TOURISTS ARE TRAVELLING WITH EMPTY POCKETBOOKS.

ONE THOUSAND AMERICAN STUDENTS

WERE IN DANGER OF LOSING THEIR LIVES IN GRENADA AND THAT'S WHY BIG BROTHER INVADED GRENADA. DO YOU BELIEVE BIG BROTHER?

RONNIE DIDN'T TAKE THE ADVICE OF THE OAS WHEN HE WANTED HIS OBEDI-ENT BRITISH POODLE TO HOLD ON TO THE MALVINAS, BUT HE TOOK THE ADVICE OF FIVE BLIND CARIBBEAN MOUSES TO INVADE GRENADA...ESPE-CIALLY LADY IRON'S ADVICE!

COARD AND BISHOP, TWO LEADERS OF THE GRENADA REVOLUTION, HOW DID YOU TWO BECOME ENEMIES? I CAN'T BLAME THE CIA, BUT THEY COULDN'T HAVE ENGINEERED IT BETTER.

I BELIEVE GRENADA WAS BUILDING A MILITARY AIRPORT TO HELP CASTRO. MR. REAGAN SAID SO, AND HE DOESN'T LIE!

WHAT'S ALL THIS TALK ABOUT GRENA-DA'S ELECTION. ALLENDE DID EVERY-THING RIGHT...RIGHT INTO THE GRAVE WITH A BULLET. WAS IT THE CIA? NO COMMENT!

WHAT'S ALL THIS TALK ABOUT GRENADA IS LEANING TOWARDS THE COMMU-NISTS AND SHOULD BE PUNISHED? AMERICA HELPS RUSSIA THE FOREMOST COMMUNIST.

I'LL SAY THANK YOU, AMERICA, AFTER YOU REPAIR OUR AIRPORT. THE MAURICE BISHOP REVOLUTION PROCLAIMED 1984 TO BE THE YEAR OF THE AIRPORT, AND

YOU MADE SURE THAT WISH DIDN'T COME TRUE. SNEAKY SON OF A GUN.

GRENADA'S WATERGATE IMPORTED!

AMERICA IS A FAIR NATION. AMERICA HAS ENOUGH BOMBS TO OVERKILL, SO WHY SHOULD LITTLE GRENADA WANT GUNS.

WHY DIDN'T AMERICA WELCOME REPORTERS?

COMRADE BISHOP IS DEAD. FORWARD EVER! BACKWARD NEVER!

MOSHIACH IS ON THE WAY.

WEST INDIAN AMERICAN DAY CARNIVAL ASSOCIATION (WIADCA) WELCOMES YOU TO THE LABOR DAY BACCHANAL.

AMERICA STOLE TRINIDAD AND TOBAGO DR. R. CAPILDEO'S THEORY OF WEIGHT-LESSNESS IN SPACE, USED IT IN THEIR SPACE PROGRAM, BUT AMERICA GAVE DR. CAPILDEO NO CREDIT. I READ THAT IN A BRITISH NEWSPAPER!

OS ESPIRITOS DE NOSSA ANCESTRAIS, PROTÉJA MBITA, KASIGA, MABOTE, CHISSANO, GUEBUZA, MOCUMBI, E TODAS OS GUERREIROS DESCALÇOS QUE LUTAM PELA LIBERDADE HOMENS, MULHERES, E CRIANÇAS, EM MOÇAMBIQUE E TANZÂNIA; E OBRIGADO, DAVID MARTIN. VOCÊ É UM JORNALISTA CANADENSE JUSTO QUEM ESTA DEIXANDO O MUNDO SABER QUE OS ASSASSINOS PORTUGUESES QUE A ÁFRICA DO SUL FERMENTOU

ESTÃO LEVANDO PÉ NA BUNDA!

AMÉRICA, TOME NOTA!

AUNT GINA HATED GRENADIANS. WHY?

Lyle read the last placard very softly. The placard was lofted in the air, but he couldn't see who carried the placard. Suddenly the placard disappeared. Was his mind playing him tricks, or were there countless Aunt Ginas who hated Grenadians, Lyle thought. He controlled his thoughts when Lord Ballotbox, a member of the *Grenada Ghosts* band, screamed into the microphone.

"Attention, please!" Lord Ballotbox said. "Friends and foes know me as Lord Ballotbox. I am chosen to be the Chairman of the *Grenada Ghosts* because my very name connotes a democratic instrument, even though ballot boxes have been rigged; and I heard that in some countries dead men cast their votes in ballot boxes. As we all know, a superpower invaded tiny Grenada and one of the reasons that superpower gave for the invasion was there was anarchy in Grenada. Agreed?"

"Yes! No! Get off of it! You don't know the facts!" were shouted by the pro-Grenada invasion and anti-Grenada invasion groups.

Lord Ballotbox continued. "What was the difference in Lebanon?" He was interrupted, but he continued. "I see no difference, except, of course, that in Lebanon there was anarchy to the tenth power. But, instead, that head of the American superpower instructed his fighting marines to cover their heads with sandbags before they die. There are many ways that I can equate that, but I leave the equation to you. It could be political; it could be racial; it could be anything."

A ghost shouted: "Speak on the motion! If you forgot it, I'll tell it to you. The motion is, 'Be it resolved that our musicians play as our road march either the Mighty Sparrow's *Sol Fish* or Lord

Kitchener's *Flagwoman*."

Lord Ballotbox went back to the subject matter. "Comrades of our historic band of *Grenada Ghosts*, my purpose today is to get your vote on which calypsonian's tune should be our road march to jump up and dance on the Parkway...I am not here to 'run with the hare and chase with the hound.'"

Connie mumbled, "That's just what you're doing, Lord Ballotbox."

"...We're here to play mas'," Lord Ballotbox continued. "No one knows the origin of this band, but whosoever got us here in this cheap costume is a genius. We all resemble. Our heights are almost identical. It's only our platform shoes that vary our height. Our road march to parade will either be the Mighty Sparrow's *Sol Fish* or Lord Kitchener's *Flagwoman*. We are not going to play any other tune because they are all stink like sol fish...Do you all remember the joke about the blind man who was walking down the street? He smelled something funky like salt fish and he said, 'Good afternoon, ladies.'"

"Boo! Boo! That joke is sexist, and it is older than my great grandmother," women in the crowd shouted; but the men's ovation drowned the women's catcalls.

Without delay, Lord Ballotbox said, "All those who wish to debate the choice of the road march raise your hands."

The hands raised were Lord Belaforma, Lord Mongoose, Jr., Lord Josh, Lord Sabga, Lord Davey Marine, Lord Arrowroot, Lord Cubano, Lady Iron, The Resurrection of King Bill, Lord Backoo, Lord Big Apple, Lord X, and countless other carnival lords and ladies who pointed their fingers to the sky. Some were in favor of Sparrow's *Sol Fish*, and some liked Lord Kitchener's *Flagwoman* to be their road march.

The Chairman continued. "Lady ghosts and gentleman ghosts, remember that we have a limited time for this debate otherwise we would be late for the competition, and we wouldn't win a prize for our originality. The stage is now open for a short debate." Standing on a parked car, Lord Ballotbox looked into the band of fidgeting ghosts and said, "I recognize Lord Davey Marine of the Pitch Lake Republic as our first debater. Promise me, Lord Davey, that no matter how much you are heckled by your peers, you will not take off your mask, you will not call them by their Christian names, because if you do, and you get hit with a rock, I can assure you that rock wouldn't be Prudential's."

"Thank you, Mr. Chairman, for your kind words of advice," Lord Davey said as he waived his placard which read POWER TO THE PEOPLE. He took the microphone. "Let me introduce myself as a brother..." He was interrupted.

"Youse no bruvver," Lord X hailed. "You didn't support brother Malcolm in his struggles even though he was born in the Caribbean."

"...Neither am I a Reicht of the Third World..."

"Youse too black to be, nigger."

The Chairman butted in. "Lord X, please don't interrupt Lord Davey."

"Thank you, Mr. Chairman," Lord Davey Marine said. "Fellow lords and ladies of this prestigious band of ghosts, the very first thing people of color must remember is that although by nature we are a spiritual people, we have the wherewithal to be political. Remember the real issues of our way of life is mouthed by folks singers, and calypsonians are folk singers. Calypso is our prose and poetry. Lest Lord Josh and Lord Sabga of Port Jamaica be offended, let me say that reggae is included in that genre. The calypsonian can attack his oppressors from this very car top, which is our protected parliament, and get immunity from a jail term for speaking the truth."

"Try to speak the truth in Russia," Lord Big Apple shouted.

Lord Davey Marine ignored his detractor. "Mr. Chairman," he continued, "who needs to hear *Sol Fish* or *Flagwoman* when the road march could be about the bogus election in Jamaica, or about Sheriff Hololo of Pitch Lake Country who opened the calaboose and let loose his kith in a country where the government's motto is 'No corruption, no graft....'"

Connie whispered. "Lyle, I'd read of that, and I was appalled."

"...We all know, ladies and gentlemen, that Sheriff Hololo of my country was swapped in a cultural exchange...We are yet to know if that exchange were a good investment for taxpayers. But whether we are taxpayers or tax collectors, we all must eat." Lord Davey checked the crowd for their reaction. "It would be better if our road march today is about Santa Claus who forgets children in East Africa, or about the freedom fighters in Mozambique, or about our tropical justices in Trinidad and Tobago who are always citing Lord Goddard, a bastard limey in wigs, instead of our talented Lord Wooding, a black Caribbeanite versed in the law." Lord Davey adjusted his mask. "Brothers and sisters, let us compose our own road march now and sing about those stupid West Indians who put down their country because Uncle Sam gave them a visa to share in the pollution."

Connie again interrupted Lyle's listening pleasure. "Bruvver Lyle, I've heard enough of that West Indian hypocrite. That kwashiorkor baby, am sure, had his best meals in America."

Lyle spoke in Connie's ear. "Take notes. Don't talk."

"Shsh," an old man said.

"...Mr. Chairman," Lord Davey Marine said and wiped his masked brow, "the Mighty Sparrow's *Sol Fish* is saltless; Lord Kitchener's *Flagwoman* is catchy, but dumb. I recommend for our road march and edification Mighty Stalin's *Run Something, Mr.*

Divider. Mighty Stalin's calypso asks for small mercies for the poor."

"Whad'ya mean by small mercies?" Lady Iron shouted to Lord Davey Marine.

He replied. "Food for the poor. Lord Stalin is trying to melt the spiritual tardiness in us. Stalin wants us to forget that Sixteenth Century oratory culture. Instead of yapping, yapping, and voting for the building of institutions that favor factories to produce guns, vote for the G-7 nations to build bakeshops to produce bread for the starving people of the world."

"Mister Fool-Fool," Lady Iron took out her false teeth and shouted, "you call that small mercies? I's hot, and all I want is a man, and I can't get one."

"Lady Iron, let me tell you the best way to catch a man..."

"Lord Davey, no such explanation!" The Chairman interrupted. "You can explain your theory to Lady Iron later tonight in a Times Square motel. I can even recommend a nice motel, if you both wish."

"Thank you, Mr. Chairman, am sure Lady Iron won't mind. As I was saying, I vehemently put forward the motion that *Run Something, Mr. Divider* be our road march. That ditty warns the monkey who shares the cheese that he should not take the bigger half. That calypso is metaphorical. In a way that calypso tells us that we didn't march for black Arthur Miller who was murdered by a policeman in Brooklyn, but we've come here in droves to march, sing, eat roti and gingerbread without a purpose. Down with *Flagwoman*! Down with *Sol Fish*! These two calypsoes are not awe inspiring. The calypso *Flagwoman* is about a woman who waives a flag in front of a band, and about how she winds her body while she waives that flag. And all you Caribbean people know that when the Mighty Sparrow sings about his wood, you can use Sparrow's wood to dig a hole, but you cannot use Sparrow's wood to light a fire;

neither can you cook the kind of salt fish that Sparrow likes. The Mighty Sparrow himself said that the more he eats that kind of sol fish with his neck bent like the Frenchmen, the more his hair drops off. So why should sane people dabble in Sparrow's kind of sol fish to have their lovely curls dropped? Does that make sense, ghost people with brains? But Lord Stalin's calypso *Run Something, Mr. Divider* gives a message; and the message says that 'the poor should share in the pie.' That's all I have to say." Lord Davey jumped off the car and received a mixed ovation.

Lady Iron shouted, "Oh god! me sol fish hot right now."

Connie pulled Lyle closer. "A few minutes ago the inference was about Sparrow's salt fish. Now what does Lady Iron mean by her salt fish is hot?"

"The heat of the day is giving a boost of estrogen to Lady Iron's hairy bank." Lyle's monotone wasn't meant to be funny.

Connie, whose newspaper beat was once medical, was confused with Lyle's clinical explanation. She said, "Bruvver Lyle, yo have a calypso dictionary to len' me?"

"Sure, me have one to len' yo, white sister."

The Chairman rose and raised his voice. "There's time for two more speakers. Brief speakers! I recognize the hero from the land of wood and water."

Lord Sabga rushed to the car top. He looked priestly in his clean gown and an original Benin mask that was brought in from the African Continent. He raised his mask slightly, yawned, and blocked his mouth.

A voice in the crowd shouted, "O gosh! I didn't know that the Prime Minister from Rasta Port was so light skin. He's just like a white man—the same color as our President Reagan; and he has good manners. You see how Lord Sabga yawned and blocked his vapor."

Lord Sabga heard the well-wisher and was pleased. "Long live the new order of Jamaica! I am now in charge." Sabga began his address on the choice of the road march.

"Boo! Traitor, your belly button is buried in America. Deputy Invader of Grenada, I hope Reagan strengthens the Jamaica dollar," Lord Josh said.

"Silence! Silence!" screamed the Chairman. "You two are from the same port. I'm warning you. Don't wash your dirty linens here. Talk on the choice of the road march." After his warning, the chairman sat down on the hot car top.

"Mr. Chairman, before I broach that subject," Lord Sabga said, "let me tell you that I could take care of myself. Let me tell all you people that Lord Josh is jealous because I beat him fair and square in our last Jamaica election. Him say that I cheated in the ballot box, but the truth of the matter is that I beat his ass. I beat him in the polls in a democratic way. All Lord Josh talked about was democratic socialism, a ghost system where everybody will drink from one goblet, but that can't work. Comrade Bishop of Grenada tried that system, and that is why one of his own Communist comrades killed him. His Communist comrade realized that system cannot work in the Caribbean that is used to a market economy."

"Wash your dirty mouth. Comrade Bishop was never your friend, much more your comrade...It's your type who killed comrade Bishop," Lord Josh shouted.

"On a point of order, Mr. Chairman," Lord Arrowroot interrupted. "I know Lord Sabga has the floor—I mean the hot car top—but would you allow me to ask Lord Josh a simple question?"

"Go-ahead, Lord Arrowroot, if it is a short question," the Chairman said. Lord Sabga was glad to be temporarily relieved of his contribution to the road march debate because he knew more about American pop music than about calypso or reggae.

"I hope Lord Arrowroot doesn't ask Lord Josh a floury question," Connie quipped softly.

Lyle replied softly in her ear, "Whitey, you are the

outsider here. I'll run like hell and leave you behind for the Ghosts to cut off your braids."

"I believe you, Blackboy." She smiled, and turned her attention to Lord Arrowroot.

Lord Arrowroot, amidst the debating enthusiasts, shaped his hands like a bullhorn and put his mouth between them to gain volume. He shouted, "Lord Josh, how does democratic socialism work?"

Lord Josh jumped up on the car top without taking heed of the Chairman's objections to that question and said, "Democratic socialism means that you ain't bound to 'ave a budget before you 'ave a job. 'The earth's the Lord's and its fullness thereof'...All our people gotta eat." Lord Josh glared at Lord Sabga.

Lord Sabga jumped off the car and ran. Sabga wanted no more bandying of words with his countryman. Lord Josh cursed in unintelligible Jamaican patois, and his homeboys restrained him. "Daughter," Lord Josh addressed one of his sympathizers, "you see that Syrian who lived in America and now he's pretending that he's a Jamaican, just wait and 'ear the outcome of 'im. Look for 'im in the river. 'im blood clat!" Lord Josh raced in the direction of Lord Sabga who disappeared as the wind.

From nowhere appeared one of the *Grenada Ghosts*, drenched in perfume. That ghost stood a short distance away, yet within Connie's view. Through that ghost's hooded mask, that ghost looked at Lyle, and Lyle inhaled and exhaled the odor of that ghost.

"Why are you inhaling and exhaling, Lyle?" Connie asked.

Lyle pretended he did not hear her.

"Attention! Attention! Who's next to speak on the motion of what calypso we'd use as our road march: Be it *Sol Fish*, *Flagwoman* or *Run Something, Mr. Divider*?" The Chairman surveyed the band of *Grenada Ghosts* as he addressed them.

A pint size masquerader, who refused to dress

uniquely as the other ghosts, put up his hand and said, "I am the Resurrection of King Bill from the Republic of Trinidad and Tobago. Though King Bill is dead, whatever I say should be taken as the gospel of King Bill himself. Before I speak on the motion of the road march, first I must let you know that I was not in favor of America invading Grenada. I will never stand for a white nation bombing a black nation." The Resurrection of King Bill ignored the motion about which calypso should be the road march. Instead, the Resurrection became an instant lecturer. His treatise was on the subject *From Columbus to Castro*, and he lambasted leaders of the Caribbean community as being ignorant of the times. The Resurrection dialogued with himself and rattled relentlessly like a Good Friday ra-ra, his favorite childhood toy. His noisy excesses were more than the World Bank's calculator.

Lady Iron was tired of the Resurrection of King Bill's tirades. She shouted, "Mr. Resurrection of King Bill, dear spokesman for the deceased King Bill, am sure your partisan's money is stashed away safely in the Swiss Bank. I also know that you were dropping words for me, but I don't care. I told President Reagan then, and I'll tell him again, that he was right to bomb Communist-inclined Grenada. I told my cabinet to put into law that 'black men who braid their hair would be punished.' Men should be men, not wannabe women." Lady Iron looked at Lord Cubano and said, "I don't want to smell a Communist near my pig pen. Fidel Castro is more than enough!"

"4-Q," Lord Cubano said. Lord Cubano's drawl sounded like a Santeria blessing.

The Chairman inquired: "Lord Cubano, is that a curse word, geometry, or Spanglish? Whatever, I need decency on the Parkway today. I don't want to hear a word from you and Lady Iron for the rest of the debate."

Lord Cubano did not take heed of the Chairman's

ruling. He spoke Spanish and English as if they were one language. Interpreted, this was what Lord Cubano said: "Lady Iron, you, Lord Bim, the other Uncle Toms and bootlickers of the Reagan Administration, could have bought proper aerial maps for the Imperialist Yankee soldiers. That would have prevented the Imperialist invaders from bombing the mental hospital when they invaded little Grenada. With all their weaponry it took the Imperialist Yankees over a month to mop up a peasant Grenadian army armed with dry sticks, shovels, and unserviceable 1914 rifles. If the Yankees had come in my Cuba," he stressed the sound "Cooba," "it would have been another Bay of Pigs."

"That's unfair," Lord Bim shouted. "Our Uncle Sam should not be given a dumb rap, and Lady Iron should be treated like a lady."

"What kind of lady?" the Chairman said sarcastically. "Please continue, Mr. Resurrection of King Bill."

"Thank you, Lord Ballotbox. You are a worthy chairperson, sir," the Resurrection of King Bill said. He was about to clarify a point, but a ghost from the band waived its banner in disgust. Lord Ballotbox kept his eyes on the stray ghost with a placard that read AUNT GINA HATED GRENADIANS. WHY? The ghost weaved in and out of the crowd.

There were crosstalks, and the Chairman could not control the differing factions in the band of *Grenada Ghosts*. The impatient crowd engaged in their own sidebars. The whole psychological matrix for instant comfort was for everyone to vent his or her feelings. The crowd dabbled in a milieu of political and social matters and came to their own conclusions irrespective of facts or logic. The sweet smelling ghost with gloved hands said not one word. Enraged, it destroyed the placard, but it held on to the half-shredded pieces of the cardboard, and put the pieces of cardboard in its gown pockets. It stood a little distance away and eyed Connie. Its eyes roved under its mask. As Connie took notes of the proceedings that ghost came closer, and Connie picked up its scent.

"Order! Order!" the Chairman screamed. "It's time to get down from the platform Mr. Resurrection of King Bill. I now recognize Lord Big Apple...Lord Big Apple, you supported Comrade Bishop and his Jewel Boys in private, but in public you called him a commie. Nonetheless, ghost men and women, give a rousing hand to Lord Big Apple, our beloved host, the gatekeeper of New York City."

"Yahoo," yelled a Brooklyn accent. "Let Lord Big Apple talk about the terlit. I went to do a number in Grand Central terlit; the doors were broken; and the homeless were sleeping on the floor. In that already stink terlit, I had to do my number one in a coke bottle, and my jiggler got stuck. Thanks to that kochsucker for my cocky fate!"

"Order! Order!" The Chairman pointed to a pro-Grenada invasion group wielding their placards that read GOD BLESS PRESIDENT REAGAN.

"Don't you pro-invasion murderers hear the Chairman," Lord Backoo screamed, and he, too, ignored the Chairman's objection. "Ghost people, how can you Caribbean people support a metropolitan government that destroyed a capital investment in a black underdeveloped country like Grenada, lied about Grenada's domestic airport by calling it a military airport. Don't forget that an American citizen helped build that airport...Your Big Brother in D.C.," Lord Backoo pointed to the Pro-Grenada invasion group, "blackballed the Grenada Revolution at every lending institution, but your Big Brother showed kindness by offering the Revolution two lovely buses that were bigger than Grenada's roads. What a genius! Isn't Washington a thoughtful Big Brother?...You know something carnival comrades: Grenada reminds me of a country gal who had more cavities than teeth;

that gal had no clothes but a sexy body. Nobody looked at that gal, but as soon as a good Samaritan from out of town paid the dentist bills and bought that naked gal Gloria Vanderbilt jeans, a gun-toting bully who lived next-door came forward and claimed that gal as his woman. You people who are showing your placards, don't forget that your Uncle Sam first used the domestic airport for his military intervention...Remember the same stick that hits the black dog hits the white dog."

A member from the band shouted, "Hear who's talking! That henchman from Guyana who sent Brother Walter Rodney that renowned scholar to his grave! That golddigger! Don't tell me about the stick or about the dog. It is the blow that matters, Lord Backoo!"

The mammoth crowd was tired of the *Grenada Ghosts'* sociological drivel. The crowd refused to let any of the ghosts speak. There were chants and abuses that were hurled from all angles—from debaters, nondebaters, pro-Grenada invasion groups, anti-Grenada invasion groups, black people, white people, brown people, yellow people, natives and aliens. They out-shouted each other:

"Wetbacks! Go back to your banana republics... Ungrateful sons of bitches who bite the hands that feed all you," a woman screamed.

"*Fille de joie*," the Chairman screamed louder, "Americans live off the fat of my country too."

"Your mama is a filly, too, whatever that is," the woman replied.

"Coconut-rice-n-beans West Indians, youse can't talk Inglish rat, but youse debating," yelled a man's voice.

"I's a educated West Indian, and I can talk English

righter than you. Fukkya!"

"Fukkya back! Youse good in Inglish as Rosie Ruiz is good in marathon. Rosie started the race at the finish line. She's so dumb; she went up for a prize not knowing that she'd be caught with her bloomers down."

"Youse no soul bruvver. All you know is carnival. I's going to report youse illegal people to the Immigration…You ain't even register to vote for Jesse Jackson this coming Presidential Election."

"Me register! to be counted as a *bona fide* second class citizen like you. I was a civil servant working in Government House where I came from, stupid nigger."

"Me stupid? I was born in America, man. I ain't brung me bruvver-in-law in a suitcase from Jamaica. That's a nice way to kill youse in-laws. If you don't like what we do in America, leave, and go back to your banana republic. Come to me for advice on how to catch the plane back home."

"With a ring in your crooked nose, how much sense could you have, dummy, to advise me?"

"I may be dumb, but I sure have freedom of speech."

"Nigger, who listens to you, apart from the Burger King and White Castle waiters?"

"Look at you! You ain't have pride. You on welfare."

"The government bailed out Chrysler too. Why don't you go and look at them, pussy boy! Them on welfare too."

"You have no culture! Get out me face."

"Who say so! McDonalds is part of my culture, and I eats at McDonalds."

"Insult me one more time, and I'll go for my gun, nigger."

"Arsehole, I walked with mine. Look at the bone handle!"

Connie stopped recording the street debate. She put her mini recorder in her handbag and appealed to Lyle: "Let's go. This Labor Day carnival is getting out of hand, and I don't like the way that stray ghost who left its pack is always looking in my direction."

As the words left Connie's mouth, shots were fired in the air, and a stampede followed. Connie fell, and that sweet smelling ghost fell on her. Connie felt a tug at the belt on her waist; and the ghost was gone. More people crashed on her. Lyle plunged into the crowd, held Connie's hand, and pulled her up. She quickly grabbed her camera out of her bag and took shots of the melee from all angles. People and unmasked ghosts ran in all directions, but in the background Lord Big Apple, still masked, shouted, "People, don't go away. I have a lot to read from my recently published memoirs, but I don't like to read to a small audience. I'm not a prejudice person. Look at my placard." Lord Big Apple hoisted his placard. It read: *JEWS AND BLACKS, DESPITE THEIR LITTLE QUARRELS, ARE GOOD FRIENDS...THEY ARE PEOPLE WHO HAVE EXPERIENCED HOLOCAUSTS.* A bottle exploded on Lord Big Apple's receding forehead. He threw his placard away, and ran as if Yihye Ayyash, the Hamas bomb maker, had set foot in his kibbutz.

Lyle and Connie ran and laughed at their ludicrous distress. They made their way to the park at the back of the Brooklyn Museum. Glad to be in one piece, they threw themselves on the grass and laughed endlessly. "I really liked the way the Adult Nigger rescued me from that sweet smelly ghost." Connie welcomed the grass as a cotton bed, and she closed her eyes. After five minutes she opened her eyes and stretched for a sip of Lyle's Trinidad solo. "Oh no!" she said. The aerated beverage spilled from her hand onto her dress. "Lyle, Lyle," she dug into his flesh and whispered, "don't you think it looks shorter, and it is following us?"

"What is?"

She pointed. "That *Grenada Ghost!*"

"You should have said your prayers before you slept, Connie. Leave that masquerader alone; that reveller must have run for his or her own safety. The Parkway is for everybody today." Lyle spoke convincingly to Connie, but he, too, had his doubts when he inhaled the ghost's perfume.

Dusk came.

"What were you scribbling all that time?" Lyle asked and raised himself from the cool grass.

"A draft of Maurice Bishop's bio: Born in Aruba; moved to Grenada as a kid; scholar. If ever there's a tombstone for Bishop, on it could be written: *Coup d'etat. Coup de grace. Coup de theater.* His Jewel Boys' motto was: Forward ever! Backward Never! What else would you add to Bishop's epitaph, Lyle?"

"That Maurice Bishop met Lord Lyle at Hunter College in New York."

"Is that really so?"

"I really met Maurice Bishop there, and I was moved by his address to Caribbean people. He was a gentle man with a positive goal."

"Poor Bishop. He meant well but he went about it the wrong way."

"Once its un-American, it's the wrong way?"

"I'm not saying that, Lyle."

"Then what do you mean? Forget it. Do you need help with those code names in the *Grenada Ghosts* band?"

"I knew all those code names and aliases of those West Indian politicians. For one thing, all those island politicians obey a kind of Salic law in their banana kingdoms. Power goes from Papa Doc to Baby Doc; from Cousin Busta to Uncle Norman, then to little Mikey—all in the family. Now the native inhabitants of Jamaica, moreso the selfish politicians, are pissed because alias Lord Sabga, who is really Prime Minister Seaga, was born in the United States. The defeated Manley and his boys are annoyed because Lord Sabga, whom they deemed an outsider, is in charge of the Jamaica pie. Whether or not Lord Sabga likes the U.S. policies, that's his democratic rights".

"Seems as though I've riled you, Connie," Lyle said.

"Yes," Connie said. "The first thing that I'll tell those placard bearers in my column tomorrow is that the majority of the people who are living in Grenada welcomed America's intervention. That invasion!...And all these placards about America's Watergate disgust me! Down there in the blue waters there are more Watergates than one can imagine. Your Caribbean politicians used all those Grants-in-Aid from the British for their social parties. At those parties Caribbean wannabes show off their British accents."

"Trinbagonians included?"

"Trinbagonians ditto...All that scandal in Pitch Lake Country about the gas station racket was never unfolded. You know why? Because press releases were applied instead of laws to punish the little Caesars...Nobody dare give the little Caesars a slap on their wrists." Connie studied Lyle's demeanor. "Oh yes, except for once. I read in Pitch Lake Country a lone jurist in that famous case, *The Man of Substance versus The Man of Straw*, said in his minority decision, 'Fellow judges, don't forget a check is cash.'"

"Why don't you try to cash Sir Lancelot's check. You remember Sir Lancelot from the President Jimmy Carter's cabinet?" Lyle grinned. "Tender his checks, and see if you'll get cash."

"That ain't funny. The egg and shell are."

"What's that? Who's that?"

"The-Ezla-girl-and-Shellyann-gyul act. The two chatterboxes who saw life through their mesdames' windows."

"Let's do something else and stop this bickering."

"I expected you to turn off course now that I'm attacking the blue Caribbean kind of politics."

"I read in Chappaquiddick they turned off course too. Make sure you buy a road map when next you summer there."

Connie was shocked by Lyle's quick retort. Her objectivity showed an imbalance in the same way Lyle's did. She forced a smile and said, "You and the other Labor Day hypocrites will surely read my by-lines for the whole week."

"Like what you'll write?"

"How you found your tongue since you came to America."

"Oh yeah!"

"Oh yeah!" She looked around. "Why is that *Grenada Ghost* following us, Lyle?"

"Maybe it's Maurice Bishop, and it wants you to write the truth, lady reporter. Bishop's body wasn't found, so maybe Bishop is alive, and he is still the Prime Minister of Grenada. Or, maybe, now that he's dead, he wants you to ask the administration in Washington why are they beating his drum posthumously. When Bishop was alive nobody didn't even burp on cotton and give him to smell."

"You West Indians say the funniest things. You may never know the power of this *Grenada Ghost*." She pointed at the masquerader that lurked two yards away. "Lyle, let's try to lose it. What if I invite you to my pad to read tea leaves."

"Sounds good to me, gypsy."

"Well, boy, leh we go 'ome an' see if I 'ave kosher

'amburger. Do I sound like Lord Goddard, the English limey, or like Lord Wooding, a member of Pitch Lake Country black bourgeoisie?"

"You can't speak black Inglish right, 'oman."

"Rat," she corrected him.

They chuckled, looked at each other, and expressed their desire with their eyes as they walked out of the park. Lyle more than ever believed that the carnival day magic worked for him as it had worked for his Grappa. As Connie and Lyle moved their bodies to the strains of sweet steelband music, he put his hand gently on her shoulders, and he drew her closer. He whispered, "I'm ready for my palms to be read, gypsy." He picked a leaf off a low lying cherry blossom and said, "I'm ready for your reading of tea leaves, ma'am. Start with this one."

"Here?" she asked.

"You prefer it to be at your place?" Lyle said.

"Why not! I live..."

"Don't tell me," Lyle said. "I bet you live in a place where you have to hide from ricocheting golf balls hit by the big boys in flannel trousers."

She looked at him quizzically. "Where?"

"Constance Wagner, who only travels on the Expressway, lives close to the ocean, in a place where, when snow falls, the snow is so high that the Feds send the National Guard to shovel her snow."

"I live in Brooklyn! Right in this neighborhood of Crown Heights!"

"Don't be so abrupt, ma'am. That's how you'll treat your underpaid interpreter?"

"I can smell your angle, Blackboy."

"Hurrah! Whitey lives near black people. I guess you are a Liberal, ma'am?"

"Mr. Adult Nigger, you are such a dumb fuck!...Taxi," Connie hailed. Lyle held her hand. They giggled, and ran into a yellow cab.

The day's diaspora had ended, but one *Grenada*

Ghost, still masked, noiselessly entered a gypsy cab, paid handsomely in advance, and motioned to the driver to trail the car that was ahead.

Chapter Nine

Connie's Fate

Perched on Club Grassport's barstool was Dalgo Gibbons, drugged from the intake of loafed liquor. His saliva spewed across the floor, and his revolving stool became stationary as he watched Connie lead Lyle to her apartment. Dalgo positioned himself; his back faced the street, and his panoramic view of the crossroads was by way of the mirrors in front and behind him. He looked at his pitiless face with regret, and his stubby fingers squeezed the drained glass that he held. Dalgo curved the tip of his red cap, and his dark shades hid his sunken eyes. He pulled a cigarette stub from his shirt pocket which had long lost its original color. From where Dalgo sat, his baggy trousers touched his flaky, size thirteen shoes. He again revolved his stool and gazed at the passersby in their seductive outdoor nightgowns. The prison archive stored Dalgo's fingerprints. He was a recidivist and barroom gossiper; when his game was slow, he moonlighted as a numbers runner and police informer, and when he earnestly sweated for hard-earned cash, he preyed on parked cars, stripped their parts and sold them to competing Brooklyn junkyards. Women accessorized Dalgo's life of crime for he had an obsession to touch their flesh. In the snaking subway cars he rubbed on the women with buxom bottoms till the swelling in his sweaty crotch appeared and disappeared.

Dalgo was not satisfied with the view from the mirrors so he came out of the bar and looked up the avenue.

Connie reached her destination on Kingston Avenue. She pushed the front door of her building, and Lyle walked in first.

"Such a beautiful 3-family house without a lock in

the main entrance," Lyle said.

"This part of Crown Heights is very safe. Do you know Crown Heights was first called Cow Hill, and at that time the investors stayed away?"

"Now it's prime real estate, and the Mayor's policemen are everywhere."

"I don't need the police because my landlords never sleep. They spend their lives watching over me."

"You mean peeping at you?"

"That's how you call it in Flatbush?" She smiled. They walked another flight of stairs, and she opened her door.

"Connie, your door doesn't even have a proper lock," Lyle said.

"Who needs it! My landlords come in as they very well please."

"How do you know?"

"My tape recorder doesn't lie, Lyle."

"How clever! You'll tape my visit, too?"

"Perhaps."

"Should I shut the door now or leave it open?"

"Close it gently." She kicked off her shoes. "Thanks for being my Labor Day adviser," she said. "You and my faithful tape recorder made my task exceedingly easy." She threw herself on the loveseat.

Lyle sat next to her. "It's nice to be in a quiet place for a change," he said.

She looked at him inquiringly and said, "You believed what those two women on the Parkway said about black men who kept company with white women?"

"What women?"

"The egg and shell—the two chatterboxes." She touched her buttocks to give Lyle a clue.

He laughed, but gave no opinion. "Oh them?"

She played with her long braids. "Do you know that I had admirers?"

"Who?"

"The Rastafarian couple who served us second hand smoke admired my braids. Their gorgeous locks touched their waists."

"And I caught myself forever looking at the toothy masquerader dentist who continually touched the women's tits and said that he was testing for circulatory distress." Lyle touched his chest playfully.

"He was a winner—wasn't he, Lyle?"

"Yeah."

"You wanted to be that kind of carnival dentist, too?"

"C'mon! I've already lost my religion, Connie."

"I know that."

"Well?"

"Speak the truth, for once, Lyle ."

"You really want a truthful answer?"

"Yes."

"Given the latitude that masquerader had, my answer would be yes. Does that satisfy you?"

"Yes." Connie got up. "This is where I live. No ricocheting golf balls fall on this avenue. Make yourself at home while I take a quick shower and slip into something more comfortable." She hummed the calypso *Sol Fish* and left her bathroom door ajar. "Lyle, where did calypsonians get the title 'lord'?" she asked, and stepped into the warm tub.

"I guess it's a sideshoot of their decolonization... Your pad is gorgeous."

"Thank you. Walk through the rubble, and you'll find the bar. Mix us two drinks." Half an hour later Connie spoke from her bedroom. "Lyle, how come people from the islands can be so edifying in speech even to the point of articulation, but as soon as they become excited, or as soon as they greet a down-home buddy, they turn English into a dialect. Is there grammar to their dialect?"

"Of course. Just take Ezla-gyul as our example. Even though she spoke in the vernacular yet she obeyed the rules of syntax. The spoken word doesn't depend on grammar though, because with the spoken word one gets the feel of the other person's retort. Cold print, even grammatically written, at times conveys the wrong message. Just picture yourself"—he looked at her wall and saw that it was not adorned like Billie Zellars'—"not because you haven't a photograph of yourself on the wall that means you never existed; the same goes for the vernacular and grammar—once there's the spoken word, there is grammar which comes in the form of intonation. Grammar is for the theoretician. I'm sure you'd prefer the hands of an ungrammatical plowman than that of a bastardly scholar."

"You lost me. You are as unspecific as Henry Kissinger, if that's at all possible. Nonetheless, I must say you defend the slaughters of the English language quite well. What was your major at college?"

"Life."

"I believe you." She looked into the mirror, sprayed her body with various jars of fragrances, and squeezed droplets of water from her braids.

"Connie, I found a penny in your kitchen. Where should I put it?"

"Keep it for good luck, Lyle."

"I'll keep it to remember the day that you were my understudy in the interpretation of Trinbago patois." He put the penny in his pocket.

"Here's something else to interpret, Lyle. While we were weaving through the crowd, a man said that his cheap partner only bought kakapool when it was his partner's turn to shop. What's kakapool?"

"That's low grade rum."

"And who's a fresh water Yankee?"

"An FWY is a West Indian who landed in America for the first time last Monday; he spent three days in Queens, two days in the Bronx, and ended up in Brooklyn on Labor Day with a Texan drawl."

"That sounds creative. At least, he got rid of that heavy Jamaican accent."

"Connie, all West Indians are not Jamaicans; and you, too, have an accent. Go to Arkansas, for example."

Connie came out of the bedroom with a blue gown, and Lyle handed her a glass of wine. She sat next to him on the large couch.

"What an adorable fragrance!" Lyle sniffed and sniffed.

"Is it as bad as that strayed *Grenada Ghost's*?"

"It's heavenly. I like it."

"Let's drink to our meeting." Connie raised her glass.

"To our meeting. Cheers," Lyle said. "I'm glad you took me as your guide. Did you enjoy your day's work?" He took a sip of his wine and glanced at the curves of her body.

"I did, even though I got the jitters whenever I saw the ghost that followed us. I was glad when we finally lost him. Thank God I'll never smell him again."

"That masquerader was clownishly disguised. You saw no part of that person's body. How could you say that masquerader was a he? Did you feel his genitals? It could have been a woman."

"I saw cracks in his façade," Connie emphasized. "Furthermore, a woman knows a man's stare even if she's blindfolded."

"I felt it was a woman, and I know a woman who bought that perfume."

"To use as an air refresher, I hope? I wouldn't class that as perfume. Your girlfriend buys that yukky stuff?"

"Naw."

"All the other ghosts had political placards, but that perfumed ghost had a placard about AUNT GINA. What was his point?"

"I say it was a she."

"Probably another glass of wine may drunken me into believing that that ghost was a woman." She poured wine into both glasses.

Lyle said, "I always wanted to be friendly with someone who writes for a big newspaper."

"What views you wanted to air, Lyle? Was it why the Rams' cheerleaders stopped showing their belly buttons to the disappointment of you sexist males?"

"Nope."

"Why Walter Mondale chose a woman to be his running mate for the Vice Presidency?"

"Nope. What I wanted to air on the Op-Ed page was why white folks moved away from Brooklyn when black folks moved in."

"Me? Where have I moved? I'm surrounded and outnumbered by blacks, plus one more."

"That's my new name: Plus-One-More? I'll tell my black Congressman about you people who refer to us by code names."

"And my upbeat Mayor knows that you refer to white people as 'the Man.' He even knows what black people say when white people aren't around." They laughed heartily. "In all seriousness," she said, "Lyle, what you really wanted to know: Why President Reagan didn't send reporters to cover the Grenada invasion?"

"My mind is not on politics."

"What's on your mind? You want me to probe it?" she repeated herself.

"Go-ahead."

"Well, tell me something specific about yourself."

"I've already told you, Connie, in the park about my boyhood in knee pants. I also told you, too, that I've lost my religion since I came to America, and it's time to get back to my Spiritual Baptist religion."

"Why do you harp on that?" She smiled.

"I do not like your half smile, 'oman."

"Sorry 'bout that. Then, tell me about your happy married life—I mean without the overworked philandering men's elegy." She studied him, and kept her half smile. "Oh yes! My wife and I live in the same house, but we hate each other's guts...She pays the grocery and telephone bills, and I meet the rent and car payments...We're just sticking it out until Mary

Lou graduates from college...We fight every night, et cetera...Omit those scenes. I'm used to those choruses from the young, the old, and the hotcrotch."

"My wife and I always fight, but our fights are about the spirit. When I catch the power, the spirit leads me to a different path from her. I went to her church, and I didn't even catch the power."

Connie didn't believe what she heard. She stuck her finger into her ears and searched for wax. She repeated the question, and Lyle repeated his answer. Instantly her uncontrolled laughter caused the wine to spill all over her gown. She rested her glass on the floor, but when she recovered from the volume of her laughter, she said haltingly, "Bruvver Lyle, I'm so glad we met, but I must also tell you that that's an original. If the *Grenada Ghosts* had heard you, they would have put down Grenada's cause and their hate for Ronald Reagan and, instead, put your grievance on their placards ...Men oh men! a special hell awaits you men for the lies you tell to gullible women."

"I'm talking the gospel, 'oman."

"Which gospel? Lord Lyle's brand of the synoptic gospel?"

"It's true, Connie."

"Give it to this sucker, boy. Whe' youse brung that ain't there's more any's sweeter? Jus' lick mama as candy, bruvver...Why don't you make beer commercials and air them on Superbowl Sunday, spirit boy?" Connie threw herself on the carpet and rolled, and her exposed legs revealed her sexy physique. She eventually got up and recited like an understudy who waited all her life to get her first leading role on Broadway. "Believers and nonbelievers, X-rated, and all of Hollywood, listen to me! I bring a vision from a brethren. At the fall of the curtain you must get rid of *Sanford and Son* and hire Lord and Lady Lyle for they fight for the spirit—that sweet, unbottled spirit. Hollywood, money is the name of the game. The box office will get millions from their spirit acts, and reruns will make even more money. Hallelujah!" She bowed at the end of her extemporaneous one-act recital.

Lyle applauded. "Connie, I can better explain in the vernacular, but you won't understand," he said.

"Youse no longer a meek bruvver but my beloved brethren. Brethren, I prefer you to answer me at a time when you catch the power and when you're in the spirit." She picked up her glass from the floor. "Brethren, since you and your spiritual mama don't agree, have you been committing spousal rape?"

"Sometimes."

"What if your spiritual mama takes you downtown before Justice Bruce Wright?"

"She won't."

"Not even to please the spirit?" Connie was pink.

"If you'll shut up, I'll tell you much more of my lost religion."

"Please."

Lyle told her of his acolyte days in Fyzabad with Leader Gerrol. He went into details about his Spiritual Baptist Shouter faith, and she listened intently.

She said, "I may even change my by-line about the Parkway hypocrites and write about the sweet spirits that fight in Flatbush. Why not come tomorrow and explain the spirit, how you catch the power when you are filled with the holy ghost, the purpose of the colors of your spiritual garbs, the duty of the bellringer, the center pole, the stargazers, and other voodoo-spiritual things."

"You breached your limit, Connie." Lyle's countenance became beastlike. "Why do white people think that black people's religion is voodoo?" He raised his voice. "My Baptist Shouter religion was deemed unlawful by the white colonial masters in my native country. On the 28th day of November 1917 all facets of the Shouter religion, even the way they mourned, were deemed unlawful behavior. That evil law remained for thirty-three prosecutorial years on the statute books all because of those WASPy expatriates. Why? One: The WASPs were prejudiced jackasses; and two: because the Shouter religion took away the white churches' members and depleted the white churches' money coffers. Many days my Grandpa, Aunt Gina, and I hid in the forest when our churches were raided during worship. So when you called my religion voodoo, I felt that you have recast me and my deceased Grandpa in the 1917 concrete of those bigots. Connie, why don't we talk about the next New York census instead? Or, do you prefer me to leave right now?"

"Now I know how to get under your collar, Mr. Cool. I see religion sets you on fire."

"How would you like someone to term your religion a white-washed sepulchre?"

"I'll surely be offended."

"Well?"

"I guess am still not fully purged of my 'inbred cultural imperialism.'" She touched Lyle gently, looked at him and said, "My humble apology, Lyle."

"It is sweetly accepted." He kissed her fingers. "Am sorry for raising my voice. My apology."

"It is just as sweetly accepted. Excuse me," she said. She went into the fridge. "Not one damn thing for my sweet tooth. Can I make you a kosher hamburger, Lyle?"

Lyle's laughter cracked the ice in his glass.

"What's so funny, dear?"

"I thought kosher hamburgers were only sold in New Jersey and served by only Shellyann's madam?"

"What did you expect? I'm the same kosher type as Shellyann's madam, except..."

"What?"

"I do not work cabaret hours." They chuckled. Connie hummed Lord Kitchener's *Flagwoman*. "Make up your mind, Mr. Plus-One-More." She looked into the fridge and then sang to Lyle. "Kosher once/ Kosher twice/ Kosher unsold." She sang the words to a calypso beat and rocked her body.

Lyle answered with a chorus: "I'll go for unsold./ Bam, bam!/ I like the way you rocked your body/ Bam, bam!/ But don't forget that I ate two giant-size roti./ Bam bam!/ Come and sit on my lap,/ And don't worry about feeding my belly./ Bam, bam."

"Okay, but you need voice training," Connie said.

"What you thought of the genius masquerader with the looking glass? What you saw when you looked into that clown's looking glass, Ms. Nosy?" Lyle teased her.

"Disgusting!" she got off his lap. "You were nosy, too. You, tell me first what you saw in the clown's looking glass." She held Lyle's hand.

"Disgusting!" Lyle said. "But interesting female parts."

"Dirty ole man...Let me tell you about this amusing saying that I heard. Let me see if I could remember it." She pondered a little. "Oh yes! Do you remember the tall guy in a yellow shirt and the Trinidad and Tobago hat?"

"Yes."

"Do you remember that he went into a guttural patois and said, 'Pardner, oh pardner, len' me you chinaman to throw some ledder on Miss Dominica to buss she up.' Why he wanted his partner's leather? And how does a chinaman help?"

Lyle's smile broadened into vulgar laughter.

"Did he intend to hurt Miss Dominica? Wouldn't that be a case of physical abuse, Lyle?"

"The answer is yes and no, Connie."

"What do you mean?"

"Honey, sometimes it's easier to act a word than to explain it to a foreigner, especially those down-home words."

"You get me there. All I can say is that your patois is phenomenal."

"As you are beautiful."

"You are quick with your similes."

"You really are beautiful, and you trust me,

especially to invite me on this block in Applesville that is guarded day and night by your Mayor's policemen."

"He's your Mayor, too."

"Yours."

"Ours."

"Yours."

"Ours."

"Yours."

"Ours."

"All right, ours."

"And repeat he's fair; because he calls a spade a spade regardless of whose spade it is. Repeat it."

"And the Mayor is fair; because he calls a spade a spade regardless of whose spade it is. That's really true." Lyle embraced her. "What's this?" His outstretched hand touched the dimmer within his reach. "I love playing with your lights." He dimmed them. He embraced her tighter and gently touched the nape of her neck. She leaned forward and stared at him. "Why are we talking so much, Connie?"

"You are; I'm not." She answered softly and rested her head on his chest. "Are you still mad with me?"

"Mad about you; that's how my madness goes."

She looked at him.

"Those are eyes of the Mormons or Shouter Baptist?" He played in her damp cornrows.

"I thought religion was off limit?"

"Sorry. Are you related to the famous Waltons?"

"Am not WASPish; and surely not John Boy."

"Sure glad you ain't, ma'am." His fingers moved up and down her diaphanous gown.

"What are you testing, sir?"

"Circulatory distress."

"Wall Street stenographers do that as part of their job description? I thought only that Park Street dentist was guilty of that charge."

"Me, too. I'm losing my balance."

"Does that mean that you are falling in love?"

"Falling? Your grammar is horrible. Try the vernacular." He looked at her, then drew her closer to him. He put his nostril on her chest, inhaled the scents that came from her bosom, and nibbled on the softness of her coathook breasts. She stood. The light was at its dimmest glow. He lifted her to the bedroom and placed her on the bed. A silhouetted frame bent first, and another followed in the darkness. There were muffled murmurings; then there was a long silence. Only Barbra Streisand's voice was heard above the rustle of silk sheets as the bedhead radio softly played *People*.

Lyle broke the silence and said, "Thank you, Connie. I do like your tea-reading technique."

"You are welcome," She looked at the wall clock and alarmed, "Can't believe it's this late! You'll get in trouble when you get home, my beloved brethren. Let me hear your excuse?"

"I'm a part-time musician. I'd *ad lib* when I get to that bar."

"You're so glib, brethren."

"I use the weapon I have."

"Just like Moses, he used his rod."

"Just like Moses, my beloved sister. I'll use my smarts." He held one of her braids and said, "Connie, do you know the dude with the dark shades who sat on the barstool at Club Grassport? I caught him staring at us in the mirror, and he particularly made a deep study of me."

"You saw all that with one blink?"

"In my daily ghetto drills I learned to walk and look at my shadow and at the traffic at the same time. Do you know him?"

"His name is Dalgo Gibbons. He's a numbers runner for a friend of mine who has a business on Fulton Street."

"Boyfriend?"

"An acquaintance. What's your concern?"

"I'm scared that Dalgo may spill the beans for a

drink of kakapool?"

"Dalgo Gibbon's taste is much more expensive."

"What if he reports on you?"

"Reports what? And to whom? You are the one who lives in a psychic household. You are the one who really needs an excuse for your whereabouts."

"That's true."

"Is Elizabeth the only one you owe an excuse for your absence today...tonight?"

"Sure." The lie showed in Lyle's voice. He immediately thought of Billie. Quickly, he said, "Is that a poem in your bedhead?"

"Oh yes. Do you like poetry?"

"Am not crazy about it. An old headteacher by the name of Mr. Tellymack made a catechism out of Leigh Hunt's *Abou Ben Adhem*. He overworked that poem, and me. I think I have a testimonial somewhere for recitation. The last place I saw that Fyzabad testimonial was with the rat poison in Aunt Lily's house."

"Who's Aunt Lily?"

"Let's not get into that tonight."

"Then prove that you had a testimonial for recitation." They eased closer to the poem. "Read the poem aloud, Lyle."

"As the duo with the mandate left the stage,
The once-cheering crowd brickbatted.
That historic day, Mama had no bread;
Yet I need no bread attached to a scythe and
hammer in a land of dead Sputniks.
Offer me victual, without the taste of freedom,
And I'll opt to walk with my shadow and sinners.
I hate color codes for my Constitution is colorblind;
The stars and stripes—Old Glory—is my flag,
And this rich land of freedom is my only home."

"You read it with feeling, Lyle. You're great! Aren't

they beautiful lines?"

"Somewhat. What it's all about: That Russia is advanced in science and technology, but to get food in Russia you have to work for it? If that's the interpretation, what's so wrong about that?"

"You give me the impression that you are nihilistic?"

"Are you saying that I believe in nothing? I believe in something."

"What?"

"That in any society, be it Russia or America, whoever becomes king, we'll still be servants."

"You, not me!"

"Just as I thought. You are not with the oppressed; and you have that stone man to watch over you."

She got off the bed, walked to a large stone sculpture in her bedroom, and patted it. "Tell Lyle, Moses, that you watch over me...Back to the poem, what do you think, Lyle?"

"Are you the poet-laureate?"

"Tell me, don't you think it's great?"

"I'm sure it's not one of us who wrote that poem!"

"What do you mean by one of us?"

"Black like me!"

"A black American was the author." She stood still as if to mark the author's memory. She spoke softly and said, "Johnny was my friend. He died in Vietnam, and that verse of his poem was the only thing I salvaged to remind me of his life and our love. The wet words were in his wet pants, and I dried those words. That's why the print is so blotchy."

Lyle got off the bed and said, "I'm sorry. So many of them died in vain. We are all pawns for the prospectors and money mongrels." He walked away and showered. She followed him.

She dried her body on the bed and finished her wine. "Lyle, please fetch me my tape recorder," she said. "There's a blank 90-minute reel in it. When you leave, I'll be recording after I take a quick nap."

"The landlords' voices?"

"They don't come when I'm at home. I'm sure they had a good look at you when you came up those stairs."

"I'll make sure that I go down on my toes. What are you doing now?"

"An outline of Labor Day in Brooklyn. Should I mention you as my guide?"

Lyle didn't answer her. "Hey, sister," he caressed her face, "look at what the Labor Day sun has done to your complexion? You can now make Jet Magazine center page."

"No, brethren, right now I'm too dark for Jet center page."

"Funny, funny."

"True, true."

"I always heard that your kind are devils."

"That's the real code name for us, whiteys...This devil wants your work address and telephone number. Or, do you want to give me the code that your commercial lovers use to call your home? I want to hear more of your religion before you abscond the ship."

"I love your ship, captain." Lyle took a blank pad from Connie's night table, and he scribbled his name, office address, and office phone number. He stopped writing abruptly. "On second thought, there's no need to leave this. I'll be back tomorrow." He tore out the sheet from the pad and put the piece of paper in his hip pocket. "You'll see me tomorrow when I pick up my belt and costume. I only hope Mr. Gibbons won't be waiting around to see me leaving with less clothes."

"Why would Dalgo be waiting on you, Lyle; except, of course, he's the perfumed *Grenada Ghost* that followed us?"

"I maintain that masquerader was a woman." Lyle looked at his watch. It was 2:00 A.M. He was already dressed in his gray sweat pants and black T-shirt. "Connie," he said, "can I pick up my jumper costume tomorrow?"

"Why?"

"Because it's late; I'm out of my neighborhood; and the words 'Adult Nigger' may rile those white policemen down the block."

"I don't see how."

"You wouldn't know how. To know how is to be born black...to be on the street at nights with a black face and funny clothes...You are not on the side of the oppressed today; in Hitler's time, your people were. My kind are the eternally oppressed."

"Get off that oppressed shit! What part of you is oppressed?"

"It's too late for a debate. Just tell me, lady, if I could leave my jumpsuit costume in your home until tomorrow?"

"Suit yourself."

"I thank you kindly." He put his jumpsuit on the chair. He looked at his prize belt, and, strangely, for the first time in many years, the belt reminded him of Spree's defeat at the greasypole competition. Lyle vividly recalled the unceremonious plight of Spree's family and how Fyzabadians treated them as pariahs. "No such thing as *Payback*." he mumbled.

"Are you still there? Payback to whom?" Connie asked.

"I'm talking to myself." He moved his belt and hung it on the bedpost closer to her.

"Please leave, and stop that belt buckle from jingling in my ear...You're outliving your welcome...Don't forget to put my tape recorder near to me. I've already put a 90-minute blank tape in it." She rested her head gently on her pillow and coaxed herself to sleep.

Lyle touched her. "Connie, what's the name of the stone man in your bedroom?"

"Moses...Go away."

"Moses? What he's doing here?"

"Don't forget this is my place, sir."

"Why is Moses in your bedroom, madam?"

"That's my business."

"Do you worship him?"

"When I catch the power."

"Why don't you donate Moses to the Brooklyn Museum and claim an exemption on your taxes?"

"Are you crazy!" The sleep left Connie's eyes. "That's my handiwork. Johnny and I worked on that sculpture. It took ten men to bring the raw stone inside; it took me five years to sculpture it to this point; and it may take another five years to bring it to a Dogon *Horse and Rider*. And, furthermore, it relieves me of stress. Why am I telling you all this! Goodnight!" She wrapped herself completely in two sheets, and covered her head tightly.

"Dream of me, and not about that smelly *Grenada Ghost*," Lyle said. He went into her fridge and ate two slices of meat. "Kosher tastes good, damn good," he said, and smiled. He washed his hands. With a towel in his hand, he picked up the tape recorder. He depressed the 'record' button with the towel; his finger did not touch any part of the tape recorder. For that matter, he never touched the tape recorder for the entire day. In an imitated voice he spoke into the little recorder and said, "You'll never guess who, white girl." He inconspicuously covered the little tape recorder with the towel. He closed the door softly, and tiptoed so noiselessly that even the watchful landlords did not hear when he left Connie's apartment. He walked north on Kingston Avenue. He avoided a mumbling drunk who crouched his body, and he crossed the street and hailed a taxi as he observed three loiterers slightly ahead of him. He jumped into the taxi and went home.

Three people observed Lyle's departure: Dalgo was one of them; a blundering street walker, who submerged into the Kingston Avenue subway and again emerged, was another; and a frocked figure, who eyed the crossroads and walked up Kingston Avenue, was that third person.

It was 2.30 A.M. when Mabel and Harvey Plutz, the landlords, heard footsteps.

"It's long after midnight. See who's going upstairs again, Harvey," Mabel instructed her husband.

"My arthritis hurts, Mabel. You know she likes Sambos. Probably this Sambo went for more booze. I refuse to look at him again. This bleep Waganer woman is what reformists are all about. Riffraffs! Moshiach got to be on his way."

"You talk too much, Harvey. See who's going upstairs."

"No."

"Are you jealous because that *yakahoola* man is going upstairs to indulge in smut, Harvey?"

"Why should I be?"

"I can make you from clay, Harvey."

The footsteps echoed softly up to Connie's door. A gloved hand tested the door. The door was sturdy, but its lock was an easy mortise and tenon combination. Carefully and noiselessly, the trained fingers put a flat plastic object between the lock and the wood, and Connie's door opened with a soft snap.

The intruder walked in like a cat and groped for his or her bearings.

Connie was asleep. The dim glow of light showed her face; and her face revealed a smile of satisfaction. Her pillow held a golden strand of hair; and Lyle's masculine odor was on the sheets which thoroughly wrapped her body. The intruder came over Connie and stopped immediately. The intruder stretched for something and smiled in the darkness. The intruder remained committed and did his or her bidding in the darkness. The intruder meant to walk away, but the intruder's body knocked the bed and Lyle's belt fell on Connie. Instinctively, Connie said, "Lyle, you're still here?" None one answered. "Lyle, Lyle," Connie said again. None one answered. Connie inhaled a familiar scent. She blinked her eyes under the sheets. She opened her eyes slowly, then uttered inaudibly, confusingly, and unintelligibly, "No! No! I'm dreaming. You! You! It's you? No! Perfume! Perfume! No! Air refresher." She tried to unwrap herself from the sheets. She tried to scream, but the unknown person blocked her mouth, and kept her wrapped in a vigorous brace-hold. Connie struggled, and struggled, and finally one of her hands got free. With the last gasp of breath, and with a whirlwind pull, she pulled away, but she was still blinded by the sheets. The unknown person tried to hold her, but Connie stumbled and fell. She hit her head on the base of Moses, and the impact of the blow on the sculpture silenced her forever.

The intruder hung the belt back on the bedpost and waited quietly in the darkness. The dim room became a darkened room. There was a sporadic jingle in the darkness, and the radio gave the pre-recorded news:

This is a late news item. Labor Day in Brooklyn drew more than a million people to Eastern Parkway. The day, however, was marred by late frolicking which is commonly called Las' Lap. Hundreds of people were crushed, and it's a miracle that nobody died in the melee. Someone who refused to give his or her name, called the news desk and said that the stampede was due to the ingenuity—if I may call the trampling of human bodies ingenuity—of a member of the *Grenada Ghost* band. The caller said that the band was late for the competition because of political stomping, and in order to find a way through the crowd, a member of the band fired a shot into the air. When the crowd scattered, the Ghost band got the space that they needed to jump to their road march *Flagwoman*; and they reached the judges' platform on time...As a personal remark, one doesn't have to live in Washington to practice dirty politics...New

York's Finest is investigating.

The intruder ended the fidgeting with jingling objects. The intruder unhung the telephone. The intruder rend a letter from his or her costumed garment. The patient intruder scrawled the last three words of the poem in the bedhead, "my only home." The intruder finally fitted himself or herself in Lyle's jumpsuit costume, and the person rested the belt on Connie's neck.

"Didn't you hear something fall upstairs, Harvey?" Mabel asked. Mabel stood before the sink and gargled her throat with warm seltzer water.

"Shsh. I hear someone coming downstairs," Harvey said.

"Why don't you look this time, Harvey?"

"Harvey poked his eyes in the authentic peephole and said, "It's the Adult Nigger. He's leaving; but his clothes don't fit him now...Like he has outgrown his clothes...He's hiding his face...I'm sure that schlepp told him what we are."

"He had too much of whatever he had, Harvey, to know what we are. One piece from a real woman is never enough for that kind of man."

"Do you know about that kind of *yakahoola* man, too, Mabel?" Harvey stopped caressing his arthritic leg, and his eyes searched his wife's pupils.

"Know about him? In what sense, Harvey?" Her eyes matched his stares.

"The biblical sense, Mabel."

"What do you mean, Harvey?"

"Joseph didn't know Mary, yet the Savior was born—in that sense, Mabel?"

"You know we don't believe in myths, Harvey." She walked slowly into the kitchen and drank the remaining lukewarm seltzer water from a tumbler. They finally went to bed, but something more than his arthritic body, seriously bothered Harvey Plutz.

Chapter Ten

The Culprit

Mabel and Harvey Plutz awoke early and, as was their custom, they peeped through a crack in the door and through the carpenter's peephole to see the exits of all their tenants. Connie never came down, and not seeing her bothered Mabel.

"Harvey, you are the man in the house. Go upstairs and behave like a man. Go and tell that woman that you won't tolerate that kind of *yakahoola*, that kind of vulgarity, she had in our house last night." Mabel sat on her easy chair, sipped her coffee, and gave instructions.

"My arthritis hurts," Harvey said. "Why can't I sit and rock, too?"

"Use your cane, dammit! You need to exercise your legs."

"All right; but I'm still waiting on an answer to my question last night."

Mabel paid her husband no mind. "Go now and let that *yakahoola* woman know how she and Sambo disturbed us from sleeping last night. I'll be standing right here in front of this door if she gives you an argument. That Little-Miss-Uppity-with-the-one-short-black dress thinks because she's a reporter she alone knows the law. Tell her, Harvey, that three of my boys are DA's and my daughter is married to Judge Weinstein. Wench!"

"I'm going...I'll tell her." Harvey banged his cane in disgust as he hobbled up every treadle of the steps. He found Connie's door ajar. He knocked. She did not answer. "The door is open, but she's not answering." He shouted to Mabel.

"Go inside. It's our house. You're within your rights. Bang your cane. Wake her up. Pay her back because we couldn't sleep last night." Mabel waited on a fresh flow of air to fill her lungs, and she inhaled deeply when she felt it. After her instructions, she walked slowly to her chair and slumped in it.

Harvey mumbled to himself. "I always have to come upstairs to this woman." He hit Connie's furniture with his cane and spoke to them. "If that Waganer woman would behave, I would live in peace with my miserable wife." He hobbled to the bedroom door; he knocked the door with his cane; and there was no response to his inquiry. Slowly, he poked his head, and jerked it back. "Shit! It's Moses. That stony bastard always gives me the creeps." Harvey rested a bit. In his urgency, he put his weight on his cane and went in. He observed a long lump under a cluster of sheets. He went closer, and he looked at the sheets. He saw a belt. The belt rested across the neck of Connie's lifeless body. Harvey gasped at its sight. He became speechless. Then he spoke. "My god! My god! Sambo strangled her." He turned around in extreme haste, and his feet and his cane made staccato beats as he hop-walked down the stairs.

"You're going to damage the steps, Harvey. I just paid to have them repaired. Did you tell that no-good woman what I said?"

Harvey panted, and panted. He couldn't answer.

"Did you tell that wench what I told you, Harvey?"

He panted louder. He caught the room's air before he answered. "No."

"Why?"

"She's dead. A belt is on her neck. Sambo strangled her. Call the police...Call 911."

* * * * * *

Homicide visited the scene with its battery of experts.

* * * * * *

Detective Crobett introduced himself. "May I come in?"

"Come in, please. We are waiting on you. I am Mabel Plutz. He is Harvey. I saw the killer's face...The Adult Nigger...You can ask my husband. He saw him, too. Didn't you, Harvey?"

"Be calm, Mrs. Plutz," Detective Crobett said. "Who discovered the body?"

"Tell him, Harvey."

"I did," Harvey said.

"Did you touch her, or anything, Harvey?" Detective Crobett asked.

"No."

"You're sure now, Harvey?"

"All I touched was the door with my cane... nothing else."

"What were you doing in her apartment that early hour of the morning, Harvey?"

Harvey looked at his wife.

"Tell Mr. Crow the truth, Harvey."

The detective corrected her. "Crobett."

"What were you doing in Miss Wagner's apartment, Mr. Plutz?"

"I went to tell her about her behavior last night."

"What she did?"

Harvey did not answer.

"Did you see anybody go upstairs to her apartment?" Detective Crobett asked.

"Well...well..." Harvey fumbled. "I saw a face last night, but I don't know if...The face I saw...well...."

Mabel spoke. "Didn't you say that you saw Sambo, the one who strangled her with the belt?"

"Who's Sambo?" Detective Crobett interrupted.

"I just made up that name," Harvey answered.

"How did you know that she was strangled, Harvey?"

"I came to that conclusion by myself."

"Just like that?"

"Yes, just like that."

"You didn't touch her neck or look at bruises?"

"No."

"But you are sure, Harvey, that you saw this person who wore the costume with the writing *The Adult Nigger*?"

"Yes."

"And he went upstairs with Ms. Wagner?"

"Mr. Detective," Mabel interrupted, "I saw him through this hole, and Harvey saw him through that hole." She pointed to the peephole in the door and to a crack above the door. "He had on this cloak or costume that said 'The Adult Nigger,' and I saw his face. Harvey is afraid to talk because his arthritis is bothering him."

"Harvey, please tell me what you saw. Besides the costume, what does this person look like? His weight? His height?" Detective Crobett blocked Mabel from looking at Harvey, but Harvey looked at her nonetheless. "You'll be protected by the law, Harvey. I give you my word." Detective Crobett looked at Harvey. "Would you be able to identify the person?"

"Sure," Mabel said. "I saw him going upstairs with her. He left, and he came back because they had an argument."

"How could you tell from down here?"

"You are a detective, and you don't know what an argument sounds like, especially the *yakahoola* kind, Mr Crow?"

"Crobett."

"Whatever," Mabel continued. "Then I heard something fall. Harvey even looked after we heard the noise because they prevented us from sleeping last night. And we saw him coming down—that Adult Nigger— after they made all that *yakahoola* last night... all that sickening stuff..."

"Harvey, is that true?" Detective Crobett inquired.

"Let me sit."

"Sure. Go right ahead. Make yourself comfortable," Detective Crobett said.

Harvey continued. "The first time he went upstairs..."

"Who?" Detective Crobett asked.

"The first Adult Nigger."

"You mean there were others?"

"Mr. Crow, Harvey's arthritis is flaring up. He's getting mixed up."

"Mrs. Plutz, please let your husband continue."

"But he's making mistakes."

"That's all right. I make mistakes, too. I call people by the wrong names. I give the wrong time of the day. I, too, have arthritis, and know how difficult it is to get my train of thought flowing, especially when I'm in pain. This is just a preliminary investigation, Harvey. There's nothing to be afraid of. Be free to talk."

"The first time that he went upstairs he looked different from the second time." Harvey looked at Mabel when he spoke. Mabel did not interrupt him this time. "The second time his clothes fitted funny like if it wasn't his clothes."

Mabel interrupted her husband. "Because he was drunk! That's why! With all that liquor he swallowed down his throat, you don't expect him to wear his clothes right, Harvey," Mabel reasoned.

"May I say a word, Mrs. Plutz?" Detective Crobett said.

"Sure. I'm not preventing you." Mabel looked at the detective.

"Thank you...Mr. Plutz, if you see this person again, whether he is drunk or sober, would you be able to identify him as the person who went upstairs?" Detective Crobett waited on Harvey's answer.

"Only if he's the same person who did not hide his face. The second person could have been a man or a woman because I didn't see the second person's face."

"So you couldn't be sure if it were one and the same person, Harvey?" Detective Crobett said.

"No."

Mabel spoke with certainty. "I know the Adult Nigger is the culprit!" She looked at her husband with pity. "Time to take your pills...Harvey, you know those kind of people look different when they drink too much alcohol. You know that, too, Mr. Crow."

"No, I don't...Thank you, Mr. and Mrs. Plutz for your help. Homicide will contact you again. Goodbye."

"Goodbye, Mr. Crow," Mabel said.

"One more thing, Mabel, how do you know that— what's that word again?"

"*Yakahoola* —that vulgar thing. You never heard about *yakahoola* before?"

"Coming to think of it, yes. The word is new to me; but I did hear that word on a Bill Mazer's WEVD radio show." The detective spoke chummily for a while with Mabel, then he said casually, "Mabel, how did you find out that *yakahoola* was taking place upstairs?"

"You are a detective, but I am a woman. I saw the Adult Nigger going upstairs, and I know the difference between when a man is going to *get* instructions and when he is going to *give* instructions. Shalom, Mr. Crow."

"Shalom, Mrs. Plutz."

Detective Crobett laughed aloud when he switched on his 1969 Buick and thought of his wife. "Mr. Crow," he called himself and laughed vulgarly. "Mrs. Crow, tonight your Mr. Crow is coming home to *give* instructions...Eh, eh, listen to me, honey...Take my instructions...You better do as I say. There'll be no Christian fellowship tonight. Just *yakahoola*!"

Chapter Eleven

Two Scraps of Paper

Nigel walked into the kitchen, picked up two crumpled sheets of paper from the floor, and read them. He immediately alternated his gaze. He gazed at Lyle and then comically at the scraps of paper. "ASDFLKJ is on this sheet," Nigel said, "and, daddy, on this sheet I see your name, your business address, and phone number. Was this information for the Social Security Administration for them to calculate your nest egg?"

Lyle laughed and bit a piece of Nigel's toast. "Those scraps fell out of my pocket. Give them to me."

"Not today," Nigel said.

"Why are you keeping them?"

"As a keepsake."

"For what purpose?"

"You'd find out."

"Would you be playing those detective games as when you and Lord Meath were children?"

"Probably."

"Don't forget that I'm not Eggie and Bob, those two old people in the corner store whom you cheated and gave hell."

"You have no candies in your jar for me to steal, and I'm not in a hellish mood this morning."

"Then why do you want those two scraps of paper?"

"Because sometimes we run out of toilet paper in this joint due of your Caribbean-trained wife." Nigel pulled up his chair closer to Lyle and inhaled the aroma of the coffee, eggs, and toast that Elizabeth prepared for him. "Isn't your lovely wife a good cook?"

"Son, she's a great cook, and she's preparing something special for me to take to work this morning; but her hot mouth and nasty temper are just as great, even greater."

Nigel poured his coffee and sang an improvisation to his favorite kindergarten song. "Scraps of paper lying on the floor...lying on the floor...lying on the floor...I know why I picked them up...Don't you know?" He looked at his father quizzically and said, "Aren't you going to help me sing?"

"All right, Mr. Detective. I can read what is taking place at the back of your head. I know what you are thinking so I'll try to convince you about those two scraps of paper," Lyle said.

"No truth dumping this morning," Nigel emphasized.

"So you, too, think I tell tales." Lyle shook his head and smiled. "I can't win in this family."

Nigel dipped his finger into his coffee, and he let the coffee drip from his finger to his tongue. He stuttered and said, "I'm really enjoying this post-Labor Day breakfast with the best father in the Borough of Brooklyn."

"If you are sweet talking me for a loan, son, let me tell you that I, too, am broke. Since I got rid of Leaky it seemed as if I'm cursed. If you really need a loan, go to your mother. She has three unknown bankbooks, and, for sure, a fourth that's hidden in her mattress."

"I have a different agenda today." Nigel playfully dangled the two sheets of paper. "I'm only interested in the paper trail."

"Let me see that sheet with ASDFLKJ."

"Only from a distance." He showed it to his father. "You may begin your believable discourse. I really want to hear it."

Lyle took Nigel's fork and tasted the scrambled eggs. He again lifted the fork to his mouth, and his eyes met Nigel's. "All right. A-S-D-F-L-K-J was my first typing lesson, but I was forced to type those letters around 4.55 p.m. on Friday last to pretend to Miss Gennoyer that I was officially busy."

"Why?"

"That's a long story. I won't even go there."

"You won that round." Father and son knocked their cups and laughed like in the days when Lyle told his Fyzabad stories. "Now tell me about the other crucial scrap of paper with your handwritten name, your business address, and phone number." Again Nigel dangled the sheet of paper in front of Lyle. "A scrap of paper, eh?...It looks like an exhibit on its way to the toolbox to be safe from prying eyes." Nigel imitated his father's mannerisms. In childhood, Lyle often searched Nigel's scrappy school bag as if Nigel's school bag contained a clue to a murder.

"I see that the tail is now wagging the dog, as my Fyzabad schoolmaster, Mr. Tellymack, would say."

"Don't forget that your Mr. Tellymack also said that there were three sides to a spongy story: side A, side B, and the sponge's side. Which version of the sponge you'd be presenting today, Papa?" Nigel called his father Papa whenever he teased him.

"The truth is that I'd written that information for a friend, but I took it back."

"The friend works for the Social Security Administration? I didn't know you are sixty-five."

"No."

"He didn't need it again, my dear Papa?" Nigel smiled, but he did not look up. He stirred Elizabeth's home-made orange juice with his finger and searched for the pulps at the bottom of the glass. "So, Papa, he didn't..." Nigel was interrupted.

Elizabeth appeared from behind the opaque curtain and said sarcastically, "It's a she working bedroom hours, not a he."

"Uh-oh! Where were you, Ma?" Nigel said.

"This Caribbean-trained woman with four bankbooks that belong to her, with prying eyes, with a hot mouth, and with a nasty temper, lives here."

"I said all that, Ma?" Nigel asked apologetically.

"Whatever you said, you said. A real man backs up whatever he says."

"Excuse me, folks." Nigel got up. "It's time to get dressed. Lord Meath will be here any minute now. We have business to take care of." He walked away.

"Lord Meath still does your homework, son?" Lyle shouted.

"Yes, Papa." He answered from his old bedroom.

The buzzer rang with a familiar code ring, and Elizabeth went to the door. "That's Lord Meath's buzzes all right." She opened the door. "Lord Meath, we just called your name."

"Speak of the devil," Tommy said.

"You ain't no devil, boy," Elizabeth replied.

"That's what some people call us." Tommy smiled and kissed her.

"If a devil were like you, Lord Meath, I'll surely not want to go to heaven with my husband."

"Is something wrong, Mrs. Gordon?"

"Life couldn't be better, child...What about breakfast, m'Lord?"

"Let's give it a rain check. My loving Kate just gave me a County Meath hungerbuster. It was sumptuous."

"How is she?"

"Mother is well. She's thinking of giving up her practice."

"*Pro bono* work is getting to her? Tell her to stay on the job because I may need a lawyer soon."

"For what?"

"One can never tell...Anyhow, what brought you here this early?"

"Nigel and I have to see our favorite D.A. this morning."

"Are you referring to Kid Raggy Beerman? The kid who vomited on my new carpet after he drank his very first can of beer?"

"That's the one. He's no more a kid; he's a grown

man. His next move after D.A. is to be the Mayor of
New York, then a senator."

"I knew that kid had a head on his shoulder. Tell
Kid Raggy he owes me a visit."

"Sure will, Miss Liz. What else to tell him, Miss
Lizzy ma'am?" Tommy changed his voice and clowned.

"I see that you, too, are in the teasing mood this
morning. Your pal was just teasing Lyle about Lyle's
Labor Day frolicking absenteeism."

"What do you mean? No, no! Don't tell me. Let me
guess. You mean that your honey missed the carnival
parade on the Parkway yesterday? He had never missed
it before as far as I could remember. How come he
missed the bacchanal on the Parkway this year? You
remember in the past when he came home from the
parade he used to say, 'Bacchanal, bacchanal...That
was mas' in you wire...Put ice in you ice...Fete fo' so...'
What was the other thing that he used to say? I
remember now. 'Liz gyul, that was people galore on
the Parkway!'"

"You have a good memory. That was since we lived
in the other house, and we are living here in the
Pastalaqua House more than ten years now."

"Of course my memory is good. Am not as old
as you folks."

"Watch your mouth, young man."

"Does my breath bother you?"

"Yes." They laughed, and they remained in the foyer.

"Mrs. Gordon, your husband really missed the
parade this year?"

"He did not miss it this year either. He just did not
take me with him, and I'm still mad."

"Was there a reason why?"

"You have been around us for umpteen years.
You're family. You know why." She looked at him, and
his smile was comforting. "You are such a handsome
kid," Elizabeth said. "Tell the girl of your dreams that
Kate and I have to give the okay."

Tommy blushed and said, "Did you go to the Parkway by yourself or with Miss Hettie?" She ignored Tommy's question. She held his hand, and walked him to the kitchen.

"Good morning, Mr. Gordon," Tommy said.

"Is that you, Lord Meath?"

"In person. Here I am."

"You got to do better than that, Irish boy." Lyle got up. He and Tommy embraced, laughed, pointed their index finger at each other, sang their greeting song, and jigged: "Am gonna whip you, boy, just like Mr. Tellymack used to whip me...You! Me! You! Me!" Lyle alone said the last word, and Tommy sat on the vacant chair around the table.

Lyle said, "So you're now a big private detective. You got my boy settled in a job, I see. Are you still doing his homework?"

"He's teaching me a thing or two now."

"Nigel told me that police info is hard to come by."

"Kid Raggy Beerman is always there for us. We get the scoop from him. Incidentally, we're on our way to see him this morning on an immigration matter."

"My god! What about Kid Raggy?" Lyle said. He looked at Elizabeth. She again ignored him. "Don't tell me not to recycle the-Kid-Raggy act again." Lyle got up and said, "Look at me, Lord Meath, doing the Kid-Raggy-Beerman version with all the antics of Kid Raggy himself." Lyle looked at Elizabeth, her mouth pouted, and he said, "Those who wish to look on at what took place on that memorable day when the kid held my hand and appealed to me may do so." Lyle held on to a chair and addressed the chair. "Mr. Gordon, I'm drunk. This is how you feel, Mr. Gordon, when you, too, are drunk? I didn't know that I would feel this way after my very first beer." Lyle stumbled and pretended that he vomited. He again held the chair and spoke to it. "I'm sorry for dirtying the carpet, Mr. Gordon. I didn't like when you first called me Kid

Raggy, but you could now give me that nickname forever. You could even call me Kid Raggy Beerman, but don't tell my mother that Donald stole two cans of beer from Eggie and Bob's, and he gave me, this little sixth grader, one. If my mother knows she'll boil me in her Spanish blood. And, for sure, my mother Rita would curse Eggie and Bob in Spanish and English. And, Mr. Gordon," Lyle shook the chair to get the chair's attention, "I'll lose my little cleaning job with Eggie and Bob's. Now who would employ little me and give me real money?" Lyle released the chair, and he held Tommy's hand. Faked tears streamed from Lyle's eyes as he addressed Tommy. "Mr. Gordon, I'll clean your windows; I'll shampoo the carpet; I'll do anything, but don't tell Rita, please. You promise, Mr. Gordon." Lyle ended his show.

"I never knew all that went on when Kid Raggy vomited on your carpet?" Tommy said.

"More than that...It's ages since I've seen Kid Raggy. Tell him that he didn't keep his promise; and he still owes me one." Lyle laughed as if the incident were happening.

Nigel, fully dressed, walked into the kitchen. "Who are you talking about, Pa?"

"Kid Raggy," Lyle answered. "What's new with that kid?"

"The same thing," Tommy and Nigel chanted in unison.

"You mean he still has the same appetite for...?"

"The same thing," Nigel and Tommy said louder. "Next case," Nigel said.

"Lord Meath," Lyle said, "when are you and Nigel going to open your own detective agency and hire me as your stenographer?"

Elizabeth found her voice. Her voice was piercing. "Don't hire him. He'll be absent on Labor Days, and that's bad for your kind of business."

Nigel spoke softly and quickly to Tommy. "Oh-oh!

Let's go. I smell smoke."

"The fire is coming as soon as we leave," Tommy said in a whisper.

"Daddy, you left your I.D. at home yesterday," Nigel said.

"I know. Yesterday was Labor Day. I didn't need it," Lyle replied.

"Lord Meath and I are leaving, folks. Stay away from the patois. Talk English," Nigel said. He and Tommy eventually left and discussed Elizabeth and Lyle as they drove Downtown to meet Tito Natividad, a/k/a Kid Raggy Beerman, the prominent District Attorney. "Lord Meath," Nigel said, "if only Liz and Lyle could stay away from their Fyzabad lingo this morning, their day would go smoothly. Their patois loosens their tongues, and it becomes an aphrodisiac for their spleen."

"Liz complained to me about Lyle as I entered the door," Tommy informed his partner

"About what?"

"She didn't say, but I alluded that it was about Lyle's over friendliness with the opposite sex. She's such a beautiful woman, but..."

"She lacks confidence in herself." Nigel ended Tommy's sentence. "If that's the case, I'm sure Lyle wouldn't be eating his special breakfast or taking his special lunch to work today. He'd be snatching his briefcase alone and running off to catch the big underground 4."

"That New York City subway really carries a variety of souls in distress...Is Lyle afraid of Liz?"

"Not of her, but of her impulsive actions."

"And imagination."

Nigel looked at Tommy intently and, hesitatingly, said, "I wished I knew of the Sullivans as you know of the Gordons."

"You are to blame. You are the one who stayed away from the Sullivans as if we are lepers."

"Don't start that shit this morning."

"What shit am starting?"

"I know you."

"And we know each other."

"Why are we in this car?"

"I thought we were going to see Kid Raggy on the immigration matter." They looked at each other and smiled warmly.

"By the way," Nigel said after a short silence, "Lord Meath, cover for me for two days. I'll be out of town and cannot be reached."

"Are you going to visit your old Sunday school flame, Sheila, in Georgia?"

"No."

"Why?"

"Because Sheila is now a married woman."

"I never looked at you as a man with morals. Young man, I'm deeply touched by your utterance."

"Age brings reason even to the young."

Tommy shook his head mockingly. "Now I know the reason why you no longer go with Liz to Leader Dollon's church. Like father, like son."

"You're telling me that every apple falls near the tree trunk?"

"All I would say is that if Leader Dollon were hip to your wrongdoing when you were in his Sunday school class, he would have put a camera in the basement to follow your fingers."

"Are you going to cover for me—yes or no?"

"Yes, Sunday school playboy. With pleasure!"

"Then, driver, look at the traffic and stop your sinful talk."

Their laugher echoed throughout the downtown Brooklyn Civic Center.

* * * * * *

"What's the hurry, Lyle?" Elizabeth asked, and she cut off the space in the kitchen as if she were a trained boxer.

"I'm going to work," he answered, and he tried not to touch her. Lyle looked into the magnet mirror that was stuck on the fridge, and he straightened his silk tie. "How do you like my Sinatra knot, Liz?" He asked the question to test her receptivity.

Elizabeth paid no attention to his question. Instead, she blurted angrily, "You never left so early before. Why today?"

"I've got to take care of business. That's why."

"Is it the same kind of business that you took care of last night—the hairy bank business?"

"What are you talking about, Liz?"

"You know damn well what I'm talking about."

"No; I don't!"

"Why didn't you sleep in your bed last night?"

"I slept on the couch outside because I didn't want to disturb you."

"I thought it was because you hadn't the energy to climb up into my bed."

"I slept on the couch. All right!"

"How discreet you were. How was your Labor Day on the Parkway?"

"Fine, honey."

"Don't honey me. Take that honey back to the bee that you waxed last night."

"And how was your Labor Day on the Parkway?"

"I have nothing to say to you."

"Not one thing? Not even to talk about which carnival costume you enjoyed best?"

"You're not my doctor, my lawyer, or my Leader Dollon, so I have nothing to say to you!"

"You mean you didn't jump up in the bands on the Parkway? Not even Lord Kitchener's road march *Flagwoman* turned you on? I know you can move your waist and waive that flag." Lyle took the kitchen towel, twirled it, and danced to a jello commercial.

"Why don't you quit trying to find out about my

whereabouts yesterday?"

"What time did you get home last night?"

"I've nothing to tell you except to say that stinking whore Jacki called after you deliberately walked out on me to go and meet her. She thinks that I'm a jackiass. I know all of your tricks...all your phone codes...the ring-and-hang-up mumbo jumbo...your contrary answers when I'm around...your writing of phone numbers backwards...your hieroglyphics... Don't forget the thief is smart, but the policeman is smarter...You are the thief! Take my word! When you leave for work—if it's really work that you are going to today—I'll find that toolbox wherever it's hidden, and I'll break it open to see the other sluts' photographs that you have hidden in there." Elizabeth crashed her hand on the table.

"Why all that rage? Honey, did you go to karate class yesterday? Did you attend a prayer meeting with Leader Dollon? Did you, Hettie, and Leader Dollon view the parade on the Parkway?" Lyle's series of questions went unanswered.

"Wherever I went yesterday, whatever I did, or whomever I met were my blasted business, lover boy."

"The way the bed looks," Lyle glanced in the direction of the bedroom, "probably no one slept on it last night?"

"Your son is a detective; now you're trying to be a fucking detective too."

"I'll tell Leader Dollon that he should not give you communion on Sunday because you have a dirty tongue."

"And you have a dirtier prick. Fuck you!"

"You's a fucking vulgar 'oman." Lyle went for refuge in the patois, the vernacular, and the vulgar. He could no longer speak the corporate Wall Street English. "You's lucky this is not me day off, otherwise I woulda cuss you in Latin till you sneeze this morning."

Elizabeth loved when Lyle went base, especially

when he spoke in the vernacular. She was deft in the superlative of baseness, and she minted patois. "And you, arsehole nigger!" she began. "You think me tongue tie or it heavy? You better think again, because I would cuss you back in better Latin than the Pope could speak English. Provoke me and I'd cuss you till you shit in you pants. You's a fucking whore stick. Devil, go away and stick your penny dick in an ant's nest!" They threw salvoes at each other. "I'm warnin' you," Elizabeth continued... "Don't play wit' me nuh!" What do you mean by running off on me after I spent so much money on making me mas' clothes to go an' enjoy meself?" Elizabeth approach Lyle and pointed her fingers in his face. She blocked his movement and shouted, "Mr. Adult Nigger, I'm not that dumb Jackiass, so doh play wit' me nuh!"

"Are you something with which to play, Elizabeth?" Lyle reverted to the language of the corporate world, but it was too late. His raw patois had already evoked her acrid replies in their Fyzabad lingo.

"Drop dead! You'll get what's coming to you, lover boy." She shouted from the kitchen sink.

Lyle went to the study, snatched his briefcase, and rushed out without having his breakfast or packing his lunch in his briefcase. That morning Elizabeth prepared, especially for him, salt fish in scrambled eggs, home-made bread, an avocado salad in sweet oil, and a mini chef salad. That was his favorite dish. He called it the "QE Special."

Away from the Pastalaqua House, yet Nigel Gordon and Tommy Sullivan, like men of seance, had already rehearsed the Lyle and Elizabeth's bound-to-happen colloquy and its inflammable consequence; but the impending fate of Lyle at the end of his working day was beyond the imagination of the detective duo.

Chapter Twelve

The Absent Employee

It was the first time in his working career that Lyle was early for the train without making any effort. The IRT express halted at Wall Street station in downtown Manhattan, and Lyle detrained amidst the briefcase-toting officials, some with home-made sandwiches encased among their prospectuses. Japanese cameramen with zooming lenses, out-of-towners, and loiterers milled around on Lower Broadway. Frugal businessmen in pin-striped suits snatched recycled newspapers from the roadside and subway bins, and dope peddlers made signals to their regular customers. On Broad Street and in Merrill Lynch's gallery, tickertapes gave information on the stock market. The Dow Jones Industrials, Standard & Poor's, NADSAQ, and AMEX showed high averages, and investors were in their glee when the President of the New York Stock Exchange hammered the gavel and opened trading.

"Read this if you want to make a quick million," a street crier said and pushed flyers in the tourists' faces. Lyle took a pamphlet and quipped, "Thank you, my bruvver. Now I'm on my second million." The street crier leaned on Trinity Church rails that fenced the cemetery and the crypted dead, and the crier scratched his half-exposed back on the upright pickets. The enthralled tourists stood close to the street crier and looked up in awe at the black Gothic Revival edifice; its nave windows with myriads of stained glass and a soaring spire accented by a gilded cross were spied at and photographed from different angles by the Japanese tourists. A beggar partially blocked the Trinity entrance, smiled and bowed approvingly as if he owned the Trinity estate, and stretched his cup to the tourists who reciprocated with deeper bows and compensated only with their goodwill smiles. The tourists then turned their attention to the hucksters' wares on the sidewalk. Tax-free merchants with mobile sheds monopolized the landscape. Three-card-monty slicksters had one eye on their dexterous card games and the gullible out-of-towners who betted their precious dollars, and the other eye was on the approaching police van seen meandering through heavy traffic in the distance. A polite white trader doffed his hat to a lady and found his favorite spot on the pavement. He sat on a milk crate; he stretched his feet, and had his shoes shone by a black concessionaire. An erudite black CEO comforted himself on a rickety chair; he took off his boots, and had them polished by a white concessionaire. Both customers were pleased with the bootblacks' workmanship, and both customers tipped one buck. Business flourished on Lower Broadway, the arena of historic tickertape parades. Lyle looked at his Tom McCan's and convinced himself that they were shoes for all seasons, and, like good wine, his shoes needed no polish.

Since his employment in the Wall Street neighborhood, it was the first time that he leisurely strolled the narrow lanes. His eyes were transfixed on the bustling street business, and so were the Parisians as they ambled south on Broadway. He walked to the southernmost tip of the Island and scrutinized the historic Alexander U.S. Custom House, "a Beaux-Arts composition." Lyle gloated at the building's numerous gargoyles and its countless columns, each decorated with a head of Mercury, the Roman god of commerce; but he was taken aback by Daniel Chester French's giant sculpture *America* which incorporates people and things, but the Native American is left behind 'symbolically.' "Interesting," the Nepal visitor whispered as she viewed *America*; "*merde alors*," a Parisian said aloud and scoffed at the giant sculpture that welcomes visitors daily to the Custom House. Lyle smiled at the visitors' comments then journeyed through the Bowling Green Park. He walked beneath the unclothed trees that signalled the approach of winter, and he stopped at Castle Clinton, a product of the Napoleonic era, guarded by rusty cannons on the edge of the Bay. He had a panoramic view of the converged waterways. On the asphalt walk, he admired the suspending battle-gray Manhattan Bridge and the majestic Brooklyn Bridge seen in the distance, and he waived to his commuting friends ferried in from the Borough of Richmond.

The morning was enjoyed to the hilt. Elizabeth was no longer on his mind for he had become a part of the mix of out-of-town dwellers, shoppers, and the Japanese tourists who clicked their cameras constantly. Lyle found himself imitating the tourists' every move. He looked at the Statue of Liberty equidistanced in the Bay between the States of New York and New Jersey, and he wondered who is, rightfully, the owner of the disputed Lady with the Lamp. The tourists glared at the *Immigrants*, dedicated to the people of all nations, and sculptured by Luis Sanguino. Lyle glared at that sculpture too. The Japanese clicked their cameras at moving objects, and Lyle looked at those objects too. The tourists became his tour guide. The tourists stopped and stared at the magnificent and imposing skyline, and Lyle stopped and stared at it even longer as if he never saw it before. On the grounds of the War Memorial he read the inscription for the American heroes who permanently "sleep in the waters of the Atlantic Ocean." He stood still for a second, thought of the soldiers' bravery and of his grandfather's unmarked grave in Fyzabad before he left the park.

Lyle retraced his footsteps. He walked north, and came upon Arturo Di Mordica's beautiful *Charging Bull*. The 7,000- pound bronze sculpture which guards 26 Broadway and the Bowling Green Post Office was photographed more than the Brazilian soccer star Pele. It was one time that Lyle wished Japanese were his mother tongue, because the way the Japanese fondled the *Charging Bull*, he was sure they cloned it, and a facsimile would appear in Tokyo. Yet the Japanese's caressing of Di Mordica's masterpiece did not take the cake. Two Californians' romance of the *Charging Bull* did. Both Californians had their names and state labeled on their T-shirts. Dora of California hugged the bull, leaned on his horns, climbed on him, tugged his tail, and rubbed on the bull's snout. Dora called her buddy. "Johnny, get your camera and shoot when I tell you." What followed was sacrilege on Lower Broadway, the "Canyon of Heroes." Dora squatted below the bull. She rested her back on the concrete, put her tongue on the bull's scrotum, and shouted, "Johnny, shoot!" As Johnny's flash went off, he said, "Dora, no one can tell you that you were not bullish in New York."

The tourists were shocked at the Californians' behavior. Even Di Mordica's inanimate bull could have deciphered the tourists' disdain.

What a morning in New York, New York!

Lyle left the bullish scene. He continued north, turned on Cedar Street, and onto the Chase Manhattan Bank Plaza to the Isamu Noguchi garden. There he threw three coins in the glass-enclosed fountain and made a wish at every plunked sound: "Elizabeth, I wish that when I come home late tonight you'll not be mad with me; and I promise that I will go to church with you on Sunday and be introduced to Leader Dollon." That was his first wish. He waited until the ripple in the pool subsided before he made his second wish. "Billie, I wish that you'll understand when I tell you tomorrow that it's over between us...A gun put to a man's brain is criminalism." Lyle opened his hand over the pool and a nickel dropped out. The coin made a clonking sound and caused a wide ripple, but Lyle didn't look into the pool. He looked into the sky as if his courage to say "No" to Billie came from there. A woman threw five coins into the pool and counted in

Spanish. Lyle waited on her. Finally, the woman left after she counted backwards. Lyle delved into his pocket and found a quarter. "Connie, this is too much to spend on you...Mira! Mira! You have change?" Lyle shouted and rushed towards the woman. The woman didn't take heed. "Connie," Lyle said as he hurried back to the pool, "you owe me twenty cents. My wish shouldn't cost more than five cents. Anyhow, I wish you'll be ready tonight for spiritual instructions." He threw the quarter in the air like a gambler and hoped that it would stay in the clear side of the pool, but the quarter sunk to the bottom without generating a single ripple. "What's that supposed to mean?"

He pondered his next move. Instinctively, he walked to the intersection of Broad and Wall Streets, and listened, as was customary, to the unconvincing fundamentalist and his gnostic detractors battle over whether man's failure is as a result of sin or due to man's lack of knowledge. Hoarse-voiced, the fundamentalist orated from the steps of the Federal Memorial building. He propped the bronze statue of George Washington with his back; and, like the bronze statue, he, too, received the liquids from perched pigeons anchored atop of the building.

Instinctively, Lyle glanced at his watch, then at a woman at the traffic light. He left the street debate and planted himself at the opposite traffic light and waited on it to change from red to green. The attractive woman, balanced on high heels, cutely dressed, pulled up her back and humped like a camel when the cold breeze from the Hudson funnelled under her short skirt and flimsy top. "Miss Cute-and-Cold," Lyle whispered as they crossed each other. "It's Agnes," she replied, and quickly turned into the 148 Wall Street building. Lyle turned back, and the light changed to red. He ignored the light, and rushed into the building after the woman.

"May I see your I.D., sir." The guard of building

148 Wall politely stopped him. The pursued straightened her back as she entered the warm elevator. She waived to Lyle, her pursuer, and smiled as the elevator lifted.

"Good morning," Lyle said to the guard.

"Good morning," the guard replied, "aren't you coming in, sir?"

"After I get my coffee," Lyle said.

That guard's block, softer than New Jersey Giant's Lawrence Taylor's, ended Lyle's erstwhile tour of downtown Manhattan. He bought a cup of coffee, and he, too, humped his back as the cold blast from the East River and the Bay pushed him to work.

However, Lyle was indeed happy that he left the street activities because at his office building he witnessed a scene that remained in his cultural memory of Wall Street and its environs: That morning, too, Annie saw a bargain on Nassau Street; it was a used folding bed that cost five dollars. So afraid that the bed would be sold before she returned in the afternoon to purchase it, Annie bought the bed, pushed it on the crowded personnel elevator, and squeezed herself between the bed frame. Annie was mute to the obscenities of the well-dressed office workers who asked Pedro, the elevator operator, "Is this the cargo freight?" Annie came off on the fifty-ninth floor and lodged her "bargain" in a space near the conveyor belt.

That eventful Tuesday morning Miss Gennoyer, for the first time in her life, was late for work, and the office mice played. Annie's novel behavior was the cheese that the office mice nibbled. "Had Ripley's Believe It Or Not scouted for talent Downtown, Annie would have been chosen for setting a world record," Jodi said.

"What record?" Lyle asked.

"The World's Most Thoughtful Bed Star," Jodi answered.

"So dumb!" Phillo commented. He did not share

the spotlight and that annoyed him. His *non sequitur* followed: "All those old women, long passed menopause, were boasting to Pedro about their hectic weekend in disco clubs as if they're so hip." Phillo knew that his unprovoked remark would end the Annie-bed discussion. His remark indeed ended the Annie-bed discussion.

Only Jodi, still on overtime hours, unruffled as ever, was engaged in office duties. Jodi had come in very early. She hummed, and her typewriter made music as she banged it and made the changes in Mr. Zumzum's rush memo. Mr. Zumzum, in his umpteenth rewrite, had changed prepositions back to adverbs, semicolons to full stops, corrected his comma splices, put misplaced modifiers next to their antecedents, and, at last (but not in Jodi's favor), stamped on his rush memo, "FINAL—FORWARD TO LAWYERS IN THE LITIGATION GROUP."

Jodi, reluctantly, rolled out the last sheet of bond paper from her typewriter, turned off her machine, and went to her bag—her brown breakfast bag. Phillo squirmed. Everyone thought that he saw feces in Jodi's rancid cottage cheese. At that moment Helen walked in and was greeted with the good news of Miss Gennoyer's late arrival.

"Who cares if that slavedriver is late this morning," Helen said. She slumped her body on the typing stool which barely comforted her posterior. She poured sweet 'n low into her coffee, and lamented, "Why couldn't Rosh Hashanah and Yom Kippur follow Labor Day?"

"I thought you were Catholic?" Jodi asked. Her jaws in-and-outbounded as the crushed raw cashew nuts sometimes flew out of her spaced teeth and lodged elsewhere.

"Yes, I am," Helen answered, "but observing everybody's holidays shows tolerance."

"Where's Cakey?" Lyle asked. "Won't he be here to

do his cakey jobs today?" The phone rang as Lyle spoke, and Phillo answered the call.

"Speak of the devil," Phillo said. "That phone call was about Cakey. A woman called to say that Cakey is sick and would be in tomorrow. I guess Cakey danced too much at the West Indian Labor Day parade...Every year those West Indian people mess up the streets and..." Phillo hadn't time to finish his sentence.

Lyle snapped at him. "Phillo, I never heard your complaints when Fifth Avenue was messed up by white folks when they had their parades!"

"Hey, man, Cakey is not coming in today, and I'm mad. I'm sure GG will give me Cakey's transcribed belts with those long-winded corporate lawyers' markups for me to re-type." Phillo cocked his fingers and shook them as if they had wet nail polish. "If Cakey's sick, I'm going through menopause."

"I believe you are," Jodi said. She licked a smudge of cottage cheese off her plastic knife and ignored Phillo's stares. She made a sign to him and Lyle, and they rushed to her. Phillo and Lyle knew that Jodi signs meant hot off-the-press news. "Listen to the latest," Jodi said softly, and pulled Phillo and Lyle closer for the Tuesday tête-à-tête. "I heard this morning from the horse's mouth that Zumzum is leaving. Zumzum wasn't made a partner; only Franz Leyland made it upstairs this year; and, of course, after seven years in this law firm Zumzum has to leave so that the company can recruit fresh brains." Jodi spoke as if she were the premier planner of policy at South Opnorth, Pickdom & Cotton, a law firm that, a month ago, gave each non-legal employee one hundred dollars to mark the company's one hundredth year of lawyering in Wall Street.

Phillo framed his left hand like a cobra and swerved it in Jodi's face. "Uptown will quicker make this Jewish boy a member of the Harlem Boys Choir," he intimated. "Those WASPs in this company know that

Zumzum is Jewish, and he anglicized, or even germanized, his name not to be detected and ostracized. Never would S.O. make him a partner...probably they would, about the same time that South Africa forgets how to spell the word apartheid!" He walked to his desk, turned on his typewriter, dropped into his chair, and crossed his legs.

"There goes Mr. Rona Barrett. Mr. She had to top my news," Jodi said and went back to her overtime duties. She proofread and collated the Zumzum doctrine, and finally sent it to the xerox room to be printed and circulated to the lawyers in the litigation group.

The phone rang aloud in the adjoining office, and Mr. Bolton's secretary, Mary, snatched it. "Hello," she said. "This is Mr. Bolton's office. Can't you hear me, sir? Seems we have a bad connection, sir...This is Mr. Bolton's office...B as in bitch-O-L-T-O-N. Is that clear to you, sir?"

"Click!"

"The nerve of this other bitch to hang up on me!" Mary slammed her phone.

"Did you hear mad Mary on the phone, Phillo? Do you think her boss heard her?" Lyle waited for an answer.

"Sure," Phillo said, and he filed his nails.

"It pays to have blue eyes," Lyle commented.

"What a racist remark! Of all the days! Cakey chose Tuesday to be absent. I thought blacks' holidays were Mondays and Fridays only. I never knew Tuesdays were their holidays too. What kind of eyes Cakey has to be taking a Tuesday off to further extend his carnival weekend?"

"When Cakey comes on Wednesday, look!" Lyle said, and he turned on his typewriter when he saw the supervisor's reflection on the glass door.

In walked Miss Gennoyer. The line tamer on her face reduced her calendar age by five years. She took a quick glance at the IBM dictating banks on the wall, her pool stenographers and typists, before she sat at her desk. "Did everyone sign the attendance register? Did you, Linda Joans? How was everyone's weekend? Where is Daniel Cake after this long weekend?" GG asked her questions in rapid succession, but only one question was answered promptly.

"Some woman called to say that Daniel is ill, Miss Gennoyer," Phillo informed her.

"Then, Phillo, you'll do Daniel's returned markups from Mr. Beck and Mr. Pitt. Make sure that your transcriptions reflect the superiority of my typing pool. Don't submit that low standard of work as the other typing pools."

Lyle looked at Phillo, and Phillo read the "Take that! That's-good-good-for-ya" in Lyle's puckish face.

The beige phone rang on Miss Gennoyer's desk. It was strange to everyone that GG didn't answer with her long salutation. Instead, she stared at Lyle, pressed the phone to her tender ear, and whispered into it as if the caller had touched her erogenous zones. GG changed her gaze from Lyle to Jodi, and everyone instantly concluded that GG had finally got wind of the underground Typists and Stenographers Trade Union headquartered in the ladies' bathroom and chaired by Jodi. GG again looked at Lyle, but her expression was unreadable. He, however, interpreted her expression: That she objected to his attire, and she felt that his jazzy tie-and-jeans outfit was an "underclass" Brooklyn style that was not in conformity with the office dress code.

Miss Gennoyer's eyes were glued to the phone. She was entranced. Her forehead creased as she squeezed the beige object in her hand. She looked at her pool people. They were seated in a businesslike manner at their typewriters and dictaphones. GG appeared to be taking a head count of her staff. She listened and concentrated as if she were given by the person on the other end of the line a recipe for a cosmopolitan dinner.

(GG was the only supervisor who had end-of-season parties.) Seemingly, if it were a recipe given her, it was relayed as "Confidential," and she guarded that recipe as the ingredients given to the chefs who prepared the kosher-Arab meals at Camp David for the palates of Presidents Sadat and Begin. It was one telephonic moment that not even gossip columnist Rona Barrett herself could have lip-read. The phone conversation between the steno supervisor and the other party seemed to have been spoken in coughed codes. GG coughed one more time. Finally, she rested the phone down gently. She addressed Lyle without looking at him, and she walked away, emotionless, but drained: "Mr. Lyle Allister Gordon, please go to Room 603 and take with you all of your things."

Room 603 was Mr. Miller's Iranian-carpeted domain. A print of the Mona Lisa was the only picture on his wall. In that room you were promoted or demoted, baptized with criticisms, born again with praises, hired or fired. Lyle's last work review was exceptional. He was the only pool stenographer whom Mr. Franz Leyland, the gas and oil litigator, requested for dictation. Mr. Leyland, through an odd coincidence, had found out that Lyle grew up in an oilfield. At first, Leyland, nicknamed "Oily," was flabbergasted that Lyle knew so much about oil wells, bore holes, derricks, pumping jacks, wildcatting, and many of the tools that are used when a rig is drilled or when a dry well is uncapped. Initially, Franz Leyland viewed Lyle's knowledge as a freak of nature, but eventually acknowledged, perhaps, subconsciously, that blacks have knowledge of things other than tap dancing and balancing their bodies under limbo sticks. Soon it became a joyful occasion when Lyle came into his office. Franz Leyland told Lyle the history of the miniature derricks that he stored in a glass cage. And he romanticized about the days when he lived in Texas and moonlighted as a trainee driller. The last thing

Leyland told Lyle whenever Lyle left his room was, "Good man, Lyle."

On Miss Gennoyer's announcement that he go to Room 603, Oily's hinted promotion to the partnership rank crossed Lyle's mind. Lyle, inwardly, but happily, thought that he was called to the administrator's office to be formally apprised that he, Lyle, would be Mr. Leyland's secretary. A partner's secretary! Lyle heard his supervisor's echo: "Mr. Lyle Allister Gordon,...take with you all of your things" reverberated in his brain. He improvised on the thought of being a partner's secretary like a Fyzabad chac-chac player who makes music with seeds. Lyle's theme, "Me, this Fyzabad boy, is going places at last!" He felt that he was above the fray and immediately took charge of the office palaver. "Gang," he addressed his peers, "you heard how GG referred to me—as 'Mr. Lyle Allister Gordon.' I'll be having my own private locker upstairs. My shorthand skills are too good to be sitting in the same pew with that Fresh-Water-Yankee, Cakey. Cakey doesn't like the best bone in me because I exposed him as a sol fish eater. Later for Cakey! Who says that blue eyes are the criteria to dance in the totempole at this prestigious firm of South Opnorth, Pickdom & Cotton?"

"You just said that, Lyle!" Phillo shouted.

"I withdraw my cynicism with my humble apology, my darling Phillo," Lyle said. "But I won't kiss you, Phillo."

The stenogang laughed; and Jodi shouted, "That's not fair, Lyle; Phillo needs your lips."

"Jodi, please be quiet," Lyle said presumptuously but teasingly, "and make sure that you stop padding your overtime hours. Let Mr. Zumzum's memo be the last! I'm upstairs in management now so I'll be checking to see if you pad your overtime."

"We pad S.O. and S.O. pad their clients," she retorted. "The game is to pass the padding on. Don't tell me, Mr. Upstairs-in-Management-Now, that you don't know that the lawyers and partners take their clients to dinner and tack on the dinner checks to their clients' fees?"

"If the clients eat, they have a right to pay," Annie said faintly. She was still panting from the task of dragging her bed and maneuvering it through the Downtown traffic.

"Haven't you read, guys, that two wrongs don't make a right?" Lyle lectured on ethics.

"I don't read West Indian literature that is copied from the British, especially literature written by the sol fish eaters of the Caribbean," Jodi said, amidst the undying laughter in the room.

A paralegal left his office, his coffee and a marked-up prospectus in hand, joined the festival in the stenopool; but he could not unscramble the sol fish-garnished innuendoes that were hurled about, and no pool member volunteered interpretation of the "sol fish" parable to him. The curious paralegal shook his head and sheepishly went back to his room.

"There goes Mr. Nosy," Jodi and Phillo uttered under their breaths.

As Mr. Nosy turned his back, Lyle picked up his briefcase, smelled it, twitched his nostril, licked his lips many times with his tongue, and said softly, "Funky...Good morning, ladies."

"The men's smell worse than ours," Miriam said. "Believe me; I know." There was no drama in her voice, yet she had the stenopool's attention, except Phillo's. He had to win back their attention.

"Yo! Yo!" Phillo addressed Lyle.

"Me?" Lyle inquired.

"Who else, yo! If Cakey were here he would have asked you if that's the kind of funk that you have at home." Phillo donned a masculine voice. He had many voices, and he alternated them to suit his fancy.

"Is this personal, Phillip? Why disguise what's on your mind? Now that you speak like a man, why don't you ask me for yourself, girl."

Phillo did not answer but the stenogang immediately became tense. Jodi closed the jar with her brown water. She looked at Lyle and Phillo's muscles and was glad when Lyle said, "Guys, that's all right." Lyle's smile dimpled deeper than ever. He looked at Jodi and said, "Boys," and he paused, "who are boys, will always be boys...And, Phillip," he paused longer, "if you fall within that category, tomorrow, please, check that absent employee's-you-know-what, and if it smells like Fulton Street fish market, that means you may take him home for your sol-fish enjoyment." He walked towards Phillo.

Phillo thundered off his seat but stood at the same spot, and waived his hands incessantly as if he were stopping an already-departed Transit bus.

Jodi pushed her breakfast bag aside and blocked Lyle's movement. As Jodi mediated, the smell of sardines effused from her breath. "Both of you are sissies, and I mean it," she said. "And you, Lyle Allister Gordon, go and get all of your things. Now! I'll walk with champagne tomorrow for us to celebrate your being kicked upstairs. You know why? Don't you, Lyle?" She smiled.

"Of course, I know why, Jodi," Lyle answered. "Because now that I'm upstairs in management you want me to have your overtime hours approved quickly so that you can buy more earth shoes." Lyle picked up his briefcase and went for his jacket.

The typists and stenographers roared, "Yea! That's it." The group wished Lyle goodluck. Phillo stretched out his hand, and Lyle pushed it aside. With lightning speed, Lyle kissed Phillo on his cheeks, dashed for the elevator, and waived to the happy group.

Lyle stepped off the elevator, pushed the heavy glass door, and the receptionist on the sixtieth floor showed him the way. He knocked on Room 603. The door opened, and closed immediately behind him like a trapdoor.

"Take a seat, Mr. Gordon." Lyle looked at the person who addressed him. That man hadn't the slightest resemblance of Franz Leyland, Esq., or of M.T Miller, the competent and dynamitely-wigged office administrator, or, for that matter, any resemblance of anyone who worked in the law firm of South Opnorth, Pickdom & Cotton. To Lyle, the man in front of him, medium height, chalky, needle-nosed and fat, flaunting an executive hairstyle, looked quasi-Pentagonish; he hadn't the mark or the silk of Wall Street, except, perhaps, he looked as unpredictable both as the stock market and as the Bowling Green subway escalator that was serviceable only on certain days known to none.

"I'm Detective Crobett." The stranger introduced himself. The collar of his Wal-Mart shirt stuck out. He appeared to be one-grade taller and tidier than Hollywood's Colombo-without-his-raincoat.

"What's the matter?" Lyle asked.

"Just a routine matter."

"About what?"

"Your whereabouts yesterday."

"My whereabouts!"

"Yes. Where were you last night?"

"At my home."

"Where else?"

"That's personal."

"How did you happen to know Mrs. Constance Wagner?"

"That's personal, I said! What business of yours?"

"Here's my authority. I forgot to show you proper identification of myself, Mr. Gordon."

Lyle looked at the insignia on the badge, and then at Detective Crobett. He barely heard the next question asked.

"How did you happen to meet her, Mr. Gordon?"

Lyle hesitated at first. "I met her yesterday at the West Indian Labor Day parade on the Parkway. She's a reporter..."

"Mr. Gordon, do you have any sort of identification on you?"

"I have my job I.D." Lyle fumbled through his pockets. "Here."

Detective Crobett looked carefully at Lyle's I.D. "What scratched the plastic off?"

"I don't know."

"Furthermore, this I.D. is old; it serves no purpose. Why do you walk with it—a keepsake?" Detective Crobett paused, then finished his question, "or a sort of wedge? I'll hold it for a while."

Lyle ignored the detective's remark and gave him the active I.D. card.

"This I.D. is fine. I'll keep this one too. How did you get into Ms. Wagner's house?"

"She opened it for me."

"The second time, I mean?"

"What are you talking about? What second time? What's wrong?"

"She's dead. Mrs. Wagner is."

"Why come to me?" Lyle concealed his grief, and hid his shock.

"You left your tracks."

Lyle looked at Detective Crobett. He knew that he could have objected to those questions from the onset because the Miranda Warning was not recited to him. Foremost in his mind was the thought that he had nothing to hide, so he spoke without caution.

"I need you to come with us, Mr. Gordon."

Three detectives in plain clothes circled him, and they led him to the elevator. "No riders," Detective Crobett said quietly when the elevator came. Lyle was on his fifth morning's journey, and he sat quietly in the back seat of an unmarked car between two men. Where are they taking me? he thought, but he resigned himself and rode with them back into Brooklyn.

* * * * * *

The events of that fateful day were fast paced. Lyle was put on an identification parade with other men of similar and not-so-similar build. Two of the men were Caucasians, two were Hispanics, and four were black men. Mabel Plutz identified Lyle immediately. "I'm dead sure it's him," she told Detective Crobett. "Him! Him!" She pointed to Lyle from behind the glass screen where she could not be seen by the men who were paraded for her scrutiny.

There was another stop on the detective's itinerary.

* * * * * *

Detective Crobett uncovered the dead body and Lyle looked at it. "I didn't do it," Lyle said. He looked at the belt around the deceased's neck.

"Is this your belt, Mr. Gordon?" Detective Crobett asked.

"Yes." He glanced at the leather of the belt. The leather had a jagged edge. He knew how that jagged edge came about after he had won that belt for climbing the greasypole in Fyzabad.

"What else didn't you do, Mr. Gordon?"

Instinctively, Lyle looked around and saw the scratched poem in Connie's bedhead. "I didn't scratch those words with dye!"

Detective Crobett read the scratched words, "My only home." He asked Lyle another question. "If you were to leave Brooklyn, New York, America, this country, would you have another home to go to?"

"Sure! Didn't you research that, too: That I came to America on a banana boat? What's your next question?" Lyle was angry as a mad bull.

"When did you read the scratched poem?" Detective Crobett asked calmly. He was as cool as a Carolina cucumber.

"About twelve hours ago."

"Tell me what you read—any line?"

"You expect me to remember a stupid poem like that?"

"Tell me what's the most stupid line of that poem?"

"All I know is that I didn't scratch it with dye."

"How do you know that there's dye on it?"

"I don't know."

"We've also found here the imprint of your name, address, and office phone number on the pad on her night table." Detective Crobett behaved as if the deceased were alive. "If that information were intended for her, your friend Constance, why did you remove the piece of paper you wrote on?"

"I'm confused."

"You're not bound to answer any of these questions."

"Only now you are telling me this after you have denied me the Miranda Warning? I can answer any blasted question because I know that I'm innocent. Go-ahead and frame me."

Detective Crobett said casually, "Oh, we've found a tape. Listen, Mr. Gordon. Is this your voice?" He was about to depress the "play" button when Lyle interrupted him.

"Connie told me to pass it for her, and I put it on record. Maybe my voice came out."

Detective Crobett played the tape. "Is this your voice?"

"Could be."

"You don't know your voice, Mr. Gordon?"

Lyle didn't answer.

"You put the tape to record purposely or accidentally?"

"Purposely; and I purposely left it on."

Detective Crobett smiled. "Well, Mr. Gordon, if you did that I'm sure that your fingerprint would be good evidence in your favor. It would be proof that you were here at the invitation of your friend Connie, and she told you to fetch the tape recorder...Other than that, I'll have to say that Connie put it to record unknown to you?"

"Yes; no; I don't know." Lyle's confusion increased.

"What are you saying, Mr. Gordon: Yes; no; or you don't know? You told me that she gave you consent to come into her house; she told you to pass the tape recorder; yet your fingerprint is no where on it? How come?"

Instantly Lyle realized that the death of Constance Wagner was already thoroughly investigated by Homicide, and that he was a suspect, possibly the only suspect. He began his defence with an explanation. "Sir, this may sound childish, but I held the tape recorder with a towel...maybe a handkerchief, whatever...and then depressed the recording buttons without my fingers touching them."

"Why you went through all that trouble and made sure that no part of your person touched the cassette or the tape? Why, Mr. Gordon?" Detective Crobett toyed with him.

"Truth is stranger than fiction, sir."

"I'm beginning to realize that, too, Mr. Gordon. Then would you say that your fingerprints would not be on the belt around her neck either?"

Lyle took time to think. He felt the thick sarcasm in the detective's voice. "Of course, my fingers would be on that belt, if it's mine." As he spoke, his stomach wambled.

"Couple minutes ago you said that the belt 'is' yours; now you are saying, 'If it's mine.' Is the belt yours? I'm not forcing you to claim the belt either. So you were here yesterday?"

"At her request."

Detective Crobett made a sign and a man raised the sheet that covered the corpse.

"At her request?" Detective Crobett pointed to the dead body.

Lyle nodded.

Detective Crobett waved his hand and a man covered the body with a sheet. "Around what time you said you left here, Mr. Gordon?"

"I cannot remember now."

"Did you have a quarrel with her?"

"I wouldn't call it so."

"What was it, Mr. Gordon?"

"We threw political digs at each other. We also discussed a masquerader in the *Grenada Ghosts* band."

"You threw those digs with your fists?"

"No such thing."

Detective Scofield handed Detective Crobett an envelope. The envelope contained photographs that were developed from the pictures that were in Constance Wagner's camera. Detective Crobett shuffled the pictures. "Is this the masquerader that caused you to hit her?"

"I didn't hit anyone."

"Is that the masquerader who caused both of you to bandy all those political digs at each other. I can't make out his or her face because the face is masked. Do you know that person? Look at the picture carefully."

"No. I don't know that person." Lyle handed back the photograph.

"Did you give Ms. Wagner a sort of karate chop?"

"With these hands?" Lyle looked at his hands, and he dusted a crumb of Jodi's sardines from his right hand.

"Yes, with those hands?"

"No."

"Two civic-minded individuals saw you going in and out of Mrs. Wagner's apartment."

"They could say that they saw me, and that I made noise in Connie's apartment, but they couldn't say that I strangled her."

"I didn't say how she died. Did you tell Mr. Gordon how she died, Detective Scofield?"

"No, sir," Detective Scofield answered.

"We also found your costume, Mr. Gordon...The

Adult Nigger's," Detective Crobett said.

"I left it here."

"Intentionally?"

"Yes."

"The first time or the second time?"

"What are you talking about, sir?"

"The Adult Nigger's movements in and out of Mrs. Constance Wagner's apartment."

"When I left Connie's apartment I never returned."

"You'd have to prove that Mr. Gordon. We would like you to come with us to the precinct, Mr. Gordon." Crobett nodded to his men. Three of them came forward.

Lyle lost confidence in his truth telling and painfully acknowledged that he was in grave trouble with the law. His mind immediately flashed on the reported cruelties that take place daily in prisons; then his mind drifted and remained on the whereabouts of his officemate, the absent employee, Daniel "Cakey" Cake. Why wasn't he at work today? Lyle thought deeply. Why? "I need to call my lawyer," Lyle blurted to Detective Crobett.

"You'll not be denied that privilege, Mr. Gordon. Let's go."

Lyle was a proud and mentally strong man, but when Detective Crobett touched him, he felt disempowered and bowed like the Hunchback Quasimodo. He distinctly heard his deceased Aunt Gina's scolding words of advice as if they came from Billie Zellars' throat: "Likkle Lyle, have you noticed how your Grandpa's jackass is always rubbing his back on the earth? The jackass is telling you, Likkle Lyle, that 'the earth is not level;' and, poor jackass, he's trying to level the earth with his uneven back...Don't be a jackass, Likkle Lyle, and try to level the earth. It will never be level!" Then he remembered Billie's favorite line: "Pollyanna, one day you'll wake up in handcuffs."

As Lyle gathered his thoughts, he felt the warm tears rolled from his eyes onto his dry lips. His pulse quickened and deadened. That was his last recollection of himself as a free man.

* * * * * *

Other investigative and court proceedings on the death of Mrs. Constance Wagner took place, and the Grand Jury found that there was sufficient evidence for the indictment of Lyle Allister Gordon.

Chapter Thirteen

The Private Detectives

The year was George Orwell's *1984*, but the drama was on the American stage. It was the year that the Commander-in-Chief of the greatest nation in the world said that he would share antimissile and antisatellite technology secrets with the Evil Empire. Wow! It was also the season when Washington increased their sandbags on the Hill, put there to deter reprisals from the angry Iranian fundamentalists. It was that time, too, when the moral and silent majority took potshots at the role of the Holy See and endorsed the incumbent President, a pinup for the Pentagon. Consequently, the Pentagon had carte blanche power. They sucked the marrow from bread-and-butter programs, injected that marrow into their military boondoggle, and bought extra hardware in preparation for an early Armageddon: $3.6 billion for nuclear activities. "We would be ready for the enemy," they said. What enemy? However, the Christian women of North America knew their enemy—themselves. These women traded their mouthbites for soundbites and flooded the airwaves with their pros and cons of legislating a woman's body. Yes, in 1984, on rolled the Republican's canons. They shot at affirmative action in flight, and the Democrats countered with their smoke screens. Drowning men appealed to the naysayers, and the naysayers shouted the words that echoed from Moses' broken rod: "Down with politicians—six of one, half a dozen of the other! Follow our new direction." Yet their new direction was akin to bioengineering which put fish genes into plants which one day would harm the as-long-as-it-doesn't-bother-me generation. Surely, Orwell's *1984* motif was realized. The feared government bureaucrat, the IRS

(Internal Revenue Service), checked for loopholes in the church rat's income tax returns; and mom and pop, poorer than the church rat, quaked in their boots at the sight of bureaucrats.

In spite of Humpty-Dumpty's great rise before his unexpected fall, avant-garde film makers reeled the scene; and Michael "King of Pop" Jackson danced his way—he did not grab his crotch—into the banks.

Thank God, in 1984, there was a saving grace. *Billie Jean* was a hit on the Billboards, but Geraldine Ferraro was "the man." Ferraro became the Democratic Party's Vice Presidential candidate, the first woman in American history to achieve that feat. Her feat outshone Jesse Jackson's triumphant return from Syria where he negotiated for the release of the shot-down American pilot who invaded Syria's air space. Even a strange rainbow appeared over New York in the year Nineteen Hundred and Eighty Four to mark Ferraro's chalked-up ambition. That rainbow bellied its colors from the lower end of the East River, arched from the concrete banks of Brooklyn Heights, and spanned eight miles of New York City.

"What a beautiful rainbow!" Detective Tommy Sullivan, in awe, exclaimed, as he looked out of the office window on Cadman Plaza. "Look! Look at it, Sunday school boy."

"Lord Meath, I have more important things on my mind right now than to look up at a polluted rainbow," Detective Nigel Gordon replied. "I lost it. Oh, no, I lost it." He pulled out his desk drawers.

"Sloppy, why not look at the rainbow? If your Leader Dollon sees this rainbow, that would be his sermon for Sunday. I can hear him speaking in tongues. Do you remember that one time when I went to church with you?"

"I have no time for you, Leader Dollon, or for that acid rainbow...I can't find it. Chrise!"

"Cannot find what?" Rubin Nicholby, the head of

the Nicholby & Jordan Private Detective Agency, asked as he walked in. He did not wait for an answer. "Salt and Pepper," he said. He rested his satchel and umbrella on Tommy's desk.

"Yes, sir," replied Tommy and Nigel.

"I'm in a rush, but I've come to say that you are on. The two greenhorns are."

"On what?" Tommy asked.

"Just listen, Salt. Strange things happen in our profession, but the strangest thing happened today. Our lawyers received funds addressed to us from an unnamed source. Those funds are for us to investigate the murder of Constance Wagner. What is even funnier is that the money came in an envelope without a forwarding address."

"Was there a clue as to its origin?" Tommy asked.

"The only clue, if that's a clue, is that the envelope looks as if it were retrieved from a Texas oil well," Rubin Nicholby said.

"That's all? Just an oily envelope?" Tommy inquired.

"Yes; that's all. Except, next to the smudge of oil are the words—'Indigenous, *Pro bono*, Lyle Gordon'— written in that exact order. Both of you know that this agency intended to do some *pro bono* also, and Jimmy Fox was our investigator for that Constance Wagner murder assignment. Now I'm taking him off, because something deep down inside of me tells me that Salt and Pepper are just what are needed to unflavor that homicide. I pondered over my decision but the word 'Indigenous' had a tug on me. Pepper."

"Yes, sir," Nigel answered.

"I know your affiliation. You will be sympathetic towards your father, even bias; but being in this private eye business for so long I know that there would be clues that, as a member of Lyle's family, you alone would see the significance. I shouldn't be doing this but heck! Pepper, you have judgment, I know; but Salt, you are in charge. Bring Pepper up to date and let him know what we did for Lyle when he was arrested. We have limited time with our investigation before the trial date. A great part of the money that came in that oily envelope would go for lawyers fees if nothing turns up from your investigation. If you find the killer a bonus from that oily envelope awaits you. The police and Detective Crobett are convinced Lyle is the murderer. You two may have to 'play' police at times to get certain info or to even protect yourselves when you are in certain neighborhoods, but be extremely cautious when you pull off those stunts which can cost you your gun and your license; and, remember, that you didn't hear that from Nicholby and Jordan."

Tommy and Nigel looked at each other. They never thought such words came from the conservative man whom they nicknamed Totohead. Whenever they see Totohead they instantly recall a a men's bathroom joke.

"Don't you two greenhorns take instructions any more?"

"Yes, sir."

"Then get on the job. Salt, remember that you are in charge." He walked away and whistled, *My Way*. He ended the chorus and said, "Pepper, who's in charge?"

"Salt, sir," Nigel said and waited for Totohead's departure. "My god! I must find it." Nigel pulled out his drawers and peeped inside the roof of his desk.

"Sunday school boy, Totohead gave you an order."

"Lord Meath, for chrise sake, I'm following Totohead's order."

"By breaking up the furniture?"

Nigel pushed his index and middle fingers into a space in the roof of his middle drawer; he twisted both fingers; and then he shouted, "Ahgatit!" He kissed it.

"What's it, Sunday school boy?"

"My ASDFLKJ murder script."

"What's that for?"

"Family matters."

"And this is an appropriate time for me to talk about

your family. While you were away on your haunts and jaunts Elizabeth got a call about Lyle's arrest. She was heartbroken. She called her spiritual Leader Dollon, and she told him to call me. I told our boss, Totohead, and he immediately went to work. A lot was done in that space of time."

"Thanks, brother," Nigel said, "for being there for me. In times like these we really need our rabbis, pastors, priests, pundits and leaders. What exactly did Leader Dollon tell you?"

"Exactly what Elizabeth told him: that Lyle was arrested and where he could be found. Leader Dollon also said that Elizabeth was incoherent at times. She had a right to be incoherent with anger, because from what I've gathered, I realized that Lyle talked too much when Detective Crobett questioned him."

"At Lyle's age, he still doesn't know the system. We have argued before, and I've tried to convince him that innocence alone is not an asset that guarantees an accused exoneration from blame."

"Sometimes it's so difficult to prove your innocence. Anyhow, Totohead did some inquiry and found out that due process was not carried out to the letter of the law. There were other discrepancies by Homicide; but the Grand Jury had sufficient evidence to recommend Lyle's indictment. We have, however, received a copy of a recording on a 90-minute cassette reel found in Constance Wagner's room. We are *not* in possession of Lyle's belt and other exhibits, but we would be able to inspect them if need be. There's a way to get around many things without obtaining a subpoena, and we know a way of getting free legal advice without going to the agency's lawyers." They looked at each other, and without commenting, one individual came to their recall. That person owed Lyle Gordon a day's work when he vomited on Elizabeth's carpet.

Tommy walked to the locked cabinet and took out the notes that Rubin Nicholby gave him yesterday. "Oh yes, Totohead obtained some other information, too, but he did not divulge it."

"Why?" Nigel asked. Tommy shook his shoulders. Nigel stared at the verbatim notes of the court reporter, and his eyes found only the lines that impressed him:

Accused LYLE ALLISTER GORDON...in the death of CONSTANCE WAGNER.

Witness Mabel Plutz, Landlord.

Medic Dr. K. Hadeem. "Death was due to a blow at the back of head. Victim was pushed on, fell on, or hit by heavy blunt object."

Exhibit 1 — One belt with buckle
Exhibit 2 — Mini tape recorder
Exhibit 3 — 90-minute cassette reel
Exhibit 4 — Camera
Exhibit 5 — Photographs of the *Grenada Ghosts* band
Photo showing Masquerader with letter "R" of monogram hanging
Exhibit 6 — Strand of super curly (black) hair
Exhibit 7 — Strand of auburn (Caucasian) hair
Exhibit 8 — Poem with scratched words
Exhibit 9 — Speck of plastic found on lock
Exhibit 10 — Imprint of name, address, and phone number (i.e., Lyle Gordon's)
Fingerprint — There were three distinct fingerprints found on the belt and costume with words "THE ADULT NIGGER."
Notably, however, was the fact that Lyle Gordon's fingerprint was not on the cassette reel or on the small tape recorder (in spite of the fact that he said that he put the tape on record.)

Nigel rubbed his eyes and handed Tommy the notes.

"You read that so quickly, Nigel?"

"I only read the words that impressed me." Nigel looked out the window, but he still did not see the radiant rainbow. "Why isn't Lyle's fingerprint on the cassette or tape recorder? He held them. Sure, the Grand Jury can use that as an anomaly to indict him. Is there hope, Tommy?"

"Sure is, Nigel. We have a cassette and we can play the tape until we know it by heart as we know all of Lyle Gordon's Fyzabad tales. We have to find out the owner of one more fingerprint. Homicide probably abandoned any idea about finding out what other fingerprints are on that belt because the belt passed through so many hands. Worse still, Lyle's explanation did not make any sense to Detective Crobett and Homicide. Why did Lyle hold the tape with a towel, purposely? The battery of detectives are probably still wondering what was Lyle's motive." Tommy touched his pal, stroked his back, and looked at him as if he were thinking something homely. "This is no time to be sentimental, kid. We have a job. Go and visit your father in jail, and I'll check on Mabel and Harvey Plutz. Mabel picked out Lyle in the identification parade. Tell Lyle that I, too, still owe him a day's work for the glass pane that you broke."

"Me broke? That was the only time that you ever hit a home run."

"You never did."

"I know; and I didn't break the window pane."

"Shame on you, Sunday school boy. After all that teaching from Leader Dollon, you still lie faster than a horse trots."

"I still can't beat you in that lying department."

"All right. All right. What's on this week's agenda?"

"You have to go with me one night to Mount Signal Spiritual Baptist Church and pray with Elizabeth."

"That I'll surely do. Would Sheila be there in the basement?" Nigel returned a short grin for his answer.

"Whom do you think sent that money to Nicholby & Jordan in that oily envelope?" Tommy asked.

"Got to ask Lyle when I visit him in Rikers Island." Nigel put his hand on Tommy's shoulder and said, "Thanks, pal. Even in my absence you do my homework."

"But you still haven't told me where you were for two weeks, Sunday school boy. You said that you would have been away for just two days. You didn't call Liz; you didn't call Totohead; and you didn't call me. You are not to be trusted."

"You, too. I'm still awaiting your answer: whether Carmensita's baby's clothes were bought by you in the capacity of a thoughtful godfather, or on account of the after effect of that glorious copulation?"

"Okay. We're even." Tommy said.

"Only with our nonanswers."

They grinned, and exchanged a brotherly handshake.

"By the way, Nigel," Tommy said, "the Jews will be marching on Kingston Avenue tomorrow."

"About what?"

"About Constance Wagner's murder."

"I didn't hear that. How do you happen to know about that march that takes place tomorrow?"

"Through the white grapevine." Tommy read Nigel's face. Nigel's wears his life on his face. "Nigel, don't go there! Just as there's the black grapevine, there's the white grapevine...I'm not listening to you, Nigel. Today, I have the last word."

Chapter Fourteen

Lyle Gordon

The phone rang, and Nigel snatched it. "Hello!"

"Turn to Channel 7 quickly," Tommy said.

"I'm rushed, Lord Meath, I'm on my way to Rikers Island."

"I say turn it on," Tommy demanded.

Nigel surfed to ABC. On ABC there was a massive crowd of Hasidic Jews. They stood stoically on Eastern Parkway and blocked the southern entrance into Kingston Avenue. The Hasidims' massive black and white banner read WE ARE JEWS FIRST, AMERICANS SECOND. NO CONVICTION FOR CONSTANCE WAGNER, NO VOTE, MR. SENATOR WHOEVER YOU ARE.

In the midst of the throng of Jews and policemen was Senator Pothole. Senator Pothole who seized every opportunity to lift his staggering standing in the polls (and opportunities indeed always fall into his lap at the right time) spoke excitedly into the battery of prime time news microphones. The sun rays reflected from the Senator's forehead as his vast audience cheered his delivery for several minutes. Senator Pothole was pleased, and he continued his eloquent stomping-on-the-Parkway speech which was again interrupted by voluminous cheers. "...This is not about election or winning votes....Crown Heights is a peaceful community. No one can tell me that there is a more peaceful block than this block and its immediate environs on which we are standing...I'm going to use one of my favorite quotes which says 'Christianity is the daughter of Judaism' and that is why Christians and Jews should live in peace. Mind you, I don't want to be misquoted by you newsmen. I did not say other religions cannot apply...Blacks and Jews held hands in

Selma, Birmingham, and Montgomery during the Civil Rights Movement. Blacks and Jews were hosed upon, bullwhipped, and were bitten by Bull Connors' dogs...Blacks and Jews held hands and marched, not to be overcome, but to overcome. It can still happen...The murder of Constance Wagner was senseless. It was heinous. This is not a matter of race or religion, but a matter of justice...The act is heinous. The act is cowardly. The act is bastardly...actions committed in an unprovocative setting. The heinous murderer should pay."

"Nigel, are you listening to Senator Pothole's choice of words."

"Yes."

"Then you know what that means?"

"Sure. Constance Wagner's death is now a political matter. Washington is looking on; Albany is looking on; Gracie Mansion is looking on; and an election is around the corner. For Christ's sake, who else is looking on?"

"You can bet your bottom dollar that the Prison Administration is definitely looking on and taking notes of words like 'heinous and unprovocative.' Heinous Lyle is a CMC (Central Monitor Case). His every minute is monitored, and his cell is being bugged as we speak. Lyle would be watched like a hawk on its way to grab King Midas's gold. It is solemnly believed that Lyle killed Constance Wagner, and her death has put neighborhood politics on the front burner; and, as you know, Nigel, neighborhood politics, though local, is Federal politics. And I won't kid myself that..."

"What, Lord Meath?"

"That the Jews have clout."

"What I'm about to say now would shock you, Lord Meath."

"You could never shock me, bruvver. Let's hear it. What?"

"I like the Jews' resolve. Rightly or wrongly, they

agitate for their people. They say, 'Never again!' and they mean what they say."

"And I like Senator Pothole because he boldly takes sides. Where are your black politicians, Nigel, to at least raise a banner that says TRIAL COMES BEFORE CONVICTION?"

"Lord Meath, I know where my black politicians are."

"Tell me, Sunday school boy. You come from that psychic Pastalaqua House, and you learn the bible in a basement."

"If my black politicians are not in Israel laying a wreath on Golda Meir's grave at this minute, then they are stuck in their neutral gears...Lord Meath, I've got to go. I'm running late."

"Give Lyle my regards. Nigel! Nigel! switch to the Peacock Channel."

"Click!" Nigel was gone.

Tommy stayed with Channel 4. Groups of Spiritual Baptists who got wind of the Jews' demonstration came marching westward on the surface road of Eastern Parkway. Regaled in their spiritual garbs, the Baptist churches lifted their banner which read GOD LOVES THE VILEST SINNER. Sister Elizabeth Gordon and Sister Hettie Campbell held hands. All the Baptist leaders, including Leader Dollon, and Reverend Beresford Moore of the Methodist Church, let the women lead the march. The women of Divine Truth Assembly, Yoruba Orisha, Sankofa Peoples, and St. Francis Spiritual Baptist Churches sang *We Shall Overcome.*

Tommy stepped away when Channel 4 went to commercials. The phone rang, and he answered it. He returned to his television and shouted, "Oh no! That's not fair...Why should the police detour the Baptist people to another street to make their point." He switched back to Channel 7, and Reverend Moore was being interviewed. The veins in Reverend Moore's neck were about to burst from his outrage of being detoured to Albany Avenue. He told Channel 7 newsman some choice words, but only the likely language came on the air. "I married Lyle Gordon, the accused— and accused of what—if it were a black woman who was murdered, Eastern Parkway would not be blocked today...I am not a seerman but I'll tell all those Jews in their long, black frock-coats, earlocks, and black sombreros, that boy Lyle Allister Gordon whom I married over thirty years ago wouldn't kill a fly. The police and Senator Pothole better go and look for the real killer who is probably on the Parkway right now."

"I agree with you, Reverend Moore," Tommy said, "but they are wearing Borsolinos, *not* sombreros."

"...And, as for you, votes-ciphering Pothole, don't forget the Romans killed Jesus...The Torah says that the Messiah will come out of the loins of David, and the Jews know, just as I, that Jesus is God; but still the Jews disown Jesus."

"That's enough, Reverend Moore. Keep religion out of your speech. How do you know your religion is right and another man's is wrong? We are are all assuming, Reverend Moore." Tommy turned off his television and studied his detective notes.

* * * * * *

Lyle Gordon looked up from his cell and saw a visitor escorted in. "Son, is that you?" Lyle said.

"Yes," Nigel answered, and he embraced his father. They cried and talked at the same time.

"I'm really glad to see you, son."

"Me, too," Nigel said and unlocked their embrace.

"Make yourself comfortable on the bunk, son." Lyle smiled warmly.

Nigel's smile was even warmer. "I didn't know that they would have allowed me in here."

"Just this morning the Prison Commissioner, strangely, by-passed the rules, and that gives me the suspicion that this cell is." The words that followed "is" were Lyle's body language and the way he looked at the walls; and Nigel indeed understood the unspoken.

"Lord Meath sends his regards."

"How is he? Is he still doing your homework?"

"He's in charge of my homework now."

"What a great kid. What's buzzing in the outside world?"

"I happened to be in the Wall Street area last week, and I really enjoyed the eye food." Nigel looked at Lyle and smiled.

"Are you referring to the beautiful women downtown?"

"Sure. Wasn't eye food one of your code names?"

"How do you know that, Mr. Sneaky?" Lyle rumpled Nigel's coarse hair. "Son, I see you have some grays popping out."

"Pa, I'll dye them like you to look younger." They laughed. "Pa, you were a winner with those code names and phone numbers, but Elizabeth always decoded them when she found them in your pants pockets."

"You were a kid. How do you know that?"

"Most nights I was awake when you and Elizabeth thought that I was asleep. I used to hear her baptizing you with her blue tongue."

Lyle laughed endlessly. "What else did you hear in the night before you wet your bed?"

"About your faithful car Leaky." Nigel rambled on past incidents. He wanted to ask the question uppermost in his mind. He opened his mouth, but there was a blocking sound, and only air came out of his mouth.

"What's bothering you, son? Is there something you wish to know?"

"Not really. How many years now Elizabeth is in that church?"

"Since you were little. I was glad that she found a

place that would be a solace for her because I was always in Leaky."

"She never believed that Leaky story because most times you hardly brought home money from your moonlighting."

Lyle ignored the comment. "Like I'm seeing your mother now buying flowers for the church. She used her own money. She never took a black penny from the collection plate or from Leader Dollon. When I tried to interfere she'd say, 'Buying the flowers is my responsibility. Amen.'"

"And she got angry whenever you compared your Leader Gerrol of Fyzabad with her Leader Dollon. In what way was Leader Dollon different?"

"I can't pinpoint it now. I went to her church once, and that was the Sunday night before Labor Day."

"You saw Leader Dollon once, and yet you came to the conclusion that he was different from your Leader Gerrol?"

"Is that the question you really want to ask me, or are you just hedging and using Leader Dollon as a red herring?"

"Still, I want to know how he's so different from your Leader Gerrol?"

"He's a bit imitative."

"Whom does he imitate?"

"Your mother and I argued about that many nights, and since you pretended many nights that you were asleep when you were not, I'm sure you know the answer...Is that the question you came all this distance to ask me?"

"Well, well...Would you allow me to go into your toolbox?"

"That's my Pandora's box."

"I know; but I'm sure to find a name or names, or even a photograph."

"Whose?"

"Jackiass's."

Lyle's eyes popped. "So you remember how Elizabeth referred to Billie. Now I really believe that you didn't sleep at nights, kid."

"What's her real name, Pa?"

"Why? Are you investigating my case?"

"I just think that I should know her name."

"You'll find it in my toolbox."

"You haven't given me permission to open it."

"Okay; but keep it from Elizabeth's eyes. There's a letter in my toolbox, already addressed, to be mailed to Trinidad and Tobago. Mail it for me." He looked at Nigel and said, "That's what you wanted to know?"

"Well..."

"Have you visited the Sullivan's new home in Queens as yet?"

"Not yet."

"I hope you are not bearing a grudge because the Sullivans moved out of Brooklyn? People are free to go wherever they please. I had my hangups that way, but no more."

Nothing was said for at least five minutes. Nigel observed the luxury of Lyle's cell. There was a bunk bed attached to the wall and a small locker. The lavatory and the face bowl were both located inside the cell. There was no partition to separate the lavatory; everything was exposed to everybody, but each cell was separated by solid steel bars drilled into concrete slabs. Nigel got up and held the bars. He turned around slowly and looked at his father who seemed at ease in the twelve-foot by six-foot room. More than ever, Nigel was convinced that his father was a contented man but he missed his wife and loved her.

Lyle looked solemnly at Nigel and said, "Son, I didn't hit her, strangle her, or kill her."

"Thank you, Pa. I wanted to hear it from your lips." Nigel embraced his father and they laughed. "Out of curiosity," Nigel said, "I called your office and a Daniel Cake answered. You spoke of all your officemates to Liz, but you never called Daniel's name. Is he a new employee at South Opnorth?"

"I met him at South Opnorth. He joined that law firm before me."

Nigel took out a piece of paper from his pocket. "Do you remember this?"

"Sure. That is the scrap of paper that fell out of my pocket with ASDFLKJ."

"Well, I'm writing Jackiass's name on it. Do you have enemies on the job?"

"No."

"Was anyone on your job absent the day after Labor Day?"

"Coming to think of it, Cakey was."

"Who's Cakey?"

"Daniel Cake. A lawyer referred to Daniel's shorthand transcriptions being as cakey as his mother's fruit cake, and since then the nickname Cakey got stuck on Daniel."

"You and Cakey ever had a fight, an argument, or anything?"

"I called him Cakey, and he didn't like it. Even the Friday before Labor Day I called him so, and everyone enjoyed my tease."

"Is he black or white?"

"Black like a pot."

"American?"

"His accent is, but he is a Trini."

"What's a Trini?"

"A native of Trinidad and Tobago."

"How could you be that sure that he's a Trini?"

"By one expression."

"What was that expression?"

"He called salted fish *sol fish*."

"Other West Indian people say *sol fish* too."

"His diction was one hundred percent Trini's."

"So you won't be surprised if he danced on the Parkway with a placard in the Labor Day parade because Trinis dominated that festival?"

"If he's a true Trini, he was there."

"What motive would he have to kill Connie?" Nigel did not wait for an answer. He wrote Daniel Cake's name alongside Jackiass's on the crumpled sheet of paper. He scratched his head, and said, "Do you think Connie would have scratched that poem?"

"No way. One more thing, son."

"What?"

"I did not tell Detective Crobett that when he took me to view Connie's body that I got a whiff of the same perfume that was on that *Grenada Ghost*, and I knew that I smelled that perfume somewhere else before."

"Where? Where?" Nigel asked excitedly.

"Somewhere, but I just can't remember now."

"Try! Try!"

Lyle thought for a minute. "I really can't remember."

"You smelled it on the street, on the job, in a bar, in Leaky, where?"

"I really don't remember now."

"About how many times did you see the Ghost that day?"

"Wherever we went. Connie suspected that *Grenada Ghost* was following us, but I put her mind at ease and told her that was her imagination. That *Grenada Ghost* was a silent agitator, a sort of ubiquitous...a sullen radical...I hate agitators—all of them...the hippies, the yippies, the plait-haired black powers, the free-bed exchangers, the Rastas—they all eventually come back to the main stream after they had their fling. I don't know why they left the stream at all...Agitators! Agitators!"

Nigel studied his father's demeanor before he spoke, and when he spoke he looked him in the eye. "Pa, sometimes we agitate our coffee to mix the cream, to taste the sugar below; sometimes a woman agitates because her man is not doing right; sometimes we agitate because our elected representative is messing up, and the press is spineless; somebody has to 'bell the cat,' and that somebody may suffer or die for his or her agitation, but from his or her agitation another Rosa Parks will emerge...As a boy, didn't you tell me that your Grandpa dug up the soil to get worms to use as fish bait?"

"Yes."

"Digging up that soil was a form of agitation."

"I thought to keep silent was the best way, and in doing so the angel would write my name in gold."

"Wait a minute! I heard that gold talk from you before."

"You surely have. When you were a tot I recited a poem with those words and put you to bed. My diction was wholesale Mr. Tellymack's. Only Tellymack's students recited that poem that way." Lyle recited *Abou Ben Adhem.*

"That's beautiful. Your style and diction are really unique," Nigel said.

"That's Mr. Tellymack's for you."

"Did you see that masquerading Ghost up close? Did you notice any marks on its body?"

"Nothing whatsoever. That living apparition pulled my belt that Connie wore, but it moved so swiftly in the melee."

"What about the height of that Ghost?"

"Puzzling." They chitchatted. "You haven't mentioned anything about your mother. Tell her that I love her."

"I did not want to tell you, but she and Hettie will be coming to visit you tomorrow."

"Detective Nigel Gordon," Lyle said, "you know something, last night I was reflecting on my life. I told myself that Aunt Gina's world is no more. It is a different world. And you know something else, I, Pollyanna, am really learning my lesson in jail. You were right Billie Zellars when you quoted that 'we are just the coal for the engine of history.'"

"Who is Billie Zellars?"

"Alias Jackiass."

"I know that I'll find her name and other pertinent information in your toolbox, but I want you to tell me something about her. What you say about her doesn't even have to make sense." Nigel turned his face and held the prison bars.

"Well," Lyle began haltingly, "Billie has a lot of pictures on her wall. She's a sort of bedroom guerilla. She talks of black power, white domination, liberation...She's always quoting Ralph Nader's 'government of General Motors, by Exxon, for Du Pont...;' and she says that it's only her plastic money that separates her from the bagwoman in the subway."

"Were you supposed to meet her on the Parkway on Labor Day?"

"Yes."

"Did you meet her?"

"No."

"How long have you been seeing her?"

"Since you and Lord Meath shoveled Eggie and Bob's snow."

"That's sometime now. What else you noticed about her—at dinner time, shower time, party time, or even bedtime?"

"I have something to tell you, but I don't know if it makes sense."

"I still want to hear it."

"As long as I've known Billie, she never allowed me to go into her clothes closet."

"You mean after all these years Billie took your coat from your hand, and she hung it herself? You never hung your coat or took your coat from her closets? Strange?"

"I knew that she had a placard in her closet, but I didn't see it. I also know that she has a brother, Ruff."

"He's tough?"

"He's big, and his name is Ruff."

"Do you think that it was her good manners, or she purposely did not want you to go into her clothes closet?"

"I really don't know."

"What else you noticed, especially the last time you saw her. Did you see her the Sunday before Labor Day?"

"Yes, I saw her that Sunday. I spent a long time with her."

"Tell me what took place on that Sunday?"

Lyle looked at Nigel inquiringly. "Everything?"

Nigel smiled. "Whatever...anything, no matter how foolish it may sound."

"Well, my belt fell, and...."

"Are you referring to the same belt that was found on Connie's neck?"

"Yes."

"Go on."

"When I was leaving Billie's house on that Sunday night, my belt fell in front of her, and she did not pick it up."

"Why?"

"She attempted to pick up my belt, then she said that her back was hurting her. She was just an inch away from the belt, yet she did not pick it up."

"Were you the cause of her back pain?" Nigel turned his face, hid his smile, and deliberately changed the conversation. "By the way, our company received a large donation for the purpose of investigating your case. The donor, however, didn't leave a forwarding address."

"Not even a postmarked envelope? No sort of clue?"

"The envelope had your name, the words '*pro bono*,' and a conspicuously oily smudge."

"Oily?"

"Yes. Why are you smiling?"

"Because the envelope is oily."

"Beats me. Do you think that *Grenada Ghost* who followed you for the whole Labor Day, whom I believe was the person who went into Connie's house after you left, who probably impersonated you, do you think that person was a man or a woman?"

"Connie, before her death, said that masquerader was definitely a man."

"And what you thought?"

"Could be a woman."

"Whom should I believe: you or Connie?"

"You are the detective."

"And right now fate is the seeing-eye dog of our happenstance." Nigel looked at his father's shrunken body in his prison uniform and quickly turned his face. He called the prison guard who opened the cell door, and he walked out without looking back. Abruptly, he stopped and said, "Pa, what is odd about Daniel Cake, alias Cakey?"

"He always looked at my waist."

Chapter Fifteen

The Eyewitnesses

Detective Tommy Sullivan knocked on their door.

"Who is it?" Mabel Plutz inquired.

"Detective Sullivan."

"Wait a minute, Detective Shurvan," Mabel said. She peeped through her favorite keyhole and made a sign to her husband. He climbed on a chair and glared through the wall and nodded his approval. "I am coming, Detective Shurvan." Mabel opened the door.

"I'm Detective Sullivan. May I come in?"

Mabel measured him with her eyes. "Sure. Take a seat. I am Mabel; my husband is Harvey."

"Can I address you as Mabel and Harvey?"

"Sure. That's our name. What do you want, Mr. Shurvan?"

"Call me Tommy. Mabel, it may be difficult for you to take your mind back some six months ago, but I'd like to ask you questions about a man you identified, the man who supposedly murdered your tenant, Constance Wagner."

"That criminal is still alive?"

"He's in jail."

"I hope he rots there."

Tommy addressed Harvey. "Why didn't you go to the identification parade?"

"Nobody asked me to come," Harvey said.

"Can I hear what you have to say about the night in question, Harvey?"

Harvey looked at his wife. "Why don't you ask her? She has a good memory. She can tell you what happened on the last whaling ship."

"Mister Detective is speaking to you, Harvey. What you said your name was again?"

"Tommy Sullivan. With a memory like yours, I

didn't think you would have forgotten my name so quickly, Mrs. Plutz."

"Harvey and I were right here on that night. I can remember everything."

"Can you remember the date of the murder, Mabel?"

"He killed her. Isn't it? So what's in a date?"

"Do you know the name of the man who is accused of that murder?"

"Something Gordon...My tenant was a good woman. A decent man used to drop her home. Don't ask me his name, but I know it was a red car with a NY 04...I can't remember the rest of the number plate, but he was a good looking man like you."

"Black or white?"

"Like you, of course." Mabel emphasized.

Tommy got up from the chair and walked around the room. He admired the photographs on the wall.

"Tim," Mabel said, "you are looking at five generations. There are three judges in my family."

"That's great. Men of justice." Tommy looked at Mabel. "Mrs. Wagner's death really bothered you, I know."

"Her death bothers me every day," Mabel said, and fanned her face with her hand.

"Tell me what you really saw of that killer, Mabel." Tommy showed sorrow in his voice.

"I looked through that hole there and the keyhole." She pointed at two spots. "I saw him. He stayed a long time upstairs. You know you men."

"When I came in, the stairs and hallway were dark," Tommy said.

"Timmy, are you telling me I didn't see the Adult Nigger's face?" Mabel repeated her question.

"Of course, you did. I am just reconfirming what I heard before. Go-ahead, Mabel."

"He stayed upstairs a long time, then he went away." Mabel thought a bit before she spoke. "The first time he didn't put on the radio, but the second time when he came back, he put on the radio after something heavy fell."

"Did you look at him the second time when he came downstairs?"

"You think I'm a Peeping Tom? I am an old woman who is interested in my community. This neighborhood has to be fought for."

"God blessed the aged," Tommy said. He forced himself on Harvey. "Please tell me, Harvey, what you didn't have time to tell the police."

"The second time when the person came down that person had on a lot of powder on his or her face like a white Ju-Ju with greenish-grayish eyes..."

"Harvey, they don't have white Ju-Ju," Mabel admonished him. "Ju-Ju are black people in the jungle."

"I believe you, Mabel. Tarzan got rid of them. Tell me if you know this person, Harvey. Here." Tommy handed Harvey a photograph.

"That's Dalgo," Mabel shouted. "He drives in the red car that used to come to her."

"And..." Harvey began.

"You have no manners! The detective is talking to me, Harvey."

"What were you about to say, Harvey?" Tommy coaxed him. He didn't answer. "Tell me about how tall was that killer, Mabel?"

"About your height, Tim"

"I am five eleven."

"About what height you think he was, Harvey?"

"I am not sure," Harvey said.

"Why?" Tommy probed.

"Well, for one thing, that person could have been a woman, Tommy."

"That's an honest answer, Harvey. Harvey and Mabel, I am going outside, and I want you to close the door. Each one of you will look through the hole that you spied on the killer." Tommy closed the door himself, and he called out, "What part of me you see, Mabel? Start with the top peephole and then go to the keyhole?"

"I see your chest, your legs, hands, and part of your head."

"That's fine, Mabel. Your turn, Harvey."

"Give me some time because I have to climb up to a high hole." Harvey went for his cane.

"I understand. Take your time, Harvey, and tell me when you are up there."

"I'm getting help with my cane...I'm ready now."

"Great. What part of me you can see?"

"Your whole body."

"Let me put on my long coat. Tell me what part of me you can see?"

"Your whole body."

"What about my eyes?"

"Your eyes too."

"And you said that that person had greenish-grayish eyes. Did you see a shoe?"

"Just the tip."

"What color was it?"

"Can't remember."

"Anything else, Harvey?"

"Nothing else, except..."

"Except what?"

"At one time it looked taller than the other time."

"You may come down now, Harvey. Be careful, and use your cane for support. Please open the door, Mabel."

"Sure," Mabel said. "Aren't you coming in, Detective Shurvan?"

"Do you have more to say, Mrs. Plutz?"

"Why does this country delay justice? A man like that should be executed already, Timmy."

"Mabel, the feast is not for Abraham alone. You and Harvey have been exceedingly helpful. Good day."

"Wait a minute." She ran inside and came back.

"This was lying about some where." She handed him a piece of shredded cloth. "And this, too."

He took the four pieces of cardboard and pieced them together. "Where did you find these?"

"By my garbage."

"Why didn't you give them to Detective Crobett or to the police?"

"You are not a police, Timmy?"

"Sure, sure."

"Then that's why I'm giving it to you."

"I thank you very much, Mrs. Plutz."

"You're welcome, Detective Shurvan."

Chapter Sixteen

Billie Zellars a/k/a Jackiass

"Walk in gentlemen. My door is open. I've been expecting this." Billie Zellars smiled and welcomed her visitors.

Tommy Sullivan walked in. Nigel Gordon followed, and he bore a meaningless smile. "I am Tommy Sullivan, and this is my associate Nigel Gordon of the Nicholby and Jordan Private Detective Agency," Tommy said.

"Two rookies, I see. After all those negative things that you've heard and read of Bedford Stuyvesant and its people, both of you walked in here, abreast, none covering the other; that's no good, detectives."

"You are not insinuating that everyone in Bed Stuy is a villain?" Tommy said.

"Do I look as one, Mr. Sullivan?" She walked to her window, opened the blind, and said, "Both of you should know whether or not I'm a fiend. You knew where to find me, so I'm sure you already know my name."

"I'm just following your line of communication," Tommy replied.

"Smart man."

"Smart about what?"

She shifted the conversation. "On your way to my apartment, you should have been covering him," Billie said. She addressed Nigel, but she didn't call his name. Nigel's eyes were glued to the darkened portraits on the wall, and he paid her no attention. "Have a seat, detectives," she said pleasantly.

Tommy sat down, but Nigel's eyes were no longer on the darkened portraits; his eyes were transfixed on the grossest caricature.

"Can I offer you a drink?" She looked at Tommy.

"I'm abstaining these days," Tommy said.

"And you?" Billie addressed Nigel, but again she did not call his name.

"No, thank you," Nigel said. He didn't look at her. He looked at a beautifully sketched portrait of Maurice Bishop, the slain Grenadian Prime Minister, and he read an excerpt of Bishop's speech that was delivered at Hunter College, New York, on June 5, 1983:

"...[T]he hostile, aggressive course of destabilization against our government [Grenada] by the Ronald Reagan administration had been established...."

Nigel again looked steadfastly at that heavily detailed caricature which, when interpreted, revealed a black man who wished he had a white soul. He shook his head disgustingly because he knew that sordid caricature was his father.

Billie sipped her wine. "Why are you here, gentlemen?"

"Ms. Zellars...," Tommy began.

She interrupted him. "Not that handle. Ms. is for rich white ladies who need a gallery for their show biz and cocktail parties. If you wish to be polite, you may relax yourself, and call me sister."

Tommy looked at Nigel, and Nigel advised him with his eyes. Over the years they had grown to understand each other's body movements. Scratching the right knee had a different meaning to scratching the left knee. "Sister," Tommy said, "why were you expecting us?"

"It's logical. A certain black man came at my feet..."

Nigel immediately turned around and looked at Billie who continued her reply.

"...And that black man is in trouble, so you're coming to me to help fix the funk."

Tommy smiled. "What that black man came for, sister?"

"Knowledge."

"That's all?"

Billie sipped her wine, and pretended that there was not a follow-up question.

"Did he get that knowledge?" Tommy asked again.

"If he did, he didn't apply it."

"So you know why we are here?"

"A white woman is murdered, and two redeemers cometh."

Nigel walked away from the emboldened caricature, and he put his chair opposite Billie's loveseat.

"How long have you known Lyle Gordon?" Tommy said and pretended dust was in his eyes.

"Do you want me to blow it out?" She put down her wine and went to Tommy's aid.

"The ball of my finger will do the job. Thank you, anyhow, sister." He rubbed his eyes. "How long have you known Lyle?"

"Since my last year of high school. But I won't tell you my age."

"I won't ask you anything about your age, but the way you look shows that you are in the early second term of twenty."

"That's very kind of you."

"Forgive me for asking you this personal question, but were you in love with him?"

"Let's forget about the past."

"What about the present. Are you?" Tommy insisted.

"Are you looking for a motive? If it's jealousy, rule me out," Billie said.

"You aren't under oath, sister."

"I know that, so you can cut out the circumlocution and come to the point."

"I'm sure you know Lyle's plight. We would like whatever help you can give us because we do not think Lyle is guilty of that murder. Whatever he learned at your feet, we are willing to hear."

"He never learned the way of the big waves." She

looked at Nigel when she said that.

"How come?" Tommy applied his charming smile. "I was told that he's a humble man who sponges on knowledge."

"If so, my sponge was repelled."

"Where were you educated?"

"PS 269, Erasmus, Tilden, La Sorbonne, and I received my highest degree at The Streets of Brooklyn University, Bed Stuy Faculty."

"Quite impressive. It's a pity Lyle Gordon didn't absorb some of your fluid credits."

"What's that supposed to mean? Sarcasm?"

"Of course not, sister. I was just wondering if he did..."

"He would have been enjoying his free Saturdays." She completed Tommy's sentence.

"Probably...Accidentally, we came across a letter that you had written to Lyle sometime ago."

She interrupted Tommy. "Mr. Private Investigator, why don't you say that was an inside job. Someone broke into a toolbox." She looked sheepishly at Nigel.

"Why don't you answer his question?" Nigel said abruptly.

"Hey, brother, I don't have to," Billie snapped.

Nigel swung his chair around and pointed to her wall. "What do you mean by that caricature with the reading, 'The fool L.A.G. never graduated?'"

"Lyle Allister Gordon, the fool, never graduated into manhood. Any more questions, brother?"

Nigel did not answer, and Tommy continued his questioning. "Sister, you said in one of your letters to Lyle..."

"I won't answer unless I know the source of that letter."

"The toolbox." Tommy looked at Billie, and she nodded. "In that letter you said, 'If anything comes across my path, my brothers will ease my pain.'"

"Mark my word. I said, 'anything,' not 'anyone.'"

"When you speak of brothers, were you thinking biologically, or was it said in that camaraderie fashion?"

"Both."

"I know that it will be difficult to bring to mind all your hand-shaking brothers," Tommy looked at the silhouetted portraits on the wall, "but do you have blood brothers?"

"Yes."

"Would you mind giving me their names?"

"Ruff Gillette."

"Any other?"

"Over twenty years I have not contacted him, so I'll make no mention of him."

Nigel made a note on his ASDFLKJ scrap paper.

Tommy walked to the portraits. "These portraits are great. Who sketched them?"

"I did."

"Who are they?"

"My heroes...not the oreo cookie..."

Nigel interrupted Billie and said, "Were you that woman who called Lyle's house and left phoney names?"

"I had one alias, and that was the one given me."

"What was it?" Nigel asked. There was no humor in his voice.

"Jacki Jackiass," Billie said effortlessly. "I'm having another. Can I pour you one, gentlemen?"

"It won't be necessary," Tommy said. "We are leaving. We have to pay a visit on an eyewitness. It was nice meeting you, sister."

Billie wore a Danskin exercise suit. She got up from her favorite loveseat and stretched her hand to Nigel. He barely shook it. Tommy held her grip firmly. He eased his hand slowly out of her grip, and he smiled. She was impressed by his personality. "Lord Meath and Son, daddy's little boy..." Billie addressed them. They looked around in astonishment. "Before I wish you happy hunting," she dipped her finger in the wine and tasted her finger, "remember, gentlemen, that mysteries are not solved by reading and digesting Sherlock Holmes. We don't have the Thames River here. Do not forget that whether the murderer walked on the London Bridge or on the Brooklyn Bridge the greatest clue would be, and I stress, would be, your keen observation. Observe not where the murderer placed his or her fingers, but how he or she placed those fingers. Don't forget that you should always use your nearest object as your first target. My generals, not my oreo cookie, taught me such logic, and it paid dividends for them and me." She raised her glass to her walled generals and nodded to those portraits as if they were living beings stuck to her wall. She surveyed Tommy and Nigel as if they were her children who returned home after their first day in kindergarten. "One more thing, detectives. My Haitian girlfriend Nikki taught me this great proverb. It goes like this: 'When the blind man says that he's going to throw a rock at you, it means that he already has the rock concealed in his hand.' Think about it. Have a nice day, detectives. Don't forget to always cover your pal." She closed her door.

Nigel and Tommy came out of Building 122 in single file. They took her advice.

"Let's go in the car and talk," Nigel said.

"I'm thirsty, man. Let's go to Fulton Street," Tommy said. They walked aimlessly on Fulton Street, the capital of Black Bed Stuy, and weaved through the busy crowd of shoppers and street merchants who monopolized the sidewalks. They bought bottled water from the Korean grocer and trekked back towards the Ford. "Shit, they stopped rolling dice, and now all those guys are sitting on my car. If they scratch my baby, I'll..." Tommy raised his voice.

"Cool it. I'll handle this, Lord Meath," Nigel said, and he walked to Tommy's car.

"Hi Bruh," Nigel addressed the young adult who wore a dark shades and a wool cap with the peak facing south, "did you see Rick, man?" Nigel shook the young adult's hand with that brotherly greeting.

"Rick just left, bruh."

"Tell him Snake was here to him...You on my baby, bruh?"

"Sorry, man. I didn't know this was your car, man."

"No problem. I'm sure you didn't scratch my baby."

"No, bruh."

"Peace, bruh."

"Peace," the young adult leader replied. He moved away. His friends followed him, and they began a new game of dice.

"Nigel, how did you know which one to approach?" Tommy asked.

"Street smarts, bruh."

"You knew Rick?"

"I don't even know what Rick looks like. I heard Rick's name as a third person in their conversation when you parked the Ford, so I knew he was not around."

"And you shook Mr. Dark Shades' hands as if you knew him in kindergarten."

"All blacks are comrades, man. We have an affinity. We belong, bruh."

"Belong where?"

"It's spiritual. It's a connection."

"And where did you get that Snake name?"

"Young adults are always fascinated with bad-John names—Snake, Cutthroat, Peg Leg—and if my name is Snake, it means that I have a rep known to Rick."

"I see, bruh."

"That's the street, man."

"Let's leave this place, Snake," Tommy said jovially, and he started the Ford.

"Turn it off. Let's talk about that bitch, man," Nigel said angrily.

"Nigel, I purposely took you for water on Fulton Street because I thought the walking around and the water would cool you down, but I miscalculated your anxiety. Why call Billie a bitch?"

"You know why, man."

"You tell me."

"Couldn't you see through that cutthroat?"

"If that is what she is, she was your father's woman. That was where he was when he wasn't in Leaky. I'm sure he made his jazz sessions very interesting when Elizabeth spent her time worshipping in Leader Dollon's church. As far as I see, Lyle told her everything about us and about his home life when his gyrating waist was tired. She even knows our nicknames. Lord Meath, Son, Daddy's little boy." Tommy mimicked Billie's mezzo-soprano voice.

"I don't trust that fucking bitch."

"That's abusive language, man. You ought to show balance in this case even if Billie is a Dr. Jekyll and Mr. Hyde. Totohead expects you to."

"Why were you so soft on her?"

"What about you? All you did was to look at her generals on her wall and at Lyle's oreo-cookie caricature."

"Totohead said that you are in charge. Remember, Tommy?"

"That's a nice way to shirk your responsibility, Nigel."

"I told you why I didn't want to question that bitch."

"You've got to stop that sentimental shit!"

"Who are you shouting at, man?"

"You! I'm in charge so I can do the shouting."

"I am sentimental! and there you were smiling, shaking her hand softly, and looking at the rabbit's body, Detective Tommy Sullivan, the playboy."

"Yes, I did admire her; but I alone asked questions. Stop taking your fucking rage out on me, man. You prayed for this assignment. That's what you told me long before you were assigned, and the good Lord made it a reality. Now you are fucking up. If you want to be a patsy, why not go back to Leader Dollon's church and take a job as a Sunday school teacher."

"Don't tell me, man, what I should do."

"But you want to tell me what I should do."

"I hate that bitch."

"Don't go overboard now."

"You fell overboard and drowned before you asked her who killed that *white* woman." The word "white" sounded like leprosy when it came out of Nigel's mouth. It was as if that deceased white woman was one of those hateful white males who chased him through Marine Park when he was a school boy.

Tommy had a different interpretation for his pal's behavior. "There you go again, Son, daddy's little boy! You are always invoking color! Color! You with your black and white eyes! You are quick to say that *white* people are racists. Next you'll apply your examples of the white policemen who shot down black kids. As usual, you always forget that some of those saintly black kids have criminal records, and their toys are real guns. We went up Billie's steps and we could have been shot down. She herself told you what is likely to happen in Bed Stuy or in any neighborhood for that matter. Stop thinking like Liberal John Public. A life is a life—black, white, yellow brown...Am on your side, man. Am tired of you sounding like those law-breakers who only become philosophers and poets when their arses are behind bars, and when they are free they forget their poems."

"I hope you are not only referring to the black bruvvers?"

"I'm referring to black like you, white like me, yellow as Chin, mulatto as your father's cheeky woman...*tout bagai*, everybody, as Lyle used to say."

"Calm down. You said enough. Tomorrow we'll pay another visit to our lovely Jackiass, and I'll do the questioning. Lyle told me that she had a placard hidden in her closet. She made that placard to parade on Labor Day. I warn you: Don't go looking at her parts when we pay her a visit tomorrow." Nigel laughed at himself.

"Are you protecting her for your kind only." Tommy

said. "I thought she was the woman who caused Elizabeth pain?"

"If Elizabeth had pain, she never showed it. Bruvver, let's go to Hende's and hang out with those guys, those print journalists. We may pick up some gossips there. That was Connie's hangout. What are you waiting on, boy. Drive."

Tommy started the Ford. He looked up through the windshield. "Son," Tommy said, "daddy's little boy, do you know whom I just saw?"

"Who?"

"Our sister. She just shut her blind. She was peeping at us through her shutters."

"Lord Meath, I'm thinking of a way to scheme her."

"Son, I hope not for a piece of arse? Remember she's daddy's."

"All I want from her is a print of her index finger."

"That's lovers' dirty finger, man. Isn't that the same finger you use on Sunday school Sheila?"

"That's why I want it. We'll corner her next time."

"Save your intuition for Dalgo."

"That doctor-shop knife who cuts both ways?"

"He cuts for himself, too. Why don't you buy a bottle and lure him. A rookie like you needs to practice your skill on how to handle human behavior. Practice on Dalgo all the stuff that you learned in training. Promise me that you'll leave your gun at home because I don't like your mood today."

"Trust me. I'm cool. I'll lure Dalgo into a liquid dinner, and I won't use my gun."

"I'm taking tomorrow off. By the way, my mother told me to invite you for dinner this weekend, and to tell you that the piano is dusty."

"Tell that lovely lady that I accept."

"Call me if you need me."

"You can bet your white grits that I'll need you to search Jackiass's clothes closet. You may have to go through her stained pajamas tomorrow and clean them."

"Nigel, you were not listening to me. I said that I'm taking tomorrow off to catch up on my sleep. Tomorrow you can go closet cleaning and check on Billie's dirty pajamas for yourself."

"I'm the associate, so I'll wait on my boss who is in charge of this project."

"Puppy."

"As my West Indian great grandfather used to say, 'Ashes col', so puppy lay down dey.' I'll lie in comfort and wait until you come."

"Quack, quack, duck chicken."

"Chickens have no reason in front of cockroaches."

"Says who?"

"Says Lyle."

"Says his libido."

Chapter Seventeen
Dalgo Gibbons

At his office Nigel studied the contents of the murder file and jotted down more notes on his scrap paper. He then drove to the New York Avenue precinct, parked, and was about to ask the officer seated at the desk a question when the phone rang.

"Hello, this is bookings...Officer Dixon speaking," the desk officer answered. Officer Dixon recognized the caller whose voice echoed through the black phone. "Yes, I have booked Langston Jay for rape, sir."

"Don't you know that he's the son of Adlai Hay! What was your hurry? Don't you know that we're New York's Finest, and we are on a go slow until the Mayor gives us more money than Sanitation? They're garbage."

Officer Dixon kept the phone close to his ear, but he did not reply.

"Where have you been, Officer Dixon? Haven't you read of the Hays? They are important people!" The caller's voice pitched louder.

Officer Dixon replied. "Sir, no one left me a list of all the important bankers, senators, congressmen, their spouses, concubines, and favorite bellydancers whom I shouldn't book."

"See me in my office at once! Click."

"Bastard," Officer Dixon shouted into the dead receiver. He hung up the phone. "How may I help you?" he asked Nigel.

"Sorry, officer, but I overheard your conversation. Where can I find the books with criminals and others on the wanted list? I am a private investigator, and I want to see a close up of Dalgo Gibbons."

"You'll find his mugshot in the next room, but if you are looking for him you'll surely find him in his red cap near Club Grassport. If you find Dalgo stripping the Police Commissioner's car buy him a round of scotch for me."

"Thanks for the tip, officer."

Dalgo was not on the wanted list, but his mugshot was in the precinct's book of known women molesters, thieves, car strippers, muggers, counterfeiters, and subway turnstile jumpers. He was photographed with his red cap as that was part of his anatomy. Nigel became curious, and he turned the pages of the book. "No," he said softly to himself. "That's not true. I can't believe that my cousin John is a thief and a counterfeiter. You were a spoiled brat who got everything. Aunt Lily predicted that you'll end up in jail. Your answer for everything was, 'I'm ahead of the game.' As far as I could see the game caught up with you. I'll visit you in prison sometime John, but right now it's Dalgo's time, and I don't want him to be ahead of me." He took a long look at Dalgo Gibbons' mugshot and closed the book.

It was a warm evening, and Nigel, dressed in a rough-dry dungaree and discolored shirt, walked to Club Grassport. He looked inside the club, but he did not see Dalgo. Neon glitter brightened the evening. Ladies of the evening leaned on the club's counters and wet their throats before business peaked. Drug pushers had a field day. He went into all of the bathrooms; he flushed them; he looked around, mumbled, "Red Cap is not here;" and he walked out. He paced himself slowly to the nearby liquor store, pushed himself ahead of the long line of weekend customers, shouted as a thirsty sailor for attention, and he got it. "Give me that red label and two paper cups," he said to the liquor clerk. "Put it in a double bag. Here's your money, bruvver." He burst the whiskey seal immediately and went to the pizzeria. He looked around, and hid his smile, when he glimpsed someone with a red cap. He sensed that that someone-with-a-red-cap trailed him. Nigel headed for the Parkway bench and sat there. He exposed his whiskey and pizza, and he sipped his coffee slowly.

"I see youse a loner, bruvver," the man with the red cap said, and he sat on the bench with the baiting detective.

"Who's youse, bruvver?" Nigel asked distrustfully.

"If youse don't know me, bruvver, youse gotta be from outta town."

"Sure is, bruvver. Am having pizza. I have an extra slice. You want it?"

"Not good for my ulcers, bruvver."

"Coffee?"

"Black?"

"Regular."

"I likes mine like my complexion, bruvver—black."

Nigel ignored his companion, bit ravenously into the two slices of pizza, and drank his coffee. "This shitting fly!" He dusted the buzzing fly away, took out his pocket radio, and searched the bands until he found disco music.

"Good music, bruvver," the man in the red cap said. "Keep it on that station, bruvver."

Nigel took out his whiskey and poured a little into his coffee. "I have another cup. What about this?"

"Not really, but I'll take a little to please you, bruvver."

"Help yourself. What's your name?"

"Dalgo. Dalgo Gibbons." Dalgo took the paper cup from Nigel and brimmed it with whiskey.

"Mine's Mannou. Mannou Reese. Peace, bruh." Like an affectionate street brother, he hit Dalgo a high five. "This is a nice cool joint, man."

"You should come more often and make friends, bruh. Over there is where the action is." Dalgo pointed in the direction of Club Grassport, north of Eastern Parkway. "Over there youse got everything from a jackboot to a slipper, bruvver. Come around here on Labor Day, and here's hot with West Indians jumping as if they'd just killed the beef and drinked the blood." He scratched his head with his dirty fingers, but he didn't move his red cap.

"I don't care for island people. Island people's the pits, man." Nigel looked at his watch and capped the whiskey bottle tightly. "Got to go, Dalgo. That fucking broad stood me up again."

"Youse won't stay for me to tell youse how I'd almost see a murder from this very bench?"

"Who wants to hear about murder, man. Am just from jail and nature is calling me to have my woman, man."

"Just one more drink, bruvver. You takes one, and I takes one, and that will give the broad some time to come and meet you here. I can hook you up to a cheap motel on Franklin Avenue, man...just thirteen dollars an hour." Dalgo wiped his raw lips. "Don't be so serious, bruvver. Let's drink until the broad comes, man. The evening is still young."

Nigel looked at Dalgo as if he depended on him for a blood transfusion. "Okay, just one." He uncapped the bottle and drizzled whiskey in both cups.

"That's all, man?" Dalgo looked at Nigel, and Nigel poured more. "That's more like it. To our health, bruvver...The story I's going to tell youse is about a white broad, more the lady type."

Nigel reached for his wallet, and he purposely dropped a photograph.

Dalgo picked up the photograph. "Em! Em! Ain't she some beautiful nigger. I'll wait until tomorrow for that bitch, man. What's the hurry? Is that your woman, bruvver?"

"Sure is, but she's no bitch, man."

"Confidential?"

"What is?"

"Her name."

"Shit! No."

"C'mon. What's in a name?"

"Okay, okay. Her name is Constance Marriane. I call her my sweet Connie."

"Youse never believe it."

"What?"

"The story I's about to tell youse about that white lady, that white lady have that same name."

"C'mon! Don't make up stories, man. The name Connie is rare as hen's teeth, man."

"This white lady Connie is rare, too. I swears on my dead grandmother that I saw the masquerader who killed that white Connie. I couldn't see his face but I's sure that's the killer."

"Youse talking in riddles, man. Where was you?" He poured sparingly into Dalgo's cup.

"I wasn't on the murder scene, but I knows that masquerader killed Connie. I was here on this same bench. I had some drinks at Grassport. Youse see that building over there on Kingston Avenue," he pointed south of Eastern Parkway, "Connie got murdered there after midnight last Labor Day."

"What was you doing on the bench at that time? Watching that white broad's window is your habit, man?"

"I was enjoying the cool air on the Parkway."

"I does do the same thing in Chicago, bruh. I sits in the park at nights and watch them homos…You was alone, bruvver?"

"No; two other bruvvers was with me…That Labor Day night there was a masquerader kind of lying down; sometimes he was talking to hisself and playing drunk. I knows he killed that white lady, but bruvver to bruvver…." He slapped Nigel's upraised palm. He did not complete his sentence, but the black lingo was understood.

Nigel got up and staggered a little. "C'mon. What sort of story is this? You didn't see the face of the killer, yet you suspected him? You was too damn drunk to suspect anybody."

"Coming to think of it, I was a little drunk, but I knows that masquerader was not drunk at all. He was up to something, so I left and went home."

"Where is home?"

"In the train."

"You lives there?"

"It only cost a token to live there, man. And I don't pay!"

"Youse knows that nice white lady who got killed?"

"Sure. I brung letters to her from Vito. She was a reporter woman with plenty of news for print. Nobody messed with her. Vito had eyes all around her."

"And you was one of Vito's eyes?"

"What kind of question is that, man? Is youse a cop, bruvver?"

"What shit you's asking, man? I's waiting on my fucking woman; you start telling me them braer rabbit stories; and now youse asking me a shit question about if I's a cop. Fuck you, Dalgo."

"Sorry, bruh."

"Youse stalling with your story, because you's lying to get my whiskey. I's fucking well mad, man. I coulda save my whiskey for me and my woman."

"Cool it, bruvver. Why I ask you that is because the news I gives to cop is different from the news I gives to the bruvvers."

"What news youse giving me, man?"

"Bruvvers news. Vito's a bitch, man."

"Is he a bruvver like us, man?"

"Naw; an Italian son of a bitch."

"You sure you didn't kill that white broad for a piece of pussy, man?"

"Nah. I think the strange man who went upstairs with a costume with the words 'Adult Nigger' or something like that, and the masquerader who was playing drunk on the Parkway near to us planned that murder. Both of them was in that plan to kill Connie."

"You was drunk like hell. You don't know nottun.

Youse was just as stupid and as drunk as them island people on that Labor Day, man."

"I knows for sure that them West Indian men was hiding their rum to drunken their womens, and they was hiding their cigarettes in their pants folds. I only got a little taste from a P.R., man."

"I hope you didn't call that Puerto Rican bruvver a West Indian? Puerto Ricans are proud people. They don't like to be called West Indians, man."

"I knows better than that...Don't call him black, and don't call him a West Indian. Call him Mira Mira. He's a people, man."

"That's what you called him—Mira Mira—to get his Bacardi?"

"Sure. I go with the flow, bruvver. You gotta know how to groove to survive, bruh."

"The masquerader who was playing drunk, where he's from, man?"

"He's got to be a wet back—a West Indian."

"Did he talk to you? How could you tell his accent?"

"I could bet on my grandmother's grave that he's a West Indian, man. He was playing dead to catch vultures alive."

"That's pretty talk, man. Where you learned that talk from?"

"From a West Indian woman."

"Is she your wife?"

"Never, bruh! If I marries a wet back, I wouldn't know how to present her to my Mama, and it's good to listen to your Mama. I was even discussing with my two bruvvers that night that I would never marry a West Indian broad even if they pay me in gold."

"Me, too, man...You had two bruvvers with you watching that white lady's window?"

"We was just talking, and I was telling them to keep away from that man who was playing drunk and was saying, 'Ahno...Lawdanno,' and he was smelling sweet like shit."

"Was you three bruvvers trying to pick that drunk masquerader?"

"That's not a nice way to judge me, bruvver?"

"Look, man," Nigel ended his staggering and began a demonstration. "I's good. Look. I's putting this dollar in your back pocket, and I's going to pick it from you." Nigel performed one of his boyhood tricks. He kept the dollar bill in his left hand, pretended that he put it in Dalgo's pocket with his right hand, then he swiftly bounced Dalgo and said, "See, I got my dollar back. I's a boss, man. If you three couldn't pick that mudder fucker, I could. My pen number was 117899. The guard always used me when they couldn't open the jail's vault, man."

"How you did that, bruvver?"

"When next I'm in town I'll come and look for you and I'll teach you, man. I knows that you three tried to pick that masquerader, man."

"I'll level with you, bruh. That mudder fucker was smart, whoever he or she be."

"What you mean? He wasn't a man?"

"I couldn't tell if that M.F. was a man or a woman. That M.F. stayed a little distance away and wouldn't let us pick him or her. That was a smart mudder fucker. He had a belt with a brassy buckle, and he held it in his hand like Bruce Lee."

"Because you couldn't pick that mudder fucker, you went home?"

"All three of us."

"Don't put your hand in fire for the other two bruvvers, man."

"I could. All three of us left together when that mudder fucker grumbled, 'Ah know...Lawd, ah know.' Probably he was trying to say, 'Lord, I know,' but those wet back West Indians talk so funny...and he kept looking at Connie's window."

"Seems as if that wet back was jealous because a man went upstairs with that white broad and stayed too long in her bed?"

"Maybe; but it is nice to have a heart and speak no evil of the dead." Dalgo touched the right side of his chest and kept his hand there. "He shouldn't kill Connie."

Nigel shifted Dalgo's hand to the left side of Dalgo's chest.

"Mine beats both sides, bruvver," Dalgo said.

"I imagine so...What if Vito had come and met that mudder fucker with his reporter woman who prints good news?"

"It would of been cat piss on pepper and pizza."

"What's that?"

Dalgo shaped his hand like a pistol. "Pow! Pow!"

"I think I've heard of Zeek Morong. Is he Mr. Vito, the numbers king?"

"Youse from out of town, bruvver, and youse know him?"

Nigel was too shocked to admit his slip up. He suddenly became drunk again. He staggered more than before. "Let's have another drink. Fuck that broad! Give me the name of that motel on Franklin Avenue. I's going to take my other woman there to get rid of this heat...I knew that stink bitch had another man when I was in jail, and it is on account of her I went to jail."

"What you did, bruh?"

"Robbed an old nigger of her pension check in the bank...That bitch encouraged me to come down from Chicago, and she stood me up again. Let's take another drink to confirm that a man can never trust a beautiful broad." He poured heavily into Dalgo's cup.

Dalgo smiled, and he began a new story. "People thinks that Connie and Vito was smoochy, but eh, eh. I knows better. I brung her mail from him, and I knows that they was not in love. It was a matter of exchanging news. They was using each other. Vito wanted his news out to his enemies, and she wanted his news to sell her newspapers."

Nigel got up from the bench and staggered, but he

needed a follow up to that information. "Youse...Yo...Yo mean Vito didn't trust the mailman, but he trusted you, and you opened his mail?"

"I swears. Only once."

"And youse read Vito's love letters?"

"No, dummy. Vito gave Connie tips on his rivals in the underworld...tips on all those underworld godfathers...and she wrote about it in her crime column of her newspaper."

"And you mean downtown didn't question Connie about where she got those incriminating inside scoops?"

"Bruvver, you now sound like an out-of-towner. Youse don't know that we has a law here in New York that is called State Shield. That law does protect reporters, and Vito used that law as a loophole to marquee his underworld."

Nigel was shocked by Dalgo's knowledge of the law. He compensated Dalgo for his knowledge by pouring him a bigger drink than he poured himself. "I...I...I," Nigel stuttered, "I'd like to work for Vito. Where's he at?"

"At eleven every night you'll find him at Limbo Hook paying out money to winners. To enter the Hook, knock five times, then push the door marked OUT without waiting for an answer."

"Bruvver, he may be scared if he sees me as a stranger, and may think that I'm coming to make a holdup."

"Vito is not even afraid of God. I'll be glad if you can, but don't try. He cheated me on the doves."

"What's that?"

"Can't say."

"I'll buy another bottle."

"He's got friends in high places; and he'll know the source."

"He murdered that white lady Connie because she cut his stories loose?"

"There was no reason to."

"How do you know? Can't you tell a bruvver?"

"Can't tell a cop...a detective... an investigator...

whatever youse is, man."

"I ain't no cop...I ain't no whatever!" Nigel looked at the photograph of his make-believe girlfriend, and he pushed the last drink in the bottle for Dalgo. "Yours, bruvver."

Dalgo curved the tip of his red cap. He picked up the bottle and said, "This red label is not a good incentive." He put the bottle to his head and drained it. He looked at Nigel in a pitiless manner. "Bruvver, I don't know anything about Chicago. What you said your prison number was?" Nigel couldn't hide his shock of that question. "Don't try to remember, bruvver, because youse can't talk black English rat, and you don't know how to lie. All your good white grammar was escaping all the time. All those possessive cases you was using—jail's vault, lady's window, and all that white grammar shit!" Nigel turned white as Dalgo looked at him and continued his lecture. "Bruvver Mannou, my last three years of college in the slammer completed my education, and there I learned about survival. I cut three ways, bruvver. Some people throwed away the nutrients and thought it was the stalk, but me, Dalgo, knew better. I knew the nutrients; I ate it and became a man. The whiskey you brung me have good balance, but it was not the best to barter for information." He looked Nigel dead in the eye. "My thumb is fingerprinted everywhere, but there's something the law doesn't know about me."

"What? What, bruvver?" Nigel said. He didn't hide his excitement because he knew his cover was already blown.

"Next time we conversate I'll tell youse, bruvver." He grinned and handed his paper cup to Nigel. "I don't mind informing a detective when I've grown to trust him, but I hates to wash dirty dishes." Dalgo walked away as sober as a hungry Biafran child who had just consumed a quart of fresh cow's milk.

Nigel hated alcohol, and he hated his present

drunken state. He was shocked to stupor as he watched Dalgo trail towards the liquor store. Nigel smashed the empty bottle in the street and shouted, "Fuck it! I hate this job. Lyle, look what your promiscuous life has done to us." He shook his head. He finally quieted himself. He put his hand to his face for comfort, and the smell of Billie Zellars' perfume aroused him. "Lyle did speak of a sweet smell. Even though I barely shook your hand, Ms. Zellars, the scent is so pungent." He took out his discolored typing sheet with the words ASDFLKJ and wrote, 'Ahno...Lawd, ah know...Lord, I know.' He muttered, "It could be a clue...an American, imitating a West Indian. I thank you, Dalgo, but when next we meet, I'm sure you won't be ahead of me. You are as smart as my cousin John who is rotting in jail. Fuck you!" He turned around to see if anyone was looking at his senseless behavior.

Chapter Eighteen

The Toolbox

"Where have you been all these weeks, young man? You had an anonymous caller. I cooked your favorite dinner," Elizabeth said.

"All I need is a drink, Ma," Nigel grumbled.

"I know how you feel about your assignment...your father. The good Lord knows best."

"How do you feel about him?"

"The good Lord?"

"No. Your husband."

She looked at him sternly.

"I'm sorry, Ma. I'm not in the best of moods today."

"My Spanish rice and red snapper can change that mood."

"Put it in the oven. I'll eat later because I'm staying over tonight."

"What's bothering you, son, daddy's little boy?"

"Nothing is bothering me, but something is on my mind." He took out his scrap of paper.

"You are still transporting that ASDFLKJ stuff?"

"It's full of dog's ears, but I'm using it to type tonight. I've noted a lot of information on this sheet of paper. I'll have a quick shower, and I'll be off."

"Why didn't you tell me that someone sent money to your detective agency to help your father in his troubles?"

"It slipped me, Ma. We'll talk about it later because I have to get out of here in a minute."

"If your pal Lord Meath calls what should I tell him?"

"Tell him that I've gone to type. He'll understand. We have to exchange notes and discuss our findings as to who is guilty of that murder."

"Where are you going to discuss your findings, son?"

"Somewhere...What's your favorite perfume, Ma?"

"The same one that I've always used. Is it too pungent for your nostril?"

"No. I'm just getting to like it."

"You are no different from your father when it comes to remembering things."

"When I leave here I think I shall first go and visit Sheila. She's back in Brooklyn."

"Be careful. She's a married woman now."

"I guess I won't go again." He smiled. "Does Sheila still go to Leader Dollon's church."

"The church is not Leader Dollon's."

"All right. Does Sheila still go to Mount Signal's?"

"Something's bothering you, and it seems as though something's bothering her too. She hardly comes to church, but she sends her daughter to Sunday school. Are you two bothered because you cannot play hooky in the church basement?" Elizabeth smiled.

"That's over, Ma."

"One never knows what's over when it comes to a chip of the old block."

"That old block is your husband."

"I know. Have some of your Mama's dinner. Let's sit and talk. It's a long time that we have not laughed in this house."

"I promise. We'll even talk about the good old Fyzabad, especially Lyle's best friend, Joiner Jan, and how he and Lyle used to put a mirror below the desk to see under your dress, especially on the days when you had on *no* bloomers."

"You mean your father told you about his dirty tricks?"

"Don't forget that 'birds of a feather flock together.'"

"Then I have to pray for you, too."

"I promise we'll talk about the good old days when kids were not as nowadays kids."

"Promise?" She kissed him. "Who's Son, Daddy's Little Boy?"

Nigel smiled. "Me."

"Well, swear on your promise."

"Me, Son, Daddy's Likkle Boy, the son of Aunt Gina's nephew, swear that I will keep my promise to sleep over, and to talk to sweet Elizabeth, my Ma, about her husband. It's my solemn promise, Ma." He kissed her, and they smiled. "Bolt the door when I leave, Ma."

"What were you looking for in Lyle's toolbox?"

"Nothing."

"Did you get what you wanted?"

"Not really. I hope you haven't been prying, Ma?"

"Why should I? Have you any suspects?"

"Not me; but I think Lord Meath is considering one."

"Did he tell you?"

"Tomorrow he will."

"My fingerprint is on that toolbox. Does that make me a suspect?"

"Lord Meath didn't divulge his theory."

"What a cute kid—that Lord Meath."

"I hope he'll always remain cute to you."

"Is there a reason why he shouldn't?"

"Time to close the door, Ma." He left in a hurry.

Was he in haste? Or was it the follow-up question that he feared?

Chapter Nineteen
Ruff Gillette

Nigel walked up five flights of a Brownsville tenement, and he pounded the door of Apartment F. "Police... Open up."

"What do you want?"

"Ruff Gillette."

"He ain't here."

"Okay. You asked for it."

"Wait. Don't shoot. I'll open. Let me put on some clothes. I have no stuff, man."

"Your buddy told me where you hid it, so open up fast."

"Pete is a liar, man."

"The law will judge that."

Ruff opened the door, and a current of air sucked Nigel in. He stood before Ruff, a giant of a man, but his demeanor was that of a child's.

"What kept you so long. I think I'll have to radio for backups," Nigel bluffed.

"I was looking for my clothes, man. I'm clean."

Nigel surveyed the room. It was dirty. "Open that closet. I want to see what you have inside there."

Ruff opened his clustered closet. "What do you expect to find? I used to do a little business for myself, but I'm no liar...no murderer either."

"Would you shut up?"

"I can support my habit."

"Junkies with those habits can do pretty mean things to defenseless ladies. They choke them to death. They hit them in the back of the head."

"I don't choke people." Ruff looked at his massive punctured hands.

"Take everything out of that messy closet. Where's your belt?"

"Belt?"

"Yes. Where is it? I don't see it among your clothes."

"I don't have a belt."

"Where's the rope you use to tie your waist?"

"I don't know."

"You'd be smart to find it before I leave here."

"What Pete told you about me, man?"

"A lot...about you...about Billie."

"That's my educated sister. She's clean. You can arrest her for being a radical and for hating the government and white people, but for nothing else."

"Tell me about her. When last you saw her?"

"A long time ago."

"At a barmitzvah?"

"I'm a Christian, man."

"Snorting your way to hell."

"It's my life."

"And I'm concerned about somebody else's life too."

"If you come here to find out about a murder, not me."

"Won't you offer this pig a seat?"

"Sure, officer...I don't call cops pigs."

"How come?"

"I, too, wanted to be a policeman, and they are good people; here and there you'll find a bad apple."

"Why didn't you become one of New York's Finest?"

"It's a long story."

"I'm in no hurry."

"This long story is a woman."

"She jilted you?" He didn't answer. For a moment Nigel stopped his questioning, and he silently studied the destruction of Ruff's body. His body, a contour map, and the needles that pricked his body tracked the railroads to his grave. Nigel was entranced. He wondered what took place at Ruff's birth and if Ruff's father wept for Ruff's mother's postpartum depression. When Ruff sneezed, it rationalized Nigel's most uncharitable thoughts. "So you are clean? When last did you see your revolutionary sister—before or after you became clean?"

Ruff walked to the window. The panes were broken and stained; cloth and staples prevented the flow of fresh air. A rat passage in the brown cloth, an improvised curtain, reminded him that a bullet came through that window, and that he was lucky that day. "What does Pete know about Billie, except that they went to Erasmus? He's not even in her ball park. Pete's a police informer like Red-Cap Dalgo, but he knows nothing of my sister. For Christ's sake, he's no longer my buddy."

Nigel was pleased with his impromptu buddy story. "I believe Pete, and from what I've heard, I hate pushers especially when they trade in my neighborhood."

"Billie doesn't trade in stuffs."

"I'll bet she deals in weaponry to keep her generals alive."

"What are you talking about? She was never in the armed services."

"Pete told me that you and Billie were hanging out on Labor Day."

"What about that?"

"You can't doubt me. I have a witness."

"So?"

"That witness knows that you were with your sister Billie Zellars, and one of you went and changed your disguise after you had a great time on the Parkway on Labor Day."

"Billie and I were onlookers. I ran into her unexpectedly."

"What she had in the bag that she was carrying?"

"You expected me to open her bag? It was her costume, I suppose."

Nigel passed his hand on the bulge in his pocket and said, "It's loaded, so don't get cute...You knew she had a costume in the bag she carried?"

"She was waiting on a friend, and she intended to put on her costume when she met that friend. She told me that she wanted her costume to be a surprise to her friend."

"Was she going to strip in the street and put it on?"

"My sister is not a stripper."

"Then where was she going to put on her costume?"

"I'm sure she had a rendezvous."

"Tell me about her rendezvous?"

"That's just my assumption."

"What an assumption!" Nigel took out the typing sheet with ASDFLKJ markings. He crossed out the letter A. "What did you and Billie talk about?"

"The cost of the bands. How Caribbean people find money to buy those expensive costumes, and those same people wouldn't find money to buy books for their kids or pay their Con Edison bills."

"So you and Billie talked about money—how to spend money wisely?" He put two diagonal lines through the letter S, and made it a dollar sign. "Did you also talk about a guy named Lyle Gordon?"

"Who is he?"

"Don't you know Billie's main squeeze—the man she was waiting on when you met her on the Parkway on Labor Day?"

"You can call me a dummy."

"So you are a dummy conveniently?" Nigel filled the space in the letter D.

"That alphabet notation is for the computer?"

"Sure. This paper is scientifically coded. It is the modern way to find out filthy liars." He stressed the word filthy, and he circled the F, the fourth letter in the A-S-D-F-L-K-J formation.

"I'm not lying."

"Where does Billie live?" He underlined L.

Ruff rattled off his sister's address.

Nigel smiled. "I thought you didn't know that, too. Ruff, do you know this woman?" He handed Ruff Constance Wagner's picture, made an asterisk near the letter K and said, "The letter K and the letter C carry the same phonic sound most times...Pete said that you killed Mrs. Constance Wagner."

"Pete is a liar!" Ruff paused for breath. "My asthma is flaring up."

"Keep on talking. I'll be calling for backups if I'm not satisfied with your story. I know you love to do good deeds for your loving big sister."

"If she had a job to be done, she wouldn't give me, man. You are a cop, and you know the ropes. There's a competing market outside whenever you want to get a job done. You can tell your brethren, your boys, the idle hands who love bloody work, but I'm too clumsy to do that kind of dirty job."

"You didn't do the bloody job because you were and are clumsy, or was it because it was a dangerous job?" He inked the letter J.

"Not me."

"Who?"

"I don't know your slant, officer."

"Have you blood brothers who'd do Billie's dirty job? You know she hates white people. She says that white people are taking the kudos for black people's inventions."

"I don't know that part of her, but it's possible. Don't they now say that Egypt is not in Africa? My sister didn't have to tell me that."

"She's your half sister."

"Whatever proportion, she's still my sister."

"Does she have other blood brothers—whatever proportion?"

"He is a minister in Georgia."

"Pete told me about him." Nigel looked at Ruff's jagged arms. "I'm going to throw away this sheet of paper with all this information about you, but before I throw it away," he tore a piece of the typing sheet and wrote a number, "I want you to call this number tomorrow. It may change your powdery world into platinum. Have you read of the Jacksons, brother?" He made the letter J more indelible. "What's their job?"

"They sing, brother. Officer, I like you. I hope you find that Labor Day killer...strangler."

"I never told you that someone was strangled. Where did you hear that...see that?"

"Some of us refuse to see the forest because of the trees, brother. I learned that quotation somewhere."

"From a woman?"

"Yes."

"What was she?"

"A forest ranger."

"Was that the woman in your life?"

Ruff Gillette did not answer, but his advice to Nigel was similar to his sister's. Nigel looked at his scrap paper and the thoughts that resonated in his mind bothered him: Who was the guilty one in that love triangle? She was...No. She was...I don't know, he thought. He eventually went blank. He shook his head as if electricity flowed through his body. He looked around. Ruff was not there. He then realized that his thoughts had engulfed his time.

He walked out of Apartment F, more confused than when he first entered it.

Chapter Twenty
Zeek

The warm air added more confusion to Nigel's mind. He knew of a way to ease his tension when he saw the phone booth. He immediately dialed his pal.

"Hello...Mrs. Sullivan speaking."

"How are you, Mrs. Sullivan?"

"I can't believe my ear." She caught Nigel's voice. "When is daddy's little boy coming to look me up?"

"Very soon."

"That's all I've heard since we moved to Queens. What about dinner next week?"

"Reserve a table under the chandelier."

"I'm holding you to your word now."

"My word is my bond...Is Lord Meath there?"

"The Lord is snoring. He went out with his girlfriend last night...By the way, who is she?"

"She's a very nice girl...Could you wake him. I'm in a hurry. I'm calling from the street."

Kate rushed into the bedroom. "Lord Meath... Tommy...Tommy."

"Eh...Eh," Tommy answered faintly.

"Daddy's little boy...Nigel is on the phone. He's in a rush."

"Who? Who?"

"Your pal."

"Where? Here?"

"No...On the phone. He's in a rush."

Tommy stretched for the phone. "Yello, darkie, what's up? Are you...?" He stopped abruptly, rubbed his eyes, and he looked around to make sure that his mother had left the room. "You are not disturbing my sleep to tell me about the result of the new aphrodisiac that you are using?"

"No."

"Is it about that Mozambican woman who gave you that elephant hair bracelet for good luck?"

"Better than that...even better than having an affair with an untouched colleen."

"Don't tell me that Sunday school Sheila is back in town again, and you are?"

"Nothing like that. She's married, man."

"Shit! What?"

"I'm calling about a virgin idea."

"An I who!"

"An idea to get Zeek's fingerprint."

"With what?"

"A cold glass. And you are going to get that cold glass after he drinks from it."

"Me?"

"Yes, you. You're that good looking Irish kid who fits in handsomely among the rich and famous. You even fit in with poor black folks. Do you know that a member of my church...okay...I don't go to church...I'm a backslider...but a member of Leader Dollon's church still asks for you? She saw you once, but the beautiful sister still inquires about Blue Eyes."

"The sister inquires about me?"

"Yes, you. Sister Bernadette likes cream in her coffee. She's a mighty fine sister. She has less meat than your Mira Mira, but the sweetness of the blue crab is in the back, man."

"Keep on talking, son."

"For your popularity with the women and even with men, you're going to get that cold glass...Let me drop a quarter into Ma Bell...Yes, you...Remember, too, that I am your associate, and you are the level-headed one who does not panic. Our boss Totohead said so. Don't forget that he told us that we should improvise and take chances, and to pretend that we are New York City's policemen whenever we can get away with it. Only a clean-cut, white kid like you can pretend and not get caught."

"Is that so?"

"You got to make it so, my Lord."

"What's on your mind, Nigel?"

"Listen, man. This is important. Be at Limbo Hook at midnight, no earlier."

"Me at Zeek's place? Nobody messes with Zeek, man. He's the law in Brooklyn."

"It's your duty to neutralize Zeek with a cold glass."

"How?"

"Here's the plan. We can make adjustments as we go along. When you get into his place, stay in the bar area with the entertainment and listen to the comedienne. Her main word is doves. If she prattles and says, 'The doves are flying,' you'll enter a door marked 'OUT' to gain access into the gambling den to be with the high rollers. Behave like a regular customer and take part in the other numbers game, but keep listening to the comedienne who'll be coming over the mike. If she says, 'The doves are detained,' keep your hands on your hip and look for the exit marked 'IN.' I'll be outside somewhere waiting for you. If the going is smooth..."

"Don't you expect it to be smooth?"

"I'm leaving space for disappointment, man; but I know with your luck the going will be smooth. If the comedienne makes no mention of the doves, place a bet on any game, knock the table three times, and someone will come and take you to Zeek. Zeek in turn will take you personally to the room with the high rollers. Whatever you lose, write up a petty cash voucher, and you'll be paid with the money from that oily envelope. If you win, we'll split the spoils fifty-fifty, not an Irish potato for me and an African elephant for you, like you Irish people do in Ireland...Don't interrupt me, boy!" They laughed, and Nigel further discussed their plan to get Zeek's fingerprint on an ice-cold glass. "Zeek's real name is Vito Morong. I learned from Dalgo that..."

"Are you trusting Dalgo?"

"To a point? Yes. Dalgo thought he had the last

laugh when he drank my whiskey on the Parkway. I and some of the bruvvers in the hood set him up. They told me that he's an informer for the police and Zeek, and I used him as my conduit. So let's give the idea a try, man...I also learned from Dalgo that Zeek doesn't drink during business hours, but it is your job to make Zeek get mighty thirsty. That's where the cold glass comes in. You've got to interrogate that son of a bitch Zeek before you gamble with the high rollers, because I know he'll never take you into that room. He'll only take you into that room on recommendation."

"And can't I say that daddy's little boy, the son of Likkle Lyle from the oil town of Fyzabad, recommended me?"

"Why not take a dose of poison instead...Let me drop in another quarter into this thief...Listen, man. Do you remember that I told you when you moved out to that sissy Borough of Queens..."

"What do you have with Queens? Dapper Don lives here, so it can't be that sissy, probably Swissy with stray bullets from the Don's foes."

"You just listen, man, and stop that name calling over my phone. The only phone that I trust is the one that is not yet installed...Are you there? Remember once I told you that you cannot take ten minutes to drive from Queens to Brooklyn. I want you to prove me wrong and make it in five...A case of beer is the stake, Mick."

"Your people drink the hard stuff, man; so why not a case of the hard stuff?"

"So you have been researching my people. Totohead researched you, and the rumor is out. He found out that you took his daughter's virginity and now your eyes are on that Mira Mira."

"So what! Totohead ain't the Godfather."

"That's the spirit, bruvver. If you go, I go. I'm with you, bruvver...By the way, your mother said that you haven't introduced your Mira Mira to her."

"Honestly, she told you that?"

"Am I in the habit of inventing such stories? I'll bring Carmensita as my girl, and we'll all sit under Kate's chandelier. That's with your consent, of course."

"You're crazy, man."

"Right now let's think of this crazy bet of you reaching in Brooklyn in five minutes. I want you to win your bet, so don't bother to shower today. Come as you are."

"It's only your Fyzabad folks with dry standpipes who take *Starboy Shenkos*—that great dry clean with a damp rag that carouses the body parts."

"I'll get you for that...Ma Bell needs more money." He dropped in a quarter in the pay phone.

"Nigel, why don't you give me the phone number and let me call you right back?"

"White-boy-in-Queens, in this part of Brooklyn we scratch out the numbers on the pay phones in order that the West Indians would not be able to receive their long distance calls from overseas. The Haitians in my neighborhood are nice church-going people, but they sleep on the public phones....As I was saying, Dalgo gave me the info on Zeek and his place, and I matched it with what the bruvvers said. In my spare time I did some scouting on my own and matched notes." He looked at his scrap ASDFLKJ sheet, and he ticked off the talking points. He and Tommy also made minor adjustments on how to get into Limbo Hook without being noticed, and how Zeek could be outwitted. The two inexperienced detectives weighed the pros and cons of their veritable tyros' approach to investigative work as they plodded along on the phone. "Are you there with me, Lord Meath?"

"I'm listening."

"If you could get into Zeek's inner sanctum, that would be profound because you would be able to connect with some of Zeek's hirelings—those who do the dirty work." Nigel put a question mark on that suggestion.

"That would be suicidal. That's no way to invade Zeek's privacy, and I don't think that I'm the one for the job."

"We've got to take chances. How else can we get Zeek's fingerprint? Are you listening to me, man? We've got to take chances. And don't forget that oily envelope has mucho money for us when we solve this crime. The oily man, whoever he is, would prefer that the money he donated to the Lyle Fund goes to the true-grit detectives than to the bumbling lawyers who would spend a month on picking a jury and on *voir dire*. Those smart lawyers, especially if they're not from the hood, would dwindle the oily man's *pro bono* gift to Lyle. We have to solve this crime...You reminded me yesterday that the purpose of the Grand Jury was to see if the Prosecution had enough evidence to take the case for trial."

"My mother, the lawyer, not the cook, told me that."

"They had enough evidence because they put my father in jail. I have to get him out. If Connie had died from a heart attack due to sex administered by Lyle, I would have believed; but my father would never hit a woman. He worships women. Do it for him, man."

"Okay, okay." The mere mention of the words "my father" from Nigel's lips touched Tommy. Tommy turned on his side and closed his eyes to concentrate on what approach was best to outwit Zeek, but instead of concentrating, he fell fast asleep after he said, "Okay...Okay." The phone fell on the pillow beside him.

"Thanks, man. That's more like it, bruvver. I can always depend on an Irishman. Don't forget that the Irish and Blacks once squatted in lower Central Park when it was called Nigger Village. We would have been still neighbors in the greenery making barbecue if the darkies weren't chased uptown to Harlem. You're listening to me, Mick?" A croaking noise came through the phone. "Shit! You're snoring on me, man...Wake up! Wake up, man!" Nigel shouted into his phone. "You're snoring like a pig on me, man."

Tommy jumped up from his sleep. "I'm up. I'm up. I wasn't really sleeping, man. I was just having a vision as to how I should handle Zeek." Tommy yawned, stretched, and laughed.

Nigel laughed, too. "That's an original, boy...So having dreamed a vision, the bet is on, Mick?"

"Of course, Mose. The hard stuff is the wager, boy."

"You're on."

Things went as planned. Tommy parked at the agreed spot, and he entered Limbo Hook at midnight. He alternated between the petty gambling tables and the bar. The comedienne came on strong but she said nothing about the doves. Tommy bought a drink, and after it was half consumed, he knocked the table three times and waited to be taken to the high rollers. He waited and waited. He was about to leave when suddenly a man in formal outfit approached him and said impolitely, "Let's go." He was ushered into a luxuriously carpeted room adorned with exquisite paintings. Before he caught his bearing, he was in a dimly lit room with the man he baited.

"I've been expecting the other one," Zeek said. "I guess you are the technicolor version."

Tommy pretended that he did not understand Zeek's insinuation.

Zeek stood pompously, and his thumbs pouted his bracers. "The name is Caesar Vittorio. Welcome to the Grecian Room. Take a seat." He did not shake Tommy's hand.

"I'm Sullivan."

"The prying detective?"

"And I thought your name was...?"

"And you are right...Was!" Zeek spoke with a lateral lisp. "I'm in a good mood, so ask me the questions that you came to ask. I may even answer them. Today is your lucky day, Sullivan."

"Why the name change? I guess your friends still call you Zeek."

"What's your interest in my name?" He made a face like Herman Munster.

"I just wanted to make sure that I'm talking to the right person." Tommy's eyes fell on Zeek's seamless, silk lapel, and he glanced also at the diamond on his pinkies. His mind had already worked up schemes to make Zeek get thirsty. "What's your occupation, Mr. Vittorio? Rather, your business is under what name?"

"I paid a penalty for whatever name I carry."

"What penalty?"

"Registration fee. Licensing fee. Liquor fee."

"You call that a penalty?"

"Surely, it is."

"I didn't hear you mention a gambling fee?"

"A man should be free to do whatever he wants in this world."

"You look free in your world, and with your connections life couldn't be better."

"I don't have to listen to you, but somehow I think you possess magnetic charms."

"Thank you."

"You're welcome. Now tell me: Why are you really here, Detective Sullivan?"

"To ask you couple questions, with your permission, of course."

"Like what?"

"Your occupation?"

"I'm a businessman."

"Have you moonlighted as a professional gentleman?"

"If I did, you'd never be my client." Zeek enjoyed having said that.

"And I believe you...If you give me a moment...." Tommy searched his pocket. "Yes, here it is. Do you know this woman?" He handed Constance Wagner's photograph to Zeek.

Zeek didn't look at the picture, nor did he touch it; but he said, "I knew her quite well." He took a seat and rested his feet on the glass table.

"But you didn't even look at the picture."

"I told you that I knew her quite well."

"Look at the picture, and see if it brings back memories."

"I told you that I knew her, so why do I have to play with the photograph of a dead woman?"

"You knew of her ability? Her talent? Her expertise? Her body? Which one, Caesar?"

"The one I wanted to know."

"And of her death?"

"I read of it?"

"You mean you didn't attend her funeral? Didn't that bother you?"

"Why me?"

"Because Constance Wagner was your friend, and she was murdered."

"Life is a chance. If I were murdered, would you have gone to her and asked all these questions on my behalf?" Tommy didn't answer and Zeek said, "Coping with life is like buying saving bonds; yet some of us buy bingo tickets instead..." He searched for words to make another analogy.

"And some people, Mr. Vittorio, put their last penny in an illegal numbers scam which gives them just one chance in a million. It might have been that Brooklynite's lucky day; she might even have hit the jackpot, but instead of being paid with cash, she was paid with a blunt instrument which crashed the back of her skull, and the murderer made it look like a fall...an accidental fall, perhaps. Some of us divulge news to the enemy and get murdered for playing the-both-sides game. Some of us cannot even bear to imagine that our white women enjoy cross-culture bedding."

"This sounds like Washington-Capitol Hill rhetoric, the Sam Donaldson version. You should air it at the Kennedy Center."

"I haven't yet been invited to the Kennedy Center. I do have my bowtie in case you piggyback me on your invitation. I really want to learn how to pull coattails."

"You and your pal are moving up in the world. You should join the Democrats; he should join the Republicans; and you two can swap invitations. Let him invite you to the Republican's fund raisers, and, in turn, you invite him to the Democrats' coffees. With your good looks and your pal's intuitiveness, you two can fast forward your imaginations and make things happen." Zeek looked at Tommy and said, "I guess you'd prefer to buy red label whiskey and sit on the Parkway bench and feed the lowly pigeons."

"You get your news as the crow flies. No wonder Constance Wagner had such spicy by-lines. She marqueed your underworld and got your conflicting news across to the other people."

"What other people?"

"For want of not having a copious vocabulary, I'd say the opposing mobsters."

"Because my name ends with a vowel that makes me a mobster? I'm a New York corporation."

"Doing business as?"

"Why not call Albany?"

"You gave me a virgin idea, Mr. Vittorio."

"The Better Business Bureau has no trouble with me. I'm no fly by night who gives out pamphlets in the day. Limbo Hook has grown from a one-door operation into a Fortune 500 enterprise. Our policy is, and was, based on the old-fashioned way. We got there by our sweat and business know-how. I'd like to give you a tour."

"I'll accept your invitation if I won't be railroaded."

"There's nothing to hide."

"Not even in the cement?"

"I can see you were nursed by the television. You watched the wrong cartoons."

"Sometimes."

"Let me show you around." Zeek gave Tommy a tour of Limbo Hook, but he skipped some rooms especially that part of Limbo Hook that hugged St. John's Place and faced East New York. They eventually returned to the Grecian Room. "Are you satisfied that there's no place to mix cement here?"

"Sure...I'm impressed. Tell me about Mrs. Wagner's husband. Being so intimate with her, I'm sure you know his whereabouts."

"He died before her. For that matter, there was no need to know him; he wasn't on my roladex."

"I guess Dalgo Gibbons is?"

"From what branch of government are you: the CIA, the FBI or the IRS? Which one? Or are you being paid by the hour to chase ambulances?" Tommy's last question irked him.

Tommy was silently pleased, but his novice approach to get Zeek thirsty by forcing him to answer unnecessary questions didn't seem to be effective. "I heard you were in love with, should I say, Miss, Mrs., or Ms. Wagner?" He smiled before he asked the question.

"Young man, sometimes you are so smart, and sometimes you sound as if you just got off the bus...or even walked up here from the sticks."

"My teacher told me that in grade school...Were you in love with Ms. Wagner?"

"I omit the handles from my friends' names."

"It's hi Zeek...Oh, hi Doll?"

"Among friends, what's wrong with that?"

"Nothing. When last you saw her?"

"Who?"

"Your Connie...Hi Doll."

"Do you call a dead woman a doll?"

"Before her death, I mean." There was an angelic buzz when two beautifully dressed women came into the room and kissed Zeek on his cheek. "I'm sorry, man, to keep you away from your high rollers." Tommy forced a cough. "This cold is bothering me. May I have a glass of water before you get rid of me."

"You are ahead of me, sir. I see that you already

know what my friends do."

"A gambling man knows his kind." Tommy again forced his cough louder. "May I have a glass of water, please."

"I never drink at this time, especially with strangers, but I, too, need to wet the throat. I'll get you a bottle on the house."

"I chase with Jamaican ginger."

"You won't mind me having mine like yours? Even keel?"

"Of course not."

Zeek hooked both women as his prize, and he left the room. "What an upstart, that son of a bitch," he said to them.

"I would have that son-of-a-bitch upstart in my bed any day, Zeek. Won't you, Dolores?"

"Sure, girlfriend," Judy replied.

Within five minutes Zeek returned with a waiter, but his drink was already poured. Tommy looked at the glass in Zeek's hand, and then he looked suspiciously at the other glass, the bottle of whiskey, and the bottle of Jamaican ginger held high in the palm of the waiter's hand and balanced on a tray. "Is this even keel? Yours is poured; mine is not."

"It's obvious that you don't trust me," Zeek said, and laughed without showing his teeth. "Here's mine then. Are you satisfied?" Tommy looked at the glass in Zeek's hand. "Do you want me to sample it to prove that there's no poison?" He rested the glass on the table.

"You don't have to," Tommy said, and he took Zeek's glass. He held the glass at the extreme bottom. "You are really good at reading minds, Caesar."

"I can read what is at the back of your head right now, Sullivan." He made a sign, and the waiter put the tray on the table and left.

"Cheers to a shrewd businessman." Tommy raised his glass.

"Cheers to whatever you and your associate seek,

Mr. Detective." Zeek poured whiskey liberally into his glass. He sprinkled three drops of ginger ale on his whiskey, and he enjoyed his drink.

"Were you a priest?" Tommy asked.

"Why?"

"That's the way Father sprinkles water on the little babies when he christens them at Saint Jerome's."

"Are you Catholic?"

"I try all of the faiths. For that matter, when I leave here I'll be attending a West Indian Spiritual Baptist Church on Nostrand Avenue."

"What's the name of that church?" Zeek pressed for an answer.

"You don't know those people. They're not your type."

"Try me. I know pastors, rabbis, policemen, community board members. Believe me, I know Brooklyn and its people, directly, and indirectly, through my lavish donations. They all come to me. What's his name?"

"Leader Dollon."

"Doesn't he have another name?"

"I don't really know."

"Come closer." Zeek whispered in Tommy's ear.

"That's vulgar! That's racial, man."

"Don't say I didn't tell you." Zeek leaned forward and spoke in Tommy's ear again.

"Ridiculous! What would he want with that?"

"Why not ask him?"

"I still think that you are both vulgar and racial."

They forced conversations on each other, and Tommy tried out his overworked jokes. "What's your first name, Sullivan?" Zeek asked, and he loosened his tie.

"Tommy."

"Tommy, did you hear the one about the two rats? The town rat told the country rat that he is never called a rat whenever he goes to town."

"I never heard that one. Shoot."

"Well, the town rat took the country rat to town,

and they hid in a pothole by the traffic light. The town rat told the country rat to run across the street first. The foolish country rat obeyed, and he ran across the street first. The midday shoppers shouted hysterically, 'Look a rat! Look a rat!' and held their packages high in the air. After the commotion died down, the town rat ran across the street, and the people mildly said, 'Look another one.'"

Tommy enjoyed the joke although he had heard it before. "So the country rat is called a 'Rat' anywhere he goes, and the town rat is called 'Another One?'"

"Sure. It doesn't take a rocket scientist to see that. It's all based on movements—like the first movement of a symphony, followed by the second. The first is rigid; the second is soothing. Mind you, Tommy..." Zeek stopped talking and poured whiskey in his own glass. Tommy poured Jamaican ginger ale and adulterated the whiskey in his glass. Zeek continued: "I'm not taking credit for that joke because I don't want to be sued for plagiarizing anybody's works. My grandfather told my father that he heard that joke when he got off Ellis Island." He looked into Tommy's blue eyes as if he wanted to pluck them. "Tell me, Tommy, why didn't the Other One come to interrogate me?" Zeek's stress on "Other One" meant it to be a proper noun; and Tommy knew that proper noun was his pal, Nigel.

Nonetheless, Tommy was not shocked by the question, neither did he answer it. At that very moment, an employee burst into the room and shouted, "Boss! Boss! We have an emergency at the tables with one of those vulgar women you just brought in. She spat on a bouncer." The man pelted out of the room with the same speed that he came in.

"Excuse me, Tommy," Zeek said. "Give me a minute or two. I want to make sure that my other guests are comfortable."

Tommy smiled. "I hope it's nothing serious. If you didn't return, I'll pour myself another drink and leave in peace."

"I brought the bottle for you. Enjoy all of it. That's the brand that Senator Pothole drinks in Washington."

"I like it, but the brand name is too hard to pronounce...D-O-M." Tommy showcased his drunkenness.

"There's no D-O-M on that bottle...Just enjoy your drink and forget about the name."

"I was about to look at your beautiful paintings."

"Go right ahead, and make sure that you look at *The Goddess*. I'll soon be back, Tommy. I'm getting to like your company." He walked out with his drink in his hand.

"Stay a month," Tommy mumbled. He first studied the room to see if there were hidden cameras. Quickly, he poured the rest of the whiskey in various places on the expansive multicolored carpet. When he poured the whiskey, he crouched as if he were drinking from the whiskey bottle, and he let some of the whiskey fall on his calypso shirt. He moved around casually and tested the thickness of the carpet with his heels. "Em, em...It's too thick to say this glass fell and broke," Tommy mused. He looked at Zeek's finger impression on the glass in his hand and thought deeply. "Got to get piece of this cold glass before that devil comes back...He says the worst things about black people and Jews." Tommy whispered to himself. Suddenly, Zeek's footsteps were heard as he approached the room. "What now?" Tommy mumbled. In Tommy's right hand he held the empty glass at the rim. He put both hands behind his back; he walked to *The Goddess* and spoke to the painting. "To describe your naked beauty is impossible." He stared at the woman in oil as if he penetrated her. Zeek crept up behind Tommy and touched his left shoulder. Pretentiously shocked at being touched unexpectedly by Zeek, Tommy jumped, and he dropped the glass at the back of his right heel. He stepped backwards, and he accidentally stepped on the glass. So it seemed.

"You are not the first to lust at her," Zeek said.

"And you have prevented me from having an orgasm with your goddess," Tommy replied. "What a pity."

"Don't move, pervert. I don't want to be responsible for your worn-out soles. That kind of crystal is razor sharp, Sullivan. I'll get the cleaner." Zeek smiled quietly, patted Tommy on the back, and said, "There's always a bad omen when I drink with strangers."

"I'm sorry, man." Tommy spoke with a drunkard's tongue and waited until Zeek closed the door behind him. He took out his handkerchief and dusted his shoes. He looked around, and then he snatched two sizable pieces of the broken glass and said, "This pervert is now a splinters thief." He wrapped the choice pieces in his handkerchief and pocketed them. He stepped harder on the remains and made sure that it was difficult to detect that pieces of the broken glass were missing. The cleaner came before Zeek, and Tommy welcomed her. "I don't know how so many New Yorkers live in a liquor bottle. I should have taken water instead."

"You are not a real man," the cleaner said and swept the splinters into a closed bin.

"My mother told me that, but I never believed her."

Zeek walked in. "Be careful with the splinters, Millis." He spoke to her affectionately.

Tommy looked at Millis' pretty face. She was no older than eighteen. Millis resembled his mother Kate, as seen in the family album. The album picture with Kate noted that Kate first met his father "Robert at the sweet age of eighteen years." Tommy smiled affectionately. He looked at Millis and at the little bin in her hands and said, "You came on time. Thank you, Millis dear."

"You are welcome, sir." She looked into Tommy's blue eyes, and, very slowly, she closed the Mahogany door of the Grecian Room.

"I see you, too, are getting used to the first-name basis," Zeek said.

"Association is catchy," Tommy replied, and he resorted to his drunken act. He stumbled, and then he sat down.

"How come I'm not fighting for every cause as you are?"

"We are bitten by different bugs, Zeek."

"Yours is a black bug?"

"No; homogenous." He staggered and got up. "Thanks for the drink, buddy. I'm leaving. I'll stick to water next time."

"Where would that be, Sullivan?"

"At a bowtie gathering on Pennsylvania Avenue."

"You don't seem to forget."

"Formulas, not faces." He staggered to the door marked, "OUT."

"This drunk detective is going the wrong way." Zeek showed him the way out via the door marked "IN."

"What that highfalutin whiskey and that naked woman did to my psyche you'd never know." He swayed slightly and looked at *The Goddess* one more time.

"She's white, boy," Zeek said. "Not your type."

"Because you're white, girl, that's why I want you." Tommy winked at the portrait. He stumbled on a chair, and held on to it to regain his balance.

"You could complement the feeling with your brand of narcissism or with the Other One, Tommy boy."

"I'm too drunk to understand what you are telling me, man."

"Keep it that way, Mr. Two-Bit Detective, and don't forget to call next time."

"I give you my word, Mr. Vit-Vit-Vito Morong."

The shock of hearing his long-abandoned Christian name on the lips of a two-bit detective was portrayed in Zeek's eyes and in his reply: "You are smarter than I was informed, Detective Sullivan. Much smarter."

"I'm glad that you personally found out, Zeek."

* * * * * *

Tommy increased his staggering when he got outside. The dim glow of the early morning reflected on his face.

Parked outside within close range of the "IN" exit was Nigel, whose heart came out of his chest countless times as he waited there. He looked at his watch and doubted the time. It was 3.00 a.m. He saw an object that swayed towards him. That object stumbled, and fell. He recognized that object as a person by his paleness and the calypso shirt that was worn. The shirt was a gift from Elizabeth that Tommy wore. Their shirts were part of their game plan for the purpose of easy identification. Nigel wore a white shirt with a glittering gold collar. "Oh my God! Oh my God!" Nigel said, and he rushed to support his pal. He actually lifted Tommy. Nigel opened the car door, pitched everything aside, and struggled to put Tommy in the back seat. Nigel spoke rapidly. "What's wrong, man? Zeek and his hoods drugged and poisoned you? What's wrong?" Tommy grunted. "Tell me the color of your drink before you pass out on me, man." Nigel beseeched Tommy to talk. "I'm taking you to Kings County Hospital. Take this. I stole it from McDonald's. It's good for poisoning. Suck on it." He stuffed two packs of sugar in Tommy's mouth, and settled him in the back seat and slammed the door. Nigel pressed on the steering wheel and spoke excitedly to himself. "Where can I find a good doctor besides Kings County Hospital? Kings County would be overcrowded with gun shot victims this weekend. Who? Where?" His thoughts raced as Tommy's gagging noises increased with the packs of sugar in his mouth. "I know who," Nigel said. "Dr. Providence on Newkirk Avenue. Thank God Dr. Providence has not moved out to Queens as the other rich blacks. Lord Meath, baby, I'll get you to Dr. Providence in a jiffy, but don't pass out on me before you get there." He reversed the Ford, and burned the tires on the way to Dr. Providence. "Talk to me, Lord Meath. Talking will keep you alive. We learned that in our training, and you know that the more you talk the greater is your chance of survival. Do that for me, man...Just think of living for your beautiful Carmensita, Lord Meath...I always wished she were my girl. Are you hearing me? If you are hearing me, why don't you show your spunk and punch me in my mouth. Win this fight, man. I kicked your arse when we were boys. Get up and bloody my nose." Tommy folded his body and gagged louder; at times he shook so hard that he affected Nigel's steering. "Lord Meath, live, man, live. Talk to me!" Tommy grumbled unintelligibly. Nigel shouted, "That's it, baby. Say something again. Grumble...Grumble...Keep the lips moving. The most beautiful thing in the world is a woman, and Carmensita is the best. If you die on me, Lord Meath, I'll have to marry Carmensita in memory of your friendship, man. That is not fair to me. What would I do with Sunday school Sheila? You know that I love that jet black woman. She taught me the world. Get up and talk to me, man. Curse me for letting Sunday school Sheila get away from me and for marrying that dumb tarheel. Curse Africa. Curse America. Curse me. Curse Elizabeth. Curse Lyle for getting you poisoned. Fuck that bitch Billie, man. I don't care if she's Lyle's woman. Just do it! Curse Japan for Pearl Harbor. Curse the dyed-in-the-flag Republicans. Curse Eve for eating the apple. Fall in love with the devil, but stay alive, for my sake, Lord Meath. I love you, man. You are my brother. Do anything but don't pass out on me, man. I want you to live. We have a future business...We have to open our own detective agency, man, with the name Sullivan and Gordon...Shit, man!" The road was traffic free and the needle of the speedometer was stuck on the last number.

Nigel resorted to another form of coaxing when Tommy kicked the car door and gagged louder. "Lord Meath, I know why you love your Mira Mira. You fell in love with her because she's the essence of humanity. She takes care of handicapped children in her basement without a penny help from the city. She's the

Mother Hale of Brooklyn. Isn't that why you are in love with your Mira Mira? Then why don't you let your mother know these qualities of Carmensita, man?" He peeked into the mirror and Tommy looked as if he took his last sacrament. Nigel shouted to the top of his voice: "No!" He broke the traffic light at the intersection of New York and Newkirk Avenues and drove recklessly into Dr. Providence's garage. He looked up and said, "Thank you, God," when the lights were turned on in the doctor's bedroom. He tooted and tooted the car horn to impress upon Dr. Providence that a dying man is downstairs.

Slowly, Tommy's head ascended; then his voice is heard. "You want Sunday school Sheila and my Mira Mira, too. You dirty bigamist...Hee hee, ha ha ha...Hee hee, ha ha ha...."

"I'll be right down," Dr. Providence shouted from his window.

"Go back to sleep, African," Tommy shouted back at the doctor. "You are not a good dentist...Hee hee, ha ha, I got it! Daddy's little boy, get out of that African's garage before he calls the real police. I think you crashed his garage door."

Dr. Providence pulled in his head, pushed up his glasses on his nose, and walked to his bathroom. "Crazy people in this Brooklyn...Soon I'll be out of here." He flushed the toilet.

"What those rowdy people wanted, Eitel?" his wife inquired.

"Some crazy man and his crazier friend are looking for a dentist."

"At this hour? I told you Brooklyn is no place to live, Eitel. Come back in bed. Later today we'll talk about moving out to Queens or Staten Island."

Nigel drove to Avenue D and stopped the car. He was blue with rage.

"We have Zeek by the balls, man," Tommy boasted.

"Fuck you, man. That's no joke to play on a man

with a weak heart."

"I had advised you to go to medical school to strengthen your heart, but you were afraid when you graduated you would have cut off Lyle's balls to please Elizabeth."

"Man, I just realize that it's better to get your balls cut off than to have them squeezed. You had mine squeezed, man, and it pained like hell."

"You're such a sissy. Why don't you move to Queens?"

"Now you want me to be a double sissy."

"Drive, boy, and stop that foolish talk. Let's go to Sam the Fingerprint Thief. His private lab is on Empire Boulevard. We'll call Totohead from Sam's office and let him know that we are getting through with our police imitation." Tommy looked at his watch. "Daddy's little boy, you can park whenever you wish because I'm going to sleep till daylight."

They fell asleep in the car. Tommy remained in the back seat, and Nigel slept with his face on the steering wheel. Tommy was up at nine. "The Other One, get up." Tommy patted Nigel's coarse hair. Then he touched Nigel harder and said, "Time to get up, Other One."

"That's my new name now?"

"That's how Zeek called you."

"And you responded to that name?"

"Yes."

"You and Zeek became such buddies that you are calling me by that fucking name, too?"

"Wait a minute. Let me explain."

"You two white boys had a good time referring to black people as 'Those People' and 'the Other One.'"

"Why are you so hyper, Nigel? Give me a chance to explain." Tommy laughed at Nigel's folly. "Zeek said some awful things about black people."

"I don't fuck well want to hear. All I want is Zeek's fingerprint. He's probably the murderer."

"He didn't only speak about black people; he castigated the Jews, too. He badmouthed rabbis, mullahs, pastors, leaders, West Indians, Arabs, Puerto Ricans—and you know how I feel when anyone speaks ill of PRs. Zeek said he has Brooklyn in his hand, from the police brass to the judges. He also spoke about..."

"His own murderous deeds?"

"He said something about Leader Dollon..."

"Vulgar and racist, I'm sure?"

"Yes, Zeek was vulgar and racist; but he also said..."

"That Leader Dollon killed Constance Wagner, the Jewish woman?"

"No. He never said that; but..."

"I don't want to hear. Period!"

"Don't you want to hear what a man who has Brooklyn in his palm says?"

"Two white boys suddenly become such buddies."

"Don't you want to hear more of what Zeek had to say? After all, he spoke in my ears."

"No. I do not want to hear. I had enough of those buddy stories—white boy to white boy, birds of a feather. You got the sleep out of my eyes, so let's go by Sam. It's after nine, and Sam should be in his office now."

Tommy and Nigel walked into Sam's lab. Sam did his job once. Sam did it twice. He did it again. He finally dropped the broken pieces of glass and wiped his hands.

"What's wrong, Sam? Your great grandfather solved the cable car murder, and you are better than he," Tommy said. "You are the best, Sam. I got Zeek's pinkie, his ring, his thumb, his index, the whole hog. So what's wrong?"

Sam looked at them, individually. "Gentlemen, that hand is glazed."

"Wha...What! Zeek has no fingerprint!" Nigel exclaimed.

"They are burned out." Sam tapped his pipe and lit it.

"I'm going home," Tommy said. He walked away.

Nigel put his hand on Tommy's shoulder. "My father loves you, man. From the day he called from Wall Street and you answered the phone at my house, he wished you were his own son, man. You can't let him down now, man. You are going with me."

"Where?"

"Anywhere that we can get a clue to solve this murder. Am personally going to interrogate Zeek."

"And after that?"

"To my home to eat some good peas and rice and stew fish."

"I'd love to...just to inhale Elizabeth's perfume."

Chapter Twenty-One

Grenada Ghost

That September Sunday brought many surprises. Tulips in Elizabeth's garden blossomed for the first time. A year ago she bought a box of pink bulbs (or so she thought) at Woolworth's and planted them, but Congo blue adorned her weed infested flower garden. Congo blue was Lyle's favorite color. Elizabeth, forever psychic, did not warn herself to be aware of the unexpected as she was wont to do. The newsboy quickly rode by and hit her window with his delivery. She pushed the *Daily News* aside and re-read an old headline: POPE SAYS 'NO' TO WOMEN PRIESTS. "Leader Dollon believes in the stained-glass ceiling, too," she said softly. She got up, switched on the kitchen radio, and Southern Baptists ministers blared about hell's fire and man's damnation. As she went about her morning chores, she sang, dusted the furniture, and reminisced about Lyle's Fyzabad stories during their nocturnal fidgetings. Hettie Campbell, her friend and confidante, was expected to accompany her to church, and Elizabeth wanted her kitchen to be as clean as a Dutch oven to get Hettie's praise. She went to her bedroom, and the spotless mirror where Lyle once stood to fix his tie reminded her of Lyle's lukewarm compliments. She stood before that mirror, pulled in her stomach, spoke to Lyle as if her reflection were his, then mimicked Lyle's likely replies.

"How doah look, Lyle?" she began her one-man dialogue.

"As usual, Liz."

"That's all you have to say about my looks, Lyle?"

"Don't disturb me, Liz. Can't you see that I'm listening to Howard Cosell's sports interview with Muhammad Ali?" She was vintage Lyle.

"I hope Cosell cooks your fry bake and sol fish this morning."

"Honey Liz, you know that you look better than Cosell with, or without, his toupee." She went into Lyle's clothes closet, retrieved his favorite French tie, playfully choked her neck with it, and said, "Liz, how do you like my Sinatra knot, honey?" She ended her skit, chuckled, and said, "Honey, I miss you every day. There's not another man in the world like you but I." The kettle whistled. She rushed to the kitchen and turned off the fire.

"My god, tomorrow would be another Labor Day," she said, as if by rote. Immediately the whole agony of Lyle's predicament and her sparse visits to Rikers Island to see her husband arrested her thought. She was glad, however, when the buzzer rang. Hettie had arrived. "Come in, Hettie. I have what you like, but remember today is church, so be moderate in your pourings. I'm going to shower. How do you like my kitchen, girl?"

"It looks awright," Hettie said. In no time Hettie went to the kitchen cabinet, retrieved her favorite liqueur glass, and filled it with brandy. She enjoyed the first sip, shook her head contentedly, and commented, "There's nothing like Hennessy's." She was about to take the second sip when the buzzer sounded twice. Being an old friend of the Gordons' family, she knew who buzzed. "Oh hell!" she expressed her aggravation, "you mean even on Sundays the mailman and Con Edison disturb the peace. They won't even allow me to enjoy my brandy."

Elizabeth shouted from the bathroom. "Answer the buzzer, Hettie. Take that special delivery from the mailman. It may be the court papers from Lyle's attorneys; but tell Con Ed that your madam is not at home, and the basement is locked. I suspect Con Ed is coming to cut my lights for nonpayment."

"I love Con Edison," Hettie danced with her brandy

in hand. "Their blackout 1977 gave me some lovely things for my apartment. God made a way for me." Hettie took another sip of her brandy and licked her lips.

"You are not really serious about what you've just said, Hettie?" Elizabeth turned off the shower and left the bathroom door ajar.

"Dead serious, Liz!" She continued to dance.

"God doesn't like people to rob the rich or the poor. God wants us to earn our daily bread honestly."

"God doesn't like darkness either, and that is why He created the light to lighten our darkness. I can't see your logic, Liz. A brother told me that he was walking in the darkness on Flatbush Avenue, and he stumbled on some good furniture, so he sold them very cheap to me. You wanted me to refuse a once-in-a-life-time bargain like that?"

"You didn't come to church the Sunday when Leader Dollon sermonized on that. His text was about all those people who used the blackout as a window of opportunity to steal from the merchants. Now Flatbush Avenue is like a shanty town, and the merchants are moving out. Who suffers? We, the neighborhood people. No one can plump the depth of your reasoning, Hettie. Your furniture brother dabbles in the philosophy of darkness. For that matter, everybody dabbles in some form of philosophy and logic these days."

"You're surely right, girl. Philosophy is the logic of laugh and cry living in the same house."

"Says who, Hettie?"

"Says logic! If you get a good bargain in a blackout, logic will tell you that it is better to apprehend the bargain and laugh about it than to refuse the bargain and then cry about not seizing it."

"Okay, philosopher Hettie. Get the door, but don't let Con Edison in for them to cut off my lights and for me to be in darkness again."

Hettie pressed her glass as if doing so restrained her

from what she really wanted to say to her bosom friend. "The things that I've done for you, madam...But, madam, to tell Con Edison you ain't here, isn't that just as bad as buying blackout furniture from the brother who was out there helping himself?"

"No! Number one, the brother who was out there helping himself was a thief; two, you were an accomplice; but I am going to pay that electric monopoly Consolidated Edison at a later date because I don't have the cash as of today. Therefore, I would hope that with every sip of my brandy, you would become cognizant of the fact that you purchased stolen furniture from that ingenious brother knowing those furniture to be stolen. You could be put in the pen under Section 165.40."

"That section of the law doesn't relate to the underprivileged brothers, Liz."

"Please, get the door, Hettie. You know where the keys are. Put down the brandy and hurry."

"Liz, you know the brandy helps my voice, and I have to belch a solo today." Hettie found the bunch of keys, but she did not know which is which.

Elizabeth came out of the bathroom. "This key is for the first door; this key is for the outside front door; and this glass is mine." Elizabeth took the glass from Hettie's hand, poured out the brandy, and rested the glass in the kitchen sink.

"Madam, from a bunch of thirty keys, you expected me to pick two winners. I betted on a sure thing at Belmont, and that horse came in last." Hettie went to the front door, opened it, and without looking up at the men at the door, she said, "Mr. Postman, I'll take the priority mail...Con Edison, my madam is not here, and her basement is locked tight."

"We gotcha!" Nigel said. "Shsh." He put his hand on Hettie's lips. "We wanted to trick Elizabeth, and that's why we buzzed the way the mailman and Con Ed usually do." He kissed her.

"Hi, Lord Meath," Hettie said. "I didn't know that you still visit this Foster-breeze Pastalaqua House."

"These days the breeze blows stronger on the Pastalaqua House, but it hasn't blown me away." Tommy spoke softly in Hettie's ear and said, "I've come to smell your madam's perfume." He kissed her.

"So you heard us from outside?"

Tommy pointed to two missing panes of glass in the vestibule.

"Mr. Postman and Mr. Con Edison, please hide inside, and let me trick my madam, too. My madam is getting ready for us to go to church." They tiptoed in. The aroma of Elizabeth's perfume punched the air, and Tommy sniffed like an East German Stasi dog in search of stowaways at the Berlin Wall. He sniffed until his lungs were filled with all the compositions of the fragrance.

"Who was it, Hettie?" Elizabeth asked, as she painstakingly creamed her body and put on her makeup in the bathroom.

"Two letter carriers brought a big box, and they want you to sign for it personally."

"A big box? From whom? What could it be?"

"How would I know, madam?"

"Since when I'm your madam, Hettie?"

"Since you taught me how to lie conveniently; and it's not the first time either, madam."

"I didn't hear what you just said, Hettie. Anyhow, where are the letter carriers?"

Hettie was least concerned about Elizabeth's anxiety. She went into the kitchen and got a clean glass. She poured her last shot of brandy, and she questioned a boxing caricature that Lyle had longsince pasted on the wall: "How could he call himself Foreman when his back is on the ground like the laborer? Muhammad Ali couldn't do that to me, not even if I were wearing my ugly tapping shoes."

"Today is Sunday. Stop imbibing the wrong spirit

on a church day, Hettie. Did you hear me?"

"Yes, madam. I'll wash my mouth before I go to church, madam."

"Where are the men with that heavy package?"

Hettie pointed to the bedroom.

"What are they doing in my bedroom? Daddy's little boy moved out, and Lyle is in jail. What got into your head to send two strange men into my bedroom, Hettie?" Elizabeth closed her robe tightly, dragged on one side of her slipper, and marched frantically into her bedroom. "Oh no!" she shouted. "So you two are the mailmen?"

Nigel and Tommy hugged her. "Don't you feel like a package now?" Tommy said.

"Just don't wrap me," Elizabeth said.

"How can we mail Cinderella to the handsome prince with only one side of slipper?" Tommy said.

"I know where my prince is, Lord Meath."

Hettie walked into the bedroom. "When I visit Lyle on Rikers Island on Wednesday," she threatened, "I'll tell him where his wife has been receiving her mail."

"Getouta here," Elizabeth said.

"I'm leaving right now for church to practice my solo. Today I'll be belching out *Amazing Grace* better than Mahalia Jackson. Don't let those two Romeos delay you, madam dear. We have a long program today, and Leader Dollon would be preaching on the plight of angels."

"Didn't Leader Dollon preach on that before, Hettie?"

"Seems as if you're losing it, girl. Hell no! He preached on the fall of angels, not their plight."

"That's true," Elizabeth said.

"Bye, Lord Meath; bye, daddy's little boy."

"Don't forget to wash your mouth to get rid of the scent of the bottled spirit, Hettie," Tommy said; and he and Nigel came out of the bedroom.

"Thanks for reminding me, Lord Meath, but I like to feel the taste in my mouth," Hettie said. She tightened her yellow and white headtie and demonstrated for them her improved Nicholas Brothers strides. "I wish I had my tapping shoes, man." She tapped out of the house.

"What a surprise," Elizabeth said as she came out of the bedroom. "I thought you two had given me up." In a house dress, her head was wrapped with the same fabric of yellow and white that Hettie wore.

"I like your headwrap, Liz," Tommy said. "I wish my mother would dress up on Sundays and go some place. She's always in a law book. The last thing she told me before I got here was the Grand Jury should be abolished. Everything she talks about is this jurisprudence and that jurisprudence...work, work, work, but no play. But whenever I see you, you are always so attractively appealing. If I didn't know my age, I would not have been able to guess yours."

"Thank you kindly, Lord Meath. Come again. My Lord, this headtie is part of our Spiritual Baptist garb."

"Ma, don't let that white boy sugar you into telling him your business," Nigel said. "He is sugaring you up into believing that your beauty is your equity, but Ma Sullivan's equity is her worth."

"Nigel, you are the worst! You have a flip side for everything. You turn everything into politics or race. Your problem is that you don't even know how to tell a woman that she's beautiful. When my Ma invites you to dinner in Queens, I'll make sure she puts you to sit in the kitchen."

"Ma Elizabeth of Brooklyn, your son comes first; and he's hungry."

"All right, kids, stop fighting. I cooked enough food for those who want to eat in the kitchen and put their elbows on the table, those who want to sit on the stoop and crack bones, and for those who want to dine with me in style. Make your choice, gentlemen."

Elizabeth, Nigel, and Tommy sat down to an early dinner. They spoke about everything, even about the

Royal Family's woes and wealth, but no one broached Lyle's incarceration. Whenever a television station hinted anything about a crime, Elizabeth used the remote control and switched to another station. Her dessert was channel surfing. Eventually she said, "Apart from the two mavericks who popped in on me today, I had another September surprise."

"What?" asked Tommy.

"I was sure I bought pink bulbs, but the garden is bursting out with Congo blue tulips."

"Did you plant what you bought?" Tommy took a keen interest in the conversation.

"I thought so, Lord Meath."

"You never know what this earth has in store for us," Nigel said, and he changed the topic.

Dinner was over. Tommy accidentally dragged his chair and said, "Kate would surely put me in the kitchen to eat if she heard me drag this chair."

"Lord Meath, I'm not your mother, and in my house you can drag your chair, and eat with your hat on. You can do anything, absent etiquette or not, once you say that you enjoy my cooking."

"I can even vomit on your carpet?" Tommy said.

"You can even do the Raggy Beerman." They laughed.

"I enjoyed your callaloo and crab, Liz," Tommy said. "The macaroni pie was great. The stew peas and beef was yum yum. That mixed rice was made in heaven. Your carrot juice has a secret recipe that I'll want to buy from you before you return to your country. Your West Indian cooking is the best, Liz." Tommy jokingly licked his five fingers. "When you go back home, Liz, I've got to visit you in the West Indies."

"Puerto Rico is also in the West Indies," Elizabeth replied.

"That was a great one-liner, Liz," Tommy said. The group laughed, but Nigel laughed the longest and the loudest. Tommy said, "Liz, Raggy Beerman once told me that you and Lyle should go on the road with your show. When next I see Raggy I'll tell him that you are now the house clown doing a dual role."

"Don't you know that I'm versatile, Lord Meath?" Elizabeth reminded him.

"And psychic," Tommy added.

"That, too. And my psyche tells me that Lord Meath wants to be excused to see those mysterious tulips."

"They had been on my mind. I must see them."

"Go through the back door," Elizabeth said, "and see for yourself, Lord Meath. Watch your steps. Lyle should have fixed those steps long ago."

"I'll be careful." Tommy left the table.

"Ma, as soon as Lord Meath returns from seeing your tulips, we'll drop you to church."

"You forgot I have to buy flowers."

"You still pay for the flowers with your own money?"

"I took that responsibility since you were a tot, and I love doing it. Nobody else buys flowers, but me. Buying flowers is my gift to God. I never take the church's money to buy flowers."

Tommy walked in. "What did I miss? The tulips are just lovely, Liz."

"Aren't they, even among the weeds?" Elizabeth said.

"I guess it's my time to see those mysterious tulips," Nigel said. He went to see them.

"Liz, I'll help you clean up," Tommy said.

"Where have you seen a white private detective doing domestic duties, Lord Meath?"

"Detectives do menial tasks when they want to get information."

"Like what?"

"How come you and Hettie are so close after all these years?"

"We just happen to be compatible."

"In everything?"

"Except in our love for brandy. Hettie even remembered that tonight would be one year since Lyle picked me up in church. That was the first and the last time that he came."

"He never picked you up before and got some of that ol' time religion?"

"That was the only time. Like I'm seeing Lyle now; he sat in the front pew; he was sweaty, more like sloppy, except for his glittering belt."

"I remember the one time that I went to your church. I was tired after church."

"Why not say bored?"

"I wasn't really bored."

"The adverb 'really' meant that you were bored, but not much."

"Do you juggle other things as you do with words?"

"Like?"

"Life's fate."

"We were tossed in that fatal mode from inside the womb."

"Do you work in the legal department at Chase?"

"Which section?"

Tommy laughed. "Let me get back to what I really wanted to ask you. What the kids do when church is in late sessions?"

"The kids who stay over from Sunday school wait for their parents in the basement. Your pal used to enjoy going to Sunday school. One of these days the things that Nigel learned at Sunday school would be of benefit to him. I must confess that Leader Dollon performs too long sometimes, and the services are really too long for the children."

"Because the adults have to wait until the spirit manifests itself?"

"You know a lot about my church."

"You know who told me?"

"When would you two stop fighting? You fight like siblings trying to take your parents' love from one another."

"We have been fighting lately about the best way to apprehend Constance Wagner's murderer. Nigel and I are sure about one thing, and that is Lyle is not guilty of that act."

"I can well imagine. I pray every night for my husband."

"Eggie and Bob still carry on business on the block?"

"Yes. That's a faithful mom-and-pop store in Flatbush. You gave those two old people hell when you thought they shortchanged you for the snow shoveling jobs. You were a Shylock from birth, Lord Meath. You and Nigel even prevented the other kids from working for them. That wasn't nice what you and daddy's little boy did. Eggie and Bob really helped the neighborhood kids. They are good people...And don't tell me they are foreigners!"

"Do they still sell booze?"

"C'mon, Lord Meath! That was a wild rumor. You and Nigel were two bad boys who fanned that rumor."

Tommy inhaled deeply. "We were always sweet like you. I really like your perfume. It smells like the fresh fragrance from France flowing in my face. I'm sure it lingers after you leave the scene."

"Is it that good? Probably that's why Hettie won't stay away from my perfume. I deeply suspect that she has a small phial, and she pours out my perfume in it."

"So she, too, uses your perfume? I see; I see. It's really feminine."

"I had another bottle, but I cannot remember what I did with it."

"What!" Tommy's shout shocked Elizabeth, and she dropped the dish and spoon that were in her hands.

Nigel rushed inside. "Leave those dishes alone, Ma. I'll clean up. Go and get dressed for church at once!" He commanded his mother.

"All right, Nigel," Elizabeth said. She remembered that she once disobeyed his command. She had asked him on that occasion, "Nigel, are you the tail wagging the dog?" Nigel didn't answer his mother then, but he stayed away from her for one year. She forthrightly apologized to him for her dog-and-tail remark, and ever since Elizabeth had been jumping to his every command. "All right, son...All right, son," she repeated herself. "I'll get dressed right away. When I'm leaving I'll walk with my keys. Just pull in the door, son. Strange, do you know, son, that I put the church keys in the very pants that your father wore the day that he came to church."

"That's the meeting of minds," Tommy chimed in. "Lyle is thinking of you at this very minute. Let me walk you to the door and tell you how sentimental your son is."

"Let her go, Lord Meath. You'll tell her another time. Maybe tonight, if we pick her and Hettie up at the church."

"No ifs. I'll tell Leader Dollon that both of you will be picking us up, and how both of you are fighting over me."

"Tell Leader Dollon that the ex-Sunday school boy is a greenhorn detective," Tommy said.

"And, Ma, tell Leader Dollon that the white boy is greener, and he did not learn his catechisms at Saint Jerome's."

"I'll tell Leader Dollon how two private detectives tricked me. Son, come and give your loving Ma a kiss before she leaves." Nigel kissed her, and she waited until he walked away. "You, too, Lord Meath." Elizabeth kissed Tommy, and whispered in his ear. "What do you really like about my perfume, Mr. Detective?"

"The missing bottle, Mrs. Gordon." Tommy's whisper was even softer.

Elizabeth pulled Tommy's cheek. "Go play the piano and improvise, Lord Meath. You may quicker find the lost chord."

"Proctor and Sullivan's *The Lost Chord*? That's a song."

"Mr. Tellymack taught his students that song many years ago...'Seated one day at the organ,/ I was weary and ill at ease.'" Elizabeth sang two bars of the song and left to buy her flowers.

Tommy walked to the kitchen. He took the liqueur glass from the kitchen sink and picked up the spoon from the floor. "Two birds with one shot...another September surprise," he said softly, and he put the glass and the spoon in his over-sized army shirt. "These are for Sam the fingerprint expert." He hummed *The Lost Chord*, washed the dishes, and then he played the piano.

Nigel was slumped in Lyle's favorite easy chair, and he fell into a dream. As Nigel dreamed, he relived a day when, as a boy, Elizabeth had taken him to church in a gypsy cab. This was part of his dream which was a snapshot of his boyhood:

"How much for you, driver?" Elizabeth asked when the gypsy cabdriver stopped at her church on Nostrand Avenue.

"Tree dowlars," the cabby said.

"Gawddamit! I always pay a yellow cab one twenty five. You charge people by counting the traffic lights?"

"Tree dowlars ah say, lady!"

"Here! You son of a Haitian bitch!" Elizabeth dropped three dollars on the back seat.

"No teep?"

"Tip you, robber?"

"Cheap West Indian bitch!"

"And you's a half-baked, Papa Doc zombie who's accustomed to sleeping on a clothes line in Haiti. Why don't you go back and drive the tap-tap bus in your country?"

The gypsy cabdriver cursed Elizabeth in creole. He thought he had the last word, and felt Elizabeth didn't know a word of his native tongue. She shocked the cabby. She eased out of his car. She took a deep breath and pulled out Nigel with her. "*Pa ou!*" she shouted to him, and slammed the car door.

"Ma, what *Pa ou* means in patois?" Nigel asked.

"It means 'same to you,' son."

Nigel's dream suddenly ended when Tommy

banged the piano. "Why were you smiling in your sleep, Sunday school boy?" Tommy asked.

"Your piano playing had me ill at ease and made me dream of my Christian days."

"You had that, too?"

"Every Sunday for a long, long time. I prayed to become a man so that I would not have to go to church with my mother."

"Or was it because Sunday school Sheila got hip to your sugarcake gifts in exchange for her forced favors, and she wouldn't allow you to use the basement to your slick advantage?" Tommy played the piano softly and dramatically.

Nigel did not answer the question. "What are you playing, man?"

"Guess?"

"*Slow Boat to China*."

"You are tone deaf, man. Can't you recognize *Mary Had a Little Lamb*, man...Now let me improvise on how to find a murderer...probably a strangler...probably a cute lefthander who came up from behind and hit Constance Wagner in her head." Tommy played all the inversions of the C and E minor chords. "You see the beauty of C and E?"

"You are too late to be a Horowitz, Lord Meath. Today is the Christian's Sabbath. Why not play a hymn, devil."

"Hypocrite, I don't know whether I should blame the Serpent, Adam and Eve, or the fruit of the poison tree for your shortsightedness."

"If you join the Order of Melchizedek, the greatest order of Spiritual Baptist, you'll know who to blame, Lord Meath. You'll learn the truth about many things."

"I'll cut corners and ask Elizabeth." Tommy struck a chord.

"That's A augmented. Your chords are thin, Lord Meath. Your chords should be heavy if you want to be really dramatic, and you'd be better able to hide your discordant movements."

"So you know movements?" He closed the piano. "Daddy's little boy, let me show you this. In your lifetime have you ever seen a similar scrap of cloth?" Tommy pushed his hand into his army shirt pocket and pulled out a scrap of cloth from an envelope. He rested the flimsy piece of cloth on the upright piano.

"Where did you get it?" Nigel asked.

"From Mabel Plutz. She said she found it in a crease in Connie's apartment." He sniffed the cloth twice. "Perfumy...You want to smell it, Nigel?"

"No! You never showed it to me before." Nigel showed his annoyance.

"It just slipped me, man. What do you make of it, Sunday school boy?"

"It's a scrap of cloth all right...It looks as if it were rubbed on a hard surface until it was worn thin...It's cheap material...It looks like a Y...It looks like a V...or an upside down V with a tail with something missing."

"What if we put a loop by the tail?" Tommy raised the shred of cloth carefully, rested it on a piece of paper, and he made a loop with his pen. "What does it look like now?"

"The letter R."

"I believe that this is the piece of cloth that was used to scratch the poem in Connie's bedhead. I had it analyzed."

"When?"

"On one of those days when you could not be found on earth or in the sky. Where do you really go, man?" The way Nigel looked at him, Tommy dropped the question. "Since we are here, and Liz isn't around, let's check Lyle's toolbox."

"The key is hidden, but I coaxed Lyle into telling me where he hid it."

They ransacked Lyle's toolbox, and they carefully examined every scribbling that journalized Lyle's life from the day he left Fyzabad.

"Here's a letter addressed to Jan Noble in Trinidad and Tobago," Nigel said. "Lyle hadn't time to mail the letter to him." Nigel looked at the envelope. "I see that his friend Joiner Jan now lives in the town of San Fernando. He moved out of Fyzabad."

"Who's Joiner Jan?" Tommy asked.

"Jan Noble. The town of Fyzabad calls him Joiner Jan, and he is still Lyle's best friend."

"Why such a name?"

"As a little boy, Noble used to eat out the center of his mother's half-cooked bake, and then he would patch the bake with raw flour. Lyle relayed Noble's special skill to the village, and that's how Jan Noble got the name Joiner Jan."

"I thought the kids nowadays were cute."

"You better change that thought. And if you thought Lyle and Joiner Jan were cute, you should hear about Elizabeth's cuteness."

"How did you happen to hear of Elizabeth's cuteness? You weren't born in her time."

"At nights when Lyle and Liz thought I was sound asleep."

"So you are a chip of two cute blocks?"

Nigel looked at Tommy critically.

"I didn't mean it that way, man," Tommy said. "You're so thin skin."

"Forget about my skin. What do we do now?"

"For now, just open the envelope, Nigel, and let's see what Lyle wrote to Joiner Jan."

Nigel ripped the envelope and read the letter. "Everything is readable, Lord Meath, except the last word or two. Lyle came to the end of the paper, and with the limited space, he wrote the last word or words in shorthand. Sometimes when Lyle and Joiner Jan are speaking on the phone, they talk in shorthand."

"Let me see the letter." Tommy read the letter, and he stared at the hieroglyphics. "I see what you mean, son. This is Pitman's shorthand. This letter is very interesting. Let's call Joiner Jan in Pitch Lake Country."

"Liz hasn't a phone. She took out the phone because she was getting too many anonymous calls. Liz told me that she recognized Billie Zellars' voice, and she'd love to put her hands on Billie but she doesn't know where she lives."

"Who nearby could read shorthand?" Tommy scratched his head and found the answer. "Let's go by Eggie and Bob's. Their daughter Suzie is a whiz." He paused. "Do you think they'd recognize us, Nigel?"

"Your blue eyes," Nigel said.

"You kicked down their door, not me," Tommy reminded Nigel.

"And why don't you say that Eggie would remember you aptly for what you did, and always wanted to do."

"Are you going or not? They can't remember us, man."

"And if Suzie doesn't live there anymore?"

"I spent a semester in a shorthand lab, so I'll call Joiner Jan. I'll describe the shorthand strokes. Or do you want us to go to the court stenographer?"

"This letter is private, man. Those Pitman strokes that we cannot understand may sink Lyle *or other members of his family*, man." Nigel immediately realized what he said, but it was too late to retract the statement that was sunk into Tommy's brain.

"What *other members of his family*? Your family was always made up of three people. Do you want to explain your last statement?"

"Ignore what I've said. Just ignore completely what I've said. I trust your expertise, man."

Tommy looked at his detective pal and smiled. "Then trust me. I'm as good as Pitman himself. The way history is changing its face, that Englishman could have been the son of an Egyptian."

"And you know Egypt is in Africa?"

"What's the beef, man?"

"Nothing, man. Let's go, Mr. Pitman." In their trek to Eggie and Bob's, though Nigel clowned with his friends from the neighborhood, he turned over in his mind what he really meant by "...*may sink Lyle and other members of his family.*"

As soon as the detective duo walked into the candy store, Eggie and Bob recognized them, and welcomed them with their cheerfulness. Like innocent choir boys who rehearsed their parts, the duo chorused a contrapuntal melody: "Good afternoon, Miss Eggie; good afternoon, Mr. Bob."

"Gootafnoon." The elderly couple answered with joy. They were very happy to see their once-upon-a-time disgruntled employees who once upon a time ate at their table.

"Tommy, no more here?" Bob, the elder block watcher asked.

"I live in Queens now, Mr. Bob. Where's Suzie?"

"Suzie no here. Married. Livin' far. Connecut."

"Her husband treats her well in Connecticut?"

"No troubel. She doctor-professor. She know if troubel, come home."

"That's good advice to your daughter, Mr. Bob."

"An' you fadder still in troubel, Nigel? Good man. Me no believe he do dat."

"Yes, my father is still in jail, and I, too, don't believe that he did that, Mr. Bob. Have change for five dollars, Mr Bob? I want to call my father from the telephone booth outside."

"You vant to use the phone? No go boot. Come 'side."

"Are you sure that you want us to use your phone, Mr. Bob?"

"Too sure. Vant a veer? Come in."

"Yes, a beer would be nice," Nigel said.

They went to the back of the store, and Eggie brought out two labelless bottles. "See you's still goot frenz. We like you two. We no get goot snow boys 'gain." Eggie left them inside and went to attend to the customers.

Pepper touched Salt and said, "You told me in fifth

grade that you must pull Eggie's breast one more time if it is the last thing you do before you leave this earth. Be a man and honor your word, Lord Meath. Do it today, man."

Eggie brought two more bottles of beer, name brand, and handed Tommy his, but Tommy kept his clean hands close to Eggie's bosom as Rochester, New York's Asian roaches were close to San Juan, Puerto Rico's long neck pullets.

"You's a chicken, man," Nigel said.

"With what this home-made brew is doing to me, let's make the call before I ask Eggie to sleep on her bed with Bob. They don't know that we are calling long distance, so this is another way to get back our snow money."

"Tom-Tom, you not goot boy. You teef."

"You 'complice."

Nigel and Tommy ended their clowning, and Tommy dialed Jan Noble in San Fernando, the second largest town of the Republic of Trinidad and Tobago. Nigel jammed his ear to the black rotary phone.

"Hello," a voice answered.

"Is that Mr. Jan Noble?" Tommy asked.

"Jan is in the toilet. Who's calling?"

"Get him out. America is calling. Long distance." Tommy lowered his voice when he said "long distance."

In less than a minute someone picked up the phone and said, "Hello. Jan Noble's speaking."

Nigel took the phone from Tommy and said, "Mr. Noble, this is Lyle Gordon's boy calling from New York. Lyle is fine."

"Whenever your father calls me, he speaks proudly of you, son."

"Thanks, Mr. Noble. He speaks a lot about you, too. He wrote you a letter, Mr. Noble, and you'll soon get it in the mail. Elizabeth is also fine. She's just as beautiful now as when Lyle climbed the greasypole."

"Son, you throw my mind back more than fifty years ago. I still can't believe that Lyle beat Spree and won that Mondesir gold belt. Did Lyle tell you that Fyzabad people ran Spree and his Grenadian family out of town? Tell Lyle that Spree's stepfather and his mother died from grief because Spree turned out to be a vagabond."

"Mr. Noble, Lyle told me that story many times. I know that story by heart. I'm calling long distance, and my money is running out. I made a bet with my pal that if nobody knows shorthand, you know it with your eyes closed, with your hands locked behind your back, and no matter how anyone describes a shorthand stroke, you could transcribe that outline in long hand. Are you ready to hear that shorthand outline, Mr. Noble?"

"Is it Pitman's?"

"Sure. I'm putting on my friend, Tommy, an expert, to describe that shorthand stroke." Nigel handed Tommy the phone.

"Are you ready, Mr. Noble?" Tommy said. "I am going to read you a passage, and I want you to put in the missing word or words after the word, 'Lord.' I will describe the stroke that is written in shorthand. Here's a paragraph from a famous author. Open quote: 'I took Connie home, and I left her house around midnight. Do you know, like in Pitch Lake Country, three people were *liming...*' Do you know what *liming* means, Mr. Noble?"

"Sure! That word was coined in my country. It means hanging out in a care-free manner."

"Okay. Let's continue with the exact quote. 'Three people were *liming* on the sidewalk; one of them, drunk like a fish, was mumbling to himself or herself saying Lord,....' That's the end of the quote. The shorthand character that follows the word 'Lord' is a very small 'V' attached to a horizontal stroke. The horizontal stroke is like the concave of a circle...normal length...not doubled...not halved." Tommy looked at Nigel and winked. He proved to his pal that he, Tommy, was really an expert in the winged art.

"In other words, the stroke is bellied?" Jan Noble's voice came crashing through the phone.

"What do you mean by bellied, Mr. Noble?"

"Is that shorthand stroke hollow?"

"Yes! Yes!"

"Is the character resembling a 'V' very small?"

Nigel snatched the phone from Tommy's hand and said, "Mr. Noble, is it chinkee...like when you and Lyle were boys, and you teased the Chinese immigrants and said, 'Chinee Chinee, never die, with flat nose and chinkee eye?' The 'V' is chinkee chinkee like Chinee eye? " Nigel smiled and handed back the phone to Tommy. He indeed felt proud of his contribution in the trans-Atlantic relay.

"And, Mr. Noble," Tommy continued, "don't forget that those two characters are linked as one stroke, and they are written above the line. If you didn't answer in ten seconds what those characters are, Lyle Gordon's boy would lose a large fortune. I can't tell you the fortune right now because some nosy people are nearby listening to our conversation." Nigel and Tommy's exhaled air was heard as they jammed their ears to the black phone. They counted the ticking seconds on their watches.

Noble's voice came through fervently. "I know," he said.

"Tell us what you know, Mr. Noble," Tommy shouted into the phone. "It is important to know. A life depends on it."

"The shorthand characters you described are transcribed as 'I know...Lord, I know.'"

"Are you positive, Mr. Noble?"

"I am as positive as the Adult Nigger's grandfather was positive that one day his grandson would live to play with John Wayne in America. Incidentally, tell Lyle that he wouldn't believe who came into my life. Over the years that person asked about him, but I always hid it from him."

"Click!" Tommy cut Noble off. "Who else but Archer Daniels Midland and White Rose Flour Company came into your life and competed to supply you with whole grain wheat to patch your mother's bake."

"You no goot boy, Tom-Tom. You cut off Joiner Jan, Fyzabad's original smart man. That could have been a clue that he was about to tell you."

"This is long distance, man. We are already abusing Bob's kindness. And, furthermore, extra dough talk from Joiner Jan could cause constipation." Tommy, somehow, felt Joiner Jan's transcription was important. He addressed Nigel as if he, Tommy, were Ralph Bunche who had just brokered an agreement for peace in the Middle East. "Daddy's little boy," Tommy said, "if I didn't live in your West Indian backyard, I would have thought Joiner Jan said, 'Lord Anno' or 'Lawdanno....' Your island people talk funny. Lyle, after all these years in America, still pronounces 'Father' as 'Farder' whenever he delves into his improved Ebonics."

"I could always count on you and your snide remarks, Lord Meath."

"Who is better in snide than you, sir?"

"You protestant Ulsters talk funny, too." Nigel imitated an Irish disc jockey he once heard.

"I'm Catholic, and I don't sound constipated like the bake thief. I had to tickle him to force out the raw flour."

"Lord Meath, the Irishman, is so metaphorical."

"Nigel Gordon, the African, is so pastoral."

"Oh yeah?"

"Oh yeah!"

Eggie whispered to Bob, and Bob looked through his bone glasses as he spoke. "See what I tell you. Before they leave store, they fight, fight, fight...."

"But goot boys," Eggie replied.

Tommy and Nigel purposely shook hands for Eggie and Bob to see. "Thank you and goodbye, Miss Eggie, and Mr. Bob for allowing us to make a quick call." To access the street, the childlike detectives raised their feet high above the door block that Bob had chiseled out over twenty five years ago.

"Goot bye."

"Goot bye."

The detectives went back to Elizabeth's house, picked up their belongings, and drove off. In the car Nigel spoke first. "At least Dalgo was right about something. He said the masked man said, 'Lawdanno.'"

"Could be a woman. Forget?" Tommy said.

"No. I didn't forget, Lord Meath. The next time I'll say 'The masked person.' Drop me at Dalgo's favorite hole, and pick me up in one hour."

"I think I'll go and check my mail, and see if Totohead has any new leads for us to work on. Totohead took us away from this investigation for six months, and now he suddenly throws it in our laps again. Why do you think he did that?" Tommy asked.

"Totohead is the boss. Ask him."

"What do you think of my shorthand, bruvver?"

"Great, bruvver. Lord Meath, why don't you join your mother's law practice and be her private secretary? Don't tell me, man. I know why. You are afraid your Mira Mira may unexpectedly drop by on the Penthouse floor."

"Do you wish to ask me a direct question, Mr. Nigel Gordon?"

"Mr. Thomas Sullivan, it would you be so kind of you to drop me in front of Club Grassport. I have to meet a client." The black Ford pulled up in front of Club Grassport. "Thank you, Lord Meath. See you in a few." They laughed at each other and clenched their fists as the Sixties' black power militants.

Nigel walked casually into Club Grassport. Tom the Regular was on the floor. His friendship liquor was in one hand, and his grass joint was in the other. "Men," Tom addressed his audience, "I loves these kinds of makeups that the ladies uses these days. When

I beats my woman in her face, she puts on all that Avon makeup shit, and nobody knows that her blue and black eyes is from my fists."

"Give me five, bruvver. Slap me on the black hand side," Dalgo said. Tom the Regular displayed his pimp walk, moved towards Dalgo, and slapped Dalgo gently on his black hand. "Youse a good man, bruvver," Dalgo said. Dalgo, his back turned to Nigel, felt rewarded when Tom the Regular poured whiskey into his dry glass.

"That's sure cool, bruvver," another bar patron said, and filled his glass with Tom's friendship whiskey. He called out, "Hi! Sarah."

"Hi! Sam," Sarah answered. "If my ol' man dies, I's sure goin' to have an affair with youse. That West Indian that I forced myself to marry, all he does is to go from one job to another, seven days a week. He's thinking of buying another property in Canarsie." Sarah threw the liquor down her throat.

"Whitey will burn him out if he moves to Canarsie. Those honkeys don't want niggers up there among them. Why don't you get rid of that monkey chaser, mudder fucker?"

"Why don't you get rid of him for me, honey Sam?"

"Put me in his insurance, and I'll surely get rid of that M.F." The bar boys burst into steady laughter.

"Whenever youse ready, youse know where to find me, honey Sam." Sarah gave Sam that coquettish look, and he replied with a half wink from his boiled-fish eyes.

Nigel went to the counter and stood. He did not order a drink. A patron said to him, "Hey, nigger! You either buy a drink or buy some ties." He touched Nigel. "Youse want ties, man?"

"I'm not a scab. I don't buy imported goods, man. I always look for the union label. If your hands are cleaner than your garlic breath, you can turn down my white shirt collar and see for yourself that this is made in the U.S. of A, not in those child-labor countries."

The regulars laughed barishly, and the reefer salesman

was hurt. Patrons of the club called the reefer salesman Mr. Hammer, and Mr. Hammer pointed his quail finger in Nigel's face. "Don't be a smart ass, nigger. I's talking about Thai sticks, Chinese reefers, mudder fucker!"

"That's out of date, Mr. Halitosis. And whose mudder you's fucking, man?"

"Yours, nigger!" He plunged at Nigel, who sidestepped, and hammered him. Mr. Hammer dropped like loose limestone separated from porous concrete onto tractor feed paper.

The manager came out of his cage. Two women, in shiny outfits which once fitted them, followed him. "You, mister. We don't accommodate loafers here. If you are waiting on the show, buy a drink, or be on your way."

"Barman, mix me a glass of water with a toothpick. Take your money from this." Nigel put twenty dollars on the counter. "I'm waiting on my woman, Jamaica Gal. She's doing dirty dancing here tonight."

"You don't have that kind of bread to wait on Jamaica Gal. Beat it. It's raining, and your hair needs washing," Sam said.

"Why don't you wash it for me, man?"

"Why don't you pick up your year's savings and leave? White Shirt, Lawrence Welk has a show on tonight. It's about that time."

"Are you talking to me, or to Sarah's husband?" At that moment Nigel spotted Tommy in his oversized army shirt as he weaved through the smoke filled room. Even under the dim lights of Club Grassport, Tommy's clean hands stood out. Nigel took his twenty dollars off the counter and hobbled in the direction of Dalgo. He stopped suddenly.

"Keep walking troublemaker," Jim, in his half-dirty- half-clean bouncer uniform, said. He ended his buddy talk with Dalgo, came towards Nigel, and uttered profanities.

"Another shithound in my way?" Nigel said. As Jim raised his eyebrow, he received a left cross and a right hook. "Who's next?" Nigel asked.

Dalgo pulled his knife, and he held it as a true brawler and whorehouse combatant. He meant to prove his loyalty to his buddy, Jim. "Leave that nigger to me. Let me carve that mudder fucker." Dalgo rushed forward, and stopped dead in his track.

"Go right ahead, Zeek's boy, and carve me, like your friends carved Pedro," Nigel said.

Dalgo was speechless. He was sure that he saw a ghost.

Tommy raised his voice, and he flashed his fake police badge. "This is the police." He pulled his gun. "Nobody moves. Drop your knife, Dalgo."

Dalgo dropped his switchblade on his uncolored shoes. Talkative Sam became a mute. Bar men became bar mice. The Thai smoke which filled the dark room disappeared, and Sarah who was about to feed the jukebox to play *Ring My Bell*, dropped her quarter into her pocketbook and said, "Officer, I was on my way to cook my loving husband's dinner. Would you please excuse me, sir."

"We would excuse everyone except the man who drew that switchblade on me," Nigel said. He collared Dalgo and dragged him. "And, as for you," he pointed to Sam, "this monkey chaser will be back for your black ass as soon as I'm through cutting off piece of this Mafia informer's tongue."

They planted Dalgo in the front seat between them, and Tommy drove deep into Prospect Park. "Sit." Nigel commanded Dalgo.

"This bench is wet, bruvver," Dalgo said.

"I don't care." Nigel pushed him down.

"Bruvver," Dalgo addressed Nigel, "I always knows youse a cop, man. I wasn't going to cut you, man."

"I'm going to hurt him," Nigel said to Tommy.

"Don't go for your gun, man," Tommy said. "Let's hear what Dalgo has to say first." He appealed to Nigel to show tolerance. The good-cop-bad-cop ordeal was applied.

"That no-good nigger pulled a knife on me, Captain. That nigger was about to carve my face, and, Captain, you are preventing me from hurting that piece of slime. You can report me to Head Office. For sure, I'm going to have an accident with my gun aiming at Dalgo's balls." Nigel took out his gun from his leg holster.

"Not yet," Tommy said. "Why are you so hasty, officer? It's the same way you killed that man in Chicago. Don't let the same fucking thing happen in New York, man. This time you'll be thrown out of the force, man. Be decent sometimes. Let me talk to Dalgo. You won't always get away with your police brutality, man. At least you could be reasonable for once and listen to what he has to say." Tommy took Dalgo by the arm and walked him a yard away from his game pal. "Dalgo, listen to what I'm saying to you."

"I'm listening, Captain," Dalgo said. He wiped his raw lips with his shirt sleeve, and then spat in the grass.

"You fucked up that mean bruvver before. You made him knock three times at Limbo Hook so that Zeek would know that he was a cop in plain clothes. Now you pulled a knife on him. Tell me what you prefer. You want to be at the mercy of that mean bruvver who killed before, or you want to be at the mercy of those body boys who are waiting for you at Rikers. They all know it was because of you that Pedro was knifed, man."

"What you want from me, Captain?"

"Tell me who killed Connie, Dalgo. No lies!"

"I ain't kill her. She was my friend, man. The dude I suspected, like he belonged to the old world. He was dressed funny, in black, with pointed-tip shoes. He had a belt in his hand. He, too, looked funny, and he talked all kind of funny shit. I swears on my grandfather's grave that he went into Connie's apartment."

"It could have been your boss Zeek who disguised himself."

"Zeek won't kill Connie, man."

"What about his hoods—Tito, Willy, Bobo,

Deadpan, and even Pedro, before he was knifed by your friends?"

"Zeek wouldn't let anybody kill Connie, man. Zeek was using Connie to his advantage. Youse don't kill the goose that hatches more golden feathers, man."

"If you are holding out on me, I'll turn you over to that bad bruvver. He's ready to draw blood, man."

Dalgo looked at Nigel. "Youse a bruvver. I'll never cut a bruvver, man."

Tommy pulled out his knife from his waist. He rested the tip of the knife on Dalgo's nose and said, "I want you to take this knife to the bruvver." Tommy looked at Nigel, and they read each other's bluff.

Dalgo, trembling, addressed Nigel, and his eyes begged for mercy. He trembled more when he handed Nigel the knife, and, stutteringly, he said, "Br-Br-Bruvver, I'll be on the look out for you. I heard it is your father who is charged for Connie's murder. I know that it is not your father who did that, and I told Detective Crobett so. I give you my word, bruvver man."

"Dalgo, you are a liar, and you are not my fucking brother." Nigel called each word distinctly. "Get away from my face before I blow your fucking brains."

Dalgo dropped the knife, and he ran faster than a sped arrow through the thick bushes of Prospect Park. He tripped on the knotted grass. He stumbled, stumbled, and fell; but Dalgo got up even faster than when he fell.

"Hey, bruvver," Tommy teased as they sat on the wet bench, "could you imagine seeing your face carved like that Mozambican woman that you're flirting with now? That would have been your goodluck scarification. Is she from the Maconde tribe?" Nigel didn't answer. "Dalgo didn't cut you, so why the unnecessary fuss, man?"

"I wished he did."

"C'mon. Let's go and have a drink. I have your namesake, Gordon's, in the car." Tommy broke the seal of the Gordon's gin as soon as they got into the car. He gulped a mouthful, and passed the bottle. "You think we can try that police shit one more time, man?"

"Why not. I like it. I may even join up with New York's Finest after this."

They drank and talked, sense and nonsense.

"What's the time, man?" Nigel asked.

"Time for me to shit in the grass like a lizard, man. Get me the toilet paper in the trunk."

"I'm serious, Lord Meath."

"How come after all these years you never told me why Leader Gerrol called his belly brains? We're pals, and you have no right to hide from me what Lyle told you about his Fyzabad days."

"I told you nearly everything of Lyle's boyhood."

"Not about Leader Gerrol."

"After I tell you about Leader Gerrol, we are leaving these mosquitoes. Okay?" He hit his hand and killed a singing mosquito. "These mosquitoes have real blood, man."

"Kill one more mosquito, and then tell me about Leader Gerrol."

"Okay."

Nigel related one of his father's bedtime stories. It was about Leader Gerrol, Lyle's Spiritual Baptist leader. Leader Adolphus Ignatius Gerrol was a Baptist preacher who practiced his illegal religion in a mud camp in the backwoods of Fyzabad. In the Thirties, Police "Dog" Riley raided Leader Gerrol's prayerhouse late one night. On Dog Riley's approach, a brethren on the lookout screamed as if he saw Lucifer himself. "Oh god! The Dog is here." The proclamation brought the unlawful worshippers to their mundane senses. The members in the faith—the sisters, the brethren, the teachers, the elders, the stargazers, the pompers, the warriors, the healers, the hunters, the bellringers, the shepherds and the watchmen—sprinted out of the one-door mud camp. "Lord Meath, are you listening?"

"I am," Tommy said, and he took another shot of the gin.

"In those days an Englishman, an expatriate, was the police commissioner, and stripes and promotion were rewarded for police brutality or for arresting lawbreakers like Leader Gerrol. Only the white man's religion was legal. Dog Riley looked on as Leader Gerrol's flock scampered. To Dog Riley, the fleeing Spiritual Baptists were the small fries. Riley's big bait for promotion was Leader Gerrol himself; and Leader Gerrol knew that fact more than Riley or the framers of that unjust law. Leader Gerrol also knew that the white man's law stipulated that an arrest should not be made while the preacher is in the power or in the performance of his spiritual duties...Lord Meath, you know what the power is?"

"Sure. When those Baptist people are jumping and shaking like this." Tommy jumped and danced with the music of the mosquitoes.

"In our kind of rejoicing we move on the off beat, man. This is no rock 'n roll boom-boom-boom shit. It is like this. It's a pity that I don't have Hettie's pointed-tip tapping shoes." Nigel sang his favorite Spiritual Baptist Shouters hymn, *I Have a Sword in My Hand, Help Me to Use it, Lord* to a calypso beat, and he performed as a man possessed with the Holy Ghost power. Tommy joined in, and they were the Bojangles and Gene Kelly who danced in the rain and trampled the shrubbery in Prospect Park. "Okay, Lord Meath, if you want to hear the rest of the Leader Gerrol story, you have to get out of the power immediately." Nigel wiped the mockery from his face.

"So quickly, man? I like to be in the power, man."

"One more mocking step of my Ma's religion, and no more story." Tommy stopped his prancing, and Nigel continued his story. "Leader Gerrol knew that Dog Riley couldn't arrest him while he, Leader Gerrol, was full of the power and the Holy Ghost, so the

Leader preached and performed nonstop. The patient Dog was in no hurry. Dog sat on the church bench and waited on his 'cocksure' prisoner. Dog Riley smoked a pack, then he closed his eyes as a sort of relaxation. Then the inevitable!"

"Tell me. What!"

"Sleep overpowered the Dog. When the Dog awoke in the morning, he found himself alone in the prayerhouse." Nigel poured some gin in his hand and sapped his face. "That cuts the chill, man."

"How Leader Dollon got away from Dog Riley?"

"When Leader Gerrol was really sure, not cocksure, mind you, that Dog Riley was sound asleep, Leader Gerrol tiptoed out of the mud camp, and he ran through the swamp like a deer with wet feet."

"No deer can run faster than the Gordons can lie, man."

"Are you calling me a liar, Lord Meath?"

"Are you rubbing my mouth with shit and calling it butter? Sorry, son. I forgot that's Elizabeth's kind of cute story that you heard at nights when she thought you were sound asleep."

"She didn't tell me that."

"Then that was Lyle's lullaby to put his baby son to sleep."

"That's a true story. You can call Joiner Jan in San Fernando, and he'll confirm it. You don't know how the white man used his colonial powers in the Caribbean, man."

"You still haven't told me why Leader Gerrol pointed to his belly and called it his brains."

"Some days later, Dog Riley arrested Leader Gerrol on a trumped-up charge. In court, the magistrate asked Leader Gerrol, 'Old man, do you have any brains?' Leader Gerrol answered, 'Yes, your honor.' The magistrate said, 'Old man, if you have brains, then show me your brains.' Leader Gerrol convincingly pointed to his belly. The magistrate dismissed the case and said,

'Old man, you are crazy.'"

"So the belly-brain allegory became the Fyzabad paradigm?"

"It surely did."

"Coming to think of it, Lyle is in jail because his dick was his brains. Trial is scheduled for next week. Which juror would believe Lyle's story: That he held the tape and cassette with a towel intentionally; he was kidding around when he did that; Connie invited him in her house; and yet he did everything to hide his fingerprint. The juror will certainly buy what they hear on that tape recorder, and listening to what is recorded, the guilt points to Lyle. Lyle's account of himself beats me, man. Sometimes I get the feeling that he's protecting someone. All those are valid reasons why the Grand Jury indicted him. What do you think, Nigel?"

"I won't buy that story from another man accused of the same crime, but I believe in my father. I know him, and of him. If Liz finds my father on top of a woman, he'll shield that woman because at that moment the safety of that woman is his responsibility. My father would defend that woman from his wife's wrath. My father would never murder a woman, and if Constance Wagner had died in his presence, he'd never walk away. I, too, have a lot of his likeness in most things." There was such a familial flair of a son's belief in his father that Tommy for the first time in all his life divulged his hidden grief.

"That is a feeling of which I'm devoid. My father never called from the day he left home. Yet my mother still loves him. I guess that's why she spends so much time with her law practice. Kate is a great mother, a brilliant lawyer, but a lousy judge of mankind. I hope she never gets a judgeship. She doesn't know law and love are not synonymous. Every living relative, and even her in-laws, told her not to marry my father, but love is like a hot shit, when you got to go, you got to go. I love your father, Nigel, for so many things that I see in a human being. One of these days Raggy will tell you what your father has done for him. Your father never talks about the good things he does. That is why I'm so vigilant in finding out Connie's murderer. Lyle must be exonerated!"

"You love your father, too, Lord Meath, and dearly. Do you remember the second week when we became friends, when we were coming home on the bus from school? A man, he was wearing a red sports shirt...That's all I saw of his body...You looked at him—he didn't see you—he stopped at the intersection of Nostrand and Flatbush Avenues, and a woman in a blue dress got into his car...Do you remember what happened after that?"

"Remind me."

"You really want me to?"

"You can tell me anything today."

"We walked from the junction. You said not a word to me. That evening you gave Eggie and Bob hell. You broke up the cardboard boxes that we were supposed to take outside, and you blocked their doors. You called them foreigners. We fought that evening. You punched out my teeth, and you gave me all the money for that day's work. You said that you worked that day because you always kept your word, other than that, you never would have worked at all for the foreigners. You refused to do my homework. Do you remember what's the last thing you told me?"

"Yes."

"What?"

"Let your father do your homework; my father's doing somebody else's."

"I knew right away that the man who picked up that woman at Flatbush Junction was your father because you never spoke of your father before, even when I asked about him. Your blue eyes were red and teary. They were mixed with water. It was the very day that Lyle called from Wall Street, and you answered the phone and said,

'This is the Gordons' residence. May I help you,' and the caller hung up on you. You did your homework; you fell asleep in Lyle's easy chair; and when you got up, you helped me with my math."

Tommy kept his eyes fixed on the swaying branches in the rainy park, and Nigel put his hand on his pal's shoulder and said, "It's raining and cold. This is Mira Mira time. Don't you feel like having her now?"

"It's more like Sunday school Sheila time."

Nigel skillfully changed the mood and said, "Lord Meath, I have a hunch. Let's go and check some business registrations and charters. Let's call Albany to get information on some people."

"Today is Sunday. You don't have sufficient lulus to wake up those fat cats in Albany. What do you want from Albany, man?"

"I want to check some names tonight—the spelling and the former addresses of couple people I know. Give me the car keys."

"You are too drunk to drive. I'll take you to the Telephone Company, and you can look up some old directories. They keep them in stock." Tommy drove recklessly, and he parked in the Telephone Company's compound.

"Death takes a holiday whenever you drive," Nigel said.

"Aren't you happy? I'm staying out here. Wake me up when you are through with your research, detective." Tommy took off his shoes, and he fell asleep immediately.

Nigel stated his case, and the supervisor gave him access to the storeroom. He leafed through the white and yellow pages of the phone books. He went back five years and came upon a name. He looked at two names in a more recent telephone listing. "Strange," Nigel said, "in 1984 I see one name, and in the preceding years I see other names." He ripped out five pages from the phone book, one for each year. "I never knew this." He walked to the Telephone Company's supervisor and said, "Madam, before I thank you, I want to ask you a very private question."

"Like?" she asked.

"Did your husband tell you how pretty you are today?"

"He knew you'd tell me. So why don't you?"

"Tell the brother that I say hi."

"He's a white man."

"Sister, if he treats you good, he's my bruvver." She was about to continue the conversation. "Thanks, sis," Nigel said. "The phone books are all intact." He went into the hard top Ford and slammed the door.

"What's wrong with you, man? It's month end. Are you seeing it? You can use the paper towel on the back seat."

"Lord Meath, I feel as confused as when I read the inscription on that Plymouth tomb."

"Where's that tomb?"

"In Tobago, the sister country of Trinidad; that place where legend has it that Robinson Crusoe, his dog, and his friend Friday once lived."

"You mean down in the islands where those two tankers collided recently...where they have that unbelievable undersea kingdom?"

"You are great with current events, and better with your geography than with your detective work. That's the place, bruvver man."

"What about the inscription on that tomb that has your mind so boggled?"

"I'll only tell you if you can unravel it."

"Call me the Tobago Ombudsman. Shoot."

"The inscription says, 'She was a mother without knowing it, and a wife, without letting her husband know it, except by her kind indulgence to him.' Isn't that baffling, my Lord?"

"What's so baffling about that inscription?"

"If you could make sense from the words written on

that Plymouth tomb, then you also know who killed Connie."

"The answer is easy."

"Tell me, my Lord."

"Which answer?"

"The tomb's first."

"It's simple! Here's the explanation. First, let's handle that tomb as an algebra problem. Agreed, Sunday school boy?"

"Agreed."

"In all problems you have to find the unknown quantity. Agreed?"

"Agreed."

"Since I already know the answer to the tomb problem, I'll make it easy and tell you that the unknown quantity is Mulatto Reggie, something like Jimmy, Chinee Chin's boy. Okay?"

"It's not okay, Lord Meath, but I'll say okay to see your angle."

"Then it's okay?"

"Okay."

"Son, I'll give you the solution of that tomb problem, the long version; and then I'll simplify it by giving you the short version. Here's the long version: An English cockney who once lived in Tobago wrote that inscription for his black Tobagonian mistress as a reminder of their tryst. The cockney never screwed his mistress as a real stud would, but his woman got full with child for him. The woman's Tobagonian husband claimed the horn child. As I said before, the horn child's name is Mulatto Reggie."

"Continue, my Lord?"

"The Englishman's mistress was a thoroughbred Tobagonian woman who, when in heat, asked her English lover who had a baby's pecker—he wasn't endowed as legend has it that your people are endowed..."

"That is why you went to the urologist for a penile enlargement?"

"Raggy told you that, but that is a stinking lie. I don't want to be disturbed again."

"Okay, Mr. Large."

"The Tobagonian woman told her cockney lover, in the grass, on the very spot where the tomb is, 'Honey, you said that the full monty was in, but I didn't feel it?' The Englishman, like a thief, broke as soon as he entered into the black hole, and his hot liquid became life. As a crafty mistress, before her death, she told her dumb Tobagonian husband that he's surely the father of Mulatto Reggie. Miss Tobago convinced her husband and told him, 'Jack boy, Reggie took after my great grandfather. Reggie even has a mold just like Great Grandpa Boysie.' Are you following me, Nigel?"

"Sure. At this time of the day what can I do but listen to a wood chopper."

"Keep on doing that...The Englishman left Tobago, but as a parting gift to his biological offspring, he wrote that inscription on his mistress' tomb with the hope that Mulatto Reggie would one day read that inscription, and he would think about the wording on that tomb...That's the long version to the inscription of the tomb."

"Lord Meath, I'm ready for the short version. I hope I'll understand it better."

"Son, here is it: Open quote, 'She was a mother without knowing it' means the cockney with his baby pecker rained very slightly in Miss Tobago; Miss Tobago did not feel the rain; and when she was impregnated she did not know. Does that make sense, son?"

"Kind of."

"Open quote, '...and a wife, without letting her husband know it,...' means you can only consummate a marriage with sex. I don't have to read and spell for you, boy. Understand my drift, Sunday school boy?"

"The wind is blowing; I'm drifting; but continue, Father Finnessy, with your divulgings of stories from the confession box."

"The final quote is, '...except by her kind indulgence to him [Jack]' means that Miss Tobago indulged in domestic duties around the house: She washed Jack's khaki pants in the river, and she cooked Jack's peas and rice, et cetera, et cetera."

"Lord Meath, you left me hanging. How did Mulatto Reggie get to find out about this *yakahoola* affair which brought about his existence?"

"You very well know the answer, Nigel."

"You are solving the problem, so I want you to tell me, Sherlock Holmes."

"That's elementary, Watson. You know, ingrained in the culture of Caribbean people, is their love of yap. Mind you, there's exception to every rule. But when it comes to yap, West Indians love to yap. They talk their business very loud on the trains, on the buses, on the streets, everywhere; so the Tobagonian women while washing their clothes in the Courland River would definitely talk about Mulatto Reggie especially when he's within earshot: either when Reggie is bathing in the river next to them, or when Reggie is looking for cray fish between the river stones. Reggie will hear his countrywomen talking about the inscription on the Plymouth tomb, and he'll understand. Worst still, the washerwoman who would spread that toxic secret would be Reggie's maternal aunt. Doesn't that give all the threads to the sweater, man?"

"As my great Grappa used to end his Fyzabad stories, 'Crick crack, monkey break he back./ Ah ben' de wire, an' de wire ben.'/ An' dat's de way me story ends.' That's the way your solution to the inscription on the Plymouth tomb ends, Lord Meath?"

"There's no other way, son. Do you now wish to hear who murdered Constance Wagner? Incidentally, I forgot to tell you that when you rushed off to see Lyle that day, Reverend Moore told Channel 7 News that he was sure Constance Wagner's killer was on the Parkway that very day. What do you have to say about this

Tobago Ombudsman, the tombstone seance man?"

"Next time make sure that you walk with orange juice to mix with the gin."

"I'm serious about my theory. I studied Egyptian triangles. Billie Zellars could never be the murderer. I checked her fingerprint."

"When?"

"The day I shook her hand."

"How? You didn't use your broken-and-stolen glass routine."

"Certain spots on my hand were pasted with soft scotch tape. When I romantically held her hands, and she looked into my eyes, I wiggled my palm artfully onto the tip of her fingers. That's how I got her fingerprints. Furthermore, Billie Zellars is as bad as steam emoting from the radiators of cold Harlem apartments."

"Why don't you drop your fancy talk and talk like Kojac. I have a lollypop if that would help. She's still my first suspect. She probably saw Lyle parading with Connie, and she hates white women who invade her territory. She didn't hide to say that. She's a revolutionary, man. She'll do anything for the Grenada cause especially as she felt a white administration exploited Grenada. She probably felt America did everything to overthrow Maurice Bishop because he had communist leanings, and America felt if Bishop survived there would have been the domino effect in the Caribbean."

"Armchair revolutionaries only damage their furniture, and when we saw Billie even her wicker chairs were well polished. She could never be that *Grenada Ghost* because she doesn't have the patience to laywait. I saw it in her personality. And I'll tell you something: All that jive she has on her wall about black is beautiful, she's one who is glad that her blackness is sunrise yellow."

"What about Lord X? He was on Lyle and Connie's

heels. You seem to know more about the bruvvers than I."

"He's an ex-con. His real name is Sixley. He no longer talks about 'Burn, bruvver, burn.' He's with the mainstream now."

"Stop this car. My belly feels like my brains." Nigel put his hand in his pocket and pulled out his scrap paper.

Tommy slammed the brakes and pulled on the service road on Eastern Parkway. "What do you have there, Sunday school boy?"

"Do you know this poem?" Nigel had an outline of the poem on his scrap paper.

"What does that poem have to do with Connie's murder?"

"Did I ask you what 'Burn, brother, burn' has to do with Constance Wagner's murder?"

"Okay. Let me hear your poem."

"I don't want you to think that I'm sentimental, Lord Meath."

"Did I say anything? Go-ahead with your recitation, please."

"In a murder, everything is centered around the accused or the victim, and this poem that I'm going to talk about is Lyle's favorite poem. Lyle even recited this poem for me when I visited him in jail. He acted the poem with his hand gestures, and his voicings were unique. Who knows, we may hear someone reciting that poem just like Lyle. Are you ready to hear it, Lord Meath?"

"Some clue, bruvver."

"This poem is about an angel writing in a book of gold. I think the angel told someone who questioned him when he came on earth that he, the angel, was writing the names of those who love the Lord. That someone told the angel to write his name as someone who loves his fellowmen..."

"Then the angel wrote and vanished, and when the angel came back on earth the angel told that someone that his name headed the list of the Lord's people...."

"So you know the poem?"

"That's Leigh Hunt's immortal *Abou Ben Adhem*."

"Where did you learn that poem?"

"Don't you know that policemen, detectives, people who protect our presidents with their lives, and citizens who do our kind of investigative work are multifaceted? We are poets, nursemaids, midwives, delivery boys, tag-alongs, and square pegs who fit in round holes. Where are you going to tag this poem? Did Lyle recite that poem for his bedroom guerilla or for his cunning wife?"

"As a boy, he lullabyed it and put me to bed."

"Now we have a square rather than a triangle."

"Billie Zellars never allowed Lyle to hang or take out his clothes out of her closets. She was hiding something, probably her Labor Day costume."

"Could be. And what Elizabeth did with her costume?"

"She told me that she gave it to a tourist. I'm certain that is what she told me."

"You *never* told me this. We promised to pick her up and hear some of the ol' time religion. Let's do that tonight."

"You said that you know who the murderer is."

"Was I that precise? I remember saying that it is not Billie Zellars, alias Jackiass; not Dalgo, the doctor shop knife; and Zeek was never on my list of the two likely suspects."

"What about Daniel "Cakey" Cake. We haven't investigated him. What about checking him out tomorrow. It's a good occasion to visit Wall Street. Furthermore, he's always looking at Lyle's waist as if he wants to steal Lyle's gold belt."

"The day that we visit Wall Street, Wall Street will end up in a minus column."

"For marginal investors like ourselves?"

"No. For prying detectives like ourselves."

"Let's still try our luck with Daniel Cake. His alibi may be as cakey as his typing skills." Nigel studied the talking notes on his scrap paper, and he spoke with quick unpunctuated sentences: "It gotta be that *Grenada Ghost*. It smelled good. It had greenish-grayish eyes. It dressed funny. It talked funny. The parade belonged to Caribbean people, especially people from Trinidad and Tobago, and Lyle suspected that Cakey migrated from Trinidad and Tobago. Cakey hated Lyle, and he did not come to work the day *after* Labor Day...The Killer Ghost could be a woman...a man...I give up."

They came out of the car and Nigel spread his scrap paper on the car hood. "Look at these two drawings, Lord Meath. Take your time and decipher my intent."

Ten minutes elapsed before Tommy spoke. Tommy rubbed his forehead and said, "As far as I see, you have two drawings. In these two separate sketches, there's a dead woman, and a belt is placed over her neck. Am I with your project?"

"Sure. Go on, Lord Meath."

Tommy looked critically at both sketches on Nigel's scrap paper. "Where do I go from here, daddy's little boy?"

"Let's suppose the murderer rested the belt on Connie's neck, which one of these two sketches would reveal whether the murderer is righthanded or lefthanded? Take your time."

Tommy studied the sketches carefully. He turned over the scrap paper, read Nigel's jottings and was impressed with the amount of clues that Nigel noted, clues that he had overlooked. Tommy turned over the sheet and again studied the sketches diligently. His forehead literally pained, but he came up with a clear observation. "Mr. Gordon," he said, and Nigel knew that whenever Tommy called him Mr. Gordon, Tommy was dead serious about a matter, "in the sketches it cannot be determined as a fact whether the Killer

Ghost took the belt from Connie's table and then rested it on Connie's neck, or if the Killer Ghost took the belt from his or her waist and then rested it on Connie's neck. The reason I say this is because each way would tend to put the belt buckle at a different spot."

Nigel thought deeply. He scratched his mopy head, and he, too, put a new interpretation to his sketches. He realized that Tommy's observation was indeed pertinent. "That's true...If the Killer Ghost picked up the belt from the floor and rested it on Connie's neck, the belt buckle would be placed in any direction; but if the Killer Ghost took the belt off of his or her waist, if he or she is lefthanded, it is quite likely the buckle of the belt would be here, facing east." Nigel pointed to where it would be in the sketch. "If the Killer Ghost is righthanded, it is quite likely the buckle would be this way, facing west." He again demonstrated physically.

"I'm righthanded," Tommy said. "I use my right hand to put my belt into my loops; and I go from left to right. When I'm taking it off, I hold the buckle and pull this way which is the more likely way. To do otherwise makes you an oddball." Tommy demonstrated in slow motion. "Therefore, according to this sketch, as a righthanded person, I'll put the belt around Connie's neck this way. Mind you, that is if I took the belt off of my waist and rested it on the body. Then the opposite is true for the lefthanded person."

"I agree with you, Lord Meath. I never thought of that."

"Let's suppose, for argument's sake, that the *Grenada Ghost* took off the belt from his or her waist, which picture is that?"

"This one."

"Okay. Let's be realistic now. According to the crime lab's photos, which photo is it?"

"This one; the lefthanded one."

"Is Billie Zellars righthanded or lefthanded, Nigel?"

"I observed her, and she is definitely righthanded."

"And Elizabeth?"

Nigel paused; then he said softly, "Lefthanded."

"And her bosom friend, the brandy drinker?"

"Hettie Campbell?"

"Yes."

It took Nigel a split second to answer. "She, too, is lefthanded. But we don't know what Daniel Cakey is."

"We also don't know a lot of things. We don't know if the belt were taken from the Killer Ghost's waist or if the Killer Ghost picked up the belt and then rested it on Connie's neck. That makes a big difference."

Nigel felt relieved by Tommy's last conclusion, but he said nothing to rekindle the discussion. He was drained. His drunkenness left him, but he felt nauseated.

"There were no ligature marks on Connie's neck which proved that she was not strangled. The blow to the back of her head caused her death. I'm not a doctor, but I'm sure that is what caused Connie's death. It's quite likely from the photographs seen of her body, partly wrapped in sheets, that she was not able to help herself when she fell." He looked at Nigel's scrap paper. "What's this note about?"

"I went to the Labor Day Carnival Committee and did some investigation. The secretary of the West Indian American Day Carnival Association told me that the *Grenada Ghost* band was not registered with them. That band copied their costumes from the KKK outfitters, except for their face masks which were Halloween, African, Metropolitan, multicolored, and numerous. I also checked with the Grenada Mission in New York, and before I asked the first question, I received the answer that I expected from those career politicians at the Mission."

"What was that answer?"

"'No comments...Let the law handle the matter.'"

"Did you ask the Grenada Mission if any of their employees played in the *Grenada Ghost* band?"

"Their answer to that question, too, was 'No

comments.' I waited around till the end of the working day and asked an employee of the Mission..."

"A woman, I'm sure?"

"You're right again. I asked her when we came through the subway turnstile, after some introductory flirting and wooing, of course, if the Grenada Mission worded any of those placards. She gave me a sort of equivocating answer: 'That if the Mission did, it would be the placards that praised the Ronald Reagan Administration.'"

"What Liz did with her placard?"

"She told me that she designed one but lost it a week before Labor Day."

"What was written on her placard?"

"I didn't ask her."

"Then I would ask her and Hettie when we pick them up tonight. If you were outside looking in, whom would you say would be most hurt by Lyle's unfaithfulness?"

"The woman who lost Lyle's favor."

"Who?"

"Billie Zellars." Nigel paused as soon as he called her name.

"Nobody else, Nigel?"

"Are...Are...You are not thinking about Elizabeth?"

"I could be even thinking about the brandy lady who would do anything for her madam. As Americanized as Hettie is, I've heard her relapse into West Indianism."

"Like what?"

"Her 'Lawdanno,' in patois, which meant 'Lord, I know,' in English."

"Know what, Lord Meath?"

"It's time to pick them up and make a decision."

"I'm not going, man."

"You have to. I'm in charge. Here's your scrap paper."

"I told you that I'm not going."

"Didn't you promise to pick them up at the church

so that they wouldn't have to pay the Haitian gypsy cab driver tree dowlars for driving past three traffic lights?"

"Yes; but I don't feel like going again. You go and satisfy yourself."

"I'll do just that. It's a job." Tommy started the Ford. "I have a placard to show and ask Hettie whether it's hers. I got it from Mrs. Plutz. Hettie would know whether it's her placard or her madam's. Don't you want to see it, Nigel?" Tommy revved the engine.

"Lord Meath, wait." Nigel jumped into the car, and Tommy made a right on Nostrand Avenue. Neither of them said a word. Nigel looked straight ahead and spoke when the Ford stopped. He addressed the wind. "If only I could go and check one more time what's in Lyle's file...probably play the tape, and see if I missed a clue. After that, the ball is in your court, man." He looked at Tommy, and his eyes were filled with the tears he fought to hold.

The Ford was parked in front of the church, and Tommy read the bold sign aloud: "MT. SIGNAL SPIRITUAL BAPTIST CHURCH, ELIAS S. DOLLON, LEADER...Nigel, I have something to show you. Let's go and look at it. I have it in the car trunk." Tommy put on his gloves, and he fitted the torn pieces of cardboard together until all the wordings made sense. The words not only made sense, but those words crawled Nigel's blood. The words read: AUNT GINA HATED GRENADIANS, WHY?

Nigel had heard Lyle's stories of Aunt Gina so many times that all he said was, "I see what you mean...That's family...The thing is, who dropped it in front of Mabel Plutz's door?" His last sentence was instinctive, and it was predicated on hope.

They went back into the car, and Tommy surfed the AM and FM bands. "Nice social music is coming over WBLS, son. Isn't social music a crossover of calypso?" Tommy purposely said the word, "Social."

"How many times do I have I to tell you, white

boy, it is soca music, not social music!" He replaced his tears with his anger.

"You see," Tommy said, "darkies are the ones who are supposed to know about music. All I know is that rock 'n roll boom-boom-boom shit, man, which is the second blueprint of jazz. I told you many times that I'm human. I'm not perfect. The same way that I make mistakes about the blues, I could be making a big mistake about who is the *Grenada Ghost* who must be unmasked. Let's take your advice and go back to the office and study the contents of Lyle's file, and then we'll play the tape. That tape is responsible for Lyle's arrest." Tommy drove off; and Nigel felt the weight of the Titanic lifted off his legs. He even smiled. "Thank you, Lord Meath," he said, "I'll always remember this."

In the office, Nigel first checked for mail in his In-box. "Lord Meath, our boss Totohead wants to see me. He put a memo in my box."

Tommy read the memo that was put in his box. "Me, too."

"Probably it's curtains for us. The matter goes to court in days, and the prosecutor will have his field day...Lyle the criminal versus the State of New York. I can hear it."

"Please, don't say that...What's in this job after all?"

"Heartaches plus headaches multiplied by belly gripes."

"More belly aches. Let's collect the stuff and go at it."

They were both tired. Both had to unite their strength to open and close the office door. They examined thoroughly copies of the photographs that Connie took of the *Grenada Ghost* band and of the crowd.

"Here's something. Look, the 'R' on the logo GRENADA is hanging from this masquerader. If that masquerader was the Killer Ghost, it was easy for him to pull off that letter from *his* clothes and scratch the poem in Connie's bedhead." Tommy purposely used the pronoun "his." "Let's listen to the copy of the tape that we received from Detective Crobett with the permission of the Justice Department." He put the tape into the player and looked at the revolutions of the reel, but no sound came forth. "Are you sure this isn't Rosemary Woods' tape that Nixon left in the White House?"

"Tommy, for my sake, I hope not." Nigel smiled awkwardly and relieved some of his tenseness. He pressed the forward button, and then he stopped it. A reporter came on and spoke of Labor Day.

"Nigel, run it farther back to when Lyle and Connie's conversation ended."

Nigel pressed the play button, and he became extra nervous. "Here it comes."

The recording was: "YOU'LL NEVER GUESS WHO, WHITE GIRL...."

"Who's that?" Tommy asked. "That's definitely a woman's voice."

"That's Lyle's voice. He does that tremolo to his voice. I've heard him speak that way many times especially when he's in a jovial mood." He looked at Tommy for he wanted Tommy as a friend, not in the capacity of a detective, to sincerely believe him. He stopped the tape abruptly.

"But we didn't hear when the door was closed, if that's supposed to be Lyle's voice, and his last words to Connie in jest...I'm doubtful...Would he lie on himself to protect someone?"

Nigel did not answer. He pressed the play button and waited. The next sounds that were heard were the soft opening sound of the door and the words:

"LYLE, YOU'RE STILL HERE?...LYLE, LYLE...NO! NO! I'M DREAMING. YOU! YOU! IT'S YOU? NO! PERFUME! PERFUME! NO! AIR REFRESHER."

Tommy stopped the player. "What do you make of that, Nigel?"

"Connie behaved as if she had seen her assailant before, and she was trying to describe that masked person." He looked at Tommy when he said "masked person." "Connie was probably drowsy when that masked person accosted her. She was sort of between sleep and wake, and the word 'Perfume!' was her keyword. It was as if she smelled that masked person on the Parkway, and she was shocked that that very sweet-smelling person was in her bedroom. That person's scent—that familiar perfume—is the key to her gibberish."

"I'm thinking like you, Nigel."

"Start over the tape, and let the tape run to the end, Tommy." There were long gaps in the recording, and they chitchatted.

"I'd rather be a checkbook journalist than a detective at this moment," Tommy said.

"I should have been that surgeon and cut off Lyle's balls...Wait...Hush." The room became so quiet that the flutter of their eyelashes was noisy. "I hear a rattling, man. Turn up the volume."

"Sssh, sssh. The sound died."

"The sound is going and coming. You hear it, and then you don't hear it. Rewind it to that spot, Tommy."

"Okay."

"You hear the rattling...It's faint sometimes, barely heard sometimes. What do you think, Tommy?"

"The Killer Ghost is adjusting or changing something brassy in the stillness of the room. That adjusting or changing was definitely done after Connie was knocked cold."

"Could be...Could be." Nigel panted like a dying man. He lost his breath and broke out in a cold sweat.

Tommy stopped the machine. "What's wrong, man? Is it too hot in here for you? Let me put on the fan."

"No," Nigel said. "I need fresh air. I need clean air. Help me to the window." Nigel's body went limp.

"I never knew you suffered from asthma attacks, man." Tommy held Nigel's arm gently and walked him to the window. Tommy pushed open the window and a draft of air, lodged the viaducts of the highrisers, blew in their faces and into the office and toppled pencils, pens, paper, and portraits of families placed on desks and tables.

"I feel better already," Nigel said. They looked out at the civic center in Downtown Brooklyn and commented on the motley colors of the people who walked in the streets. "Take me in, Lord Meath. My lungs are filled. It's now do or die." They walked back into the room and left the door wide open.

"Start the player on the exact spot, Lord Meath."

Tommy obeyed. At that moment he would have done anything not to aggravate Nigel's unwholesomeness. "Are your ready?"

"Yes, I'm ready. This is it. Lord, I know. Let it be."

Tommy looked at his pal. He was afraid to depress the play button. "You do it, man."

"Okay. I'll start it. I thank you, Lord."

"You are not in Leader Dollon's church. What are you thanking the Lord for, Sunday school boy?"

"For allowing me to discern that rattling, brassy sound." Nigel stopped the player. "Lord Meath, do you agree that rattling, brassy sound was the noise of the belt buckle?"

"Yes."

"That's the greatest lead. I was too prejudiced not to take Billie Zellars' words of advice."

"Is she the murderer?"

"I don't know. Do you remember that she told us to forget about that academic stuff and be more observant. She was right."

"Right about what? What are you hiding from me? What have you found in that toolbox that you haven't told me about? We are supposed to be on this case together...togetherness, man."

"You hid couple of leads from me, too, man...Lyle told me that one of the *Grenada Ghosts* pulled at Connie's waist. Probably that was the Killer Ghost who wanted Connie's belt. Today is Sunday and the court is closed, and we have to find a way to check the court's exhibits, especially Lyle's belt and buckle. We must. We can't wait till tomorrow. I'm nervous, and when I'm nervous my instinct is usually right."

"You still haven't told me what you found out by listening to the tape."

"This is not grudge coming from the Gordons, man. I must see that belt tonight, especially as Cakey always looked at Lyle's waist"

"It is seven o'clock. We have to pick up Elizabeth and Hettie at the church."

"Mt. Signal goes to late hours; and this week the service will be longer. Hettie has to sing a solo, and she usually ends up getting three encores. Don't forget she had her full share of brandy."

"Then how could we get the court to open for us is late hour, or wherever those exhibits are secured in the property room?"

"Lord Meath, you are in charge. That's your department to make things happen. Find out who, where, how, why...Just make a miracle happen now!"

Tommy leaned on his desk and racked his brain. In a quick minute, he shouted, "I know who."

"Who?"

"That Mr. Who who owes Lyle one."

"My god! My god!" Nigel shouted. "D.A. Raggy Beerman of New York State Supreme Court, Kings County, Second Division!"

"Be informed about your protocol. Mr. D.A. is no longer in your league. He'll soon be running in the mayoralty race. His name is?"

"D.A. Tito Natividad. Mr. District Attorney, when you were but a naughty boy recently boated in from Puerto Rico with holes in your pants, shirt, and shoes, you vomited on my mother's carpet. You didn't clean it up; Lyle did; and you promised Lyle, after he cleaned your vomit then, that you'd do anything to repay that debt. That then is now. It's dangerous territory; it's risking your integrity; but we know that you won't let Lyle down. Where do you booze up, Mr. D.A.?"

"The same place," Tommy answered. "The same Waterhole downtown."

The detectives were on their way. The faithful Ford took them there by way of the Parkway, the most beautiful tree-lined carriageway in Brooklyn.

Tommy and Nigel walked into the Waterhole. There was an empty stool next to the District Attorney, and both rushed noisily for the stool. The D.A. didn't look at them. He sipped his beer and looked at the wide screen before him. There was a New York Knicks-Los Angeles Lakers game, and the noisy bar was crowded. The bar was a meeting place of yuppies, post yuppies, and the baby boomers who no longer wanted to look at their overweight wives. Young women with an eye on eligible rich bachelors and sugar daddies frequented the Waterhole.

"I have no money, and I need a beer," Tommy said.

"Why not ask that bum next to you?" Pepper advised Salt, and the bar patrons looked at Nigel as if to say, 'How dare you call a man of repute a bum!'

"Which one? This one?" Tommy touched the D.A. and changed his voice "Sir, that black drunkard wants a beer. I don't know what this Rastaman is doing in this place. He doesn't belong."

"Why don't you buy the beer for the Rastaman? If you are for the Lakers, at least you could be quiet, or have the courtesy to leave," the D.A. said. Walt Fraser sunk a basket, and the D.A. shouted, "Take that, Kareem!"

Tommy touched the D.A. harder and said, "That Rastaman said you have to buy him a beer because you owe his mother one."

"Did I screw his mother?"

"Probably you did, sir. You vomited on her new carpet, and her husband cleaned up your stinking vomit, cocksucker."

The D.A. put down his beer and looked into

Tommy's blue eyes. "You son of a bitch, Lord Meath. What are you doing here?"

"Mr. Raggy Beerman, may I introduce you to the Rastaman."

"That asshole son...daddy's little boy."

"Yes, vomit," Nigel said.

The Waterhole became a noisy hole, and the trio's joy was in contrast to the disappointed Knicks fans. Knicks was down by twenty points with five minutes left on the game clock. "We'll be safer outside," Tommy said when he looked into the New York fans' faces. "These people will blame us if mercurial Knicks loses."

Raggy snatched his beer. He called out to the bartender and said, "Give these two bums what they want on my account."

"We are in a hurry," Nigel said. "Another time, Raggy."

Outside Nigel and Tommy jockeyed for Raggy's attention. "One at a time," Raggy said. "What you are trying to tell me must make sense. This is not when we trash talked, and when you two had the first and last say over me. I give the orders Downtown."

"Yes, Mr. D.A." Nigel said. He shortened his version about why they came to see him. "Raggy, all we want to see tonight is Lyle's belt wherever it is. That's all."

"And you, Lord Meath?" Raggy asked.

"Daddy's likkle boy is in charge of this Downtown operation. Whatever he says goes."

"Let's go. It's a problem, but not a problem. I owe Lyle one. I must repay him tonight because tomorrow I'll be out of town on an important political matter. No one must know that I did this. Stay right here. Don't move. I'm going to make a call. Don't even look at what direction I'm walking."

"Soon you'll be Mayor of New York, how do you expect us to spy on your fat arse," Nigel said.

"Watch your language with me, nigger. This PR

would put you in handcuffs right now. You are not talking to Raggy Beerman who once got drunk on a sip of beer. You knew Eggie and Bob spiked that beef with a Polish recipe, and you did not tell me."

"C'mon, Raggy. Why not say the Puerto Rican kid was only used to drinking goat milk when he came from the island in patches," Nigel said.

"You are asking for a favor, and you are still so darn fresh, pussy boy. Not because you had a penile enlargement that makes yours bigger than mine," Raggy said.

"Nigel, I thought you said you didn't need that?" Tommy inquired.

"Don't listen to that Puerto Rican liar," Nigel replied. "He's the one who wanted the dick enlargement. I gave him the doctor's address, but I didn't go."

The trash talk continued.

Eventually Raggy left on his secret mission. He made the call, and he returned.

"Raggy Beerman, where are you taking us?" Tommy asked.

"There...and with my car." Raggy was abrupt in his manner.

Nigel and Tommy immediately knew that their friend and buddy reverted to the D.A.'s mode, and they realized the D.A. did not want to be questioned.

Raggy took them there. "I'm taking you through the back door," he said, "because I don't even want you to observe the building. Stand here for a minute. I don't want you to even hear who I'm talking to." He left Tommy and Nigel downstairs and went upstairs in a building on Schermerhorn Street.

"Raggy, you are a politician," Tommy said, when Raggy walked away.

"Don't forget to tell your Irish folks to vote for this PR next term. My logo would be the axe. I'll be cutting down on corruption and breaking down those bridges that divide all peoples."

"You are an American now," Tommy raised his voice. "Whatever you are going to do for Puerto Rico has to be in your manifesto, Mr. District Attorney. If it's not written in, don't count on me, man. Make Puerto Rico a state, and give them nationhood, if they need that as a bonus!"

"You got it, Lord Meath," Raggy said. "Whatever that Mira Mira is putting in your face is really working in Puerto Rico's favor. Cocksuckers, stay there till I return. From now on, treat me as a D.A." The D.A. spoke to someone who opened the property room, and he returned for them. "Let's go, cocksuckers," the D.A. said. "What about Sunday school Sheila, son?"

"I don't know a thing about that woman since she moved to south, Raggy?" Nigel said. They completed two flights of stairs.

"Lying son of a bitch," Raggy said. "When you were a Baptist Shouter in Leader Dollon's church you spoke the truth. But now you ain't shit. You lie faster than— how they use to say it in Puerto Rico again—damn, I can't remember."

"Don't say it in Spanglish, please, Raggy," Nigel said, "because I know you'll start with your pappy's home-grown jokes, and I'm busy tonight. The one that your pappy told you about the man and the goat he stole is nasty, man. Don't tell us any Puerto Rico shit tonight."

"Okay, daddy's little boy. By the way, why does Lyle call you 'Daddy's little boy' and Liz call you 'Son?' Or is it the other way round?"

"Not tonight, Raggy. Time is of the essence."

"Let's go through this door," Raggy said. "This is the place. Look at your stuff quickly. Over a certain time, I'll have to log in and give an account of my stewardship, so I want you to do it faster than you did it to Sheila in the basement, son."

"It will only take me one minute to look at the belt, Raggy."

"That's all it took in Mt. Signal's basement, daddy's

little boy...son?"

Nigel smiled when Raggy showed him the belt.

"It's yours to see, gentlemen?" Raggy said, and he walked to the window. "I was sorry to hear about your father, man. I hated myself for not dropping by. Every time I made up my mind to drop by and see Elizabeth, a lump came to my throat."

"Lyle would be thrilled to hear what you've done for him tonight, Raggy. He'll be grateful for this risk that you are taking unknown to the authorities...I'm too nervous to look at the belt, Lord Meath. I walked with a glove. Put it on, Lord Meath. Turn over the belt, and look at the buckle. For my sake, please, Lord Meath." Nigel turned his back.

Tommy took a pencil from his pocket and flipped over the belt. "What's wrong with it, Nigel?"

"Lawdanno means Lord, I know."

"Let's be serious now. Know what?"

"That Elizabeth's fingers are on that belt."

"That's true. You took so long to realize that."

"I'm glad I did. Now I can solve the case. Thanks to you, Raggy. Even my fingerprints are on that leather strap. That's Lyle's leather strap, but not his gold buckle." Nigel turned away from the wall, and he looked at Tommy and said, "The Killer *Grenada Ghost* who must be unmasked between today and tomorrow went to Connie's house for one thing—Lyle's belt buckle. These are the longtime buckles, turned out by apprentices on lathes in the machine shops of Apex Oilfields, Fyzabad, Texaco Oilfields, and Shell Oilfields in Pitch Lake Country. These buckles carry the hook-and-eye fasteners. The Killer Ghost has to be Lyle's contemporary. That kind of belt buckle is not made in this country. The Killer Ghost purposely exchanged the buckle. He took Lyle's buckle and put his buckle on Lyle's belt. I'm one hundred percent sure that's what the rattling sound was all about. The Killer Ghost was exchanging belt buckles. This thing here is brass, man."

"How could you tell brass from gold in the night? You were never a jeweler as far as I know."

"I just have to look at the secret Mondesir trademark. Do you see it there? Do you see a little *M* on any part of the buckle?" Nigel held his breath. This was his last break with hope. Reality had to be the factor, and he knew that. "Look carefully at the buckle, Tommy." Nigel held his breath and prayed to his mother's God; he didn't trust his.

"Not one shit on it!" Tommy emphasized. "No *M* is on this brass buckle."

"Are you sure?"

"Do you want to call the D.A. to have me swear to a solemn affidavit?"

"I don't want to get the D.A. involved any more. That kid is going to be our future senator to take over from Senator Pothole...Incidentally, Pothole would be talking on the Puerto Rican plebiscite next week. Last week he was on the Jews' bandstand, next week the PR's...the following week the West Indians' immigration problem...Whatta a professional! If Senator Pothole hears of this, it's all over for our man, Raggy."

"Then look for yourself, Nigel. I didn't see the trademark *M*."

"I trust you with all my heart, Lord Meath. I'm taking your word. Then this is not Lyle's buckle. This is not the Adult Nigger's prize belt buckle...The jagged leather, yes; the buckle, no. Lord Meath, I thank you from the bottom of my heart. I love you as a brother for your patience with me. I know how I treated you whenever you got close to Elizabeth and Hettie, because they are two people with, but one mind. I became angry and insulted not only you, but your race, whenever I thought your focus was on Elizabeth and Hettie. I was nervous, man, and I hope you'll forgive me for my unkind words at times. You always helped me with my homework. The motive for the murder was jealousy, but not the love-triangle type.

The Killer Ghost came looking for the buckle from the outset. That *Grenada Ghost* would have killed anybody to get that buckle once *he* or *she* had devised a scheme." This time Nigel said the word "She" without fear. "Connie was just the unlucky one, and I am sure the Killer Ghost had *his* plan in cold storage years ago. Though I have never said it publicly, I grieve for Connie. Somehow, even though I never met her, I feel for her. It's a father-and-son thing. We love people. I'm sure Connie was a great soul."

"I'm trying to believe you," Tommy said.

"To recognize that belt buckle in a parade of a million people on the Parkway, you've got to come from Pitch Lake Country, and specifically from Tubal Uriah Buzz Butler's Fyzabad, the home of the greasypole art...And, of course, you've got to be a contestant."

"Winner or loser," Tommy chimed, slightly convinced.

"In Lyle's triumph, a man was the sour loser, not a woman."

"So that clears Billie Zellars, the lovely Jackiass, too?"

"Sure. She could have stolen that buckle many years ago. I'm not trying to discredit her honesty or knowledge, but I'm sure she, too, thought that belt buckle was made of brass. And, about Elizabeth?" Nigel looked at his associate.

"I'm sorry, man, for the way I was thinking. I was vigilant for Lyle's sake, man, and I'll continue to be."

Nigel hugged Tommy like a lifebelt; the same way he did after Tommy accosted Ricco on his behalf. "You are a good man, Lord Meath. The evidence was so strong against my mother and Hettie, yet you gave me the ball at the line of scrimmage. I love you, man." They held back their tears. Raggy looked on, bewildered.

"You are a thinker, Nigel," Tommy said. "That's why I gave you the ball...Besides, associate means equal."

Nigel let Tommy go. "Lord Meath, you were not

bound to come and listen to the tape and help me with my homework."

"Homework about a family vine can never be done by outsiders, man. That's why Africa is in all this mess today, even the missionaires know that."

"Ireland, too, man."

"Stop that womanish shit, pussy boys," Raggy shouted. He came closer to them. "If I stay around you two one more hour, I'll puke. Right now I prefer to ring the Salvation Army's gong bell in front of Macy's than to be near you sissies. We have to get out of this building now, otherwise I'd have to log why I was in here. Sissies, do you want me to put in the log book that I was watching two pussy boys make love in the property room? Let's go." The D.A. passed Nigel and Tommy through another door in order that they would not see the person who opened the property room. "Take this elevator, ladies. You're on your own. I never met you two before."

Nigel moved forward to hug and thank his friend. "Get away with that sissy shit, asshole," Raggy said. As the elevator descended, Raggy shouted, "Daddy's little boy, tell Lyle goodluck. He was the only non-family who showed me kindness when I came from Puerto Rico. I love him." Tito Natividad, the respected District Attorney of New York State Supreme Court, Kings County, Second Department, took his shirt sleeve and wiped his teary eyes. "Lyle wouldn't kill a fly," he whispered. "He and Liz were made for each other."

Nigel drove the Ford and whistled, *Ring My Bell*. He felt relieved that Elizabeth was no longer a suspect. "Lord Meath," he said, "what about the fresh water Yankee Cakey, who always looked at Lyle's waist. If I knew his address, I'd go there right now. Cakey hated Lyle, and his accent was always suspect. For that matter, Cakey was not at work the day Lyle was arrested, and Lyle told me that up to the day that he was arrested, Cakey had the best attendance on his job. Cakey never missed a day at work before. Prior to that day, Cakey got a clock from the company for his perfect attendance in twenty five years. Most important, Lyle believes that Cakey is a native of Trinidad and Tobago."

"Did Lyle wear his gold belt to work?"

"Lyle never put it down, and he often boasted to some of his officemates of his greasypole adventure."

"I guess we'll visit the financial district and talk to Daniel Cake tomorrow."

"Sure thing."

"Then I guess it's time to pick up Elizabeth and Hettie. I know Leader Dollon would be glad to see his ex-acolyte who played hookey in the basement. Tell me about the cracks in the basement, boy."

Nigel was in a happy mood, even his hidden dimple deepened. From the day that he took on the assignment to find Constance Wagner's murderer, he hid behind a façade. "Lord Meath, I feel like kicking youse arse. When youse was supposed to check that tape with a fine tooth comb where was youse, boy?"

"Massa, I went to a baby baptism, sar."

"The young'un is youse, Mandingo? How would youse call a PR crossed with an Irish transplant of royal birth, boy?"

"Massa, youse didn't teach me how to read, sar...An' ah doh care if youse hang me on ah pepper tree, sar; but that's not your honky business, sar."

"Youse got to talk the truth, bruvver Mandingo, before youse cross the door of my church."

In spite of their comedy, Tommy's focus was on finding out who murdered Constance Wagner. Casually, Tommy said, "Nigel, from what Elizabeth told me, the last group of people who saw Lyle's belt before Labor Day were the church members. Are the members of that church natives of Trinidad and Tobago, and particularly from the village of Fyzabad?"

"I'm a backslider. We would have to ask Elizabeth and Hettie when we pick them up. It's a long time since I've last been to Mt. Signal."

"All you know is how to get in and out of the cracks in the church basement without being noticed?"

"My boy, at this moment you should be thinking of your own bloody business."

"What business?"

"How to introduce your woman Carmensita to the Sullivans. I told Ma Sullivan that your Mira Mira would be coming to dinner the same day with me."

"You lie. You didn't!"

"Do you know me to lie about family matters, Lord Meath?"

"Of course, you do, man."

"When? Like what?"

"You said that you never went out of town recently, one; you said that you didn't know where Sunday school Sheila lived in North Carolina, two; you said that you have an aversion to married woman, three; when a kid, you said that your main reason for going to Sunday school was to learn of Jesus, four. Do you want me to continue, or are you satisfied with the abridged version, Sunday school boy? I guess with our individual sins neither of us can cast the first stone."

"Seems as if Saint Jerome's Sunday school taught you the catechisms. So how can we overcome our transgressions?"

"Transgressions or not, at least I'll have the opportunity to see daddy's little boy shake, catch the power in real, and talk in tongues when Leader Dollon pipes the gospel about a backslider who has returned to the faithful flock."

"Take care I don't have to say a prayer for you, devil."

"For me? Nunca!"

"You learned that Spanish word at the baby's christening, Irish Mandingo?"

"Get off my back, man. I'm a good Catholic."

"Good to throw 'way." Nigel slowed the Ford. "Let's park on Snyder and walk over to Nostrand. The exercise is good for you, daddy. We're just one block away from Mt. Signal. In fact, about this time Leader Dollon is about to end his sermon. But whatever you hear from that holy man will stimulate your soul, devil."

"All right, Saint Martin."

The greenhorn detectives entered the church through the front door and seated themselves in the last two rows of pews. Their faces were as pious as the Pope's. Tommy sat behind Nigel. After their meeting with Billie Zellars, they never sat in the same seat in a public building or walked abreast in a crowd.

Leader Dollon was in the middle of his sermon. He continued: "Ohhhh Lord, I feel the spirit." Leader Dollon paused, and he looked at the new arrivals. "Ohhhh Lord, what a morning...."

Tommy was not used to Leader Dollon's style so he looked at his watch. It was nine o'clock on that warm September Sunday night.

"...Last night, one of our sisters had a vision. Ah know, Lord." Leader Dollon walked forward and surveyed his congregation.

Elizabeth in her psyche shouted, "Yes, Lord. Tomorrow would bring a new dawn." She took a leaf out of the lota that was next to the centerpole, and she put it in her mouth. Then she dipped the leaf in the lota, wet the floor with the water that remained on the leaf, and went into a deep thought.

"Why Elizabeth did that?" Tommy whispered in Nigel's ear.

"That's her libation to our ancestors. Be quiet and listen to the Leader."

Leader Dollon wiped his sweat with his heavy fingers and said, "Yeeees, Loooord. Last night one of God's children had a vision..."

Tommy put his finger in his ear, and he checked his ear for hard wax. He bent over Nigel and said, "Sunday school boy, who really had that vision?"

"That's the Leader's preaching style, man," Nigel

mumbled. "Why don't you listen and learn something. This is not about Hail Marys and about rolling those beads, man."

"...Ohhhh Farder, dear Lord..." Leader Dollon said.

Tommy kicked Nigel's heels. "Nigel, Leader Dollon pronounced 'Father' just like Lyle, and he pronounced 'Lord' funny. He's from the islands, I'm sure."

"So what! His grammar is good; his audience is receptive."

"So was Jim Jones's," Tommy mumbled.

"...Oh Farder, dear Lord...Last night a great someone ...a great earthly being had a vision. Yeeees, Loooord. Let the church say Amen."

"Amen!" the congregation shouted. "Hallelujah!"

Leader Dollon paused, his body shook, and he looked at the rafters. There were all sorts of scriptural writings, Rosicrucian markings, and other undecipherable marks on the ceiling and on the walls; but most prominent on the eastern wall was the first verse of Psalm 1, and he recited it: "Blessed is the man that walketh not in the counsel of the ungodly, nor standeth in the way of sinners, nor sitteth in the seat of the scornful." Leader Dollon stretched out his hands, and Hettie knew what he wanted. Hettie rushed to Leader Dollon's aid. She handed him a glass of water with a white rose, and he took seven savory sips of the sanctified water.

Tommy spoke in Nigel's ear. "Who really had that vision? Even as a backslider, you should know."

"You'll soon find out."

"And why Leader Dollon took seven sips of water?"

"Seven is the number of completion."

"Completion of what?"

"Whatever it is, there'll be completion in our lives, and it will be tonight!"

"Completion in whose life?"

"Maybe yours. Irish Mandingo may summon the courage to take home his future bride tonight and introduce her to the matriarch, not as Mira Mira, but as the future Mrs. Thomas Sullivan."

"I see that you are psychic like Elizabeth and neither of you could lead me to the murderer. Why don't you psyche the murderer?"

Before Tommy got an answer to his question, Leader Dollon pirouetted and stopped. He moved forward, backward, east and west. He completed the shape of a cross. It was as if Leader Dollon invoked the spirits of his ancestors of the Upper Volta. Immediately the congregation shook their bodies. They screamed; they sang; they ad libbed *a cappella*; they jumped and manifested in tongues. A male worshipper rushed to a heap of white candles that dripped and glowed in the lota. He grabbed the lota and sprinkled water first in the center of the church and then poured three drops of water in the corners of the building. The sweaty male worshipper twirled like a top in all of his movements. The glow of the candles in the lota formed a rainbow from the candle grease; and the candle grease burned him. The bellringer caught the power. He ran down the aisle and stared in Tommy's blue eyes. He rang the bell successively as if to warn: The British are here. Beware! A sister screamed, "Jeeezazazas!" and fell. Her body, fraught with sweat, tattooed to the floor, jumped like the severed neck of a dead fowl. A brethren took her up. She faced him. With clasped hands, he put his neck on her right shoulder as their feet moved rhythmically, and then on her left shoulder. She reciprocated his movements. They remained still and close. The two worshippers curtsied and went to their ordained spaces.

"Amen!" Leader Dollon shouted. The commotion died, and Leader Dollon continued. "One night, a traveller had a vision. Ohhh yes, Lord...."

"Oh yes, Lord," the congregation echoed with gusto.

Leader Dollon pumped his body like a soldier ready for battle. "...That earthly traveller awoke from that vision and saw a celestial body in his domain...Oh, yes Lord."

"Oh, yes Lord," the members reciprocated.

"Brethren," Tommy said to Nigel, "I now see really why you like the Leader's narrative structure. His cadences; his leaps; his dramatization; his poetic delivery; the words he mints; his mannerisms. Wow! He leads us to the object, but he presents prisms first. This is Broadway on Nostrand Avenue. Whew!"

Nigel shifted his body slightly and spoke softly. "I'm confused. I'm hearing things. My stomach is turning."

"Constipated, brethren?"

Nigel didn't answer. It was as if Nigel went into a trance in which he heard his father's bedtime stories being told to him by someone else: How Mr. Tellymack told his students that they could use that certain poem in their preaching...in their daily lives...in their...

The bellringer peeled the bell in sixty-fourth staccato rhythms, and the decibel of the sounds interrupted Nigel's train of thought. Tommy touched him and said, "I am healed, brethren." Nigel again did not answer. Instead, he looked at Leader Dollon's pyramidical movements.

Leader Dollon walked to the four corners of his crooked altar. He cut the longest distance with his diagonal strides, and he made two triangles out of the squared space. He stood at the farthest corner of his altar and said, "Forgiveness, dearrrr Lord, for we know not what we do. Do right, and right will fall in our baskets. Do evil, and evil would be our portion. Love your neighbor—all your neighbors, black and white, yellow and brown, fellowmen and nonfellowmen, and you'll head the Lord's roster." He paused, and he threw his eyes in the direction of the last two pews.

Nigel's eyes were closed, and he kept mumbling, "Couldn't be...Couldn't be...He's Tellymack's carbon copy...Lyle tried to tell Elizabeth that the very first night he heard Leader Dollon preach on Ezekiel...Couldn't be...Tellymack's..."

"Couldn't be what? Tellymack was a pastor here, too, Sunday school boy?" Tommy asked.

"I'm going outside for air, Lord Meath. I need to sort things out in my mind."

"Who's the devil now? You can't even take in the word. 'Thy word is a lamp unto my feet, and a light unto my path.' You didn't think Irish Mandingo could quote from the bible." Tommy realized that Nigel didn't hear a word of what he said. Nonetheless, he spoke to Nigel again. "When you come back from outside, I'll be right here taking in the Leader's spiritual food. I've already begun to feel a vibration in my body."

Under the Arab's store Nigel lit a cigarette and dragged in all the nicotine he could get in one breath. He thought of his boyhood when he saw the children of church members congregate in a huddle in and out of Hamid's. "Hi, kids!" Nigel said. "Why aren't you in the basement or in the nursery? Isn't it a bit too late to be in and out of Hamid's?"

"Hamid's things are cheap," a little boy said.

"My mother told me not to buy anything at Hamid's because he has a big cat in the store that licks everything there, especially the cookies," another boy said. "And, furthermore, my history teacher told me that those Arabs enslave the black Sudanese in Africa and kill them for nothing. I hate Hamid because his people want to take back Africa from us."

"I want to go home! I'm tired!" A little girl spoke the loudest.

Nigel liked the little girl's frankness, and he replied to her. "I used to come to Sunday school here, and I remained for the night service. I never got tired because I used to play in the basement."

"True?" the little girl asked.

Nigel threw away his stub cigarette. "True. True. I cross my heart."

"Who used to bring you?" the little girl asked.

"Sister Elizabeth. And who brought you?"

"My grandmother brought me today; but my mammie used to bring me."

"What's your mammie's name?"

"Sheila Sanders."

"Pretty Sheila is your mother?" Nigel was shocked. "If Sheila is your mother, you have to give me a big kiss, girl. Sheila and I used to come here to Sunday school. Your mammie is my friend. We used to play in the basement. We had fun, and we never wanted to go home."

"What's your name?"

"Nigel Gordon. Tell Sheila that I send my regards. And what's your name?"

The little girl giggled. "Adanna Ashaki."

"Do you like Leader Dollon, Adanna?"

"No. He didn't leave the basement open for us to play tonight."

"And because of that your mammie didn't come to church? She doesn't like Leader Dollon any more?"

"Since we came back from south last year mammie goes to Mother Vie's Spiritual Baptist Church. She told Grandma that Leader Dollon doesn't take off his gown and shout no more. He just runs around acting in his Kente cloth as if he's an African king. He's so stiff now. Mammie liked Leader Dollon when he shouted, when he caught the power, and when he fell down on the floor like everybody else. My mammie says Leader Dollon behaves as if he's hiding something below his African cloth."

"Your mammie said that?"

"True, true. I cross my heart."

"Do you like icecream, Adanna?"

"My mammie told me not to take anything from bad men, because they kidnap little girls. But you're a nice man; you know my mammie; and my mammie knows you."

"Sure, I'm a nice man. Put this in your purse, Adanna,

and let's go inside and have a chat with my friend Hamid. You must come and give me a big kiss when church is over. Don't you forget now." Nigel told all the kids to follow him into Hamid's, and the kid who once heeded the advice of his mother and history teacher, led the pack into the store. The crew ordered icecream on the stick and candy. They remained outside in the open air and enjoyed their gifts from Nigel, the ex-Sunday school boy.

"Come go inside with me, Adanna." Nigel held Adanna's hand, and they walked inside the church. She went by her grandmother, and he went back to his seat.

"Lord Meath," Nigel spoke softly into his cuffed fingers, "I must talk to you now."

"I hope it is about that pretty sister in white. Is she sister Bernadette?" Tommy let his eyes do the pointing. "I like the way she wraps her head. The yellow is showing evenly with the white. That's neat, man. You missed a great part of the sermon...Sssh. Listen to the Leader, man. You should have heard his elucidation on the plight of angels. He's about to end the Preached Word."

"...'What's hidden from the wise and prudent is now revealed unto babes and sucklings.'" Leader Dollon paused, and he looked directly at Nigel. "Yes, Lord, I know. Amen."

He ended the Preached Word so soulfully that Tommy was about to cheer, but the congregation burst into their closing hymn, *The Day Thou Givest Lord is Ended.*

"Let's leave now, Lord Meath," Nigel said.

"I'm waiting for Sister Elizabeth to introduce me to that pretty sister in white, man. This is a charismatic gathering, and I'll be back every week. I'll bring my Mira Mira here to worship and for our marriage."

"Outside!" Nigel again spoke in his hand like if he were a member of President Reagan's Secret Service.

"Okay, okay. But let it be something good that you want to talk about."

"It would be disastrous to embarrass Elizabeth here."

"Embarrass her for what? I already said that she's innocent. So what's the hurry?"

"Just to listen to what I have to say."

"Listen to Gordon's gin?"

"I'm not drunk, Lord Meath." Nigel controlled his temper. "Let's check out Leader Dollon before we check out Daniel Cake. Dollon recited Lyle's favorite poem *Abou Ben Adhem* in disguise."

"I didn't hear it."

"Because you filled your brain with the aesthetics and your stomach with the substance a *le* Gerrol. Dollon's hand movements, diction, and mannerisms were similar to Lyle's. Lyle made those same gestures whenever he recited that poem with long vowels. It's likely that Lyle and Dollon's style is a prototype of the Tellymack style. Mr. Tellymack of Fyzabad was Lyle's headmaster; probably Dollon passed under Mr. Tellymack's hands, too. Dollon is definitely older than Lyle. Lyle did not remember Dollon, but probably Dollon never forgot Lyle...Crazy things happen over the years, man. Maybe Dollon was a Fyzabad boy who migrated to these shores before or after Lyle...Probably he was the sore loser who fell down from the greasypole. I'm gripping at any straw, man. I know that we have to talk to Cakey tomorrow at his job in Wall Street, but there's nothing wrong in setting Dollon up, and tonight."

"You are not calling Leader Dollon by his religious title anymore? You are behaving as if you are so sure of his misdeeds."

Nigel did not answer. "We have nothing to lose, so let's do it." Tommy looked at his pal warily. "Let's do it, Lord Meath. I'll leave now after drawing attention to my departure. You will run after me, and I'll drive off but I'll be waiting for you at the left turn of the next block. We'll discuss further there. I'm depending on you to do my homework."

"Okay." Now Tommy was the confused detective. He felt like hot salt in ice water; but his pal was peppered with positiveness.

Nigel left his pew in a rage. "I don't want to hear of it, Tommy," Nigel said as he walked out. "That's nonsense what you're telling me, man!" Nonetheless, Tommy looked at Leader Dollon's pointed-tip shoes.

Nigel's angry departure was noticed. He called out to Adanna. "Adanna, don't forget to tell your mammie that you saw me." Adanna rushed behind him. He ignored her, ran outside, and drove off in a hurry. Snubbing little Adanna was part of the detectives' game plan.

Tommy stepped briskly outside and pretended that he pursued Nigel. He crossed the street, stood there, and counted the congregants in the open church.

Elizabeth and Hettie were the first of the congregants to walk out of the church. Leader Dollon accompanied them and showered his blessings on them. He shook their hands, and he waited outside and chitchatted with other members as they filed out of the church and discussed the Sunday's text: The Power of the Plight of Angels.

"Sister Elizabeth and Sister Hettie," Tommy shouted to their amazement, "I have to take you home by taxi. Nigel, for no good reason, left in a hurry." Before Tommy said another word, a taxi pulled up. "The taxi is here," he shouted. "Let's go." Elizabeth and Hettie rushed across the street. "Goodnight, Leader Dollon," they said, and the taxi drove off. Tommy kept looking back, and he spoke to the taxi driver at the same time. "Make a left on the next block and stop, driver... Elizabeth, what you did with your Labor Day placard...the one about Aunt Gina?"

"I lost it somewhere between my way to church and home or vice versa," she answered. "Why are you asking me that question, Lord Meath? It's a year ago since I lost that placard."

Tommy did not answer Elizabeth's question. "Hettie," he said, "what you did with your pointed-tip shoes, the one you used to tap in?"

"That pair of disgusting male shoes? I couldn't for sure tell you what I did with it, but if I'm not mistaken, I think I put it in one of our charity bins. No; I gave them to Leader Dollon to have them repaired and given to charity."

"Turn here, driver, and stop." Tommy jumped out before the taxi stopped. He rushed back to the intersection of Tilden and Nostrand Avenues and looked up the street in the direction of Mt. Signal Spiritual Baptist Church.

The taxi stopped, and Nigel appeared from nowhere. "Ma, how did Leader Dollon address Lyle the only day that he came to church?"

"As a visiting shepherd."

"How did Dollon know that my father was a shepherd in the faith?"

Elizabeth shrugged her shoulder.

Nigel shouted louder. "Did you tell him?"

"No. I did not."

"Give me the bunch of church keys."

It was his second command to his mother for the day.

"What's wrong, son? Why?" Hettie hit Elizabeth's leg with her leg, and Elizabeth realized that Hettie was telling her that Nigel was in one of those crazy moods. Elizabeth said not another word.

"Hurry, Ma. Just give them to me." Nigel grabbed the keys from her hand. "Where's the red key to the basement?"

"Leader Dollon mislaid his, so he borrowed mine...only for today until he makes a copy, son."

Nigel took the keys as his sacrament. Overtly, he threatened the white cabdriver. "Cabby, I want you to look at my black face and nappy head." The taxi driver looked at Nigel's face and left his meter running. "Here," Nigel said. "A metered taxi takes three dollars to drop them. I'm giving you ten for their safety. If they didn't get there, consider yourself a dead man."

"Thank you, sir. This is not those foreigners' gypsy

cabs. Your family will always be safe in a yellow cab."

Nigel ran to the corner and met Tommy. They crouched and walked at the sides of parked cars until they were obliquely opposite the church. Leader Dollon's back was turned to them, and he shook the hands of his church members, advised them about many things, and wished them God's speed.

"Tommy, this is the last time you'll be doing my homework in a long time. Did you count all the members who were in the church?"

"Yes."

"Who came out first?"

"Hettie and Liz."

"Did anyone come out of the church while you drove to meet me?"

"Only two people. It was easy to count them because all of the female members were dressed in white with their yellow and white headties, and the men were dressed in easily discernible outfits."

"Good. How many people were there in full?"

"Forty."

"Let me know when the last person comes out."

Tommy counted carefully as each member came out. He peered through the glass of a parked car. Suddenly, he said, "Thirty nine, forty...the little girl and her grandmother. He's talking to the little girl."

"Let Dollon talk. You got my instructions about the church's layout?"

"Sure, but..."

"It's your time to trust me, Lord Meath. I trusted your shorthand skill. I know this church. I know Dollon's habits. The church has a night lock, so let's give him time to go to the robing room and change." Nervously, they dallied for ten minutes and rehearsed their plan. They crossed the street, and Nigel opened the door. He made a sign to Tommy which meant, 'I'll stay here by the step that leads to the basement while you go in there after him.' Nigel pointed and whispered, "He can't see us out here."

Leader Dollon was still robed when he stared into the large wall mirror. He held one side of his contact lenses in his hand, and he saw Tommy's full figure in the mirror. Leader Dollon continued with what he was currently doing and displayed no signs of panic or shock at Tommy's sudden appearance.

"Good evening, Leader Dollon. I've come to pay my respects."

"That's very nice of you. The last time I saw you, you were about eight, young man."

"That's a long time ago. I never knew that you wore contact lenses, Leader Dollon."

"There are so many things that you don't know about me."

"Like what kept your britches up?"

"You are so poetic. Why would you want to know that? Make yourself comfortable, and just give me a minute to change these robes." Dollon smiled amiable. He smoothly changed the subject and took Tommy off guard. "I'm glad you are here, young man. Before I change my robe, Tommy, let me give you some money to take to faithful Sister Elizabeth to buy flowers for next week's service. She left in such a hurry. Would you mind?"

"Of course not, Leader Dollon."

Leader Dollon finally took out both of his contact lenses, and he rested them in a case on the table. He picked up two two-dollar bills from the table and handed them to Tommy.

"The flowers that I see on your altar cost more than that, I'm sure."

"Forty dollars are more than sufficient," Leader Dollon emphasized. "That's what I always give Sister Elizabeth to buy flowers."

"But these are two two-dollar bills," Tommy showed the two bills to him.

Leader Dollon looked at the bills. "That's why I should always keep on my contact lenses, but they are so itchy at times. Please take the money from the church offering that is near to you, Tommy."

There were two sets of donations on the table, one at each end of the table. One was near to Tommy, and the other was nearer to Leader Dollon. The two sets of donations were in silver platters and each was covered with a coarse, but lily white cloth. "Go ahead, Tommy, raise the cloth and take the money for the flowers." He spoke to Tommy in a chummy manner. "You need only thirty six dollars more. Count the money while I drop some liquid into my eyes." He faced Tommy and dropped Visine into his eyes.

Tommy raised the cloth willingly. "This is only small change. Surely, you don't expect me to count thirty six dollars from this small change, Leader Dollon."

"Oh my! That money is collected from the children for the Sunday school outing fund. We use that money to take the kids on trips. This is a living church. We have rallies, outings, days in the park, and we sometimes invite the reformed rabbis and other churches to join us in our community discussions. No doubt, these hard-working ushers separated the money to save me the trouble. May God bless them for the work that they do in Mount Signal." Leader Dollon made one step to the other covered platter. "This is the tithes, the Lord's money, and it should always be blessed before it is put to use. Give me a short minute, young man, to bless the tithes. Only then can I give you the money to give Sister Elizabeth to buy flowers for next week's service. It's a pity that Sister Elizabeth, faithful Sister Elizabeth, had to rush for that taxi before taking the money with her." Leader Dollon prayed softly, and with both hands outstretched, he blessed the vessel covered with the lily white cloth that was before him. "Dear Lord, you sent a raven to feed Elijah; you used a donkey to speak to Balaam; and you sent Sister Elizabeth as faithful as Sarah and Rebecca combined with her flowers...."

Tommy bent his head, and he, too, said a silent

prayer. He asked the Lord to forgive him for pre-judging Leader Dollon. He was convinced that he was in the company of the Lord's anointed, and the Lord's anointed should not be harmed.

Nigel, in a cramped position, heard their conversations. He knew Elizabeth always bought flowers for the church with her own money. That was her responsibility from the day she joined Mount Signal Spiritual Baptist Church. Nigel was on the opposite end of the spectrum. He was convinced that his partner was in serious trouble, and one false move would be fatal. He pictured a tragedy. For one? For both? Nigel could not say. He mumbled, "If only Lord Meath didn't go to see those wretched Congo flowers in the garden, he would have heard that Elizabeth always donated the flowers to her church." Nigel inhaled and exhaled. His breath was hot. "Lord, don't let me panic today. Give me, Lord, the ability of David."

Nigel knew that he now had all the missing links to the Constance Wagner puzzle. But now his pal Lord Meath was none the wiser. Lord Meath could pay the price, fatally, because he was, like others, trustful of the gown. Confused, he crawled up to his favorite pew, the pew which he and Elizabeth occupied when he was a little boy, and words came voluntarily from his lips. "Dear Lord,..." he prayed in a whisper with the thought that his pal was already dead for he instantly remembered a tradition of Fyzabad, *Payback*. Nigel began afresh and prayed to his God. "Dear Lord, my God, Thomas Sullivan, Lord Meath, was my friend, my confidant, my brother. I loved him. We did good things together...and bad things, too, unworthy to mention even though you know of them...But dear Lord, make a way for Lord Meath in your kingdom.

"Dear God, Lord Meath and I heeded the ad of the citrus grower who wanted two robust males with penile enlargement to pick her fruit after hours. We masturbated together...Lord, Lord Meath and I did not discover the stolen fissionable material in the hands of evil scientists who want to destroy the world with bombs, but Lord Meath and I have discovered that peace is a good thing for the world over.

"Dear Lord, Lord Meath and I have differed bitterly on *Bakke*. Lord in heaven looking down upon us, I'm sure you know who Mr. Bakke is...I believe that affirmative action would help the poor, the underprivileged, and the denied, but Lord Meath felt affirmative action is reversed discrimination. Lord, Lord Meath and I differed in our many beliefs since we were boys, but there was no hate when we differed. We have fought fist fights and bloodied each other's nose, but we shared our cookie soon after we fought. Lord, I want to tell you this: If you give back Lord Meath his life and both of us leave here alive, I won't say anything bad about the Borough of Queens, white people, or, for that matter, anybody. For that matter, I'll turn the other cheek. Are you listening, Lord?

"Lord, break this cycle of impending pain today as you broke it for Jesse Jackson in Syria, but make a miracle and don't let me leave empty handed as Jesse left empty handed when he left the Democratic Convention. And, Lord, I know Lord Meath was destroyed with a bullet. The media and critics also thought they destroyed the first black woman who was crowned Miss America. The media and critics thought they destroyed that beautiful black woman with their newsprint and bias journalism...But that beautiful black woman rose from the burns and hot ashes of newsprint to be famous. Now that black woman is a movie star, a Broadway star, a hit parade singer, and a lady. Lord, it is you who did that for that black woman, Miss America, and I know you'll let Lord Meath survive the wound from Leader Dollon's gun. Lord, Lord Meath and I are two greenhorn detectives who are not wise to the intricate foibles of mankind, and that's the cause of our dilemma today. You have to correct our mistakes, Lord. Lord, I've forgotten how to pray, but help me to make the right decision at this hour.

"Lord, you know that I was a bad Sunday school boy; Pa was a good shepherd in spiritual Leader Gerrol's mud camp in the backwoods of Fyzabad; and Ma loves you...Ma said, in Fyzabad patois, that you ain't have *cokey* (crooked) eyes. Lord, you know why Ma told me that you ain't have *cokey* eyes? Ma told me that when I was a Sunday school boy. I wanted to play ungodly in the basement with Sheila. Ma told me that I was like Paul heading down the Damascus Road and you were watching me. Immediately I stopped going down that Damascus Road. I stopped bullying Sheila to kiss her in the basement, Lord, and I stopped lying and telling Lord Meath and Raggy Beerman that I put my hand below Sheila's dress. I told them that to feel like a man. After that I began to learn of Jesus. Lord, I know John 3:16 by heart. You want me to say it for you to hear, Lord: 'God so loved the world, that He gave his only begotten Son, that whosoever believeth in him shall not perish but have everlasting life.' You know that is true, Lord.

"But you know, Lord, since I became a backslider and stopped attending church I've started to do bad things again. Now I go by Sheila's house down South when her husband leaves for army training. Save Lord Meath, Lord, and I promise you that I'll never do that again. Lord, if you bring back Lord Meath to life, I'll stop going by Sheila for *yakahoola* as I stopped bullying her in the church basement to get a little kiss."

The very mention of the name "Sheila" and the word "basement" in Nigel's confused eulogy of Thomas "Lord Meath" Sullivan brought him to his mundane senses. His spiritual thoughts became carnal. He instantly remembered, as a boy, when he played in the church basement and Sheila hid behind a certain door, he was never able to find her, but he always ended up in Leader Dollon's robing room that was blocked by a black curtain.

At that very moment Thomas "Lord Meath" Sullivan was relaxed. He raised his head when Leader Dollon said, "Amen...Here's the money for the flowers, Detective Sullivan." Leader Dollon raised the cloth with the supposed offering and picked up something. "Sister Elizabeth and songbird Hettie excitedly told me that you and your pal were coming to pay me a visit today. Why? I asked myself. As a good boy scout, I prepared myself because I was also told by Sister Elizabeth and songbird Hettie that you and Nigel tricked them today." Dollon smiled.

Tommy, shocked from this unbelieveable September surprise, glared at the object in Leader Dollon's hand. He forced out the words, "Leader Dollon, a gun to buy flowers?" Tommy immediately remembered his encounter with Zeek: Zeek had told him in his ear that his underlings had sold a preacher on Nostrand Avenue a gun, and, from description, that preacher was Dollon, known to Zeek by another name. Tommy remembered he called Zeek a racist when Zeek told him of Dollon.

"Stop daydreaming, Mr. Detective. Yes; a gun to buy flowers."

"Is that the gun you bought at Limbo Hook from Zeek's boys?"

"Batman, you talk too fancy to have much sense. That is why Robin ran off on you." Dollon locked the door. "Black Robin, even if he changes his mind and returns, will never find you. Detective Batman, you want to hear a little history. My one-way ticket to Fyzabad is already bought, not in the names you probably know. Right now I can see very well. Sometimes my contact lenses are gray; sometimes they are like your Irish eyes...You won't believe this: I never lost a battle; I never lost a prize; and America is not my only home."

"So it was you who scratched the poem in

Constance Wagner's apartment?"

"You are catching on."

"Leader Dollon, please put that gun away. You just preached a lovely sermon about angels writing in a book of gold. Your sermon converted me."

"I'm glad it did. Now you are fit for heaven."

"Aren't you giving me the money to buy flowers again?"

"Faithful Sister Elizabeth always bought the flowers with her own money, but in future I won't need her flowers."

"So you planned this scheme to get Lyle's belt? Probably you were the one who trumped up that *Grenada Ghosts* Labor Day band?"

"You are right again."

"In other words, you used Grenada to your advantage?"

"Didn't the American invaders do the same? Maurice Bishop, another Anwar Sadat, was a visionary, not a pragmatist. Sadat thought he could put Jews and Arabs to sit on the same log of wood and make a bonfire of friendship. Maurice Bishop, with Big Brother looking over him, thought he could reform those black hens and their chickens who, all their natural lives, sang *God Save our Gracious King and Queen*."

"Maurice Bishop should have done like you: Dress British, think crookish, and laywait?"

"You learned that line from conservative George Will, I suppose?"

"No. I heard it on Johnny Carson's."

"Bah! Try again...Let me tell you a little about me."

"That Mr. Tellymack taught you and Lyle the same poem...That you were born in Grenada and migrated to the oiltown of Fyzabad? When did you come to New York?"

"I'll give that information to your undertaker."

"Why so much hate and vengeance, Leader Dollon?"

"You have no idea how my family suffered...all

because of Lyle Gordon and the Boys of Fyzabad. They turned my entire family into pariahs. The Boys of Fyzabad gave the East Indians an opportunity to make money on my failure...So many Africans lost their entire savings...The Boys of Fyzabad engineered my failure and caused the people of Fyzabad to chase my family out of town. If I'm a criminal today, the Boys of Fyzabad are responsible. My mother and stepfather died in disgrace as a result of the suffering meted out to them. I did my secret investigation, and I found out that only Joiner Jan and Lyle are alive; and I got my information clandestinely. Poor, unsuspecting, Hettie was my final conduit. That's how Fyzabad's *Payback* works. Slow, but sure. Yesterday for the Boys of Fyzabad and their trickery; today for me with my sweet *payback*."

"You all were children. It meant that you were scheming for over half a century. How could you nurse that sore!"

"Don't shout in here."

"Constance Wagner was innocent. You didn't have to kill her. She had nothing to do with your parents' hurt."

"Miss Wagner killed herself. It was dark. She tripped and fell on a marble sculpture."

"Due to you," Tommy said. He was happy that Dollon engaged him in conversations. It gave him time to think out a plan for his escape, without Nigel. "Give yourself up. Leader Dollon, hate is a cancer. Don't use religion to destroy yourself and others."

"The white man did the same. See how they divided up Africa? Come closer, young man. Don't show no punkness." Dollon smiled. "See how hip I am. Did your pal Robin tell you about my secret door to my robing room?"

"That dumb fool, Nigel! I told him that I suspected you, and he jumped in his car and ran like a poor church rat. A black dumb-dumb for a detective...an affirmative action nigger...a detective emerging from the quota system...This government with their quota shit robbed a bright white man of a place in the business world and gave that employment opportunity to that dumb church nigger. I can't see how you people could be equal to us." Tommy's theatrics was superb. It was really Off-Broadway on Nostrand Avenue, Brooklyn. Tommy's sincerity of his hatred for his pal even convinced himself. He learned in his war training that to kill the enemy you had to hate him, and now he hated his pal Nigel. It was momentary, but it was done right. As he spoke, he kept his eyes on the wall. He looked for cracks in it with the hope that Nigel was somewhere listening to his predicament.

"Looking for something, detective? The good thing is that your pal, the dumb, black fool, like Napoleon, will live to fight another day. Not you! I knew what the black fool did in the church basement, but I also knew if I chased away the chick, the mother hen would leave for good. I was always a patient man. You can see that. Can't you?"

There was a built-in closet equidistanced between Leader Dollon and Tommy. The door was slightly ajar. Tommy did mathematics in his brain without looking at the door. Whether the length of the door would reach his target was Tommy's dilemma.

"Come closer, detective."

Tommy did not move. He attempted to put up his hand voluntarily, but he changed his mind. His mind raced. He inhaled the air, and he studied the air drafts that seeped in. He again studied the dimension of the closet door. He put his hand behind his back to annoy Dollon, and he stood still.

"Put your hands up and walk towards me. I want my target to be close. All the preaching is over, just as the lies and deception of Vietnam and Watergate are over. Forget your tricks. Charge in with your head, and I'll show you that I am good. I can use a lead pencil to block a bayonet, so you can just imagine what I'll do to your white skull. I learned strategy from the British.

Your American soldiers ran from disgrace in Lebanon, and then they came to my country Grenada to avenge their defeat. The Americans took advantage of old men who fought with 1914 rifles and firewood. The Americans killed innocent people with their heavy guns. I want you to know that I'm a Corinthian Christian. I want you to go into your pocket nice and easy. Take out your gun and kick it to me. Don't try to be John Wayne. This is not Hollywood. This is I, Elias S. Dollon with a gun. Do you know what the 'S' stands for? Guess."

Tommy obeyed the order. He dropped his gun and kicked it to the preacher man.

"Nice. Yours is too noisy, Batman. Mine has a silencer." He kicked Tommy's gun away.

"You're doing the wrong thing, Leader Dollon." Tommy glanced at the closet.

"That closet will soon be your burden."

"I'll make it my bridge," Tommy said in his mind.

"I'm a born leader," Leader Dollon said.

"You are a leader of your people, and you are doing this?"

"Your white leaders mined civilian harbors and invaded weak nations. Your white leaders dropped bombs and killed babies. Your white leaders shot down passenger planes and called those planes spy planes. So my leadership is not too bad after all."

"You have good souls in your flock like Sister Elizabeth and Sister Hettie."

"I knew through Sister Elizabeth that one day I'd get what I needed. My sister first befriended stupid Joiner Jan in Trinidad, and he told her all of Lyle's addresses in New York. Whenever and wherever smelly Lyle moved to, I knew his place of abode. Lyle hasn't changed his ways. When he smelled the water in the holy lota, I knew that was my man, Smelly. I knew his address even before Sister Elizabeth joined my church."

"It is not your church, Leader Dollon. It is

God's church."

"White boy, I'm not listening to you...How to get the Gordons into my church was my daily concern, and, as I just told you, tapping Hettie was the final lead conduit. When I conscripted Hettie, she fell for my ploy. I used the church just like the white man to get what I wanted. What was I saying? Yes! Hettie was my final conduit to the Gordons...*Payback*, the Fyzabad phenomenon, was on my sister's agenda as much as it was on mine. My sister Louise created the first move by befriending Joiner Jan and eliciting information from him. Lyle and the Boys of Fyzabad destroyed my family. Someone said, 'Family is the first organized structure of homo sapiens; it is the first structure of social engineering;' Lyle and the Boys of Fyzabad had their families; and mine was destroyed due to them. It's *payback* time."

"You got the belt, Leader Dollon. What more do you need?"

"Let me decide that, blue eyes."

"The good book tells you, Leader Dollon, 'If any man be in Christ, he is a new creature: old things are passed away;...all things are become new.' It is not too late to be a new creature and rid yourself of hatred, Leader Dollon."

Leader Dollon smiled. "I see the detective knows the scripture. Too bad."

Tommy was at the spot he earmarked. That blessed spot. He stood beside the closet door that was slightly ajar. He measured the length of the door from the corners of his eyes and was sure of his next move. With lightning speed, his right hand pushed the solid wooden door forcefully. The door hit Dollon's wrist and knocked the gun from his hand. A shot from his gun went off. Dollon was lefthanded, and his left hand was badly hurt, but he was also extremely athletic. Dollon outbounced Tommy as they scrambled for the gun. Dollon dove for the gun, and Tommy pulled back his leg. For three minutes both men fought fiercely. They were two desperate men fighting for their lives. One was John Wayne, the other Randolph Scott. Blows were evenly distributed as bibles, bells, books, trays and lotas with and without water rained down on them. Dollon was surprised at Tommy's tactics, smarts, and strength. Tommy used his wit, his academic and judo training, and he gained the upperhand on his foe; but Tommy got cocky, and made one mistake: He began his trash talk and treated Dollon like if he were Raggy Beerman.

"In what part of Africa did you buy your pointed-tip shoes, Dollon? I more believe you took it out of the charity box. Are you Puerto Rican? I'm in love with one."

Dollon didn't answer.

"Aren't you a mulatto, Dollon? Sometimes you have gray eyes, but you maintain your straight hair. Your features are quite chiseled, I see. Your Sunday school boy said that you people are the original man, and I'm sure that you are the original murderer of that beautiful and productive Jewish woman. Dig it, murderer?"

"I can block a bayonet with a stick of chalk, white boy. I'm warning you." Dollon spoke softly and conserved his energy as he looked at his walking stick tucked conveniently in a corner of his robing room. Tommy looked at it, too. They raised from the ground, locked in each other's hand grip. Dollon, an old stick fighter, sensed that his combatant was losing his strength as he listened to Tommy's uneven breathing.

"I don't believe your embroidered stories, Dollon." Tommy felt his fading strength and tried to camouflage it. "Don't forget that I'm the stick of chalk, murderer."

The preacher man, the sly fox, slackened his handgrip for a reason. Tommy responded and showed Dollon that he, Tommy, was young and strong. Dollon slackened his handgrip again. He pulled away from Tommy but shifted the leverage of his body to the right side. Tommy responded one more time to Dollon's movements. Tommy brought Dollon closer to him to show Dollon his strength and mastery of the clinches. Dollon pretended that he was falling and shifted his weight to his left side in the direction of the walking stick. Tommy fell for all of Dollon's ploy. Dollon slackened his hold on Tommy's right arm even more, and Tommy with renewed vigor, pulled him in with his left hand and went for the jugular. That was Tommy's crucial mistake.

Dollon used his cranial box as a sledge hammer on the detective's forehead. The blow separated Tommy Sullivan from his senses. Like a bombed aircraft, down Tommy went in a dizzy nosedive, momentarily comatozed. "White boy, you are so used to those Latin capping verses during the Hail Marys that you forgot that you were in a black church where we improvise. You should have asked Smelly about me. I meant to kill Smelly on the Parkway on Labor Day last year, but he eluded me." Dollon muttered those words and fell on the ground from exhaustion.

The force of the blow also affected foxy Dollon. He was blistered. His left hand was swollen and bloody, and his body was too weak to stand upright. He crawled and rested. To retrieve his gun was now his only aim in life. He crawled again and stopped. Dollon's last move would be to hold his gun and fire it.

Nigel took advantage of the noisy tumblings that were made upstairs. There was no reason for him to be extra silent in his movements in the basement. He lifted the rows of chairs which blocked the entrance to the basement door. He tried every key in his possession but none worked. He took out the five bullets from his gun, put them in his breast pocket, and he broke the basement lock with the gun butt. There was no light in the basement, and he was careful not to stumble against the scattered furniture. In desperation, he searched for the door where Sheila Sanders used to hide, but he became worried when he heard no movements upstairs. I hope Tommy is not dead and Dollon escaped, he thought. He used the nozzle of his gun, twisted loose a wire latch, and a door gave way. Light came peeping into the basement. He knew where he was, and he moved with lightning speed through the passageway in the basement. He ran through the nursery door that Sheila always made her escape from him. He stopped. He mused for a quick second: "This way. That way." He remembered that he went in the other door whenever he went behind Sheila. He followed his instincts, and he was right. He took off his shoes the same way he did as a boy when he entered the robing room, and he tiptoed up the steps that led to the clothes closet. He peeped from behind the black curtains in the clothes closet.

Two limp and battered bodies were on the floor. Tommy appeared to be dead, and Dollon showed a mere semblance of life. Dollon painfully eased his body off the floor. He was in pain. He was angry and bruised, but he forced his body to move one more time. He crawled slowly for his gun. He was a finger tip away from that precious object, his own silencer, and he stretched for it.

A voice is heard. "If you twitch a muscle, I'll have to buy you flowers, Spreewell." Nigel pushed the black curtains aside and walked through the clothes closet. His eyes, red as blood, he aimed his gun at Dollon's brain.

Tommy heard his partner's voice, grit in pain, and rose from the floor. "How you got here, man?"

"Through a crack in the basement."

"Thank God...Oh thank you, Jesus, for giving Nigel the vision to play with Sheila in that blessed basement. Hail Mary, 'Hitherto hath the Lord helped us.'" Tommy thanked God as he never did before. "It was the plight of angels, Lord," he affirmed.

"Stay right where you are, Leader Dollon...Get both guns, Tommy." Nigel's aimed at his target.

Tommy retrieved his own gun, and he stepped on Dollon's blistered left hand when he picked up Dollon's gun.

"Police brutality," Leader Dollon said.

"Neither of us is a policeman, Leader Dollon," Tommy replied. He looked at Dollon who laid there as a turtle turned upside down. "Won't you get up and rend your garment, Leader Dollon? What if I stand on your face by mistake. That's not fair, white boy. What about a fair fist fight with this dumb fool, bad Dollon?"

"Let me get up," Dollon pleaded. He writhed in pain.

"To drop your belt, I hope, and to show what kept your britches up. See how this white boy can still talk fancy."

Leader Dollon got up. He reeled off the many yards of his African print until his trousers were seen. An ordinary-looking belt buckle, but an exact replica of the one that was left on Constance Wagner's neck, was fastened to Dollon's leather strap. The strap went through the loops of Dollon's serge pants. The tightness of the belt around Dollon's waist kept his gun-mouth pants bottom two inches above his pointed-tip black shoes. He stood straight and proud until he felt the full force of Tommy's high school ring on his nose. It was a bloody and unexpected blow.

"That's for your coconut, Dollon." He touched his head. "Isn't that what you call it in Trinidad and Tobago?"

"That's enough, Tommy! Stop it right now!" Nigel shouted. Nigel looked at Leader Dollon, and Dollon understood Nigel's unspoken lingo. Dollon unbuckled his belt, and the once-fumbling detectives looked at the way the lefthanded Leader Dollon took off his belt.

"Don't hold the belt, Leader Dollon. Drop it at your feet, and take four steps backwards." Nigel commanded him.

The belt fell noiselessly on the carpeted floor. The Mondesir trademark on the buckle stood out boldly.

"I see the *M* trademark on the buckle, Nigel." Tommy spoke excitedly.

"I need my lawyer," Leader Dollon said.

Tommy replied. "Lawd, ah know...To tell your

lawyer that Spree, the 'sounding brass and tinkling cymbal' never climbed that greasypole. A likkle boy by the name of Smelly did...Spree, like Moses who never crossed over to Jordan, will never cross over the Atlantic to flee to Fyzabad. Spreewell, you are going to jail, and we are going to Disney World...Ha ha ha."

Nigel faced Leader Dollon. He put his hand in his breast pocket, took out all the bullets from his pocket, counted them, and put them one by one, slowly, into the chamber of his empty gun. Leader Dollon's eyes bulged bigger and bigger as Nigel counted every replaced bullet. Dollon was convinced that he was again tricked, not by the Boys of Fyzabad, but by Likkle Lyle's son himself.

"Leader Dollon, I once believed in you, but it is now my duty to make a call." Nigel dialed the police. "Leader Dollon, what should I tell your faithful flock: That it is not how they jump and catch the Holy Ghost Power on Sunday, but how they walk on Monday."

He did not answer. He was still thinking of Nigel's empty pistol...or, perhaps, he was thinking of the hands of fate.

Tommy went through the clothes closet. "Nigel, look what I've found. Here's the costume with the missing R from the word Grenada...even a scratched credit card...How many names do you have, Sprewell?" Tommy asked politely.

"Why don't you ask the last two unfair Boys of Fyzabad?"

"What would smelly Lyle and the bake man know about your spiritual malpractice? They don't even know that you, fitted in five yards of Kente cloth, have less brains than Leader Gerrol's belly." Tommy put his hand in his pocket and said, "Leader Dollon, I forgot to put my tithes and offering in the collection plate." Out from his cargo pants pocket came a mini tape recorder. He rested it in the silver platter and scratched his buzz haircut. "You may cover it with the lily white cloth, if you wish, Leader

Dollon." That was the last September surprise.

Dollon bent his head in shame. He was indeed shocked by the thought that a white man in Brooklyn knew so much of the doings and undoings of the people of Fyzabad, a village unknown to the majority of the people of Trinidad and Tobago and frequented by self-serving politicians only at election time.

There was a knocking on the door. It was Detective Crobett of the NYPD who entered the room and read the Miranda Warning to the stowaway from Fyzabad.

"Gentlemen, do you happen to know Dalgo Red-Cap Gibbons?" Crobett asked wryly as an interviewer on National Public Radio."

"That's our bruvver," Salt and Pepper replied and high-fived noisily with their black and white palms.

Chapter Twenty-Two

The Placard and the Perfume

Lyle beamed in the Pastalaqua House. "It's a shame that Liz and I did not recognize our schoolmate Spree," Lyle said. "We look different when we age, and we get ugly when we hate. Tell me, Lord Meath, what led you to that crook?"

"Your Aunt Gina stories," Tommy said.

"And I trusted my Ma," Nigel butted in. He looked at Tommy and winked. "Ma, tell them about the misplaced placard."

"Gentlemen of the jury," Elizabeth began, "I wanted to be unique at the Labor Day parade with my presentation. I knew how Lyle's Aunt Gina hated immigrants, especially Grenadians, so I got a sign painter to print on cardboard AUNT GINA HATED GRENADIANS. WHY? The thing is I'd absent-mindedly left the wrapped placard in a taxi. A very handsome Haitian taxi driver did not remember my address, but he remembered that he picked me up in front of Mount Signal Spiritual Baptist Church, and I was dressed in my church garb. Therefore, the nice cabdriver took the wrapped package to the church, and he gave it to Leader Dollon. All that time, I was sure that I had the placard safely hidden under my bed away from the prying eyes of my husband. When I didn't find the placard on sweet Labor Day morning, and I realized that Lyle ran out on me, I took off my clothes and went straight to bed in the back room. It so happened that a tourist who got lost on my block, rang my bell at that very moment. She asked me for directions to the Parkway. I told her that I would give her more than directions. I went inside, brought out my costume, and gave my costume to her. It was only after the tourist left I remembered that Leader Dollon was on the Parkway waiting to be introduced to Lyle...And, Lyle," Elizabeth addressed her husband personally, "that was the surprise that I had for you on the Parkway."

"Thank God I did not meet that crook. He would have murdered me then. That bastard murdered an innocent woman. I hope he rots in jail."

"Any more questions for my Ma, gentlemen?" Nigel asked.

"Liz, why did you give Leader Dollon your perfume in the first place?" Lyle, lounged in his easy chair, asked.

"Lyle, if you had dropped..."

Nigel noticed his mother's anxiety. "Ma, take your time. Remember, no patois today."

"I promise you, son. No patois." She smiled. "Lyle, my friend," Elizabeth looked at him, "if you had dropped Hettie and me to church that morning I would have told you about the gift that I had in my hand. The first time that I met Leader Dollon, he told me that he liked my perfume and to buy the same fragrance for him. The perfume was to be given to his mother as a birthday gift."

"The perfect con," Lyle said. "Joiner Jan told me that Spree's mother died long ago. He allowed time to elapse to see whether you or I remembered him."

"And it was through Joiner Jan that he found out everything about the Gordons...Their addresses, you name it," Tommy said.

"When did Dollon talk to Jan, Lord Meath?" Lyle asked.

"He never spoke to the flour man, Mr. Gordon," Tommy laughed as he spoke.

"But how Dollon found out about us?" Lyle got up from his easy chair.

"Through a woman."

"Who?"

"His sister Louise."

"How?"

"Louise now roasts Joiner Jan's bakes."

"Carrajo!"

"Pa," Nigel said, "no patois today."

"Honey," Elizabeth addressed Lyle affectionately, "how come you didn't recognize the smell of my perfume on that worthless *Grenada Ghost*?"

"I knew all along that it was your perfume, doll."

"And you said nothing, honey?"

"When I made my oath under the weeping willow, I meant it. That's the folly of a man in love. He'll die for..."

Tommy and Nigel did not want to share in that sentimental moment so, as usual, the boyish detectives pulled off another of their distraction stunts. "Liz," Tommy said, "here's Hettie's brandy glass and the spoon that I took from your kitchen to stir my troubles."

"I knew when you stole them, Lord Meath." She smiled.

"And Pa," Nigel said, "here's your ASDFLKJ scrap paper to lock away as a souvenir in your toolbox. The case is solved, and now we are leaving."

"You all are leaving so quickly?" Elizabeth said.

"Yes, Ma."

"Why, son?"

Tommy answered. "Because my lovely Ma, the lawyer, is preparing the Le Bec-Fin's recipe that she read in a cookbook, and we have to pick up some of the ingredients for dinner."

"I hope the bruvver's collard greens and chitterlings are part of that recipe, man; otherwise that dinner would be soulless. " Nigel squinted his nose. "I never heard of a white lawyer who could cook."

"Nigel, you are always talking down my people! I'm tired of it! Why? Why, man?" Tommy was furious.

"Lord Meath, it is because your people don't keep their promise." Nigel matched Tommy's rage.

"What promise, Nigel?"

"After slavery, your people promised to give my people forty acres of land and a mule, white boy."

"Well...right now...." Tommy thought deeply for a second then he blurted, "Blackboy, your people would have to treat that promise as a postdated check, man."

"Pa, you see what I always tell you, and you never believe me. His people are devils!"

"You are always looking down on my people, man! I hate you for that."

Lyle got off his easy chair and put his arms around the playful detectives. "My sons, if you two want me to be a stenographer in your private detective agency, before I even consider, let me give you an advice that Mr. Tellymack gave me years ago: 'Never look down on people unless you are going to pick them up.' If both of you agree to follow that advice, I'll be your employee. If not, I'll have to whip you right now like Mr. Tellymack whipped me for learning that blessed poem."

Nigel broke loose of his father's grip. He looked at Tommy, winked, and said, "Lord Meath, don't forget that we are running late, and we have to pick up Mira Mira." He spoke in a whisper.

"What's mora mora, Lord Meath?" Elizabeth inquired.

"An Italian sauce...Just an ingredient for dinner tonight...Mr. Gordon, why did they call you Smelly at school?"

"Come tomorrow, Lord Meath, and I'll end the Fyzabad chapter."

Elizabeth and Lyle hugged Tommy affectionately and thanked him for what he had done for them. Neither wanted to end his or her "Thank you, Lord Meath...Thank you, Lord Meath."

Tommy didn't want to be caught up in any sort of emotions. "Ma and Pa, you know when daddy's little boy is in a hurry what that means? I've got to go now," he said and smiled. He literally ripped himself from Lyle and Elizabeth's arms for he refused to join in their joyous tears. He ran outside and into the driver's seat of the Ford.

"Where to, darkie?" Tommy said.

"To under Ma Sullivan's chandelier," Nigel answered. "It's time to partake of the Le-Bec Fin's recipe."

"I hope my Ma puts you to sit in the kitchen."

"Ma Sullivan loves me as her own son...Bruvver Tommy, how come you happen to know so many scripture verses?"

"Because my Ma sent her decent, blue eye son to a Sunday school in St. Jerome's that didn't have a basement where he could learn spinal gymnastics in the Christian pose, Nigel Atiba."

"Lord Meath, you have an unruly tongue."

"Me have an unruly tongue...or you?"

There was a thunder of laughter as the Ford sped down the Brooklyn-Queens Expressway and was washed by the sudden downpour that burst from the sky. Tommy took his clean left hand, washed it playfully in the huge raindrops, and said slowly, haltingly, as if he worked on the cadence of his speech, "Nigel, what about that solemn promise that you made to the Lord above concerning staying away from Sunday school Sheila?"

"Lord Meath boy, you think He'll remember that part of my promise?" Nigel said in a mood of paradox.

Lightning flashed brilliantly. Tommy pulled his hand inside, wound up the glass, and said, "Sunday school boy, it is you who have aluminum in your brain, not the Lord." The Ford was rocked with their laughter. Its hubcap flew off, bumped rhythmically, as if to a calyspo beat, and trailed the detective duo for a good distance.

Chapter Twenty-Three

The Future

The silhouetted cloud disappeared. A chilly breeze blew, and Elizabeth closed the door. "Honey, where are you?"

"I'm writing a thank you letter to Mr. Oily," Lyle said.

"Is there such a person?"

"I'll put the letter in my toolbox until I find out, Liz."

"That's really a safe place to keep things, honey."

"Come over here, Lizzy, and let me show you what I've been hiding from you. Here. Look at it. Read the words carefully, gyul."

"Oh no! You composed this song for me: *Sing Me Mama's Song*. You composed it in jail...on Rikers Island? You composed this lovely song for me?"

"Who else, honey?"

"See, you did not have to go gallivanting on Saturdays to write music." She bent and kissed him in his easy chair.

He got up and walked to the door. He put his hand in his pocket and caressed the penny that he had picked up in Constance Wagner's kitchen. "Won't it be nice, Liz, if we call our first granddaughter Elizabeth Constance. Isn't that name just adorable, honey?" Lyle embraced his wife with both arms, and he squeezed her tenderly.

Elizabeth looked into her husband's eyes; she smiled effusively and said, "And jazzy."

Lyle looked up at the remains of Aunt Gina's rat trap, in deep thought. "Thank you, Fyzabad," he said. "I'm now your harvest, and I'm coming home."

Lloyd Hollis Crooks is an exciting new voice in Caribbean literature. His language is rich and evocative, and his multi-layered story of the immigrant experience is one to which all can relate.

—Dr. Andrea Freud Loewenstein
Associate Professor,
Medgar Evers College, CUNY

**Author: *This Place,* and
*The Worry Girl.***

A People in Diaspora, their lives as colorful as the rainbow. More than a million bodies gyrating...the biggest Woodstock/USA.

A. Taariq
Freelance Reporter

ABOUT THE AUTHOR

Lloyd Hollis Crooks was born in Fyzabad in the Republic of Trinidad and Tobago. He received his early education at the Fyzabad Canadian Mission School and Forest Reserve E.C. School. Later he attended Fyzabad Secondary E.C. School and Oxford Commercial College. Lloyd also attended Medgar Evers College of the City University of New York.

Mr. Crooks was employed as a Hansard (Parliament) Reporter, Court Reporter, and a Secretary in the Office of the Prime Minister of Trinidad and Tobago. He also worked as a Legal Secretary in various Wall Street law firms.